BETA

CW00409588

Wow! What an epic. It's a h[...]
and always engaging and g[...]
good balance of dialogue and description. Brilliantly done.
Jim Hawkins – TV dramatist and author of ALMOND

I really enjoyed this book. The writing is engaging and had me gripped right from the start, the storyline is compelling and the characters are well developed. I couldn't put this down and read it in almost one sitting. The descriptions are vivid and the imagery is rich and I felt like I was back in the tropical heat of Cuba.

A really enjoyable read that I would recommend if you like historical fiction.
Fiction Vixen Book Blog

I'm going to start off with this front cover, it's gorgeous! If you look closely, you will see the outline of a gun that's blended in, you could easily mistake that for an island, very clever design.
Straight away I was hooked to this storyline. The writing was captivating, the descriptions, the characters, everything.
I would highly recommend this fantastic book, especially if you're a lover of historical fiction.
Layla Penfold Book Blog

Island of Dreams is a really interesting read, relating the story of a family – the Muellers – during the Cuban Revolution. It's a huge journey the reader goes on with the characters. The characters are well developed. The descriptions are vivid and the imagery is rich. The writing is engaging and the storyline is compelling and always engaging and good to read. It's very well written, with a good balance of dialogue and description.

I would highly recommend this fantastic book.
Bookish Dreamer

Out of the fire and into the frying pan – I expect that's what the Mueller family felt like when the path to freedom ends up landing them in a political inferno, one that threatens to swallow up dissenters whole.

The older children are already set on different paths by the time the family reaches their new destination. When it comes to ideals, politics and beliefs – even at such a young age core memories have left their mark. Those differences lead to further division as they settle into a life in a new country, which has its own powder keg waiting to implode.

War, trauma, fractured relationships and the way each family unit creates a tentacled system of connections and relationships. It would probably make a great mini tv series.
Cheryl's' M-M Book Blog

If you're a fan of historical fiction this story will be one for you. I was interested in this because it's set in a place and time period I don't know a lot about, so that intrigued me.

I think the writer has put a lot of time into all the characters as they are detailed and the reader is able to care about them as the story progresses.

I found this to be a very interesting and absorbing read and I'm glad I signed onto the tour and discovered this book.
Libraryoflouise blogger

An intriguing story about the Mueller family as they flee Germany and find refuge in Cuba during the Cuban Revolution. We meet Professor Mueller and his family as they move to Cuba with hopes for a new start. I enjoyed learning the backstories of each family member.

Had me hooked from start to finish. I enjoyed the writing style and found it easy to read. The book is fast paced, full of tension and gives the reader insight into what it was really like to live during this time. The characters are brilliantly written, and I enjoyed the family dynamics between each character.

I highly recommend this book to anyone who loves historical fiction with an international flair.
Charlie Hodges - Author of 'The Vanishing Act' and 'Live Bait'
[A Tom Knight Mystery Series]

ISLAND

OF

DREAMS

Harry Duffin

CUMULUS PUBLISHING LIMITED

Copyright

PROLOGUE

She would come, he knew it. Despite the danger, she would come. As the black-frocked priest droned beneath the fierce sky, Freddie stood back from the other mourners and surveyed the vast sweep of marble tombs, cool even in heat of the sun, that surrounded the tiny group. The ancient cemetery looked deserted, but he knew they were there. Invisible and deadly, concealed among the lavish monuments to Havana's wealthy dead; crouching beside the weeping angels, praying Madonna's, mock castles of granite and the towering black pyramid, last resting place of the city's most celebrated and scandalous lovers - they were there. Hiding behind those final monuments to vanity, cradling their weapons, confident she would take up the challenge.

His heart thumped heavily inside the damp cotton shirt and linen jacket. She was brave and headstrong, and he knew she would come. He craved and feared it at the same time. 'Craved' – the word revealed his age as much as his feelings. Foolish old man, harbouring such dreams. Dreams he had promised himself she would never know. But they were dreams she had given him. For he had none when the ship sailed into the harbour all those years ago. She had brought him her dreams, bright as that May morning, as innocent as he was corrupt...

Harry Duffin

CHAPTER ONE

May 1939, Havana, Cuba

'It's so warm, Papa. It's still night, but it's so warm!'

Professor Carl Mueller smiled down at his daughter, holding his hand at the rail of the s.s. St Louis, the ship that had been their refuge, their salvation, as it slipped slowly through the darkness towards the sleeping city. A sense of relief washed over him, like the caress of the tropical breeze.

'We're in the Tropics, Anna. It's always warm here.'

Anna gazed at the shimmering lights of the city strung out along the shore. 'Look! It's like one of Mama's diamond necklaces!'

'She hasn't got them anymore!' snapped her elder brother, Hans, in German. 'We had to sell them to get on the boat!'

'Because of your stupid Nazis!' replied Anna fierily.

'The Nazis are not stupid!'

'Children, children, don't fight!' said their father firmly, but gently. 'And please remember we must speak English now.'

Hans snorted his annoyance, but said nothing.

As the deep throb of the engines slackened below their feet, they fell quiet. The scent of wet palms and exotic blooms filled Anna's nostrils. She breathed deeply. At twelve years old her life was beginning again. She breathed deeply once more. It was the smell of freedom.

'It looks so beautiful, Papa. Our new home.'

'It isn't our home!' retorted Hans. His father looked at him. Hans continued in English. 'Germany is our home, isn't it, Father! Our Fatherland.'

'Perhaps one day, my son, it will be again. Until then...' Professor Mueller's voice tailed off.

'I want to explore everything, Papa!' Anna said excitedly. 'I shall learn Spanish and learn everything about Cuba!'

3

Her father smiled at her again, but beneath the smile there was deep sadness. There was one person who could teach Anna everything about the island. A charming, lively, intelligent man who would make the perfect guide to their new home. He didn't know if the man had ever returned to the island, his home. But, if he had, Carl Mueller fervently hoped that they would never meet him.

The cab splashed to a halt, waking Freddie Sanchez as he was thrown against the back of the driver's seat. Streetlights dazzled him from the wet, empty sidewalk. He felt disorientated and a little sick. That last daiquiri was one too many. The last half dozen, really.

'Thank you, Carlos,' he muttered, groping for the door handle.'Put it on my tab.'

'Señor Sánchez –'

'Mañana, Carlos. Mañana, I promise.'

'I have a family to keep, Senor Sanchez –'

'You're a lucky man, Carlos. A lucky man. I have no one.'

He stumbled from the cab, ignoring the muttered Spanish oath behind his back. Freddie understood. Being half-Cuban, of course he understood. But at such moments he leaned on his English side and played the colonial.

The cab squealed into a turn and roared back along the deserted sea-front towards the casinos.

Leaning against the harbour wall to support himself Freddie recalled falling headlong down the stairs of the Hotel Nacional, and the young policeman catching him, saving him from breaking his neck.

'You have to be more careful, Senor Sanchez', said the young man as he helped him to a taxi.

'Thanks, Ramos,' he had said. 'I'm...er, just a little tired.'

Freddie remembered the flash of gleaming white teeth, the sarcastic smile. Why did he still pretend with people like Ramos, who must know as many gutter secrets as anyone on the island. Ramos could care less about him being a drunk, so why did Freddie pretend? Perhaps because the years of excess still hadn't quite left their tell-tale traces, and the last thing to leave him was his vanity. From his medical training, Freddie knew he'd been born lucky. He had a constitution like the sea wall he was leaning against. Solid, resistant, able to take anything that life threw at him. In body at least, if not in mind.

The faint strains of 'Moonlight Serenade' drifted from deep inside the narrow streets of the Old City. In the dark blue of the west a lone star was fading.Fading like him. But in broad daylight it would still be there, shining invisibly, long after he was gone. Freddie Sanchez would leave no trace.

The klaxon on the s.s. St Louis broke into his self-pity. Out in the dark ocean, like a birthday cake ablaze with candles, the ship stole into the arms of the harbour, the smoke from its stacks ghostly wraiths against the night sky.

Nearly a thousand refugees, the papers said, escaping from the Nazis. German families like the one he once knew as a student in London. Where were they now? Safe, he was certain. He was sure Professor Carl Mueller's family would be safe...Despite the warmth of the night, at the thought of the Mueller's, Freddie shivered. After so many years, the cold chill of self-disgust still lingered.

CHAPTER TWO

The ship's breakfast gong had roused those passengers not already on deck watching their sanctuary appear out of the night like a mirage. As the Mueller's ate their breakfast, among the other excited passengers, the sudden rattle of the anchor splashing into the water far below broke through the noisy salon.

'W-W-What's that, Papa?' stammered Carl's youngest son, Klaus, nervously.

'It's the anchor, dummy!' Hans snapped.

'Hans!' his mother reproved, taking Klaus' hand protectively and patting it. 'Your brother is not a dummy! You are not to say such things!'

Anna frowned. She had raced through her breakfast so she could get back on deck. 'But we're not there yet! Why have we stopped?' She got up to go outside.

'Sit down, Anna,' said her mother.

Carl looked at his wife, elegant in her Parisian chiffon. Despite the early hour, she may have been back in her beloved Vienna. Esther Rosenberg, the belle of the ball, the raven-haired beauty who had stolen his heart so long ago. Then broken it, like a wilful child a toy.

'It's been a long voyage, my dear. We must allow them a little excitement.' He smiled at Anna. 'Go on, but be careful.'

Anna went out, annoyed that the ship had stopped in the middle of the harbour some distance from the quay. She leant on the rail, looking beyond the harbour to the broad, tree-lined square, where the domes of the Presidential Palace and Cathedral were being touched by the rising sun. To the west, where the Old World met the New, tall American hotels thrust brashly upwards. She wanted to explore everything, now.

In the salon Esther repeated Anna's question, impatiently. 'Why *have* we stopped, Father?'

Carl paused, the crystal water glass at his lips, and gazed at his wife. Like all thoroughbreds she was highly strung. Right now, with her deep brown eyes wide open, she looked like a gazelle startled at the water's edge.

'Just routine, my dear, I'm sure. There's nothing to be concerned about'.

The hubbub in the salon sprung up again, but now the excitement was flecked with a trace of anxiety. Carl watched people turning to each other enquiringly. One or two were talking in whispers.

Were the rumours really true, he thought?

His heart was pounding, shaking his whole body. Lungs bursting, he made a last desperate effort to reach the surface, as disembodied hands grasped for his limbs to drag him back into the depths.

'Wake up, Senor Freddie! Wake up!'

Freddie jolted awake. Conchita let go his shoulders and stepped back.

'Uhh?' He sat up and gasped as the pain hit his head like a mallet. He lay back and groaned, shielding his eyes from the shimmering barbs of sunlight piercing the cracks of the shutters.

'Here. Drink!' Conchita thrust an earthenware mug in his face. His stomach heaved at the acrid smell of her patent hangover cure. Pushing the mug away, he groped for the bottle on the floor beside his bed.

'No, no, Señor Freddie! No more! You get up. You get up for ship!'

He shot upright, ignoring the fact that his brain had just exploded inside his skull.

'The ship! – Have they disembarked yet?'

'Dis-imback?'

Conchita's English had never improved and he'd long since given up trying. Whores didn't need to be fluent linguists. Not harbour whores at any rate. The ones who prowled the roulette tables of the city, sniffing out rich Americans, were a different matter. But whether they were any more fluent at their principal trade Freddie had never bothered to investigate. He'd had his fill of sophisticated women. He preferred the honest, earthiness of Conchita and her friends. They only lied for money.

'The people. Have they got off the ship?'

'No. It there still.'

Freddie forced himself to squint through shutter's glare. The ship lay stationary in the middle of the harbour. He sank back on the pillow, an arm covering his face.

'Conchita – '

'You tell me! Make me promise. You shave. I make suit nice. Your hair needs cut...' Freddie groaned again. 'You look nice for job. You need money.'

Beneath his elbow Freddie sighed. That much was certain.

CHAPTER THREE

Gripping the ship's rail excitedly, her eyes wide in wonder, Anna turned to her brother. 'Hans! Look!'

Below them, circling the ship's black sides like a multi-coloured bangle, dozens of small craft began to arrive over the sparkling water. Traders crowded the swaying boats shouting up to the passengers gathered at the rails of the decks, offering a bewildering array of fruit, ornaments, straw hats and carved effigies of every kind. Guitars played, small drums and tin cans beat time. Waif-like boys dove into the water after coins thrown from the ship.

Hans glowered at the sea of black faces beaming up at them. 'Niggers! Dirty niggers!'

Anna glared at him. 'You're not to say such things! They are not dirty.'

'The Fuhrer says that – '

'Stop that!' she said angrily. 'We are not in Germany now!'

A scowl marred the young boy's handsome features. He marched away with a toss of his head, shunning the colourful spectacle below.

Anna turned back to the scene below her, intoxicated. When were they going to land, she thought? She couldn't wait to join in the carnival atmosphere.

Scrubbed, shaven, and nursing the mother of all hangovers, Freddie had waited all morning. Despite sitting in the shade outside his habitual harbour café, his light cotton suit, so lovingly pressed by Conchita, had grown damp and limp in the relentless summer sun.

At lunchtime the ship remained stubbornly marooned like a still life, and he desperately wanted a drink. Just one to bring his system into equilibrium. But the last thing he needed was potential customers to smell booze on his breath. The Jews would pay well for an interpreter, and his rudimentary German would at last be of some use, if it wasn't too rusted with alcohol and lack of practice.

It was ten years since he'd used it regularly teaching English to the beautiful young wife, in exchange for German lessons and her heart-stopping smiles, her bright, frivolous company, and... He shook his head to banish the memory. He definitely needed a drink.

Anna rushed the news to her parents, who were drinking iced tea in the salon.

'What's the matter, Anna?' said Carl. 'You look upset.'

'Father, the policeman on deck said we won't be able to get off until Monday!'

'Monday!' exclaimed Esther. 'That's preposterous!'

'He said it's the weekend. Everyone goes to the country.'

'They can't do that! Father, go and see the captain at once. We can't stay here until then.'

Carl placed a hand gently on his wife's cool forearm. 'My dear, I'm sure he's doing all he can.'

'Can I go and play in the pool then, Mama?' asked Hans.

'Oh, yes, please, Mama,' pleaded Anna. Her high-necked dress had caused a rash in the stifling heat. 'It's very hot.'

'No.'

'My dear, we must let them relax a little, if we're going to be here for the weekend. I really do think they'll have time to get dressed again, if the man's wrong, and things start to move.'

Esther relented, 'Very well. Tell Nanny Price to get you your costumes.' She dabbed Klaus' brow with her lace handkerchief. 'I will retire to our cabin. Can you please try and find out what's happening, Father?'

'I'll ask the passengers' committee, my dear.'

Esther rose regally. 'Come, Klaus. We'll have a little nap together.'

'I want to go to the pool, Mama,' said the boy, timidly.

'Not on your own, my dear. Come along.'

Hans laughed and pulled a face at his younger brother.

Cowed, the young boy followed his mother from the salon. Anna and Hans looked expectantly at their father.

'Run along. But take care. Water can be dangerous.'

'Thank you, Papa.'

Brother and sister hurried off, jostling each other on the way out the door.

Carl sat alone thinking of the headline he'd read in the newspaper that had been brought on board the ship. Despite their visas Decree 937 forbade refugees from Europe to land in Cuba, and no other country had been willing to take them in. What if no one took pity on these weary, displaced, hounded people? Surely the world would never allow them to be sent back to Germany and the rumours of the camps?... Would it? As a young medic in the mud-filled trenches of the Great War, Carl had seen countless young men die needlessly to satisfy the whims of their leaders. He had no illusions about the depths to which presidents and politicians could sink.

In the air-conditioned American Club, Freddie's usual bar stool was occupied by a large U.S. Navy lieutenant buying his way into the favours of one of the stunning local girls.

'Freddie!'

Juan Mendez, half hidden by a fringed palm, waved him over. He was seated with another official from the immigration department. As Juan made room for Freddie on the cool leather sofa, a white jacketed waiter appeared at Freddie's elbow.

'A daiquiri, and..?' Freddie waved his hand to his two companions.

'Will you be paying cash, Senor Sanchez?'

Freddie's hand stopped in mid-air. 'What?'

'Sorry, senor, but the manager says - '

Juan intervened. 'Put it on my tab, George'.

'Very good, Senor Mendez.'

Freddie's hand returned to his lap, his muttered 'Thanks' lost in the noise of the bar.

'And the same again for you both, sir?'

Juan shook his head. 'We have to get back after this'.

'Back?' Freddie queried. 'It's Friday. It's the weekend.'

'Tell that to the crowd at the enquiry desk. "What's going on," they say. "Why hasn't the ship docked?"'

'Why hasn't it?'

Juan shrugged. 'Decree 937.'

Freddie knew that President Bru had issued a decree banning future refugees from landing on the island, but he'd heard it wasn't retrospective.

'But the passengers have valid permits, don't they?' he said.

'A matter of debate, my friend. Benitez issued the permits himself.'

'At one hundred and fifty dollars a throw,' added his companion.

'Into his back pocket.'

'So, where's Benitez now?' enquired Freddie.

'Scuttling backwards and forwards trying to see the President. Like a beggar on the Paseo de Prado'.

'What about Batista? Surely, he can't let a thousand refugees just sit out there slowly cooking?'

Juan drained his glass and stood up, smoothing down the sides of his uniform.

'Batista's gone to ground, Freddie. Our brave General is letting Mr President fight this battle alone. There's an election next year, my friend.'

As the two men moved away through the throng, the waiter returned with Freddie's drink, and left leaving an air of disapproval behind. Freddie held the glass by the slender stem and swirled the liquid, resisting the temptation drink it straight down. He sighed heavily, shaking his head. If the Germans weren't allowed off the ship he'd have to rely on Conchita until he found a patient who could afford to pay him for his services. What did that make him? To hell with it! He swallowed the drink at one go. Freddie Sanchez the alcoholic pimp. His parents would have been so proud!

CHAPTER FOUR

Anna's initial excitement had long since turned to frustration. The carnival had continued unabated all weekend and she longed to be part of this fascinating, vibrant new world, tantalizingly just out of reach. The colours, music and brightness of light lifted her spirits in a way she had never felt in the dark, fear-ridden streets of her homeland.

While the bustling horde of revellers surrounding the boat and on the shore became more vocal and excitable, the mood of the waiting passengers aboard grew increasingly sombre.

On Monday afternoon as groups of passengers huddled conspiratorially, spreading rumours and speculation like wildfire, Anna leant on the stern rail, watching the traders' tireless efforts to sell just one more coconut, hand of bananas, or the red-green mango fruit that Anna had yet to taste.

Suddenly a woman behind her screamed. Anna heard a terrifying cry like that of a wounded beast. She half turned, but felt a blow which pushed her onto her knees.

A middle-aged man scrambled up onto the rail beside her, blood dripping from both his wrists.

'They won't get me! I'll die first!' he screamed. Before anyone could move, the man leapt from the rail and, cart-wheeling over and over, plunged into the dark green water beneath the towering stern.

Anna struggled up, shocked and alarmed. A crewman appeared beside her, throwing off his jacket. Mounting the rail, he dove expertly into the water far below. Passengers crushed to the rail to watch the drama, crying out and weeping in panic and fear.

As the man in the water screamed and tore at his bleeding wrists, the crewman locked a burly arm around him and struck out for a police launch racing towards the scene. Still screaming his defiance, the man was hauled aboard the launch, which turned and sped away towards the quay.

Anna looked down at her dress. The white lace was spattered with bright crimson blood.

In the family cabin, Esther cried out, terrified. 'It's an omen! It's an omen! Nanny, burn the dress immediately!'

As Nanny Price helped the distraught young girl out of the blood-smeared dress, Esther sank into a tragic posture on the chaise longue and screamed at Carl, 'Do something, Father! Do something! Before we are all killed!'

After dinner the head of the passengers' committee discreetly invited Carl to join their suicide patrol to help the local police watch the ship overnight. Carl declined. With Esther's rising panic he felt he was on a suicide patrol of his own.

The next day, with Esther refusing to stir from her bed, Nanny Price bustled about ministering to Esther's needs, and keeping a tight rein on her three young charges. While other children played 'chase' with the friendly policemen posted around the decks, the Mueller children were confined to their stuffy cabins.

Anna was playing a tedious game of cards with Nanny Price.

'But why can't we go on deck, Nanny, or in the pool?' Anna complained.

'Your poor mother has got enough to worry about without you getting up to mischief.'

Throwing her cards on the table Anna huddled herself into a tight ball on her bed. 'I don't want to play anymore.'

'Well, just sit quietly then, and don't disturb your mother.'

Carl had spent the day in earnest debate with members of the passengers' committee, who had access to the latest, most reliable information. It was clear that the 'tourist' permits, which many people had paid their last Deutschmarks for, were not worth the flimsy paper they were printed on. It seemed that

Benitez had taken his money and fled Havana. Everything now depended on the two negotiators from the Jewish Committee, who had arrived from New York in a flying boat to try and broker a deal with the obstinate President Bru.

'But don't get your hopes up,' said the committee chairman, 'America's not offering to take us in. They don't want to get involved in Europe's "little squabbles" after the last time.'

After the meeting broke up, Carl sought out one of the Cuban policemen guarding the deck rails. The man's answer to Carl's discreet enquiry made him determined to act.

That evening, when Nanny Price had taken the children to their beds, Carl poured himself and Esther a schnapps and sat down on the bed beside her. He handed her the glass and a small pink pill.

'Take this, my dear. It will help you sleep.' Carl was thankful he'd been allowed to bring his medical equipment and a few drugs out of Germany, even though the customs had charged him a thousand Deutschmarks for the privilege. He waited as Esther swallowed the pill and sipped the drink. Then he broached the subject that had been on both their minds since they boarded the ship over three weeks ago.

'My dear,' he began quietly, 'I talked to the committee today. I'm afraid the news is not good. They don't want panic breaking out on the ship, so they say everything will be all right, to keep us calm. But...' he paused, then took the plunge, 'I keep asking myself, what if it isn't all right? What if they send us away, back to Germany?'

Esther sobbed and clutched his sleeve. Through the fabric he could feel the sharp points of her manicured nails bite into his flesh.

'No! They can't do that! We can't go back! We must get off! There must be a way!' she cried.

He let her lean against him for a moment. Such intimacy had become so rare, and then only at times of crisis.

'Perhaps there is,' he went on gently. 'Perhaps there is a way...for us...' Carl felt his wife stiffen beside him. He paused and then went on cautiously, 'There maybe, maybe...Maybe there is someone ashore who could perhaps help us.'

She looked at him sharply, 'No! No!'

'My darling – '

Esther broke away and stared at him.

'No. Never! I will not have any contact with that man! Ever! Ever!

'Esther, my dear –'

'How could you think of it? How could you even have the nerve even to suggest it.'

'Because I'm thinking of the children, my dear.' he said gravely. 'It's hardly a thing I would suggest lightly. I still feel deeply wronged, as you do.'

'You didn't have to endure the torment I suffered. That I still suffer every day.'

'I know that, my dearest. Believe me I would never try to make light of that in any way. But surely we must try, for the sake of the children, to swallow our pride just this once?'

'Never! Would you shame me before the whole world?'

Carl laid his hand gently on hers. She drew it away sharply. He pressed on, softly pleading. 'Esther, the Cuban people have been poisoned with lies. The President has set his face against us. Should we sit quietly and risk sending our children to their...to their deaths, without even lifting a finger? Knowing perhaps there could be a way?'

Esther sat up, her full lips drawn tightly in a thin line. Carl recognised the expression well. She hugged the ivory silk dressing gown around her knees, like a stubborn child and said, without looking at her husband, 'Something will happen. It must do. We will be saved...'

17

'But what if -'

'I forbid you to make contact with him, ever! Do you hear me? Ever!' Turning her back, she lay down on her side, snatching the sheets furiously around her like a cocoon. Carl looked at her shoulders tensed with anger, and sighed.

CHAPTER FIVE

Late that night Anna was woken by a bright beam of light through the porthole. The light flared, faded, then moved on. Sitting up she looked out through the thick glass. In the darkness, a posse of police launches had surrounded the ship, playing searchlights over the superstructure.

Fear started in her chest. Back home in Germany she had seen what the police had done to the Jews. From her bedroom window she'd watched the almost nightly raids and beatings by the light of the street lamps. Even though she had been brought up a Protestant, and had been shunned by her maternal grandparents, Anna still felt a kinship with the people from whom her mother came. They had become victims. And she, because of an accident of birth, was counted as one of them.

Anna crept from her warm bunk, slipped out the door and across the narrow corridor to her parents' room. Gently she knocked on their door. It opened almost immediately. Her father was in his dressing gown, looking tired.

'Papa? she whispered nervously. 'What's happening? The lights?'

Carl let her in and took her in his arms. 'It's nothing, my love. They just want to discourage anyone else from trying to jump from the ship.'

'I'm frightened, Papa.'

'There's no need, Liebchen. You're quite safe.'

Anna relaxed against the warmth of her father's dressing gown. He rocked her gently.

Carl watched the searchlight beam cross the cabin wall again, and thought of the dark figures of the police patrolling the decks of the sleeping ship, with guns at their hip. Despite the warmth of the cabin and Anna cuddled against his chest, he felt cold. The ship had become a floating prison.

Just before dawn, after he had soothed Anna and put her to sleep in her cabin, he returned to his own. Checking Esther was still heavy in her drugged sleep, Carl noiselessly drew back the closet door and lifted her silver-blue mink coat from its hanger. With a small silver pocket-knife, he cut neatly through the fine stitches that held the lining. His fingers drew out a long roll of tissue paper. Slipping the roll inside a brown paper packet, he sealed it carefully. Then, silently, he left the cabin.

If her last client didn't leave too late Conchita often came to sleep beside Freddie. Not for the sex, though that occasional act with him seemed to cleanse the bad thoughts she sometimes had about her work. He had saved her life years ago and, always, sleeping beside him she felt safe. But an American frigate had docked the day before and Conchita and another girl had gone with its officers to an all-night party at the Hotel Sevilla. So, Freddie had slept alone that night.

The s.s. St Louis remained besieged in the harbour. That was frustrating for two reasons. With no passengers allowed to leave, Freddie's dreams of easy money had faded, while at the same time its presence brought unwelcome memories to the surface.

It was ten years almost to the day since he had last seen the Mueller's. He thought with irony that it was their anniversary. A celebration of the horrendous parting that had left him at first in tears for weeks, and then inside a bottle ever since. He knew it was self-indulgent and weak to blame others for one's own downfall, but when drunk Freddie cultivated that side of his nature, and fuelled it with bitterness over his ruined career. He preferred that state to his guilt and regret when sober.

Strangely for him, he had woken very early and was brewing a pot of rich black coffee when he saw the young policeman arrive and enter the building down below. There were footsteps on the stair and moments later a knock on the door. Freddie crossed the tiny room to open it. Though they had a deserved reputation for casual brutality, the police didn't alarm him.

The man was holding a brown paper packet which he held out to Freddie.

'Senor Sanchez.'

'Yes? What's this?'

'From the ship, senor. A man sent it.'

Freddie gazed at the package transfixed.

'A man? From the ship? What man?'

'A doctor, like you, senor. Professor Carl Mueller.'

Freddie felt as if he had been electrocuted. For a moment he thought he must be still dreaming. He'd been having nightmares about the Mueller's all weekend.

'Don't you want it?'

After a moment Freddie reached out and took the package. It felt real. But dreams always did.

'I er...don't have...any...'

'The other doctor paid me.'

After the policeman had left, Freddie closed the door and locked it, an unusual precaution for him. He gazed at the package for a long time, until the coffee burnt in the saucepan.

As he held the scalded pan beneath the cold water, he continued to stare at the package which, though small, seemed to fill the entire room.

It was too incredible that the Mueller's were actually on the marooned ship. At first, he thought he had misheard. But the policeman had described Carl exactly. Tall, thin, distinguished, but now with thick greying hair, not the jet black he had known. Was the rest of the family with him? Being half-Jewish perhaps they'd not been one of the lucky ones allowed to leave? But Carl would never desert his family, not even if it meant his own life. No. They were on the boat. Only a couple of hundred metres across the water, Esther Mueller was there.

Freddie lit another cigarette, sucked the poisonous smoke deep into his lungs and exhaled long and slowly. At last, he picked up the package and turned it over in his hands. Something soft, and something long, thin and hard. With fingers he couldn't stop trembling, Freddie tore open the packet.

The note inside was brief, but unmistakably from his old tutor. Slowly he unwrapped the thin roll of tissue paper and revealed its contents. Freddie felt a terrible weight descend on him and crush his chest like a vice. His heart pounded insanely. The man who ten years ago had banished him from his life and ruined his prospects of a fine career, was now begging him to save his family. Just as Carl Mueller once held Freddie's future in his hands, now the Mueller's fate was in his, in the form of a sparkling diamond necklace.

CHAPTER SIX

Anna had been the first to see the memo, posted on a notice board outside the ship's salon. Carl opened the cabin door to her frantic knock. She was pale and breathless. Hans stood behind her, with a glint in his eyes.

'Papa, papa! There's a notice!' Anna gasped. 'You've got to see!'

Esther called out from the bed. 'What notice? What is it?'

Aware of the alarm in her voice, Carl reassured her. 'It's alright, my dear. I'll go and see.'

Carl hurried with the children to join the crowd of anxious passengers, all craning to read the captain's message, which read,

"The Cuban Government has ordered us to leave the harbour. After we have refuelled and taken on provisions, we depart at 10am the day after tomorrow."

He had no need to read more.

'Papa, look!'

Anna pointed to the police launches, which had begun to shepherd the small craft packed with traders away from the ship's side. They were now effectively quarantined, with no hope of escape.

'Papa? What's going to happen to us?

Anna was trying hard to be brave, but Carl could hear the echo of fear in his daughter's voice.

'Hans says we are going back to Germany. We're not are we, Papa?'

Hans folded his arms across his chest. 'No one wants us. We have to go back'.

'But we can't, Papa. You saw! The people beaten in the streets. Our friends being dragged away in the night.'

'They were communists,' snarled Hans. 'Enemies of the Fatherland.'

'No. They were Jews!' shouted Anna. 'Like us.'

'We are not Jews!' Hans snapped, indignantly. 'Ask Mama. Tell her, Father!'

'Hans,' Carl said wearily, 'we have been through all this before.'

'We are not Jews!' the youth repeated.

'Hans, your mother gave up her faith when she left her family and married me. But nevertheless, in Germany, she is still seen as a Jew. And as a family, we are all in this together.'

Hans' mouth set in a thin ugly line. 'I am not a Jew,' he said fiercely. 'I am a member of the Hitler Youth. Jews can't join.'

Carl was silent. His son's implacable loyalty to the monster that had usurped his country, and was now threatening the whole of Europe, made him despair. He sensed that Hans fierce commitment wasn't just the naivety of youth, but sprang from a deeper, darker side of his son's nature that made Carl fearful for his future.

Anna didn't share her father's reticence. 'That won't stop you being killed like the rest of us!' she said angrily.

Hans glared at his sister, turned on his heel and strode away. Anna looked at her father, her bright eyes anxious for reassurance. With none to give, Carl hugged his daughter to his chest and stroked her hair.

Freddie found him in the Hotel Nacional's casino. The Mafia's chief fence on the island was playing blackjack in the room reserved for the world's high-rollers. For those people who liked to mix with the Hollywood stars and visiting international cabaret artistes.

'Have you got a minute, Alfred?'

Alfredo Santini looked up from his cards. Freddie had made an effort to conform to the dress code, though his tux had seen better days.

'Don't see you here no more, doc.'

'It's just something I'd like your opinion on.'

Having already bust, Alfredo threw in his cards. 'Deal me out', he said to the dealer.

Alfredo led the way into the sumptuous 'Gentlemen's' Facilities'.

'Can I do for ya, doc?' Five years on the island hadn't changed the Brooklyn twang.

'What d'you make of this?' Freddie produced the brown paper packet from his pocket and slipped the necklace into Alfredo's hand.

'Ice? Nice!'

'Worth, what?'

Alfredo fished in his inside pocket. 'Lucky I carry these around, doc.' He put the glass to his good eye and squinted. He let out a long, low whistle.

'Good? Genuine?' Freddie tried to hide his excitement, his anxiety, the crazy mixture of emotions since he'd first set eyes on the necklace.

'Where d'ya get it?'

'From a friend.'

Alfredo raised an eyebrow. 'Generous friend.'

'How much, do you think?'

'D'you want it split?'

'Either way,' Freddie was impatient.

'Either way, doc, with this baby you ain't gonna worry 'bout going hungry. Not for a long time.'

Freddie took the necklace back eagerly.

'Want me to handle it?'

'It's not stolen, Alfred.'

'That case, double. I can get you top dollar.'

'No. Thanks.'

'Ya welcome, doc. Take it easy. And if you change your mind.'

CHAPTER SEVEN

'Esther, Esther, please calm down,' Carl implored. 'You'll wake the whole ship.'

When Esther woke she had demanded that Carl take some action, and now she was storming round their stateroom in fury.

'You gave him my necklace! You trusted that man with - That was a gift from my father! And he's just made off with it! How could you!'

'My dear, we don't even know if he got it. Maybe the policeman...who knows...? It was a gamble I felt I had to take. I had to try.'

'With my jewellery! To him!' Her dark eyes flashed venomously and she whispered in a voice deep with tragedy. 'How could you! How could you!'

'But you yourself said –'

'I said we must try him as a last resort! For the sake of the children! I swallowed my pride, as you asked. But to give him my necklace!'

'I knew he would need something substantial as a bribe. That is how it works here, I'm told.'

'What do you know about how anything works, you foolish, stupid old man!'

She slumped onto the bed sobbing. Carl stood helplessly, knowing it was futile to try and comfort her until she had wrung the last morsel of tragedy from the scene. He had come to believe that his wife never really felt anything truly. Even now when their lives could be in peril, she was playing the role of the tragic romantic heroine she had been groomed to by her indulgent parents.

He sat down in a chair and waited, watching the woman he had once adored more than anything in the world, wondering if she had ever felt anything real for him. In Vienna where she had stolen his heart at the masked ball, or in the daring clandestine courtship frowned upon by all society, or in her breathless dash to follow him to London, renouncing her family, her religion and demanding to become his lover. Had any of it been real, or just a girlish fantasy inspired by her trashy bedside novels? Perhaps the next stage of their ordeal, with its very real fear of death, would finally break the brittle, dazzling dream. But what would happen to Esther if it did?

At last the sobbing subsided. 'Damn Freddie! she said in a voice thick with tears. 'Damn him! Damn you!'

Dressing in his one decent suit, the light-weight cream linen that Conchita had so lovingly pressed, Freddie spent the whole day trying to gain an interview with the Secretary of State, Juan Remos. A close ally of the President, Remos alone had the power to intercede for the Mueller's.

For effect Freddie had put on a tie from one of the elite London clubs he'd known during his wild student days in the Twenties. Hardly anyone in Havana would recognise it, but it made him feel temporarily like the young man he had once been; charismatic, adventurous, brimming with life and optimism.

But despite hours waiting in the cool marbled halls of the Secretariat, he saw no one who could help. President Bru was out of reach at his country estate. The crooked immigration chief, Benitez, had fled, and the real ruler of the island, General Batista, was letting his troublesome President sweat out the international crisis unaided. Freddie was out of his league. He was a waster, a drunk. Despite his privileged background and his educated accent, he was a low-life. Everyone knew that. Freddie Sanchez the alcoholic. Freddie the Pimp. Who would listen to him?

That night, back in his room, he watched the floodlit ship lying motionless in the harbour, like a huge, wounded animal caught in the glare of headlights. He tried to imagine the Mueller's waiting on board, waiting for him to rescue them.

Freddie took the necklace from his pocket and stroked the hard stones that had hung around the soft, warm neck he had once caressed. She had worn the necklace that evening.

He knew it was pointless offering these riches to some petty official, who would have pocketed them and done nothing. He had tried his best. He had tried and the jewels were still in his safekeeping.

With the diamond necklace, he had enough money to drink himself to death in luxury.

He could set Conchita up in her own little house, where she could ply her trade in safety, if that's what she chose to do. If not, she could just look after him until he passed on. That wouldn't be too long.

But it was not his to sell. It belonged to Carl Mueller's wife, the astonishingly beautiful Esther, or so she had been the first time he set eyes on her. What did she look like now?

Could he return the necklace to its rightful owner before the ship sailed in the morning? Should he? No one knew where the ship was bound. Perhaps the necklace was safer with him. If the Mueller's found a safe haven, they could send for it... That was best.

As he reached for the bottle beside his bed, the low drumming of expensive tyres approached and stopped outside. Looking out, he recognised the Bel-Air Cadillac beneath his window. The uniformed, black chauffeur glanced up and saw Freddie framed against the glass, bare-chested, in the glow of the street light. Raising a white-gloved hand, the chauffeur crooked a finger.

They drove swiftly alongside the dark ocean, heading for the mansions of Miramar. Luckily, perhaps because of his crushing sense of guilt, he hadn't started to drink in earnest. But it would only be a temporary stay. By morning he would be insensible.

In five minutes the limousine was slipping smoothly down the deserted boulevard, its headlights picking out ornate wrought iron gates and glimpses of palatial residences set back beyond well-tended lawns. The chauffeur made a left and stopped before double golden gates, almost twice as tall as Freddie. After a moment the gates swung silently open and the car cruised inside.

'Doctor Freddie!' Tony Trevianni extended his chubby arms and lightly clasped Freddie to his corpulent torso. His host smelt of Parisian cologne, expensive cognac and the finest Cuban cigars.

'A drink?'

'That depends, Tony. On why I'm here.'

Tony shrugged and smiled uncomfortably, a flash of gold among the straight white teeth, complementing the cluster of gold chains that hung at his throat. He waved his hand.

'Sit. Sit down.'

Freddie chose the white leather sofa, twice as long as his own bed.

Tony heaved a deep sigh. 'It's bad, doc. Very bad. You must say nothing. Nothing.'

'Would you have brought me here if I were a gossip?'

'No. Of course not. You're a good man, Senor Freddie. An honest man.'

It was Freddie's turn to smile uncomfortably, thinking of the necklace hidden beneath his mattress and the ship that would be gone in the morning.

Tony clenched his chubby fists. 'I'm ashamed to be a father. What did I do wrong? Tell me. I bring my children up to be good Catholics. To respect their father and their mother. What did I do wrong?'

Freddie thought of the Trevianni children. There was only one girl of age.

'Isadora?'

Tony let out a little cry and thumped his palm with his fist. 'How could he do that? To my daughter. Eh?'

Freddie shrugged sympathetically. Precocious, flirty, brown-eyed Isadora had long been an accident waiting to happen. Apparently, it finally had.

Tony gave a short, ugly laugh. 'But he won't do it again. Not unless he fucks fishes.'

'I'm sorry,' Freddie said, hoping that Tony would never have cause to bear him a grudge.

'But you can help, doc? She's not a bad girl. I don't want her life ruined, Senor Freddie. She's my daughter.'

The image of another daughter flashed into Freddie's mind. A dark-eyed, chubby child, the image of her beautiful mother. Was Carl Mueller thinking about his daughter Anna now? Was he too praying for her to be saved? Not from social disgrace, but from the places whispered about by the German agents who swarmed like smooth rats round the casinos and bars of the city? Saved from the places they joked of as 'death camps.'

'Where is she?'

'She's upstairs. You've got everything you need?'

Freddie nodded and patted his doctor's bag beside him.

'You save her, doc, I give you anything you want. Anything. You name it. Anything at all.'

Freddie rose and paused before he left the room. 'Tony,' he said, knowing the answer before he asked. 'How well do you know the President?'

CHAPTER EIGHT

Anna was woken by the dull throb of the engines deep down in the ship. The sound mingled with the sorrowful wailing that had not ceased since the time she had read the notice.

She was up in an instant. Were they moving? Had the ship sailed while she was asleep? She looked from the window. In the early dawn the police launches still bobbed in their cordon, sealing off the anchored ship. Throwing on her dressing gown she hurried to her parents' cabin.

They were already up, sitting on the bed. Esther was cradled in Carl's arms, weeping softly.

'Papa? Are we going?

'Not yet, precious.'

'But the engines - '

'They will have to warm them up. They have to test them, before we sail'.

Esther sobbed, muffled, in his arms.

Anna felt helpless. 'Can I go up on deck, Papa? I want to see the island one last time, so I can remember it.'

'Of course, Liebchen. But take care.'

The Bureau of Immigration hadn't opened when Freddie arrived, but he was very early. He stayed inside the car in the shade, opened another pack of cigarettes, and looked out across the bay to where the ship lay with its stacks idly smoking. The notice had said it was to sail at ten and, knowing the damned German mania for order, it would leave on time.

Freddie waited and fretted, but he would have plenty of time if someone would only come and open up.

Tony Trevianni had been very intrigued when Freddie had asked for the favour instead of his usual fee. But he was a man who knew the value of contacts, and made the call.

'Sure hope your old friends are grateful', he said when he'd fixed it with his good friend, the President.

Freddie had wanted the Mueller's freed that night, but everything had to be done officially, by the book. He thought, ironically, that an illegal abortion had gained their release, but everything had to be seen to be done correctly. Politics was like an elegant white glove hiding rough, cracked hands and dirty fingernails beneath. He loathed himself for having to use the same squalid tactics.

Juan Mendez arrived twenty minutes late. Freddie quizzed him as he unlocked the ornate wrought-iron shutters that protected the heavy walnut door.

'No, my friend, I haven't had any instructions about issuing any visas'.

'It's from the President himself.'

'Have you any documentation?'

'No, Juan. It was a phone call late last night.'

Juan shrugged his plump shoulders as he opened the door and went inside the cool, shadowed entrance hall.

'Then I'm afraid I can do nothing.'

Freddie followed him in anxiously. 'But the President –'

'Maybe my boss has been told. I'll ask him when he comes in.'

'When will that be?'

Juan shrugged again, and opened the window shutters to let the morning sun flood the room a bright yellow.

'He's the boss, Freddie. Whenever he likes.'

The deck was already full of passengers mostly standing in silence, like Anna, taking their last look at the island. She found a space at the rail facing the shore. The rising sun was turning the grand buildings of Presidential Plaza to gold.

The ship was divided between wailing and deep silence. Somewhere Anna could hear a rhythmic chant –

'We cannot sail. We must not die -'

Anna choked back tears. How she longed to set foot on the island. To walk under the palms, to be lost in the bustle, the sounds, the music of these vibrant people. She stood silently, the tears hot on her cheeks. She looked past the line of police boats to the shore and remembered her first sight of the island. It had looked so welcoming, so free. She could make out the line of tall palm trees beyond the harbour, their long fronds waving in the gentle breeze. She had never stood beneath a palm tree. Were there coconuts clustered at the top? She'd never know, now.

'We cannot sail. We must not die -'continued the chant.

But they were to sail. Were they also to die?

The ship's klaxon startled them all. A long, mournful moan. A deeper silence followed the deafening noise. Then the panic and the prayers rose again, louder, from deep inside the ship. Suddenly, the note of the engines changed, higher, louder, more insistent. It couldn't be long now.

Juan's boss, Fernando Mestre, arrived thirty minutes before the ship was due to sail. By then Freddie was frantic.

He'd sat in the lobby jumping up at each new arrival, but each time Juan, seated at his solid, walnut desk in the corner, had shook his head. Mestre was small and ill-formed, Juan had finally told him, like a tiny insect with a moustache. You couldn't miss him.

But Freddie did.

He was in the washroom cooling his hot cheeks and forehead and snorting the last of his cocaine when Mestre

arrived. Freddie looked at himself in the mirror as he rubbed
the remains of the white powder around his gums. He'd slept
badly, thinking about facing the Mueller's. He looked like his
suit, crumpled and tired. But his concern at meeting them was
nothing to the thought of facing himself if he failed to set them
free. Straightening his tie, he took a deep breath and went out
to find Juan indicating an open office door.

'He's here. Waiting.'

Yes, Mestre informed Freddie, the message about the
Mueller's had been relayed to him, but there were the usual
formalities to be gone through before he could issue the visas.

'But the ship sails in twenty minutes,' said Freddie, trying
to sound urgent and not weak at the same time.

'Senor Sanchez, a man of your intelligence must appreciate
I cannot issue visas without completing all the necessary
documentation,' said the swarthy insect with the moustache.
'There are regulations –'

'Damn the regulations!'

The moustache twitched. Freddie had lost it. Juan had
warned that anger would put Mestre's back up, but Freddie
was no longer in control.

'This is an order direct from the President! What's he going
to say if the ship sails with those people still on board?'

In reply Mestre slowly opened the top drawer of his large
desk and withdrew a sheaf of official-coloured forms. 'The visa
applications have to be made out in triplicate. One for each
of the passengers,' he said grimly, placing the forms under
Freddie's nose.

Freddie stared at the forms, then snatched up the phone on
Mestre's desk and dialled 0.

'Miramar 247', he snapped when the operator answered.

'Yes, I know that's the President's house! Just dial it! Now!
And tell them it's Dr Freddie Sanchez for President Bru!'

CHAPTER NINE

The crowd at the harbour had increased with the news that the ship was about to depart. By the time Freddie arrived it was so dense he had to abandon his car and shove his way to the harbour edge, where people were in danger of being pushed into the water by the crush.

The ship was still there, with thick smoke belching from its twin stacks, clearly ready to sail. His telephone bluff had worked and the six visas were safely in his pocket, stamped unceremoniously by Mestre as soon as Freddie had put the receiver down. Freddie didn't want to fail on the last lap.

Scanning the dock-side he saw what he was looking for. 'Lardy' Brown had his boat tied up at the quay and was sitting aboard alone watching events along with the rest. Freddie pushed through and jumped aboard, landing with a thump that surprised the old boat owner and made him spin round with a start.

'Hola! Senor Freddie?'

'Lardy, I need to get out to the ship. I've got visas to take six people off.'

'Off? She's just leaving.'

'I know. That's why I need to get to it now.' He took the clutch of visas from his pocket and waved them under Lardy's nose. 'Look, visas.'

'How much you pay?'

'Anything you like, but I need to go now.'

'Twenty dollars?'

It was a question because it was an extortionate amount, even by Lardy's standards. But at this moment Freddie didn't care.

'All right. Let's go.'

'Twenty dollars.' This time the chubby black hand was extended, pink palm upwards.

'I don't have it right now. Later.'

Lardy smiled, black gaps where teeth should have been. He knew Freddie's reputation for credit. 'Twenty dollars, Senor Freddie,' he said evenly.

'I don't have it, Lardy. Look, these visas are direct from the President himself. I'll pay you later.' Freddie thrust the papers into his face again, knowing it was useless as the old man couldn't read.

Lardy grinned, 'Thirty dollars.'

Freddie glared at him. 'And how would you like the President to know you ignored his direct order and that the ship sailed with these people still on board?'

Lardy continued to grin at him, but the smile was a little less cocky now.

'You got trouble, Senor Sanchez?' It was the young policeman, Ramos, standing beside the boat, looking cool and relaxed in his neat khaki uniform. A black, evil-looking service revolver nestled in the stiff, brown leather holster at his hip.

'Do you know how to use that thing, Ramos?' asked Freddie nodding at the weapon.

Ramos smiled smugly. 'I am the best shot on the island.'

'Then jump aboard. I may need you if there's any trouble on the ship.' He thrust the visas at Ramos. 'Direct from Bru. And Lardy is just taking me out there, that right, Lardy?'

Ramos glanced at the official visas and then stepped on board. With a surly glance at Freddie, Lardy flicked the ignition and started the boat's engine.

As the wailing combined with the throb of the engines, Anna turned away from the crowd lining the rails. She felt her parents needed her and she needed to be with them. If they were to die, they would begin their final journey together as a family.

She had just reached the main stairway to go back inside the ship, when she heard a man cry out. Fearing another suicide attempt she turned to look.

'Look!' the man shouted again, excitedly.

All eyes followed his pointing finger. Anna went back to the agitated crowd and wormed her way through to see the cause of the excitement.

A stubby boat was racing through the water towards them. As the craft grew larger, approaching the cordon of police boats still surrounding the ship, the passengers started chattering excitedly. The helmsman of the boat was a plump black man. Beside him stood a young policeman and another man in a crumpled, cotton suit, his shock of straw-coloured hair flattened to his brow by the speed of the boat.

As the boat raced through a gap made by the police launches, the man looked up at the passengers crowding the rails. His handsome face looked tired, worn, but triumphant. Cupping his hands to his mouth, he shouted excitedly, 'The Mueller family! Professor Carl Mueller!'

CHAPTER TEN

The atmosphere in the Mueller's cabin was electric.

'He's said he's got visas for us to leave the ship!' gasped Anna, breathless from dashing the news to her parents.

Carl and Esther looked at each other, a mixture of shock, joy and disbelief. But it was true. A steward, hurrying after Anna, confirmed the good news. They were to take their luggage to the ship's ladder and disembark. All the Mueller family and Nanny Price too.

The next few minutes were a blur. Carl, Hans, Nanny and the steward stumbled up the companionway to the boat deck, hauling various brown leather cases. Bringing up the rear behind Esther, Anna and Klaus, two more stewards carried Esther's trunk.

Having climbed the ladder to the ship's deck, Freddie looked through the excited crowd. Carl was easy to see, being over six foot and wearing a silver-grey homburg, but the rest of the family were hidden in the milling throng. Anger was rising as the crowd grew, demanding to know why they weren't allowed to leave too. Freddie had expected it. He glanced at Ramos, who smoothly slipped his gun from its holster and fired one deafening shot into the air. The effect at such close quarters was immediate. The crowd took a pace back, allowing Carl to shepherd his flock to the ladder where another policeman was waiting to help them down to Lardy's boat.

Freddie only glimpsed Esther, tearful and near to panic, as she was jostled through into the arms of the policeman. Out of Freddie's sight, Anna had wrestled her arm from her father's grip.

'No!' he heard her shout angrily. 'I'm not leaving without the others. It isn't fair!'

Carl, occupied with the bemused Klaus, had become separated from his daughter, who was about to become submerged in the crowd.

'Anna!' he cried.

Esther's cry of panic pierced the hubbub. Freddie forced himself into the scrum, grabbed the young girl firmly round the waist and carried her, kicking and screaming, to the top of the ladder where Ramos helped him carry her down the precarious steps. They were all in danger of falling as Anna struck out furiously, catching Freddie full in the face, and knocking Ramos's cap into the water.

'No, no!' she cried. 'We can't leave them! They're our friends!'

Somehow, they were all suddenly in the swaying boat, the luggage was tumbled in after them and Lardy gunned the craft away from the sheer, black wall of the ship.

The family huddled towards the prow in silence, listening to the howls of anger and outrage coming from the passengers they had abandoned. Carl hugged the sobbing Anna to his chest and held Esther in an embrace all the way. Freddie sat in the stern with Ramos and Lardy. No one spoke on the short journey.

Ramos, aware of the danger of the large, excitable crowd gathered at the quay, told Lardy to take the boat through the harbour channel and up the river leading through the Old City.

As they entered the mouth of the narrow river and the s.s. St Louis disappeared from view behind the dockside warehouses, Anna let out a little cry, 'Papa!'

Carl hugged her closer. 'Hush, Liebchen,' he murmured. 'There was nothing we could do.'

After Lardy had tied up at the small jetty, Freddie quickly found two taxis. He and Ramos crammed into the front seat of the first, with Anna and Nanny Price in the back.

'Hotel Ingleterre,' Freddie instructed the driver.

As the two cabs wound through the narrow shadowed Spanish style streets, that made up the ancient and most beautiful part of Havana, Freddie became aware for the first time that his nose was violently throbbing. Touching it he realised it had bled. He took out a handkerchief and dabbed it gently. The faint red smudge on the white cotton told him the blood had already dried.

The ship's klaxon sounded one final echoing blast. Glancing behind Freddie looked straight into the wide dark eyes of Anna, glaring hatred at him from the shadow of the rear seat.

'You had no right to drag me from the ship!' she said coldly. 'I wanted to stay.'

'I understand how you feel –,' began Freddie, but Ramos, squashed at his side, snapped without turning his head.

'You should be grateful! I would have left you there!'

Anna was about to respond, but felt Nanny Price's hand gently squeeze her own. She contented herself with staring hard at the back of Ramos' bare head, pleased that she'd knocked the man's hat into the water.

Uniformed porters scurried from the imposing 'Hotel Ingleterre', which looked out on the tree-lined central square leading to the Paseo de Prado, the finest colonial avenue in the city. If Esther was annoyed it wasn't the Biltmore Hotel, she didn't show it. She was helped from the cab by Carl and ushered from the burning sun into the cool reception hall, replete with palms, baroque marble statues and Moorish wrought-iron. A few elegantly dressed guests, seated amid the sumptuous sofas and deep armchairs, glanced up at their arrival, then cast their eyes away, affecting the indifference of their class.

The family waited seated in the lobby while Freddie took charge asking at reception for the finest suite and bedrooms the hotel had to offer. Though he had hardly exchanged a word with Carl, he assumed the Mueller's would expect the best. Having completed the formalities, he approached the family. He was no longer conscious of his throbbing nose, facing them in the cool calm of the lobby had driven everything else from his mind.

'They've given you one of their finest suites and two other bedrooms. I hope that's sufficient,' he said, avoiding looking at Esther.

'Thank you,' said Carl stiffly.

'The porter will take you up. They'll charge the taxis to your bill. I'm afraid I'm a little short –'

'That's quite all right,' the icy voice replied. 'I will pay them.'

'You'll find that most of the staff speak English and a little German.'

'English will suffice,' replied Carl, clearly anxious to take charge of the situation.

Freddie risked a glance at Esther, but her eyes, beneath her wide-brimmed hat, were fixed firmly on the white gloved hands resting in her lap.

'As you probably know,' Freddie continued, looking back into Carl's cold eyes, 'there are German agents on the island who have been spreading propaganda against, er...I'm sure you're safe now, but be on your guard.'

'German agents?' said Hans excitedly. Carl shot his son a stern glance. The boy looked away with a scowl.

'If there's anything else I can do for you –'

'Thank you,' said Carl coolly, 'I'm sure we will be able to manage very well from now on.'

It was a dismissal. Freddie was shocked at its abruptness, but was thankful for the excuse to get away from Carl's glacial presence. He nodded, feeling almost like clicking his heels at Carl's Teutonic tone.

'Fine...Well, welcome to Havana.' Turning away, he walked briskly from the hotel.

As Carl watched him go, Anna looked at her father. She had only ever known him as gentle, warm man, with a good word for almost everyone. This cold, ungrateful figure standing before her was a complete stranger.

CHAPTER ELEVEN

Once outside the hotel Freddie slowed down and drew breath. Even beneath the shady canopy of the almond trees that ran the length of the Paseo de Prado, it was sultry and too airless to hurry. But the heat wasn't what caused Freddie to drop his pace to a slow, almost trance-like, walk.

He had expected embarrassment and awkwardness from the dignified Carl, and the total snub that he had received from Esther. But Carl's coldness still enveloped him like a shroud. He had saved their lives and done everything that had been asked of him. Despite their past history, he expected a little more gratitude. He walked on, feeling hurt.

As he made his way slowly back to his car, Freddie tried to piece together his initial impressions of the family.

Carl hadn't changed, except for the steel grey hair which gave him an even more distinguished appearance than he'd remembered. Esther, hidden beneath her wide-brimmed hat, he'd hardly had chance to observe. He couldn't tell how ten years had changed her, if at all. But already young Anna was taking after her mother; the same determined olive-skinned oval face, straight emphatic nose and those wide round eyes that seemed almost purple in their depth. She clearly had the same fiery temperament too, as the ache in his nose testified. He felt it gently. It wasn't broken, but he'd have two black eyes by the morning.

The older son, Hans, whom he'd last seen as a young child, was going to be as tall, dark and handsome as his father. But there was a hint of arrogance there that could only have come from his mother's side. Of the youngest son, Freddie had hardly gained an impression, except that he seemed to cling to his mother's arm too childishly for a boy who looked about nine years or ten years old. Unlike his siblings, he was looked plump. His hair was covered by a large hat, but his fair skin was a surprise, among the olive shades of the rest of the family. A throwback to another generation? Perhaps an ancestral peccadillo resurfaced to remind even the proudest family that even they are human. Esther Mueller needed no reminder of that. She had been so very human once, and being close to her again reminded Freddie of how he had once felt.

But that was in the past. In the sharply class-divided city, it was unlikely their paths would ever cross again, for Carl had made it quite plain that Freddie was still an outcast.

In the excitement of the previous forty-eight hours Freddie had forgotten the necklace. So, it was two days later before Conchita, putting Freddie's mattress out the window to air, found the necklace lying underneath. She picked it up and was standing gazing at it when Freddie came back from collecting his monthly allowance at the bank. A small sum left in trust from his father which barely lasted him a week.

'Freddie,' she said, eyes shining. 'This for Conchita?'

Freddie laughed. 'You?' he said, not meaning to sound unkind.

The young woman nodded. 'Tomorrow my birthday'.

He grimaced. It was almost three years since he'd saved Conchita's life, after he found her in a pool of blood where her pimp had left her. She, grateful to the gentle 'gringo' who had taken her to his room, and stitched her up, had stayed the night and afterwards moved into the room below his. Along with booze, Conchita was a fixture in Freddie's life. A habit he hadn't bothered to break. And, until now, he had never forgotten her birthday. Perhaps because, apart from his own, it was the only one he had to remember.

'No, Conchita. That belongs to someone else.'

Her eyes flashed jealously, 'Who?'

45

'The lady I helped get off the ship.' The story was all round the harbour by now, though Freddie had spoken to no one about it. 'Her husband sent it so I could pay for the visas. But I didn't need it.'

'You not give it back?' said Conchita incredulously, clutching the necklace to her breast.

Having forgotten it, Freddie hadn't thought what to do with it until this moment. It was true the Mueller's didn't know he hadn't needed it to gain their release, so they wouldn't be expecting it back. And, they had been less than grateful for his help for saving them. There had been no word from them since he'd left them at the hotel, so he could certainly keep it, without too much remorse.

Not, of course, as a present for Conchita. That would be as absurd as cloaking a pack mule in ermine instead of a rough saddle cloth. Alfredo Santini said the necklace was worth a small fortune. Enough to keep him for the rest of his life. So, there would be no more cutting looks from waiters at the American Club. No. He would buy a house, where Conchita could 'entertain' safely, or just retire. When Santini sold it.

The Mueller's were at dinner in the dining room of the parents' hotel suite. Still feeling out of place and on show, they had kept themselves to themselves since their arrival. Or at least Esther had, and the children were forced to follow suit.

Carl had ventured out that day to the American Embassy to enquire about immigration to the United States. But, as he told them solemnly over dinner, that was impossible. There was a waiting list of many years and, since the family were now considered safe, they would not be a priority.

'It looks like Cuba is to be our home,' he said. 'At least for the foreseeable future. So, we had better make some plans.'

The family greeted the news in silence. From the little they had experienced of Havana it was a strange, alien world to them. It was fiercely hot, with bouts of torrential rain. They had to sleep under huge hanging mosquito nets, listening to strange cries and music drifting up to them from the busy streets below, at all hours of the day and night.

Anna was the only one truly excited. 'I'm learning Spanish from the chambermaids,' she announced. 'And we'll have to find a home, won't we, Mama? Perhaps that man Freddie can help? I think he's rather nice really and I'm sorry I hurt him. Can we go and ask him if his nose is better?'

Esther remained silent. Carl wondered how far the next tantrum was away. There was a knock at the door and Nanny bustled from her chair in the ante-room to open it. She returned holding a white envelope which she handed to Carl.

'This was handed in at reception, Herr Mueller.'

'*Mr* Mueller, Nanny,' Carl corrected. With a World War seemingly inevitable he wanted to distance his family as far as possible from their past life. Carl opened the envelope and shook it. With a sharp clatter the diamond necklace dropped onto his plate.

It was late. Esther was in their bedroom in her cream silk nightgown and jacket, staring stubbornly at her husband, still dressed in his shirt sleeves and trousers.

'But, Esther, he had no need to return it. He could have kept it and we would never have known.'

'No.' The voice, though high, was not yet at danger pitch.

He pressed on. 'He saved our lives, my dear. The lives of our children. And now, he's given us back a fortune he could well have kept as a legitimate reward. The least I can do is give him our sincere thanks.'

Her tone rose dramatically, 'If you love me. If you have ever cared for me and your children at all,' she said, 'you will not see him, or mention his name, or communicate with him again, in any way! Ever!'

CHAPTER TWELVE

The invitation came out of the blue. Standing by the Italian marble fireplace in their suite, Carl read aloud from the stiff, gold-edged card in his hand.

'Senora Isabel Luisa Gonzales Rio de Cruz has the pleasure of inviting the distinguished Professor Carl Mueller, his wife, Esther Mueller, and their family to be her special guests at her annual garden party –'

'When?' Esther asked excitedly.

He checked the date. 'Next Saturday.'

It was the Mueller's third week on the island and, apart from rebuffing calls from various newspaper reporters, this was their first real contact outside the hotel. Esther had not set foot beyond the entrance, complaining of the heat, the noise, the fumes and the beggars. She spent her days in the cool elegance of her suite reading romantic novels, or playing bezique and canasta with Nanny Price and the children. Little Klaus was kept constantly at her side, petted and pampered with sweet titbits provided by the hotel chef.

A representative from the island's small Jewish community had left his card, but Esther had told Carl to ignore it. Having abandoned her race and faith when she married Carl, and with anti-Semitism seemingly endemic, she wanted to distance herself as far as possible from her roots.

But this invitation was entirely different. From the hotel reception Carl learnt that Isabel Luisa Gonzales Rio de Cruz was the premier hostess of Cuba's elite.

'She owns a mansion in Miramar,' he said, 'as well as the island's largest country estate. She even has her own box in the city's Catholic cathedral.'

Esther clasped her hands with pleasure, thrilled that the Mueller's had been singled out. At last Esther would have a setting in which to shine again. And she was certain from what she had seen of the dishevelled Freddie that he would not be among the invited guests of the city's elite.

The occasion was all that Esther had dreamed of. They were met at the hotel by their hostess's uniformed Spanish chauffeur and driven in her custom-built Hispana Suisa along the gently curving boulevard beside the sparkling ocean, into the tall-palmed suburb. Home to the island's ultra-rich.

Isabel's mansion, a sprawling Moorish extravagance in white and pink, was hidden from the road by a forbidding granite wall topped with teeming crimson bougainvillea. As they drove up the gravelled drive leading to the house, they saw armed policemen strategically placed among the trees and flowered shrubs that surrounded the estate.

Incongruously, in this exotic setting, an English butler complete with white tie and tails greeted them at the door. He escorted the family through the vast cool entrance hall to the rear terrace, where the scene before them made Esther give a tiny gasp of delight.

In the brilliant afternoon sunshine, the huge pink and white awnings decked with profuse blossoms, mirrored on the tables and surrounding trees, with the turquoise pool of the swimming pool, the lush greens of the garden and lawn stretching to the distant Moorish gazebo, were a kaleidoscope of vibrant colour. At one end of the huge patio, a seven-piece Cuban band played popular melodies for several couples who glided before them with practised ease. The rest of the guests were standing and seated beneath the awnings, everyone in their brightest summer clothes.

Even Carl, accustomed to the finest Bavarian house parties, was impressed. Only the full splendour of a Viennese Ball could match the vitality of the scene before them.

Before the butler had finished his announcement, their hostess was descending upon them, arms open wide.

'Professor Carl Mueller, Mrs Esther Mueller and family,' the butler announced solemnly.

'Professor Mueller!' exclaimed Isabel, a tall, slim vision in diaphanous cerise, with matching mantilla framing the tight black swept hair. 'And Mrs Mueller,' she continued, having caressed Carl's proffered hand with the most delicate touch.

'Esther, please,' said Esther, taking her hostess's hand between her own two white gloves, and adding in perfectly accented Spanish, 'I am most honoured and delighted to meet you, Senora de Cruz.'

Carl smiled to himself. For a moment he was almost filled with pride again for his elegant, beautiful wife who, in her stylish Parisian gown with its discreet décolletage, had immediately become the focus of attention for all the men in sight.

'You speak Spanish!' said Isabel delightedly.

'I'm afraid not. My daughter Anna taught it to me. She is learning, as I hope to.'

'Anna,' said Isabel fondly, touching the girl's cheek.

Anna noticed that, despite the warmth of the day, her skin felt hard and cold.

'This is Hans, and this my youngest son, Klaus,' Esther continued.

Hans eyes were riveted on the vast, heart-shaped pool beyond the terrace, where a bronzed young man, who could have modelled for Michelangelo, had just performed a flawless dive from the springboard.

'A swimming-pool!' said Hans in awe.

'Of course,' smiled Isabel, showing unexpectedly tobacco-stained teeth. 'Do you swim?'

It was settled. Hans and Anna were found swimsuits to join the others in the pool and, while Nanny Price watched over

Klaus in the shade, Isabel introduced the new guests to her charmed circle of Cuba's ruling elite.

After they had been shown off, leaving Carl feeling rather like their hostess's newest pets, Isabel installed them at a white damask table crowned with a centrepiece of fragrant blooms. She had already decided that when Carl set up his practice all her circle would patronise him. Now, she was arranging with Esther to view a modest but elegant villa, ideal for the family, which was currently for rent.

'Well, Professor Mueller, is there going to be a war?' asked Ronaldo de Cruz, impatient with his wife's domestic chatter.

'If Hitler is to be stopped, I fear that's the only way,' replied Carl.

'Shame. I like the guy,' said the short stout Italian, Tony Trevianni, seated across the table.

Carl looked at him sharply.

'Don't get me wrong, doc. I don't like what he's doing to your people. The Jews. But he sure gets things done.'

Esther had been distracted from Isabel by Tony's words. 'We are not Jews, Mr Trevianni!' she said, in that pitch of voice that always gave Carl concern.

'Call me Tony,' said the fat man, waving his huge Havana cigar through a little circle in the air.

'My husband is a Protestant and I renounced the Jewish faith before I married,' said Esther crisply.

'Good thing,' replied the mobster. 'It's the Jews what´s causing all the trouble, if you ask me. Them and the commies.'

Isabel rose with a bored, dismissive air. 'Politics. We have enough of those with that tedious man Batista.'

'Another communist,' grunted Trevianni.

'Come. Let me show you the house,' Isabel said, taking Esther's hand proprietorially. 'I have some wonderful designs you could copy for your own. We'll leave the men to be boring.'

Carl watched apprehensively as his wife was led away across the perfect lawn. Isabel Luisa Gonzales Rio de Cruz was as sharp as a surgeon's scalpel, and clearly intent on interrogating her newest friend.

Giorgio Trevianni performed a stylish somersault from the board. Turning smoothly beneath the water, he surfaced beside Hans who was seated at the edge, feet dangling in the sparkling clear pool. The young Italian flicked his tight curls, blinked the water from his eyes and smiled his perfect smile at the admiring boy.

He reminded Hans of the posters promoting the Hitler Youth he'd seen back in Germany. Giorgio would look splendid in the black S.S. uniform. Hans resolved to hone his body to the same perfect physique.

'Here's the guys I told you about,' said Giorgio, nodding behind Hans. 'The spies.'

Hans turned and saw two men, in their mid-twenties, tanned and casually dressed, heading their way.

'Dieter! Franz!' called Giorgio and waved.

The men stopped beside the pool, looking down at them. Hans glanced across the pool at Anna. She was in the pool preoccupied playing 'catch' with Giorgio's younger sisters. He got up and put out his hand.

'This is Hans Mueller,' Giorgio said. The two men tensed imperceptibly. Giorgio smiled. 'It's okay, I think he's on your side.'

Isabel had shown Esther every inch of her impressively vulgar mansion and the two women were about to emerge onto the sunlit terrace.

'Oh,' said Isabel, 'I forgot. We must toast to celebrate for your friends.'

'My friends?'

'The other passengers on your ship.'

'Oh, yes, of course.'

The news had come the day before that the s.s. St Louis passengers were to be allowed to disembark in friendly European countries, and not be returned to Germany.

'Would you have rather stayed with them, if you had known?'

'No!' Esther said. 'I think I am going to adore your island.'

'I'm sure it is going to adore you.' Isabel smiled and took Esther's arm. 'It's lucky for us that Freddie was able to get you off the ship.'

Esther started. 'You know him?'

Isabel smiled and looked piercingly into Esther's eyes. 'He's not invited, Esther. But everyone in Havana knows Freddie Sanchez. I didn't realise, however, that his fame had spread as far as Germany,' Isabel probed.

Esther felt herself grow hot under her gaze. 'He was a student of my husbands in London.'

'Ah. But not a friend apparently.'

'What do you mean?' Esther's voice betraying her concern.

They were standing in the shadow of the French windows leading to the terrace. Isabel still had hold of Esther's arm. She lowered her voice. 'I have to warn you as a friend. Soon to be a close friend, I hope.' She moved closer to Esther and put her other hand on her arm. 'The gossip in this city is terrible. Too many people with too little to do. They can hurt, just for the fun of it. But my husband is very powerful and I have much influence. I can help my friends in many ways. I just want you to know that I am always – '

She stopped as Esther went rigid beneath her hands. Esther was staring beyond her, the colour draining from her cheeks.

Isabel turned. Standing at the edge of the terrace was Freddie Sanchez.

CHAPTER THIRTEEN

Conchita had pressed his suit again and yesterday Freddie had bought a new shirt, an event she had never witnessed before.

'Why you go?' she pouted. 'You no like that Isabel woman.'

'I'm going, Conchita, because she hasn't invited me,' he said, adjusting his tie.

'Them people. They be there?'

Freddie had told her their name, but ever since the row over the necklace, Conchita had referred to the Mueller's as 'them people'.

'Undoubtedly, yes. They'll be the newest exhibits in Saint Isabel's zoo.'

'Zoo? You crazy.'

She took his hands from his tie and placed them on her firm round buttocks. He could feel the heat of her flesh through the thin cotton of her dress. 'You no go. Stay with Conchita. She no work today.'

Gently he removed his hands. 'You have to work. I can't afford to keep you.'

She stroked his tie. 'We get married. Conchita keep you always.'

Freddie kissed the vivid pink scar that began at her forehead and ended at her jaw. 'I have to go,' he said and moved away to pick up his hat.

'They no nice. Them people. You give back necklace. They no thank you.'

Which was precisely why he was going. He had checked with the hotel reception that the Mueller's had received the necklace, but there had been no word of acknowledgement from Carl. Not the briefest note of thanks. Surely what he had done for them deserved that? So, he was going. Not for the party. He loathed Isabel and her cronies, who took from the island's riches and never gave back. But Carl Mueller had never been like that, and Freddie wanted to know why he had changed. And, of course despite himself, he was curious to see her again.

It had been easier to talk his way in than he'd expected, as if the guards at the gates were waiting for him. He'd skirted the house just in case Isabel's pompous English butler threw up a last line of defence, and emerged at the end of the terrace behind the band, who had just begun a soulful Gershwin medley 'The Man I Love'. It was then that he saw her, standing shadowed in the doorway in close conversation with Isabel.

If it were possible, the strain of recent events, the persecution in Germany, the flight on the ship and the agony of their week-long 'imprisonment' in the harbour, had increased Esther's beauty. The smooth cheeks were a shade more-hollow, the high cheekbones a little more pronounced, the eyes more deeply set and the figure an ounce fuller.

As if sensing his gaze Esther looked up, straight into his eyes. Isabel followed her look.

'Freddie!' called Isabel, as if she'd expected him to arrive. He hadn't wanted their first meeting to be under Isabel's scrutiny, but there was no choice. He made his way over to them, took Isabel's proffered hand, feigned to kiss it, then turned to Esther.

'Frau Mueller. What a delight.'

She had regained her regal composure and greeted him as a visiting dignitary would a primitive tribesman, extending a white gloved hand and saying coolly, 'Mr Sanchez.'

Freddie touched her fingers lightly and withdrew his hand. Isabel regarded them like a vulture its prey.

'I see you're settling in well,' he said, inclining his head towards their hostess.

'Senora de Cruz has been most kind,' she responded, as if reading a particularly bland inscription.

'I was just learning of your…past relationship,' said Isabel, with a mischievous pause.

Freddie glanced at Esther who betrayed no emotion.

'A student of the distinguished Professor Mueller.'

'Yes. A very poor one, I'm afraid,' he said, with a trace of an apologetic smile to Esther. 'I deserted.'

'But you have redeemed yourself, now at least, bringing the most charming family to our little island.'

'It was a pleasure to be able to help.'

'Yes,' said Esther awkwardly.

'Freddie!' Carl had seen them and hurried over to his wife's side.

'Professor Mueller. Delighted.' The two men shook hands briefly.

'But you have no drink,' said Carl briskly. 'Come. Let me find you a glass of champagne.' With a nod to the two women, Carl led Freddie away towards a white-coated waiter weaving among the guests, glass-filled tray held high.

Isabel watched Esther follow them with her eyes. 'Such a shame,' said the hostess. 'He came from such a good family, as you know.'

'No. I know very little about Mr Sanchez,' Esther said, and then lifting her voice to delight chimed, 'Oh, what are those most beautiful blossoms? I must have some for my own garden.'

As she hurried to smell the extravagant blooms that fringed the terrace, the band segued into 'Lady Be good.'

Carl handed Freddie a glass and the two men made their way through the guests to a less crowded spot near the sparkling pool. There was an uncomfortable pause. Both men knew that

Carl had hurried Freddie away with no other thought than to shield his wife from a potentially embarrassing situation. And now, alone together, Carl realised he had nothing to say.

'A very impressive gathering,' he said lamely.

Freddie nodded. He was not here for small talk.

'You are looking well,' Carl went on uncertainly.

'Carl, you're a brilliant doctor, but a terrible liar. I look like shit.'

Carl grimaced at the obscenity and turned it into an attempt at a smile, 'Well, none of us are...in the first flush of youth.'

'But some of us are in the first flush of alcoholism,' said Freddie, emptying his glass in one go.

He beckoned a drinks waiter and took two glasses from his silver tray. Keeping both glasses, he drank half the first, cursing himself inside. He'd promised Conchita he wouldn't drink and make a scene.

Carl went on uncomfortably, 'It was very good of you to return the necklace.'

'Yes, wasn't it,' said Freddie unhelpfully.

'I was wondering how you managed it without a bribe.'

Freddie gave him a cold look and emptied his first glass. 'You don't want to know.'

Carl frowned.

'There are many things about this island you don't want to know, Carl. Your gracious hostess could tell you most of them.' Freddie waved his glass in the direction of two men, Dieter and Franz, who were making their way from the pool area towards the cavernous food marquee. 'German agents.'

Carl stiffened.

'Oh, don't worry. Saint Isabel won't allow a scene. Everything is done undercover in our little paradise.'

Freddie surveyed the grounds and started on his second glass. Carl cleared his throat. To hell with it, he'd say it once, get it over with and then he could leave satisfied he'd done all he could to placate the man.

'Freddie,' he began, 'I would like to say, on behalf of all my family…just how much we deeply appreciate –'

But Freddie wasn't listening. He'd spotted Anna and the dog a few seconds earlier, but at first his distracted mind hadn't processed the information. The stray dog emerging from the shrubbery, Anna climbing from the pool, hair still dripping, to coax the dog nearer. The dog's twisted stance. The curled lips caked with foam.

'Oh, poor thing. Are you thirsty?' he heard the girl say. Suddenly his mind returned to the present.

'Anna! No!' Freddie yelled.

Anna froze as the rabid animal crouched to spring at her.

Hurling himself through the air, Freddie snatched Anna around the waist. His momentum flung them both tumbling head over heels into the shrubbery. Scrambling up, Freddie shoved himself between Anna and the dog, which faced him with bared teeth and wild eyes. A deafening shot rang out, startling them both. The dog was thrown into the air by the impact of the bullet. It fell and lay still on the grass. Ramos crossed to the dog and rolled it over with his boot. It was quite dead. Putting his pistol back in his holster, he shrugged to Freddie. Taking the animal by the tail, Ramos dragged it out of sight behind the high hibiscus bushes, leaving a thin bloody trail in the bright green grass.

Then everyone was surrounding them. Anna was shaken, but unhurt. Freddie sat on the grass beside her, trembling from the unaccustomed exertion, the adrenalin still surging in his blood.

'Stand back, please. Give them air. Let them breathe,' said Carl taking charge.

Suddenly young Klaus, having raced away from Nanny Price, burst through to his sister, hugging her in fright.

'You hurt? You hurt, Anna?' said the anxious boy.

'No, no. It's all right, Klaus,' said Anna, still a little breathless. 'I'm not hurt.'

Klaus hugged his big sister and smiled a huge smile of relief. Freddie, seated beside them, smiled too at the touching scene. In the forefront of the onlookers, Isabel stared at the sight.

Suddenly Esther took control. Taking Anna and Klaus by the hand, she hurried them away towards the house, with Nanny Price in close attendance. Isabel followed after them, and having organised a warm bath and a hot, sweet drink for Anna, she re-entered the garden and sought out Freddie.

She found him still pestered by a group of admirers reliving the event, and he was initially grateful as Isabel steered him away to a secluded table beneath the trees.

'So, you're a double hero to the Mueller's,' she began. 'I trust they appreciate it.'

Freddie studied his drink and said nothing. He'd moved from champagne to his usual daiquiri, of which Isabel's cocktail waiter was an acknowledged master.

'I heard they haven't contacted you since you so gallantly rescued them from the ship.'

'If war breaks out, Isabel, you should hire your spies to the British...And the Germans,' he added.

'So, it is true.'

Freddie looked across the table into Isabel's ice blue eyes. 'Take care, Isabel,' he said evenly. 'You have secrets that I doubt you even mention in your confessions.'

Her eyes didn't blink. 'Strange that with such a brilliant tutor you never graduated.'

Freddie shrugged. 'I guess I just wasn't clever enough.'

'You're not being clever enough now, Freddie. I saw the way the beautiful Frau Mueller looked when she saw you.'

'Isabel - ' he began to protest.

'I felt it in her body. I am a woman too, Freddie.'

'No, Isabel,' he said getting to his feet, trying to look calm. 'You are an evil bitch.'

'Such a pity about the youngest son,' she said in a voice that stopped him from moving away. 'I gather he isn't very clever either.'

She let the words hang in the air between them. Freddie turned slowly and looked down at her with a slight frown.

'Is it possible you don't know?' said Isabel. 'Or is it just my evil imagination, seeing a likeness that isn't there.'

Freddie continued to stare at her, glass half-raised to his lips. Isabel rose abruptly, with an air of a mission completed.

She stroked his sleeve, 'Poor Freddie,' and glided smugly away over the grass.

Nanny Price was telling Klaus a fairy story more suitable for a toddler, in a quiet, shaded spot close to the gazebo, when Freddie found them. She had her back to him as he walked towards them over the soft grass, but Klaus looked up at his approach, and for the first time Freddie took a proper look at the boy's face. Despite the hot sun on his shoulders, a cold shiver ran down Freddie's spine as he found himself staring at himself as a child.

The hair, the complexion, the jaw, the eyes. None of the dark, almost Mediterranean look of the Mueller family. But his medical training had taught him throwbacks to previous generations were common among all families. Looks alone could be deceiving.

When Nanny Price turned and saw him her face set in the pursed-mask he remembered from years ago. It wasn't inconceivable that anything had ever been said between her and her employers, but she knew, and she made no effort to hide her disapproval of him.

'Mrs Price,' he said pleasantly. 'How are you enjoying Cuba?'

'It's very hot,' was the starched reply.

'And how is this young chap enjoying the sunshine?'

Klaus looked at him blankly. Mrs Price's lips were squeezed into a tight thin line.

'Do you like the sun?' Freddie asked more slowly, looking into the boy's green eyes. Klaus looked at Nanny and nodded shyly.

'My name is Freddie,' he said gently, holding out his hand. 'Hello, Klaus.'

Timidly the boy held out his hand. As Freddie's fingers grasped the tiny hand there was a flurry in the air as Esther burst between them like an avenging angel.

'Mrs Price!' she almost screamed, 'Take Klaus into the house immediately! It's far too hot for him out here.'

With mumbled apologies and excuses, Mrs Price gathered herself and, with a last glare at Freddie, took Klaus by the hand and led him away.

Freddie and Esther stared at each other for a long moment. Her nostrils flared like a thoroughbred, her full breasts heaving beneath the Parisian chiffon. She had seen them at a distance and had run all the way.

'I –' He got no further.

Her voice, breathless, was barely controlled hysteria. 'Don't you ever, *ever* touch that child again! Don't you ever even try to talk to him! D'you hear! Ever. *Not ever!*'

Turning away in a fury, she almost raced back over the grass towards the house.

Freddie stood for a moment, catching his breath. He was conscious of the heat, the buzz of the insects and the distant sound of the band playing one of his favourite melodies. But at

63

that moment he couldn't remember which. It was true. He was a father. Poor little Klaus Mueller was his son.

CHAPTER FOURTEEN

Carl frowned at his wife. 'Leave, my dear?'

'I can't stand it a moment longer,' Esther gasped, breathlessly. 'Gather up the children!'

Before he could respond, Isabel gushed up to them. 'Esther, my darling! There you are! You must meet my ladies!' She took Esther by the arm and smiled winningly at Carl, 'You don't mind if I kidnap your beautiful wife for a moment, do you Professor?'

'I...I'll be with you in a moment, Isabel,' said Esther, flustered. She made as if to kiss her husband on the cheek, and whispered, 'Keep Freddie away from Klaus!'

Carl watched his wife being led away again like a prize pet, and then went in search of Freddie. He found him at last, an empty bottle by his side, unconscious behind the shrubbery bordering the pool. With the help of the young policeman who had shot the dog, he bundled him into the back of a taxi.

'Si, Senor Freddie, I know,' the driver grinned. 'I take him home many times like that.'

At the last moment Carl got in beside the slumped Freddie. The least he could do was see him safely home. He turned to the policeman. 'Could you please tell my wife that I have taken this gentleman home?'

Ramos nodded sardonically and the cab drew away.

As they drove back towards Old Havana, Carl reflected at his guilt for not having thanked Freddie properly for his help. It was unforgivable, but he wasn't expecting to see Freddie at the party, and had been taken off-guard. He didn't know what had happened with Esther, but from her agitation he guessed she and Freddie had exchanged words. He knew that Freddie had really only seen Klaus, briefly, when he rescued them from the ship, but he had seen him closely when the boy was together with Anna. Had Freddie suspected the truth? Was that what Esther meant about keeping them apart? Had Freddie guessed their secret?

Carl was still pondering the implications of that when the taxi drew up beside a row of shabby cafes and bars fronting the harbour. He thought that the driver had made a diversion on some errand of his own. This obviously couldn't be where Freddie lived.

The harbour side was alive with humanity, loitering in the late afternoon sun. Young, skimpily dressed whores posed provocatively by the harbour wall, or in dark, open doorways invitingly. Swarthy, sharp-suited pimps watched idly from their shiny cars, or sat at bar tables doing deals with sailors, or with furtive male passengers from the cruise ships that lay anchored in the harbour. By a hydrant on the corner a black man was tempting a group of balding, paunchy American men with obscene postcards, while another exchanged a small packet of white powder with a young, racy couple. Among the adults, small barefoot children ran, pestering the prurient tourists for nickels, dimes and gum.

The taxi driver looked back at Carl and muttered something unintelligible in Spanish.

'Que?...Qui passa?' said Carl haltingly.

The man rattled off something that Carl couldn't catch. He looked at Carl's uncomprehending expression and gestured out of his window.

'Senor Freddie. His house.'

Carl looked to where the man's finger was pointing. Above a seedy café, flanked by a small bar and what was clearly a brothel, two stories of shabby windows looked blindly out across the harbour.

'There?' he said disbelieving. 'Senor Freddie lives there?'

'Si. His house. There.'

It was a moment before Carl could collect his thoughts. The heat, the noise and the movement disorientated him. Seedy, lascivious humanity swarmed at either side. And Freddie lived here?

'Two dollar fifty,' said the driver.

Carl paid the man and struggled to get the semi-conscious Freddie from the cab. For a moment no one came forward to help, then two lean black men, casually but neatly dressed, eased alongside and, taking an arm each, hoisted Freddie to his feet.

'Take it easy, man.'

As the men half-carried, half-dragged Freddie to the open door beside the café, Carl found himself following as in a trance. He had to see. He followed them up the dark narrow stairs past a closed first floor door, to another flight of stairs leading to a single door at the top. Its brown varnish had long lost its lustre, the brass handle was tarnished green from neglect. One of the men opened the door. They carried Freddie over to the iron double bed and flopped him onto the thin flock mattress. With a grin and a shrug to Carl, the two men left. They had clearly done this before.

Carl stood taking in the room. It was larger than it looked from the outside. Room enough for the bed, a wardrobe, a chest of drawers with a basin and jug on top, a small bookcase containing dusty volumes piled haphazardly on the shelves and a tiny wooden table with two cane chairs. A faded, worn Persian carpet covered the boards between the door and the bed. Slatted blinds kept out the heat of the day and motes of dust floated and sparkled in the sunbeams that pierced the shadows. Beside the bed an empty bottle lay on its side.

'Que passa?'

Carl turned at the woman's sharp voice. She was in her early-twenties, dressed only in a white satin shift which delineated her brown, rounded body. She would have been pretty but for the hideous scar that ran the length of her face, bisecting her full mouth so that her top lip was left puckered to one side.

'Pardon?' he said. 'Me habla no Espanol,' Carl stumbled.

'What you do here?' asked Conchita suspiciously.

'I'm Professor Carl Mueller. I...er, know Senor Sanchez. I brought him home. He's not well.'

Conchita crossed to Freddie, leaned over and smelt his breath.

'He drink?' she asked, eyes narrowed.

Carl nodded. 'I'm afraid so, yes.'

Conchita crossed to the chest of drawers, snatched up the jug and flung its contents into Freddie's face.

Freddie jerked and shuddered half-awake. He tried to focus, wiping the water from his eyes. When his vision cleared, he saw Carl.

'Carl?'

Carl stood awkwardly in the middle of the room, lost for words. He looked about him. Anywhere than look at Freddie. What could he say to the man he had helped bring to this place? The brilliant young student whose career he had shattered and led him to this?

They all turned at a movement by the door. An old man, clothes hanging in rags around his thin bent body, was standing like a penitent before the altar.

'Dr Freddie,' he croaked, eyes wide with hope and tears.

Freddie propped himself up unsteadily on one arm, 'Si, Manuel.'

The old man mumbled in Spanish and showed them his leg. On the skeletal shin an old wound had re-opened and was ulcerating.

'Vamos! Manana!' said Conchita, waving her arms as if shooing chickens from a farmyard.

'No, Conchita,' said Freddie. He motioned to the old man, who shambled to the bedside like a whipped dog. Freddie tried to sit up higher, but sank back on the pillow and groaned, battling nausea.

'Carl,' he said, his forearm shielding his eyes. 'I have iodine and bandage in my top drawer.'

Without a word Carl went to the chest of drawers and opened the top one. Inside were a variety of bottles and rolls of bandage. Selecting a dark brown bottle and a roll of bandage, Carl took them back to the bed. Freddie attempted to sit up.

'Wait, Freddie,' said Carl. 'I can do it. You just lie down.'

Freddie looked at Carl. Their eyes met and, for a moment in the shabby gloom, there was a light of recognition, memories of things past, little triumphs shared, of mutual respect, bright hopes and lost dreams. Freddie smiled weakly and lay back.

'Proceed, Professor Mueller,' he said, and closed his eyes.

By the time Carl had finished treating the old beggar, Freddie was sound asleep, snoring loudly on his back. When Conchita had fetched Carl hot water to clean the wound, she told him she was Freddie's woman. She would take care of Freddie now, she said, and Carl wasn't going to argue with those fierce, dark eyes.

Carl took his time walking back to the hotel. By the time he reached its elaborate wrought-iron entrance he was resolved.

'No, no, no!' screamed Esther. 'I forbid you to contact him again!'

She paced the carpet of their bedroom, her ivory-coloured peignoir flowing behind like waves of her anger. Usually, he just gave in before the onslaught, but for once Carl stood his ground.

'You didn't see, Esther. Where he lives! *How* he lives!'

'I don't care! I don't care!' she screeched.

This time his voice was louder than hers. 'But I do!' he roared.

There was silence. Esther stopped her pacing and looked at him in surprise. In all their years her husband had never once raised his voice to her. He was standing in the middle of their bedroom, still wearing the formal suit he had worn to the garden party. Eyes alive with indignation, he looked taller than his six feet.

'Do you think that Freddie Sanchez would be where he is now, in the gutter with pimps and whores and beggars, if I hadn't acted as I did?'

'You had to throw him out! You had to!'

'But not as I did it. Not as he went. With my word blackening every step he took, my reputation closing every door in his face. I didn't have to ruin his future, Esther! To destroy the career I knew he had set his heart on. That he would have been so splendid at..!'

He paused and then went on more calmly, but with fierce determination. 'Esther, I am not asking you to play any part in this. Indeed, it would be abominable if I did. You need never ever see him again but, as God is my judge, I am going to try my utmost to help undo the damage I have done.'

CHAPTER FIFTEEN

Freddie kept his eyes tightly shut as Conchita bustled about the room, tidying the debris of his life. Outside in the dusty street below urchins shrieked and yelled, either for joy, or in agony inflicted by their bigger, brutal companions. Flies buzzed the room, spiralling in the hot humid air. The summer was going to be unbearable. His brain felt hot and swollen in his skull. It hurt like hell, but that was nothing to the pain he felt about Klaus.

He was in shock. Surprised. It would have been so easy for Carl to dispose of the evidence of their disgrace. And yet he had chosen to keep the child. Freddie's bastard, backward child. Perhaps he hadn't realised the situation until it was too late? But if Esther could be believed, and that was a question one always had to ask, there had been no sexual contact between husband and wife for more than a year. So why? Why hadn't Esther insisted he perform the operation? It would have been so much better for all of them, including the poor cosseted little boy. What kind of life was it for him, the lapdog of a demanding, selfish mother? His own treachery, the betrayal of his friend and mentor, had left them all with a living reminder, a sad burden each had to carry in their own way to their graves. His son who Freddie wished, like himself, had never been born.

Playing dead, he waited until Conchita left for the market. Then he rose, unsteadily, and searched for the bottle in the slats of the sloping ceiling. But no matter how clever he thought he was, she invariably found it. He cursed. She had this morning. Poor bitch. Clinging to the fantasy that she could save him, as he had once saved her. Well, he was determined. No one would save him now.

He was grateful his parents had not lived to see this final fall into disgrace. His doting parents with such high hopes for their only child, sacrificing so much for his future. His father, a minor official in the Cuban Embassy, had glimpsed what glittering prizes could be had by those from a 'proper' background. Together with his wife, he had scrimped and saved to send their golden boy to the best public school in England that they could afford. Well aware of the privilege, Freddie had rewarded their sacrifice by excelling at his school and then later at St Bart's, the premier teaching school for his chosen profession, medicine.

Freddie knew what had drawn him to that career. Growing up in his beloved Cuba, he was conscious of the great divide between the 'haves' and the 'have-nots'. Life expectancy for the poor was short, with disease often fatal from lack of doctors and medicines. To his great surprise, Freddie had found the same conditions in England. The slums of London were a shock and a revelation to the young impressionable student. After witnessing the prolonged death of a child wracked with consumption, he resolved to shake the medical world from its complacency and indifference towards the poor. But then his world collided with that of Carl and Esther Mueller.

At first, the combination of brilliant student and master tutor had the rest of the faculty buzzing with anticipation. There was a symbiosis between pupil and teacher which was the stuff that legends were made of. Then it happened. News of his parent's tragic death in a car accident, just outside Havana, left Freddie orphaned and grieving deeply for the parents who he had not seen since his arrival in England a dozen years before. That evening Carl, now more a friend than a superior, invited his young star pupil to his home. And, for the very first time, Freddie Sanchez met the dazzlingly beautiful wife of his friend. His nemesis, Esther Mueller.

Struggling into his cotton slacks, he was slipping on a pair of word-down loafers when the knock came at the door. What he didn't need now was another bloodied peasant seeking 'Doctor Freddie.'

'Go away', he called in Spanish. 'Not today'.

The knock was repeated.

'Go away! Vamos!'

A pause, then the door opened slowly. Freddie looked up and felt a stab of alarm. Standing in the doorway was Carl Mueller.

CHAPTER SIXTEEN

Giorgio Treviani roared up to the hotel just before dawn, waking most of the guests with the sound of the V8 engine and the squeal of his tyres as he slammed the car to a halt. By then Hans was already dressed and waiting for him in the lobby.

'You wanna to catch fish, you have to surprise them while they're half asleep', Giorgio had told Hans.

Carl had initially objected to the trip.

'My dear,' he said to his wife, 'Hans is only fourteen. That Trevianni boy must be nearly twenty.'

Esther was dismissive. 'Hans has been torn away from all his friends in Germany. He needs an older boy to look after him in this city.'

'But he seems altogether too wild, too reckless. His father looks like a gangster.'

'The Trevianni's are one of the richest, most powerful families on the island!' Esther snapped. 'Who do you want him to mix with, the urchins and villains at the harbour where you new 'friend' lives!' she added bitterly.

Guilty about his determination to see Freddie, Carl backed down.

Hans' ice-blue eyes widened when he saw the gleaming white roadster standing outside the Hotel Ingleterre. He'd only ever seen an open-topped limousine once before. One memorable day in Berlin when he had attended the parade against his father's wish. That day the car had been the darkest black and standing in it saluting the throng was his beloved Fuehrer, Adolf Hitler.

Giorgio led him to the car and with a gymnast's grace, leapt into the driver's white leather seat without opening the door. He motioned to Hans, who hurried eagerly around the other side. As he put his hand on the door handle Giorgio clicked his fingers in an upward gesture. Hans hesitated. Giorgio being a good six inches taller, had easily cleared the high door. Hans put his foot on the running board and leapt.

The young Italian's high-pitched laughter shattered the morning calm as his new friend pitched head-first into the passenger seat. With a roar the roadster leapt away from the kerb, with Hans' legs still waving in the air, and Giorgio's laughter rising above the engine's growl.

From the window of his hotel suite, Carl watched the car disappear beneath the row of almond trees with a deep sense of foreboding.

Dieter and Franz were waiting for them at the harbour, lounging in the well of the cabin cruiser, when Giorgio raced up and stopped with his trademark squeal of brakes. The rest of the party was made up of two dark-skinned Cuban youths who were waiting to cast off the boat fore and aft. Hans followed Giorgio on board where the two Germans greeted them both with a formal handshake.

Hans had only been on one boat before. The ill-fated s.s. St Louis that had carried him away from his homeland. He felt a tug of apprehension as the engine spluttered into life, the lines were dropped and Giorgio wheeled the boat away from the jetty. The swell heeled the tiny boat immediately and Hans found himself hurled into the arms of Dieter. Giorgio's laughter floated out over the waves.

'Hans has trouble staying on his feet', he grinned to the others. 'Too much drink!' he laughed.

Hans extricated himself from Dieter's embrace. The man smelt heavily of cologne. Not the subtle, exotic fragrance that Giorgio wore. This was a hard, pungent smell that left a taste in the mouth. A German agent wearing scent? It was a good job for Dieter they were in Cuba, not Germany.

Giorgio steered the boat out into the shimmering Caribbean Ocean, as the other three men assembled the fishing gear. Hans looked on. He was feeling a little queasy and tried to concentrate on the talk which was of a recent fatal incident. A local girl had got herself involved with some American sailors and her naked body had been found floating among the harbour rocks after the destroyer had sailed. There were no marks of foul play and the autopsy proved she must have been reeling drunk.

'Americans are all cowardly pigs', said Franz.

Dieter nodded agreement. 'They had better stay out of the war if they know what's good for them'.

'Will there be a war?' asked Hans, still tasting an echo of the pungent cologne at the back of his throat.

'Of course. How else can we get rid of all the filthy Jews that are poisoning our country?' Franz's face was a mask of hatred.

'Hold on!' said Giorgio. 'Hans is a Jew'.

'I'm not!' Hans blurted out in panic. 'We are Christians! German Christians.'

'Loyal to the Fatherland', said Dieter.

It wasn't really a question, but Hans felt the need to reply.

'Yes! Yes! Heil Hitler!' He gave the traditional salute that he had practised so often before the mirror.

Giorgio grinned. 'Poor Hans. He's terrified he's going to be found floating in the harbour like that poor tart. Relax, buddy. The only thing that's going in the water is fish bait.'

'And puke', laughed Dieter, as Hans lurched to the side and retched foul-tasting green bile into the clear blue water.

Though deeply embarrassed in front of his older companions, he felt much better after he'd thrown up. But by the time that he had landed his first marlin, with a little help from Giorgio, Hans began to feel 'one of the boys'.

The fish had been stubborn. Almost half his size. His young muscles had burned with the effort of reeling it in. Now there it lay, its streamlined grey blue scales sparkling in the tropical sun. He had conquered a wonder of nature.

Giorgio slapped him hard on the shoulders. 'Well done, little Hans! We'll make a man of you yet, eh, boys?'

Dieter and Franz smiled at Hans.

By the time the trip was over, he'd promised his new friends to keep his eyes and ears open, and to report back anything that may be helpful to the cause. Though far away from home he was still going to be able to work for the Fuehrer.

CHAPTER SEVENTEEN

Carl had surprised him when he arrived unannounced at Freddie's shabby room. He stood shyly, turning his hat between his fingers, and asked the question.

'The carnival?' said Freddie, 'We're always having carnivals. Keeps the poor from revolution.'

Accepting the offer of coffee, Carl went on, 'The children, that is Anna and Hans, are very excited to see it. And I wonder, I mean, if it's not an inconvenience, if you would be our guide?'

'Your guide?'

'The city is still very strange to us. We've heard so many stories about tourists being preyed upon by unscrupulous locals and so on. So, we thought that, if we were with a local person... We'd pay you, of course, naturally.' he went on hurriedly.

As Freddie prepared his own superb coffee, Carl continued to lay it on a little too thickly. Freddie wasn't fooled. He knew the guilt between the two men was mutual. Freddie for his betrayal of the older man's trust, and Carl for what he had seen of the way Freddie lived, what he had helped reduce his former star pupil too. Despite himself Freddie couldn't quite help playing the martyr, the genius blighted by a husband's cold revenge.

'I'd be delighted, Carl,' he said. 'But I wouldn't dream of taking your money.'

Esther had kept Klaus back at the hotel with herself and Nanny Price, while Carl took Anna and Hans to the carnival. As they got out of the taxi, Hans looked surprised when Freddie came to meet them.

'It's that horrible man,' he whispered to Anna, as his father and the man shook hands.

'Shh,' she said.

'Mama hates him.'

'Shh,' Anna repeated.

Freddie had shepherded Carl and the two children through the teeming crowds with the ease and charm of a celebrity on his home turf. This was *his* city. He knew the heights it could reach and the depths it could sink too. Carnival was its pinnacle. A celebration of life that perfectly reflected the Cuban people who had forged, from the many different races, conquests and revolutions, a unique blend of beauty, grace and sensuality.

Standing beside him, Anna clapped her hands in delight watching the street filled with dancers and musicians. Multicoloured feathers spun on exotic tanned bodies, brass and steel blasted out music that she had never even imagined. Music that vibrated deep inside your body, your soul. Rhythms that echoed the pulsing hot blood in your veins, the beat of your heart. It was as if the air itself had turned into a shimmering kaleidoscope of rainbow sound.

She looked up with shining eyes at her father, standing beside Freddie Sanchez. But it was Freddie who caught her eye. He smiled at the young girl's radiant face, flushed with excitement at the sights and sounds of the city carnival. Such innocent joy. So much vitality and love of life. Like the young Esther he had first seen in London all those years ago. He caught himself blushing at the thought of the tawdry, destructive liaison this innocent girl knew nothing of. Freddie hoped it would always be that way.

Suddenly, Freddie found a small hand in his, and Anna's bright face beaming up at him.

'I want to dance,' she said.

He allowed himself to be pulled through the throng of onlookers and dragged into the gyrating, intoxicating turmoil of dancers, making their rhythmic way along the street. Anna smiled and shouted something to him that was lost in the cacophony of sounds. He grinned in reply and moved to the beat, surrounded by peacock feathers, strewn blossom and semi-naked brown bodies. Child and man danced on, lost in the throng and the magic of the moment.

Standing beside his beaming father, Hans scowled darkly. His sister was dancing with niggers and that man his mother hated. He'd tell her when they returned, and wouldn't his father get a roasting then? And he'd keep an eye on Freddie. Just in case.

Later as the children ate huge ices by the harbour wall, watching the water carnival play out below them, Freddie and Carl sat in the shade of a giant carob tree, sipping cold beers from the nearby bar. Sensing his gaze, Freddie turned to Carl. Their eyes met, looking deep into the others. Freddie felt that perhaps this was the moment, about the child who wasn't there. Something had to be said, eventually. There was no way it could be avoided forever. Now, surely, was the time. He braced himself to speak.

'Carl', he began, but something in Carl's look made him pause. There was an almost imperceptible shake of the head.

No, it said. It was not to be spoken of. Relieved, Freddie sat back. He took out his pack of cigarettes and lit one. As he blew the smoke into the early evening air, he understood it was settled between them, all the same.

When they returned to the hotel Carl found that his clothes had been transferred to the boys' room.

'Klaus is going to sleep with me,' Esther informed him coldly. 'The noise of the city frightens him. He's having nightmares and needs to be close to his mother.'

Hans scoffed. 'Das Baby!' he said to Klaus. He couldn't wait to tell his mother about that awful man. Should he tell her now? No, he'd wait 'til they were alone.

Carl knew better not to protest. Maybe he deserved it, he thought. But he was glad he'd stood up to Esther for once in his life. And grateful that poor, damaged Freddie was back in his life, whatever the consequences.

CHAPTER EIGHTEEN

'I have found the 'perfect' little home for you all!' Isabel gushed. 'And it costs practically nothing.'

Carl was standing by the marble fireplace in the lounge of their suite. 'We had thought we would wait for a while, and look around.'

Isabel was too delighted with herself to listen. 'Why wait? After all, you're here now. You can't go back home and America won't take you in. You must put down roots, become part of society. Leave it to me. I'll help you get settled.'

She patted Esther's hand.

Esther, sitting beside her, squeezed her hand in return. 'You're an angel! Saint Isabel!'

The 'little' home proved to be a rambling Gothic mansion close to the Old Town. As Isabel showed the family through the many rooms, she breathlessly informed them that the previous owner had been an American 'businessman'.

'He was a close friend of Tony Trevianni.'

Hans perked up at the mention of his new friend's father. 'Is he still on the island?'

'No,' Isabel grinned. 'He has a new residence between Havana and Florida.'

Hans frowned. 'But there's only ocean between Havana and Florida, isn't there?'

Isabel smiled sweetly at the youth. 'Yes, my darling. How clever of you knowing that.'

Leaving Hans with his jaw hanging open, she swept on up the wide staircase. Carl glanced at his wife, but she studiously avoided his eye.

When Carl suggested that selling Esther's diamond necklace would pay for the house, he was met with a point-blank refusal.

'It was a present from my father!' Esther exclaimed. 'I will never part with it!'

But with Isabel's assurance that Carl's new practice would be a great success, a bank loan was arranged, and within a month the Mueller's moved. The new house was big enough to have a large well-equipped surgery downstairs and, as she had promised, Isabel helped Carl establish a practice, using her considerable influence over the wealthy residents on the island.

'After all it's not every day we have an eminent physician coming to live among us!' she exclaimed. 'To tell you the truth the majority of doctors here are expensive, and on the whole second-rate. I personally guarantee that you will soon have the most successful practice on the whole island.'

The children adored the house from the first visit. Its rambling hallways and shadowed staircases held the promise of endless days playing secret games out of the glare of the blazing sun and the eyes of their parents.

At the top of the house a large gloomy attic instantly became the children's lair. In thick pencil Anna wrote out a message on paper and, with difficulty, pinned it into the hard-grained wood of the door.

'Keep out! Children only!'

Within twenty-four hours the three siblings had formed a secret society, with Anna and Klaus as Hans' lieutenants. It was all Anna could do to prevent Hans turning it into a branch of the Hitler Youth in exile. The glamour and excitement of guns, marching and war eluded her, just as it fascinated her elder brother. And she drew the line at saluting.

'We have to have rules! Rules and discipline,' explained Hans tetchily when challenged by his sister.

'We get enough rules from Nanny Price,' complained Anna. 'Wash your hands, blow your nose, make your bed...'

'Empty your potty', chuckled Klaus.

Hans glared at him. The young boy wilted under the cold eyes of his hero. At that moment, on cue, Nanny Price called from the landing below.

'Children! Come downstairs, please.'

'We're playing!' Hans called back, irritated.

'Your Father wants you to meet someone.' She put on her stern tone. 'Come downstairs at once!'.

'See?' said Anna, vindicated. 'Rules'.

Nanny Price ushered the three children into the large airy salon that led out, through multi-paned French windows, to the thickly overgrown garden beyond. Outside in the bright morning sunshine a small army of black gardeners toiled with machetes and axes to clear the undergrowth that had overtaken the paths and patio, that had once the pride of the deceased owner. The thwack and slash of the blades resonated in the air, like a primitive percussion section beating out the rhythm of a long-forgotten slave song. The air was thickly scented with the aroma of freshly cut stems and vines, while the cool shade inside the room was washed with the shimmering reflection of the variegated greens of the falling foliage outside.

Following Nanny Price into the room, the children stopped and stared. Their father and mother were seated separately in high brown leather armchairs. Standing on the polished wooden floor in front of them, looking slightly uncomfortable under the gaze of so many strangers' eyes, was a large jet-black woman and a waif-thin black boy of about Anna's age. The woman was dressed in a voluminous flowered dress whose faded pattern gave testimony to the many beatings it had taken on a large riverside rock. The boy wore well-worn khaki shorts held up by a length of string. Hanging over his shorts he wore a brilliant white T-shirt, that was probably once the possession of an American sailor several sizes bigger than the present owner. Against the white of the cotton the boy's skin looked blacker than the woman beside him. So black it seemed, to Anna, almost blue.

Beside her Hans gave an involuntary grunt of surprise and disgust. Anna glanced at him sharply. He returned her look defiantly.

'Children', their father began, 'this is Carlotta, our new housekeeper. And this is her nephew, Jose, who will help her about the house and run errands for all of us.'

Anna felt Hans stiffen beside her.

'Father...', he began to protest.

'Hans', his father interrupted sharply, aware of the insult that was about to burst out. Father and son locked eyes. After a moment Carl continued, 'They will live in the annex at the end of the garden.' Carl rose. 'These are our three children. Hans, Anna and Klaus.'

Carlotta beamed a large smile that lit up her face. 'I am very pleased to meet you all'.

Anna skipped across the space between them. 'And I'm very pleased to meet you, Carlotta.' She held out her tiny white hand, which the surprised woman took in her own huge black fist, after a nervous glance at Carl and Esther.

'Pleased to meet you, Missy Anna'.

'And Jose'. Anna held out her hand to the young boy who was standing looking at the floor, in which he could have seen his reflection, if he had been concentrating on that. Jose stared at the delicate white hand before him like a small animal caught in a searchlight. He glanced nervously about him, at his aunt, his new employers, the grim-faced Hans in the doorway. Anna made up his mind for him by taking his hand in hers and shaking it vigorously.

'Hello, Jose. I'm sure we're going to be great friends.'

Esther cleared her throat disapprovingly. 'Anna.'

Carl smiled at his daughter indulgently. He hoped she'd never have cause to lose her innocent generosity of spirit that accepted each and every new experience with such optimism and hope.

CHAPTER NINETEEN

Conchita knew something had happened to Freddie at the carnival. She had been very surprised to see him there with the Mueller father and two children. Freddie had even danced with the little girl on the crowded street. She had never seen him dance before, except occasionally, when listening to a blues song on the radio, he would get up and waltz her slowly around the room. After that they sometimes made love. Slow, gentle love. Nothing like the rushed, selfish, sometimes violent sex she got from her clients. She wondered why it seemed some men wanted to punish a woman with sex? They thrust hard into her, holding on to her, squeezing so much it hurt, as if they were punishing something, someone. It hurt, but it wasn't her they were really punishing.

Maybe she was lucky she had survived this long. She wouldn't have, if Freddie hadn't come along that night and found her, bleeding into the gutter. He had taken her to his room, bathed and sewn up the wound. That was so strange. Wonderful. She had never had a man care for her before. After she recovered, she moved into the room below him, and gradually paid him back the only way she knew how, with her body. Teaching him what a woman really wants.

After the carnival, Freddie didn't seem to be drinking quite as much as he used to. For a few days now he hadn't started the day drinking from the bottle which he used to keep beside his bed. She liked that because when he drank he would get very depressed and nothing she could do would help him. But he never got violent. She never felt afraid of Freddie. Not like some of the pimps she had when she started. Not like the one that made her look like a monster. How Freddie could kiss her looking like she did, she didn't know. Sometimes he gently kissed her all along the scar, from her forehead to her lips. That made her cry inside, remembering what she used to look like. He would have really loved her then. She couldn't bear to look at herself, and had smashed the only mirror in her room.

They were seated, eating a meal she had cooked for them in Freddie's room. Rice and beans. It was one of the few things she could remember as a child. Her mother cooking that. She wasn't old enough to remember very much else about her. She didn't even know what she did. She went out every day, and came back hours later with food to eat. Mostly rice and beans. Maybe her mother did the same as she did, selling her body for food.

After their mother died, her only brother didn't like having to look after his little sister, so she had to beg on the streets to eat. She was lucky that she was very pretty, and made enough to feed herself and her brother, until he left one day and didn't come back. She had no idea what had happened to him, where he had gone, or if he was still alive.

She found it was easy to flirt with the men to get money. Some of the older men really liked her, and asked her to do other things for more money. It was a simple thing for a pretty young girl to go all the way and make a lot of money. Now, with her ugly face, she had to take what business she could. But it was enough to feed Freddie rice and beans.

'You dance at carnival. With little girl.'

'You saw? Yeah. Anna, she's called. She's sweet.'

'You friends now?'

'A little...A little. With her father.'

'They thank you, for necklace?' It still hurt her that he had given it back and not to her. Not that she could wear it anywhere. If she wore it outside, it would be stolen in a moment. But she could have worn it in her room, or Freddie's. It would be nice making love with him wearing the necklace. Making her beautiful again.

'Yeah. Sort of,' Freddie said with his mouth full.

'That woman thank you?'

Freddie hesitated.

'No?'

'Not really,' he said. 'No.'

'She bad woman. Watch out.'

Freddie smiled. He didn't need to be told that about Esther Mueller.

CHAPTER TWENTY

Despite the heat of the summer, Anna was eager to explore the city that was her new home. With her father establishing his new practice, tending Havana´s social elite in his surgery at the front the house, and her mother sheltering indoors from the relentless sun, Anna and her new friend Jose roamed the narrows streets and medieval plazas of the Old City.

Initially, Esther protested this new friendship.

'It's not suitable associating with servants, Anna,' she said, as Anna was hurrying her breakfast, anxious to go out with Jose.

'But, Mama, Jose's showing me the city, and teaching me Spanish!' Anna said stubbornly. 'I want to learn it properly before I go to school.'

'I don't think it can do any harm, my dear,' said Carl.

Anna finished her last mouthful. 'Can I go now, Papa?'

'Yes, but be careful, Anna. And stick with Jose, he knows the city. And don't talk to strange men.'

Esther glared at him as Anna left the room.

'My dear, she will be mixing with her own class when she goes to school. She'll make new friends, of her own kind. And this friendship will end…Just for this summer, let her have her freedom.'

'What, playing with beggars and urchins, like your 'friend'!'

Pushing her plate away, Esther swept out of the room.

After his initial shyness with Anna, Jose was coming out of his shell and proving to be a lively and amusing companion. Having a rich white girl for his friend made him feel special. For Anna the contrast with her former life was bewildering. After the grim, austerity of Germany marching inexorably to war, and the starched, censorious regime of her private school, the vibrant optimism of Cuba and its people was intoxicating. With her olive skin turning quickly to brown, her dark shiny hair, deep brown eyes and her rapid grasp of the new language, she was soon indistinguishable from the local children, who ran in and out of the street markets and shady colonnades of the Plaza de la Catedral begging gum and candy from the swarming American tourists. Anna enjoyed joining in this game, passing herself off as a poor local girl, until some of the older kids took exception to a 'dirty' foreigner taking their trade. Risking a beating, Jose bravely stood up for her. But after the warning, Anna told him they should stop playing that game.

So, instead Jose taught her to fish from the harbour wall beside the brooding fort 'El Morro'. She was delightedly holding up her first catch, an emerald green parrot fish, aptly named because of its facial resemblance to the exotic bird, when a voice behind her called her name.

'Anna Mueller? Is that you?'

She turned and was delighted to see Freddie standing beneath the deep shade of a carob tree. She ran to him, holding the fish out proudly in her hand.

'Freddie! Look what I've caught!'

'Congratulations. Are you going to eat it?'

Anna screwed up her face. 'Uh, no I couldn't! It's alive.'

'It soon won't be unless you put it back quickly.'

'But it's caught on the hook,' she exclaimed.

'Here, let me.' Gently, Freddie plucked the homemade hook from the fish's upper jaw and handed it back to Anna. Holding the wriggling fish in both hands, she ran to the water and dropped it into the clear blue water. The fish lay on the surface for a moment, as if stunned.

Anna gasped, 'I've killed it!'

At that instant, with a flick of its tail, the fish swam off disappearing into the depths out of harm's way. Anna breathed an audible sigh of relief. She turned to Freddie.

'Thank you. I never want to kill anything, ever,' she said very seriously. 'Do you, Jose?'

'I shoot mongoose at the farm,' he replied. 'My mother puts them in a stew.'

'Well, you shouldn't,' Anna said sharply. 'People shouldn't kill things.'

'A very laudable sentiment. Deserves an ice-cream, wouldn't you say, Jose?' said Freddie, heading off the looming argument.

Jose grinned broadly, his dazzling white teeth shining from his black face.

When they were seated at the cafe overlooking the harbour, Anna looked up from her mango flavoured ice and said, 'You haven't seen our new house yet, Freddie.'

'No. I haven't been invited.'

'Well then, I'm inviting you,' said Anna firmly.

Freddie smiled. 'I think it's best to wait for an invitation from your parents.'

'I don't see why. They should invite you straight away. You saved us.'

'Well. Not exactly. All your fellow passengers are safe now.'

'But we didn't know that then, did we? We all thought we were going back to die.'

'How's the ice-cream?' asked Freddie, changing the subject.

Back home in the attic, Anna found Hans playing his favourite game of tormenting his younger brother. He was as angry and resentful as his mother about Anna's friendship with the 'nigger', the news of which had got as far as Giorgio and his friends. It was acutely embarrassing when they made sniggering remarks about his sister and Jose which he didn´t quite understand, but knew that it was something secret and disgusting.

'And then we met Freddie,' Anna went on. 'And he helped me get the fish off the hook.'

'I'm going to tell Mama about you meeting him! She hates that man,' he said vehemently.

'Why?' Anna protested. 'He's nice and kind. He saved our lives!'

'For money, I bet! That's all he cares about.'

'That´s not true! He gave Mama's necklace back, didn't he? I heard Mama and Papa arguing about it.'

'Yes, because Mama's thinks Papa's a fool for being taken in by that crook!'

'He's not a crook! You don´t know him!'

'Well Mama does! She hates him and she should know!' Hans repeated with a superior air. Leaving Anna in the attic helping the crying Klaus look for his favourite toy, which Hans had hidden, he ran downstairs keen to tell his mother about Anna meeting Freddie.

CHAPTER TWENTY-ONE

As the hot summer wore on, Carl's banishment from the marital bedroom become permanent. He didn't mind that. Sexual intimacy between them had long since disappeared. Vanished long before Freddie had succumbed to Esther's charms. He wondered how long the affair lasted? That was what he had begun to suspect was the case, not the brutal rape that Esther accused Freddie of. A brief affair that Freddie had decided to end, being too intelligent to be fooled by Esther's wiles for very long. If she had lied, Carl wondered, did she ever feel any remorse?

Relations between husband and wife were made worse when Isabel informed Esther that Carl was using Freddie's contacts to source the equipment and medicines he needed to set up his surgery.

'The Mafia run the drugs racket here,' Freddie had warned him. 'And that applies to pharmaceuticals. Stuff you'll need every day.'

As soon as she heard, Esther confronted Carl. 'Why do you deliberately go against my wishes! Doing business with that man.'

'But it makes sense, my dear. Freddie knows the suppliers who can be trusted. There are a lot of unscrupulous people on the island.'

'I don't want you having anything to do with him! Isabel is asking too many questions!'

'Then avoid seeing her.'

'What? She's my only friend on this damned island!'

'She's a manipulative gossip. I would be very careful, if I were you.'

'Careful! What about you and that drunken waster!'

'Freddie is saving us a lot of money.'

'How do you know!'

'Because I trust him.' Carl emphasized the word, as he repeated it. 'I **trust** him.'

Esther tensed. The word hung between them like a lightning bolt poised to strike. Ten years of suspicion about to unravel their lives.

She snorted. 'Do what you like! Just keep him away from this house!'

Late in the afternoon, on the third of September, Freddie pulled the ornate bronze chain hanging by the Mueller's front door. The bell echoed down the long-shadowed hallway. He had heard the news on his crackling short-wave radio and felt that he should express his sympathy at what was bound to be a difficult time for the family. He straightened his tie and brushed imaginary fluff from his jacket sleeve while he waited for the Mueller's housekeeper, Carlotta, to waddle down the hall to open the door. Freddie took off his buff Panama as Carlotta showed him into the sitting room where the Carl and Esther were seated in separate armchairs.

Esther froze when she saw him. Carl rose to greet him, extending his hand. 'Freddie. What a pleasant surprise!'

Freddie shook his hand, 'Carl.'

He turned to Esther seated regally in the large armchair. She was dressed as if for an elegant social function, in cream chiffon which emphasized her olive skin and the deep brown of her eyes. He inclined his head. 'Frau Mueller.'

Carl cleared his throat, uncomfortably. 'Under the present circumstances perhaps 'Frau' is not appropriate.'

'Ah, yes,' said Freddie. 'You´ve heard the news then? About Chamberlain's speech?'

'It was bound to happen,' said Carl resignedly. 'It was just a matter of time.'

'I just came to offer my sympathy. I'm sure you have many relatives and friends in Germany who – '

'We have no contact with anyone there!' Esther cut in sharply. 'The war has nothing to do with us.'

Freddie looked at Carl, questioningly. Carl lowered his eyes to the floor.

Breaking the awkward pause, Freddie went on, 'Well, it's a bad business, anyhow,' reverting to the traditional mode of understatement he had learnt at his English public school.

'Thank you... You'll have some tea?' asked Carl.

Esther immediately shot him a look, and ruffled the material of her dress to show her disapproval of the invitation. So different, Freddie thought, from the first time they had all been together in the same room.

On that fateful day Freddie had been listening attentively to Professor Mueller's lecture about the diseases of poverty, when a uniformed porter entered the lecture theatre and quietly informed Freddie there was an urgent telegram waiting for him in the administrative office. Irritated at having to leave the lecture, he had hurried to the office where a grim-faced secretary handed him the single sheet of buff paper. The message was brief and shattering. Both his parents had been killed in a motor accident outside Havana.

After his lecture Carl sought out Freddie and found him, white-faced and trembling, waiting for the operator to place a call to a family friend in Havana to fill in the details.

'I'll call home and have the servants make up a bed for you tonight,' Carl said, not wanting to leave the young man on his own at such a distressing time.

He took Freddie home in a taxi, where the butler opened the door to the elegant house in Eaton Square, which Carl had rented for the duration of his contract as visiting tutor at St. Bart's.

The butler preceded Freddie and Carl into the drawing room where Carl's wife, Esther, was waiting for them. She had put on her black velvet dress with a décolletage that hinted discreetly at the full bosom beneath. At her neck a diamond necklace sparkled prettily, but failed to outshine the lustre of her eyes. At twenty-two Esther Mueller had swept Belgravia off its feet with her dark beauty and vivacious charm. Despite his grief Freddie was instantly captivated, as she had intended. She'd heard stories of Carl's brilliant, dashing young student and had tentatively suggested to her husband that Freddie be invited to dinner at a convenient time. Now, in such tragic circumstances, she could be even more solicitous to the grieving, young man than she had planned.

The truth was that her husband bored her. Esther Goldberg had been determined to have Professor Carl Mueller, the most eligible man in Vienna. Her family's objections on religious grounds only spurred the wilful young girl on. The clandestine meetings and the exciting, romantic dash across Europe to join him in London had thrilled her. She was living the life of the heroines in the novels at her bedside. But in a very short time the reality of daily life with the eminent doctor evaporated the dream like so much hot air. Carl was a studious, sober man, not given to excess, except for the brief, crazy flirtation which led him to marry Esther to save her from social disgrace. They had both immediately regretted it but, respectability on Carl's part, and Esther's fear of ridicule forced them into the pretence of family harmony.

The arrival of the first two children hadn't helped. Esther was a wayward mother, obsessively doting in one instant, dismissive and distant the next. That the two children were growing up as normal as they were was testament to the sound principles and stern discipline of Nanny Price. She had answered the advertisement within two months of Hans birth and had been with them ever since. With her two offspring well cared for and out from under her feet, Esther was looking for some fun. She yearned to rekindle the heady passion that still burned deep inside her. And, from the first moment she set eyes on him, she knew that handsome, charismatic Freddie Sanchez was the one to relight her fire.

Carlotta served the tea from a silver tray, handing a china cup to Esther first. Initially, Esther had thought of retiring to her room to register her disapproval to Carl. But curiosity got the better of her. As Carl and Freddie talked about the war, she watched him through lowered lashes, idly stroking the white Persian cat on her lap. If anything, the years of dissolution had made Freddie more attractive. The boyish bloom had been replaced by a rugged, world-worn appearance. The corn-blonde hair was still artistically long. His brilliant blue eyes, once darting and mischievous, were now deeper, more sorrowful, saddened by the world he had witnessed since they were last together. There was no mistake, Freddie Sanchez was still a catch. But to show him anything other than a polite, cold exterior would be outrageous. She must maintain the pretence of tragic victim forced to endure her shame.

Anna suddenly burst into the room with a cry, 'Freddie!'

Esther watched in surprise, and a touch of jealousy, as the young girl met Freddie like a favourite uncle, throwing her arms around him and planting a kiss on his cheek.

'Anna!' she protested.

'Darling, show a little respect for your elders,' said Carl mildly. 'Think what Nanny Price would say.'

'Huh!' scoffed Anna. 'She'd just wish she was me.'

Freddie laughed out loud, showing his even white teeth and the deep lines creasing the corners of his eyes. Esther felt as if she had been struck, shocked at the sound that used to delight her and send a thrill tingling through her whole body. The laughter she hadn't heard in ten years.

'Anna, go to your room!' she commanded.

Pulling a face, Anna looked at her father. His expression was enough.

'I'm very pleased to see you in our house at last, Freddie,' she said with a touch of defiance in her voice. 'Please come again soon.' With a glare at her mother, she flounced out of the room.

Esther rose with a flurry of white fur and chiffon. 'It's far too hot in here,' she announced. 'I shall retire.'

Freddie rose. 'Mrs Mueller.'

She inclined her head towards Freddie. 'Mr Sanchez.'

Ignoring his out-stretched hand, Esther swept from the room. After the shock of the familiar laughter touching him would have been too much. Cursing herself she entered her room, threw herself onto her daybed and let the tears soothe her.

Upstairs in the attic, Hans was delighted at hearing the news.

'At last the Fuhrer is going to show the world what Germany is really made of,' he told Klaus breathlessly.

They may have taken him far away from home, but he was determined to play his part. He knew people in Havana, spies for the Fatherland. And he, Hans Mueller, was going to help them win the war. With a piece of material stolen from Nanny Price's sewing box, he had made a makeshift swastika armband, which he was now proudly wearing as he strutted before the full-length mirror waving his toy gun.

'We are going to smash France and England! We are going to conquer the whole world! Heil Hitler!'

Seated on an old rocking-horse, open-mouthed, Klaus watched his elder brother in awe.

CHAPTER TWENTY-TWO

At the outbreak of war, with Germans and Austrians being interned in many countries throughout the world Esther's paranoia blossomed. She fled through the house, wringing her hands, spreading alarm in her wake.

'They'll put us in prison!' she wailed to Nanny Price, within earshot of her three children.

Carl emerged from his surgery and tried to calm her. 'My dear, please calm down. You're frightening the children.'

'Don't tell me to calm down, you stupid man! Do something before they come to drag us all away!'

'Isn't Isabel's husband something to do with the government? Surely, he can do something?'

And so, it was resolved. Esther's friendship with Isabel and Carl's distinguished reputation not only spared the family, but gained them staunch support and commiseration from Havana's social elite.

'What a vulgar little man!' Esther's women friends said. 'It must be so galling having that man Hitler ruining your country!'

At their new schools Anna and Hans were initially treated with suspicion. But Anna's natural charm soon won her a circle of friends, while Hans' brooding, aggressive manner, and his friendship with Giorgio Trevianni made him feared among his peers, if not universally liked.

Still anxious, Esther immersed herself in Isabel's circle, determined to divorce herself from anything Germanic.

'I am converting to Catholicism!' she announced one evening to her husband.

'Very well, my dear,' Carl replied, understanding the irresistible appeal the lush ceremony of the Catholic Mass would have for her.

Esther found Isabel a willing tutor. She covered her lustrous, black hair with fine white lace and, instead of her trashy romantic novels, she encouraged her pupil to carry a book of catechisms and a rosary, at home and in public. But, delicately probing Esther's past relationship with Freddie, Isabel was met with stubborn silence. She retreated, biding her time.

With Carl absorbed growing his medical practice and Esther with her new religion and friends, the couple saw less and less of each other. Esther's continued disapproval, and secret envy, of Carl's contact with Freddie increased the distance between them. Mealtimes became tense, silent affairs, with Hans and Anna also deeply divided about the news of Germany's success in the war.

'We will not have any discussion about that subject!' Carl had to insist, after an argument almost came to blows.

Banned from glorifying his Fuhrer at home, Hans began to strut about at school revelling in his allegiance to the 'Master Race.' While Anna, deeply ashamed to be German, assiduously cultivated her friendship with Jose as a camouflage of her nationality. Being deeply tanned by now, she could easily pass as a 'white' Cuban.

As Christmas approached the mood in the house was gloomy. The daily tension, and the constant, stifling heat, made thoughts of the festive season impossible. So, when Anna suggested that Freddie be invited to share Christmas dinner with the family, she was met with a stony silence. Freddie had not set foot in the house since the day of the announcement of war.

'Why can't we invite him?' she protested sulkily. 'He's been a good friend to us, and I bet he'll be spending Christmas all alone!'

'I'm sure Freddie has many friends to spend Christmas with,' Carl replied kindly. 'In fact, he told me they were organising a big party, as they do every year,' he lied.

With resentments seething just below the surface Christmas Day was the worst the family had ever known. After Carlotta had cooked them a sumptuous meal, which none of them had any appetite for, Carl attempted to start the party games they had known back home in Germany. But memories of those happier times were so potent, compared with the present war escalating in Europe, that friction quickly developed and, by mid-afternoon, all members of the family had retreated to their own rooms to be with their separate thoughts.

In early January at Anna's insistence, Freddie drove Carl and Anna, in his battered old car, to the sugar plantation where Jose's extended family lived and worked. Freddie was a regular visitor, providing a free medical service for the impoverished estate workers who, young or old, called him 'Doctor Freddie.'

It was the first time Anna had been out of the city and she was both delighted and appalled in equal measure. Delighted at the lush, exotic greenery and wildlife, and appalled at the homes of families she saw along the way. Rough wooden cabins with patched roofs and crumbling walls were scattered at the side of the road like litter thrown from passing vehicles. Ragged children played in the dirt with emaciated dogs, idly watched by their parents who lounged despondently in the shade of their rickety wooden porches.

The young girl was appalled to find the conditions no better at the sugar estate. It was the middle of harvest, and men, women and children toiled from dawn to sunset, through the heat of the day, cutting and collecting the crop relentlessly. At night, dusty and weary, they returned to their primitive homes to eat meagre rations, then drop exhausted onto the bare boards, or thin straw mattresses inside their shacks.

'Why do they live like this?' she cried to Freddie. 'Isabel's husband owns an estate. They have lots of money. Why don´t they share it with their workers?'

Freddie shrugged. 'It's the way it is, Anna. This is Cuba. Like everywhere else, we have rich and poor.'

'But they're treated like slaves!' Anna insisted. 'It's not right. We should do something about it, Papa!'

Carl smiled indulgently at his headstrong daughter and shrugged to Freddie. 'You see what I have to put up with?'

Anna bristled. 'It's not a joke, Papa!'

Seeing Jose emerge from the family's shack, she stomped away to greet him. The two men stood watching her as she threw her arms around the little black boy.

'Why do the young want everything to happen at once?'

'I think she's inherited your sense of injustice,' Freddie replied, and then immediately regretted he said it.

Carl turned away, suddenly reminded of the wrong, that he was beginning to believe more and more, he had done his companion. His sense of injustice had deserted him then. He turned back, 'Freddie, I want to help you with your clinic.'

A week later Anna burst in on Carl and Esther as they were taking afternoon refreshments. Thick black coffee for Carl, and rich, milky chocolate with iced cakes for Esther.

'Papa, papa!' she cried breathlessly. 'The plantation is for sale! Where Jose's family live. We must buy it and help those poor people!'

'For sale? Who told you that?' Carl asked.

'Carlotta. She just told me in the kitchen.'

Esther huffed, exasperated. 'How many times have I told you not to pester Carlotta?'

'I'm not pestering her. I help- her. She lets me make bread.'

'For goodness sake, Anna, you're not a servant!'

103

'Don't be hard on the child, my dear,' Carl said mildly.

'She should be mixing people of her own kind. Not with...' She didn't finish, but her meaning hung in the air like a bad odour.

'Can we buy it, Papa! It would be fun to have an estate, wouldn't it?'

'What would we do with a plantation? I don't have time to look after it.'

'Jose's family could look after it for you. They do all the work anyway. They could do it.'

Esther joined in, her irritation fading as a new diversion beckoned. 'Isabel has a plantation, Carl. Her husband pays a manager to look after it.'

Carl turned to her, surprised. 'My dear, are you siding with Anna?'

'Isabel says it's very profitable. It's been in their family for generations and it's made them the most important family in Cuba.'

'In Isabel's eyes,' Carl responded quietly.

'How can you say that! Look what she has done for you! She's made yours the best practice on the island.'

Carl gave a wan smile. 'And I suppose I had nothing to do with it? I hadn't realised that, among her many other gifts, Isabel is an eminent doctor.'

'You know what I mean, Father!' Esther snapped. 'But if you don't want to help your family to become rich and well thought of...' She ruffled her skirts and stared sulkily out of the window at the broad palm leaves shining brightly in afternoon sun.

'Please, Papa, can we?' Anna said clasping her hands together pleadingly.

Carl turned his gaze from his wife's stern profile to the sparkling eyes of his daughter, and smiled.

CHAPTER TWENTY-THREE

Hans was restless and resentful at school. After his mother's religious conversion, she had insisted the children attend a Catholic school, and Hans hated it. He hated the priests and nuns with their self-importance and their harsh punishments. He hated the interminable repetitions of the catechisms and the endless praying. And, most of all, he hated the unwelcome hands of the priest resting heavily upon his shoulders as he stood behind the boy encouraging his devotions. In class he would gaze out the window dreaming of the day Adolf Hitler took over the world and he, Hans Mueller of the Waffen S.S, could take his revenge on his religious tormentors, with Giorgio as his second in command.

After school he was often met by Giorgio. With the help of General Batista, Cuba was rapidly becoming the Mafia's paradise of gambling, drugs and girls, and Giorgio's father was very much part of the scene. With Giorgio being the heir apparent, young men were desperate to be seen with the handsome, charismatic son of one of the island's top mobsters, so his roadster was always crammed with acolytes. Hans would have much preferred to be alone with his hero, but was happy that Giorgio always gave him the passenger seat next to him. Hans knew some of the others resented that.

The youths' favourite game was trawling the city's slums to taunt the 'niggers.' The raids frequently ended with Giorgio's mob leaving one poor, outnumbered black boy a bloody mess in the gutter. Even if the police were around they never intervened.

Despite his fiery bravado, inwardly, Hans was deeply ashamed to discover that real physical violence frightened him. During the ugly melees in the slums he kept himself on the periphery, lashing out with a boot, but never engaging hand to hand, fist to bloody fist. After one such encounter, he heard the word 'cobarde' uttered behind his back. Hans feared resentment of his cowardice would reach his favourite friend, Giorgio.

On their next foray, as dark storm clouds gathered above them, the youths cornered a skinny, black youth in a narrow alley leading to a filthy public square. As the gang moved in for the 'kill', with one deafening thunderclap the heavens opened.

Within seconds the rain became an impenetrable blanket. Soaked to the skin the youths abandoned their 'fun' and headed for the shelter of Giorgio's car. As the terrified young black took to his heels, Hans cried out after the gang. 'Come on! He's getting away!'

He took off after the boy, intending only to give token pursuit. From now on he would be seen as the leader. The most fearless and bloodthirsty. As he rounded the corner of the square through the fog of rain, he saw them. A group of large black youths sheltering under the colonnade of an abandoned building, with his wide-eyed quarry huddled between them.

Spinning on his heels Hans took off out of the square, but was knocked flying before he made ten paces. Rolling himself into a tight ball, arms protecting his head, he screamed as the blows reined in.

'Hold it steady,' instructed Jose, holding the barrel of the shotgun to help her.

'Shall I pull the trigger?' Anna asked.

'Not yet! You have to aim it first.'

'What shall I aim at? I don't want kill anything!'

With his wife and daughter pestering him incessantly, Carl had finally asked the bank for a mortgage to buy the plantation. As his medical practice was now flourishing with the city's elite as patients, it was a simple transaction.

Most weekends Anna took a bus and walked the rest of the way to the plantation. She spent as much time as she could there, helping Jose's family with their daily chores. She enjoyed washing the clothes on a stone by the river, helping prepare the evening meal, usually 'moros', consisting of black beans and rice, sometimes with meat from a mongoose, a bird, or whatever tiny mammal Jose was able to shoot.

Anna had found him stalking his prey among the palms and magnolia trees on the edge of the estate.

'You have to kill to eat!' he said, when she admonished him.

'I won't! From now on I shall just eat vegetables.'

'Then you'll die.'

'Rubbish!'

'Aim at that branch then. The dead one,' Jose said.

'Let go then!'

She swung the gun round, squinted down the barrel and pulled the trigger. The recoil jerked the weapon from her hands, as the shot flew harmlessly into the sky. Shaken, Anna spun round on the laughing Jose, indignantly.

'You didn't tell me it did that!'

Still grinning, Jose picked the weapon up. 'Girls shouldn't shoot guns anyway.'

'Why not? We're as good as boys!'

Anna watched Jose reload the gun.

'Teach me to shoot, Jose.'

'What will you give me?'

She considered. 'A kiss.'

Jose giggled.

'Don't you want one?'

The boy nodded shyly.

'Well, teach me then,' giving him a little kiss on his cheek.

Giorgio arrived at the hospital after Hans' parents had left. The patient was propped up in bed badly bruised and shaken, but with no serious damage. Fortunately, a passing policeman had stopped the attack and called an ambulance.

As usual Giorgio was immaculate in tailored shorts and matching gold beach shirt with his initials embroidered on the breast.

'Hey, amigo, you look so sad.'

'It was a trap!' snapped Hans. 'Those dirty niggers set a trap!'

'No pasa nada. Can you walk?'

'Yes, I think.'

'Come on then, amigo! Vamos!'

'The doctors say I have to stay here. In case I have a reaction.'

'What reaction! Come on, you deserve a present.'

'A present? What for?'

'You showed them you're no 'cobarde.'

The first part of the present was a visit to Giorgio's personal tailor. The man looked askance at Hans clothes, torn and dirty from the attack.

'Samuel, my friend requires a new set of duds.'

In half an hour, wearing shorts and shirt to match Giorgio's, Hans followed his benefactor back to the gleaming roadster, which this time was not filled with acolytes.

Giorgio grinned. 'Now for the real present.'

In the 1940's visiting tourists and American sailors looking for 'action' all made their way to La Playa, where every pimp, prostitute, drug dealer and low-life of the city could be found. An atmosphere of sleaze hung heavy in sultry air, day and night.

As Giorgio pulled up to the kerb, Hans gazed about him, wide-eyed at the intoxicating mixture of the cheap, garish and the exotic.

Giorgio lounged back in his seat. He nodded at the young women and girls loosely ranged in a line beneath the shade of the palms. 'Take your pick.'

Hans looked at him, puzzled.

'One, two, the whole lot if you want.'

'I...I don't understand.'

'Time to get you laid, amigo. You're getting to be a big boy now.'

'Laid?' Hans knew what the word meant. His classmates used it a lot. Bragging of their exploits.

'These pretty ladies can teach you all you need to know.'

Hans was silent.

'So, which? How many? Shall I choose a couple for you? Who can teach you real good.'

'I don't know.'

'What's the matter, bud? Don't you like girls?'

Hans shrugged. 'It's...well, they're...they're black.'

That wasn't strictly true. The line of girls ranged from deep black to mid-brown. But there were no white-skinned, blondes. No Aryans.

'So?'

Hans' ugly grimace almost made his words redundant. 'I don't want to do that with a nigger!'

Giorgio raised an eyebrow. 'Okay.' He revved the car. 'There's a place I know where they have cock-fighting.'

CHAPTER TWENTY-FOUR

'Did you say share the profits?' queried Freddie.

Carl nodded.

'With the workers?'

They were seated in the cool interior of a cafe on the Paseo de Prado, drinking black coffee. Anna was sipping an iced orange juice, freshly squeezed, through a straw.

'It was my idea!' said Anna, proudly. 'Jose's family hardly have enough to live on.'

'That's true,' Carl said. Sensing Freddie's scepticism, he went on, 'Freddie, the new president himself, Batista, supports redistribution of wealth. It's in the new constitution.'

Reaching into his pocket, Freddie brought out a pack of cigarettes. 'Batista is a general, Carl. Generals want power. He's also a politician. Politicians know what to say to get elected.'

'I don't share your cynicism, Freddie. I think Cuba's turning a new page. And I want to be on it.'

'We want to be in on it,' Anna affirmed.

'Have you thought this through, Carl? Okay, a fair wage, yes, maybe. No problem. But sharing the profits?'

Carl put down his cup. 'I think so. Each harvest makes a good profit for the estate. It's only right that the people who do the hard work get their fair share.'

Freddie shook a cigarette from the pack. He looked evenly at Carl as he lit it, sucked in and then let out a stream of blue smoke, which drifted lazily upwards into the whirling fan above and was extinguished.

'Carl, the new constitution aside, things have gone on in this island for decades, centuries.'

'Things change, Freddie,' Carl said, mildly.

'Yes. Germany changed, and not for the better.'

'I'm talking about progress.'

'But some people on the island might not see it that way. They won't like it.'

Anna finished her drink, sucking the last dregs noisily up the straw.

'Manners, Anna!' said her father.

She put her glass down firmly, as if to make a point. 'Who cares about 'some people'?'

'That's just the way it is, Anna.'

The smoke from Freddie's cigarette drifted into Anna's face. She waved it away fiercely and glared at him.

'You said that before! At the plantation! About rich and poor. Well, I think what my Papa is doing is right!'

Freddie chuckled at the young girl's stubborn expression.

'It's not funny! Stop laughing at me! We have to help the poor people!'

Freddie's grin widened and put his hands up as though praying. 'I'm sorry, Saint Anna.'

Screwing up her face, Anna flung the straw at Freddie and stomped out the door, letting in a rush of hot air as she went.

Carl rose. 'I'd better go after her.'

'Please apologise to Anna for me, Carl. I shouldn't have said that.'

Carl nodded. 'There's a lot of her mother in her.'

'And, Carl, please, think about it. God knows I'm the last one who should tell anyone what to do. And everyone admires principles. But they always have consequences.'

At Sunday Mass Esther had become accustomed to sitting with Isabel and her ladies in a private box in the soaring Cathedral. This morning she was surprised that she seated alone. She looked around, puzzled, and was about to leave when the service started.

She sat fidgeting in her seat. The priests' rituals felt interminable today. Where was Isabel? Why had she not called to say she wouldn't be there? Had something happened to her best friend? She hoped not. Isabel had been a lifeline to her. True, she was a terrible gossip, and was always prying into her relationship with Freddie, but with Isabel she felt protected. Her husband had money and influence, and Isabel used that to look after her special friends.

Esther hated the city, with its perpetual heat and dust. The traffic, the noise. The Cubans were an alien race. Their music was too loud and crude. So, unlike the wonderful concerts of Vienna and London.

She hated their 'manana' attitude, leaving for tomorrow what could be done today. So, unlike the Germans. Esther pushed that thought away. Though she tried not to listen, it was impossible not to know about the horrors in Europe. She had not heard from her family in months. No, over a year. What had happened to them? She pushed the thought away again.

At least she was safe. Her conversion had protected her, and her children, from the ugly undercurrent of hatred towards her race. It was there on the island. Isabel had told her of the German spies, spreading rumours and lies, fanning the prejudice that had existed for centuries against the Jews. She was so grateful for Isabel's protection.

Mrs Price was waiting with a message for Esther when she arrived home, feeling rather agitated, from the Mass.

'What did Isabel want, Mrs Price? Is she alright?'

'She didn't say, Mrs Mueller. She just asked you to call her when you got back.'

'How did she sound?'

'Brusque.'

Brusque? She sounded brusque?'

'Yes. But I am a servant, after all.'

Esther went to her day-room feeling a flutter of anxiety. When she dialled the number she noticed her hand was shaking. She tried to calm herself as Isabel's butler went to get his mistress. Esther waited and finally heard the phone being picked up.

'Oh, Isabel, dearest, is that you? How are you? I missed you all today. Are you not well?'

'What's this nonsense about Carl's estate?' Isabel's tone was terse. 'Is it true?'

Esther's heart was in her throat. 'Carl's estate? What about it?'

'Do you agree with this insanity? Had you anything to do with it?'

Panic was raging now. 'Agree about what? I don't know what you're talking about, Isabel! Please, tell me!'

Esther burst in on Carl talking to a patient.

'Are you insane!', Esther cried. Standing fists clenched and red-faced in the middle of the room, she didn't wait for an answer. 'Are you crazy! Sharing the profits with the peasants! Have you...Have you lost your mind!'

The patient got up and left hurriedly.

Carl was calm. 'I don't think so, my dear. Unless practising Christian values is insanity.'

'Christian values! That's not what Isabel called it! She called it "communism!"'

'Ah, Isabel.'

'I have just been given a severe dressing-down on the phone!'

Crossing the room, Carl quietly closed the heavy mahogany door. 'My dear, I don't think we want the whole house to hear.'

'You planned this behind my back! This madness! This lunacy!'

Well-practised at dealing with her ritual hysteria, Carl remained placid. 'You said you had no interest in the running of the estate.'

His calmness only served to increase her fury. 'Well, I have now! And you had better change your mind! You madman! You lunatic! You've got to change your mind!' The sobbing began. 'Isabel is refusing to have anything to do with me!' The sobs increased, shaking her whole body. 'She is cutting me off!' she wailed.

'I'm sorry to hear that, my dear. But I can't be responsible for what Isabel chooses to do.'

Knowing he should try to comfort her, he went forward, arms wide. She drove him away with flailing arms.

'Don't touch me! Don't touch me..!'

He waited for the sobbing to subside. Words useless at the moment.

Finally, she dried her eyes with a lace handkerchief, determined to regain control. Her life depended on it. The voice felt like cold steel. 'You will tell them tomorrow! You will tell them it's all nonsense! Just stupid, silly rumours!'

Carl looked puzzled. 'Tell who, my dear?'

'They are all coming to see you tomorrow! Isabel's husband and the other estate owners!'

Freddie hadn't seen Carl for weeks. Despite Carl's wish to help in his travelling clinic, Carl's practice now so flourishing that he had no time to go with Freddie into the countryside. Freddie felt a little neglected. Rekindling the friendship they had once shared had done wonders for him.

'You good now,' remarked Conchita. 'No drink much. Conchita like. Much.'

It was true. Having a purpose, regaining a dear friend, things he thought would never happen again had changed him. He had prepared for a short drunken dive into oblivion. Enjoying his martyrdom. And now?

The knowledge that he'd been forgiven lifted a burden he had carried for ten long years. After the months of drunken self-pity in the London gutters, too ashamed to return to his island home, he had tried to assuage the guilt. He worked among the poor and destitute in Europe, becoming more cynical and pessimistic day by day. Finally, more from a death wish than through idealism, he'd joined the resistance against the dictator Franco. Fighting in the snowy mountains of Catalonia, tending the sick and wounded, hoping to find the bullet with his name on it. Too cowardly to do the deed himself.

Disillusioned with the constant in-fighting between the socialists and communists fighting against Franco in Spain, and the ugly threat of Fascism in Europe, he'd worked his passage back home. There, he found his reputation had preceded him. The shining youth from Havana, destined to become one of the finest doctors the world had seen, had returned a drunken, rudderless bum.

He liked to think he had saved Conchita, but the truth he suspected, was that Conchita had saved him. She loved him, which no one else did. And now Carl's forgiveness had given him a second chance. But to do what? To begin his studies again? To become a proper doctor, with a certificate after his name? Could he do that at his age?

Hearing footsteps on the stairs, he went to open the door for Conchita. He could do with a warm, body against his to stop the endless questioning in his brain.

What he saw made him actually step back in surprise. Standing on the threshold, hand raised to knock, was Esther Mueller.

CHAPTER TWENTY-FIVE

The consequences were immediate, as Isabel had threatened they would be. Within twenty-four hours of rejecting the estate owners demands, the bulk of Carl's wealthy patients had left his practice.

It was impossible for anyone in the house not to hear the repercussions. Even hiding away in their attic sanctuary, the children couldn't ignore Esther's fury far below, as she followed Carl through the house, throwing any object that came to hand at him.

In the attic, Klaus had retreated to a corner, hands over his ears.

'Why doesn't Father just do as Mama asks?' moaned Hans.

'Because what he's doing is right!' Anna snapped. 'They should get their fair share!'

'Why? They're just niggers!'

'Don't say that!'

'Niggers! Dirty niggers!'

Anna flew at him, fists whirling like windmill sails. Hans ducked away, but a stinging blow caught him on the nose. Anna stopped at the sight of blood.

Hans tried to staunch the flow which gushed onto the monogrammed shirt Giorgio had him. 'Now look what you've done! You're crazy! Just like Father!'

He flung open the door and stormed out. His racing footsteps echoing down the stairs.

Terrified, Klaus began to wail. Anna went over to him and put her arms around him.

'It's alright. It's alright. Don't cry. It's alright.'

Klaus's anguished howls were muffled against her chest.

Finally, exhausted by her own furious anger, Esther lay on her day-bed, an arm covering her eyes. Like one of her tragic heroines, too drained to cry anymore. She had refused Carl's offer of a sedative. Telling him she didn't want anything from him. Ever again.

Her life was ruined. He had made her a social outcast. After all she had been through, just when her life was beginning again, Carl had destroyed it. She had tried everything. Anger, tears, threats, violence. An expensive Art Deco vase, intended for his stupid head, lay shattered on the hall floor.

Unless he could be made to change his mind her life was over. She may as well end it now. That would teach him. Carl had plenty of pills in his surgery. An overdose of her sedatives would be easy. But how many was enough? She didn't want to survive, like failed suicides she'd heard about, with a damaged brain. That would be unbearable. Pitiable. Just like poor Klaus.

Her son. No, she couldn't leave her helpless son. She had to carry on. She had to find a way to change his mind. Someone to persuade him.

Lying there, staring unseeingly at the ceiling, the idea came to her. She sat up, her heart now beating wildly. Going into the bathroom she cooled her cheeks with water and stared at herself in the gilded mirror. Could she? Dare she?

Angry and smarting from Anna's assault, Hans left the house as soon as he had changed. Walking quickly under the shade of the trees through the colonnades of the old city, he headed for La Playa, where Dieter and Franz had arranged to meet him. Meeting spies in a place full of such sleazy energy made the youth's pulse race.

Banned by his father from listening to the German radio in the house, he relied on his two secret friends for news of the war. Hans was thrilled at Germany's success and his Fuhrers military genius. Belgium, Holland and France had fallen like skittles. And England was being pounded day and night by the might of the Luftwaffe. The war would be over before he was able to join up. But he was doing his bit for victory.

His contacts were drinking beer outside their regular bar.

'Hans!' said Dieter, in English. 'What are you drinking?

'A beer.'

Franz frowned. 'Don't want to draw attention to yourself by breaking the law, Hans.'

'A coke, then,' Hans said, embarrassed.

As he drank, Hans listened to their latest news from Europe.

'It won't be long before we in total control of Europe,' said Dieter.

'Wonderful!'

'So, you have news for us, Hans?'

The two men listened intently as Hans recounted his father's plans for the estate.

'So, your father is a communist?'

'That's what Isabel's husband called him, Franz.'

'Who are his friends?'

'I don't think he has any. Apart from that man Freddie.'

'Freddie Sanchez?'

'You know him?' asked Hans.

'The one who pretends to be a drunk all the time,' Dieter replied.

Franz finished the sentence. 'But we're not so sure.'

'You think Freddie could be a spy?' Hans' voice was eager. This was getting better and better. Was his father and Freddie involved in a spy ring plotting against Germany? They both certainly hated Hitler and the Nazis.

'Sanchez spent a lot of time in England.'

'And he speaks good German, apparently.' Dieter added.

'Perfect credentials,' Franz concluded.

Hans was breathless. 'That's incredible!'

Dieter laid his hand on the youth's bronzed forearm and stroked it. 'Watch them, Hans. Reports any meetings, phone calls, messages.'

'I will,' said Hans, quickly, taking his arm away. He was slightly worried about the physical contact. Men didn't stroke each other. Not German men.

'You have no worries about spying on your father?' asked Franz.

'No. Not if it's for the Fatherland!' said Hans proudly.

The taxi has been waiting outside for ten minutes, but she didn't hurry. It had taken a full two hours before she knew she was ready. She had bathed, powdered her body and applied her favourite fragrance. One he would surely remember? Choosing the outfit had been difficult. Alluring but not too blatant. She chose a pale tangerine chiffon that complemented her complexion. Finally, going to a drawer she took out a slim black box. Opening it she took out the necklace.

As she fastened it around her neck, she knew he could never forget that.

CHAPTER TWENTY-SIX

Freddie stood at the doorway lost for words. If he'd been drinking, he would have known it was an hallucination. But it was real. She was real. Esther Mueller was standing at his door. All alone.

She glanced at him and then looked down at her hands. Despite the heat, they were sheathed in white lace, fingerless gloves. Her tone was subdued, almost penitent.

'Freddie, I need to talk to you.'

He stood back and said, as if it was the most natural thing in the world. 'Come in, come in.'

But there was nothing natural about it at all. It was over ten years since he and Esther Mueller had been alone together in the same room. A room so very different to the one they stood in now. Freddie glanced around, feeling embarrassed, ashamed. How had he let himself get to this state? A fall triggered by this beautiful, elegant woman standing incongruously among the meagre surroundings, like a diamond in the gutter.

'Please, sit down. Sit down,' he said, hurriedly wiping the seat of a wooden chair with his palm.

Esther sat down demurely. Her heart was thumping in her ears. She had not felt so alive, so excited since...Well, since they had been alone together the first time. She fingered her necklace nervously. The necklace she had worn that night.

'Would you like a coffee? I'm afraid I don't have anything else.'

She shook her head. 'Thank you, no...This isn't a social visit.'

Freddie stood, waiting expectantly. She looked grave, unhappy. Her cheeks were a little more sunken than before, emphasizing the perfect bone structure beneath.

'I've come...I've come to ask for your help.'

Anna was excited. The holidays were imminent and she was going to help with the cane harvest on the plantation, working out in the fields with Jose's family and relatives. This year the family would be paid a fair wage, for the first time in their lives. She was thrilled for them, and couldn't wait to start.

Jose had been astonished when Anna told him the news. They were sitting in the kitchen, tasked by Carlotta with watching the cakes baking in the oven.

'Really! You're joking?'

'No! It's true! You're going to have lots of money! All of you!'

The boy's eyes widened. It was like a dream. He knew that some people were rich, but his family had always been poor. It had been that way as long as he could remember. He had seen the long, gleaming cars gliding down the tree-lined avenues of the city. He could name them all; Plymouth Coupe, Buick Phaeton, Chevrolet Deluxe, and his favourite, the Chrysler Thunderbolt. But he had always known he would never own one. No one in his family had ever owned a car, unless you counted his uncle's ancient, rusty Ford pick-up. But now. Maybe in a few years...

'I told Papa to do it. It was my idea!' Anna said proudly.

Jose beamed at his friend. 'Thank you!'

'You're very welcome,' she grinned in return.

'Thank you, Anna... I don't know what to say.'

'You may kiss me, if you like.'

Jose looked at his beautiful friend. He had seen a film poster outside the cinema in the Old Town. The film was called 'Gone With The Wind', and the picture showed how real men did it. Before she could protest, he grabbed Anna in his arms and planted a firm kiss full on her mouth.

Anna struggled and beat him away with her fists. 'Urgh! Not like that! Urgh! That was horrid!'

She sprang up and walked away, shaking her hair indignantly.

Jose watched her go, biting his lip, humiliated.

Freddie listened without speaking as Esther told him about Carl's stubbornness, and Anna's wilful encouragement of her father's folly. About the collapse of Carl's practice and the shame and ruin the family would be brought to.

'It's dreadful,' said Esther. 'Some people shouted obscene things at him from a car. And he was pushed in the street!'

He watched intently Esther's animated face and delicate hands twisting in her lap. Her distress was evident, but she surprised him by not resorting to the usual histrionics. He guessed Esther must be very frightened.

When she had finished, she looked at him for the first time. Tears glistened in her eyes, but none fell. She looked like a lost child. An older image of her daughter. Though, he thought with a secret smile, fiery Anna was far from lost.

He flipped a cigarette from the pack, lit it and let the match burn down between his finger and thumb, savouring the moment. Enjoying the upper hand after such a long time. A little mild revenge, as Esther waited for his response.

'Well,' he began at last, 'I did warn him before about what could happen. It may be foolish and naïve of him, but I doubt he'll change his mind. We both know how intransigent Carl can be,' he added pointedly.

She looked crestfallen. Betrayed. 'But I - '

'But, I will try again...For you.'

'Oh, thank you, thank you!'

It was worth it just to catch a trace of the radiant smile he had not seen the Mueller's came to the island.

'One more thing...' she went on, hesitantly.

'Yes?'

'Please, don't tell Carl I came to see you.'

He released a cloud of smoke with his sigh. 'More lies, Esther?'

'No! Not like that! If Carl knows I asked you he won't listen. He thinks I'm a hysterical fool.'

Freddie nodded his acquiescence. Though it was uncomfortable to lie to Carl again, he could see her logic. 'Okay.'

'Thank you,' she said quietly.

So, the meeting was over. The business was done. But Esther showed no signs of leaving. She smiled timidly at him under her lashes. He returned her gaze, a tiny animal transfixed by a cobra.

Sunlight through the shutters turned the hairs on his naked forearm to gold. The hairs, the flesh she had once stroked. Her hand lay on the small table between them. Slender fingers inches from his arm. Freddie could hear her breath becoming shorter.

Stressed or not, Esther was still extraordinarily beautiful. Freddie dare not speak. One word could bring it all crashing down. One gesture.

Taking a deep breath, Esther was about to speak, but instead she spun round startled as the door swung open.

'What's this!' cried Conchita. 'Who's this!'

The slight, beautifully formed young woman was marred only by the hideous scar running from her forehead to her jaw.

'Is this her? That woman?!' Conchita snarled. 'What she do here?!'

Esther looked at Freddie for protection.

Conchita strode into the room. 'The necklace!' she said, gesticulating at Esther. 'She got my necklace!'

Alarmed, Esther leapt up and fled. Her footsteps panicking down the wooden stairway.

The look on Conchita's face told Freddie not to follow.

She found a taxi waiting by the harbour, and asked the driver to take a circuitous route back to her home.

'Take me along the ocean,' she said.

She needed time to think, to compose herself. She had almost...Unthinkably...If the woman hadn't burst in on them?

It was crazy to contemplate it even for a moment, but all her old feelings were still there. Made more intense by the circumstances of their final parting. And her betrayal of him.

As the taxi drove along the Malecón, she looked out at the calm blue ocean, at once intensely relieved and also deeply unhappy at her escape. How could she think of getting involved in Freddie's sordid existence? Esther had immediately recognised the young woman as one of the prostitutes that hung around the Hotel Ingleterre. The ugly scar unmistakeable.

Carl had not exaggerated the circumstances of Freddie's life. Where he lived, the company he kept. But she was not responsible for that. No, she couldn't be. Not after all this time. And Freddie didn't seem to bear a grudge. He had agreed to help. Pray God, Carl would listen.

Conchita was naked in his arms, placated by his profession of love. As their bodies lay entwined, he'd thought only of that time with her. That eager young body, the ripe breasts, the intoxication of her smile. Had he been close to betraying his friend once again? He mustn't go down that road, no matter how enticing. She was unstable, destructive. His own life was testament to that.

But she had come to him in desperation and he would try to help. Though he knew he would never change Carl's mind, he had promised he would try. He would go through the motions. And try to keep the dangerous Esther Mueller at a distance.

CHAPTER TWENTY-SEVEN

Hans lay back, relaxed, in the passenger seat of Giorgio's open-topped coupe. He had been delighted when Giorgio arrived that his car was not crowded with the usual acolytes. They were alone. It made him feel very special. Giorgio's special friend.

The ocean they were driving beside was as calm as a mirror, reflecting the azure sky. It was a beautiful day. He'd been telling Giorgio that Dieter had told him the war was going well for Germany in Europe. Though they had not yet invaded England, which was a disappointment for them. But Hans knew that he would rather be here than in war-torn Europe, listening as Giorgio outlined his plan for him.

'It's a breeze, Hans. You can do it after school and make tons of dough, buddy,' Giorgio said.

'What about the police?'

'My pop knows the chief. No problem. You up for it, buddy boy?'

Hans was excited and nervous at the same time. 'You bet.'

Giorgio drove through the open gates of the family villa in Miramar, adjacent to Isabel's where he had first met Giorgio.

'The family's off for the weekend on some big film star's yacht. Errol's, I think,' Giorgio added casually.

Hans was deeply impressed by his friend's familiarity with Hollywood legends.

Giorgio led the way around the side of the house to the large terrace surrounding the pool. He raised his arms to the sky. 'It's so hot. Let's hit the pool.'

'I haven't brought my swimsuit.'

Giorgio grinned at him, and in answer peeled off his sweat shirt and shorts. He had nothing underneath. 'They won't be back 'til Sunday. No one to see.'

Hans was used to male nakedness. His school in Germany, and here, had showers. But he had never been alone naked with just one boy. He glanced shyly at the thick clutch of golden hair surrounding Giorgio's semi-erect penis. One man.

Giorgio looked at him, standing awkwardly. 'Do I have to take 'em off for you?'

'No, no!' Hans said, hurriedly pulling off his sweat shirt. His hands poised at the waistband of his shorts, a tremor of excitement running through his body. He pulled them down, deeply aware of his own boyhood, shrivelled with embarrassment.

Racing down the length of the pool, Giorgio leapt onto the springboard and performed a graceful arc into the sparkling, clear water. Surfacing, he gestured to Hans to join him. Hans dived inexpertly into the pool.

Giorgio dove underneath the surface and grasped Hans by the ankle, pulling him underneath. Hans thrashed about, gulping in water, and struggled to surface. Giorgio surfaced beside him, grinning.

'Gotta teach you to swim, buddy boy!'

For twenty minutes Giorgio instructed his protégé seriously, only occasionally lapsing into fooling around, diving underneath Hans, grabbing him a bear-hug and dragging the struggling youth to the bottom at the deep end. Gasping for air and scary as it was, he was excited being so close to Giorgio's muscular body.

Afterwards Hans lay on a sun-lounger letting the hot sun warm his tingling body to a healthy glow. He looked up as Giorgio walked out from the lounge, smoking a cigarette. 'Didn't know you smoked.'

'S'not a cigarette, bud.' He held it out to Hans. 'Take a drag, and then hold it.'

The first drag made Hans cough. He tried again, and this time held the smoke inside.

127

'Now, let it out slowly.'

'That's nice.'

When they had finished the joint between them, Hans closed his eyes and drank in the sun. This was paradise. All thought of Germany's continued success in Europe seemed far, far away. With surprise, Hans found himself thinking that he may never return to his homeland. The war didn't really matter on this sun-drenched island.

He opened his eyes with a start. Giorgio was kneeling beside him, one hand holding a bottle of sun oil, the other resting lightly on Hans's thigh. Hans tried to rise. The hand was on his chest, gently restraining.

Giorgio smiled. 'Relax, bud.'

Hans lay back, feeling a little uncomfortable. The hand began smooth oil over Han's chest soothingly.

'Enjoy.'

Soft, strong hands caressed his pectorals.

'Close your eyes,' Giorgio instructed.

Hans did as he was told. The sensation was greater with closed eyes. After a moment the fingers sought out the nipples. His body tingled at the touch. Hans had never known his nipples come become erect. He sighed. The sensation was pleasurable. Slowly, he felt the hands drift down his stomach to his belly.

'Giorgio!' he tried to say, deeply embarrassed.

'Hey, looks like the big boy's come out to play!'

Hans looked down at his erect penis in alarm, and excitement.

'We should tell him 'Hello!'.

Before Hans could respond Giorgio's fingers were firmly around the shaft. Hans felt his whole body trembling. He wanted to speak, to protest, but no words came. Giorgio looked at him and licked his lips. As Giorgio's mouth closed round the swollen, purple head, Hans's voice cried out, unintelligibly.

When she came home from school, Anna was surprised to see Freddie sitting with Esther in the garden room.

'What's he doing here?' she asked tersely.

'Anna! How do dare you be so rude!' Esther exploded. 'I asked Mr Sanchez to come to see Carl about the plantation.'

'Have you come to pester Papa about the workers again!'

'Anna, go to your room at once!'

Freddie deflected Anna's aggression with a friendly smile. 'It's alright, Mrs Mueller. It was my fault.' He turned to Anna. 'I asked your father to apologise for me, Anna. About the other day in the café. Perhaps he forgot?'

Anna was not to be denied her moment of retaliation. 'You think you're so clever being cynical, don't you! Laughing at people's principles! Just because you don't have any yourself!'

Esther stood up. 'Anna! You don't know what you're talking about!' she said furiously. 'I said go to your room!'

'Why all the raised voices?' Carl had entered unnoticed. 'Hello, Freddie. How nice to see you.'

Freddie decided to get straight to the point. It was an uncomfortable situation and he wanted out of it as soon as possible. He wished he hadn't come now.

'Hello, Carl. Anna thinks, quite rightly, that I've come to ask you to reconsider your decision about sharing profits with your workers, Carl. I hear you've been having some trouble with the other estate owners.'

Carl looked at Esther, who coloured up immediately. 'Esther?'

'No, no, it wasn't your wife,' Freddie lied. 'We haven't spoken about this. Word gets around fast in this city.'

Freddie caught her glance of gratitude, before she lowered her eyes. 'And apparently Saint Isabel has been ordering her friends to leave your practice. It must be a difficult time for you.'

'Thank you for your concern, Freddie,' Carl's tone was unruffled, friendly. 'I appreciate it, but it's all under control. The estate harvest will more than make up for the loss of clients...Now would you like to stay for some tea, coffee?'

'Thanks, no. I just called because I'd heard you'd been having problems.'

'Nothing I can't handle, Freddie. But thankyou again.'

Freddie glanced at Esther, looking up at him, pleading. He went on, 'Carl, are you sure, really sure, you're doing the right thing?'

'As I said, Freddie,' his tone was a touch sharper now, 'Everything is under control. Thank you.'

Anna stared out at the garden. Esther at her hands in her lap.

Freddie broke the uncomfortable silence. 'Well.' He rose. Esther glanced up at him. He nodded to her. 'Mrs Mueller.'

She looked down again at her lap, crestfallen.

'Goodbye, Anna.'

'You will see what my father is doing is right!' said Anna, then turned away dismissively.

'I'll see you out,' Carl said.

Outside Freddie felt relieved. He had done what he had promised Esther, and he hoped that Anna was right about her father's decision. But he didn't think so.

Hans was in the dreamy state. Exhausted from the high-jinks in the pool, the warm sun on his naked belly, the haziness from the joint, but mostly from the amazing event that had just occurred.

At school in Germany boys had proudly shown off their erections in the showers, some even simulating masturbation, but he had never joined in. Though the Hitler Youth gloried in the perfect masculine body and manly strength, it frowned on homosexuality. But yet what had just happened was the most powerful, erotic moment he had ever experienced in his young life.

Afterwards, Giorgio kissed him softly on the lips and then went inside. Hans lay there feeling embarrassed and thrilled at the same time. He had admired Giorgio from the first time he saw him in Isabel's pool. He was his hero. But this feeling he had. This feeling felt like he was in love. But with a man.

Giorgio came out holding a jug and two long glasses. 'Mojito?' he said, filling the glasses and handing one to Hans.

The only alcohol Hans had ever had was a small glass of wine at Christmas. He took a long drink of the iced cocktail. 'That's nice,' he said, trying to sound cool.

'Drink up. There's plenty more.'

When they had finished the jug, and smoked some another 'weed' cigarettes, Giorgio told Hans to turn over onto his stomach.

'Don't want you burning up, buddy-boy,' Giorgio's voice was low and husky. 'You German boys aren't used to the rays.'

Once he'd turned over, he felt Giorgio's warm, soft hands begin to massage oil onto his back. He closed his eyes, enjoying the feel of smooth fingers delicately tracing his spine. Slowly the two hands were caressing his buttocks.

'Giorgio?' he began.

'Relax, buddy-boy.'

The hands became more insistent, kneading the firm flesh. Hans felt his penis strengthen again beneath his belly. He was uncomfortable now, but it was a mixture of excitement and fear. He tensed.

A long finger thrust its way between his clenched buttocks and...

'Giorgio! No!'

He tried to struggle up, but a firm hand between his shoulder blades held him down, face crushed against the fabric of the sunbed. He gasped in shock as the finger entered him.

'Giorgio!' he said, alarmed. 'No.'

'Relax. Enjoy.'

Giorgio slowly inserted his finger deep inside. Hans tried to move, but he was pinned down by the much stronger youth.

'No! Please!'

He felt mortified, but as the finger explored him, Hans felt his penis swelling larger than he'd ever felt it before. To his surprise, the pain was now mingling with unusual pleasure. Deep animal grunts began to come from his lips.

'Giorgio..! Please..! No..!'

He felt Giorgio sit astride him. Strong hands spread his buttocks wide. Giorgio's erect penis slipped between his buttocks, easily sliding up and down the oiled flesh.

'Oh, yes, Hans. Oh, yes.'

Giorgio began to breathe heavily, as the stroke of his penis became faster.

Panicked, Hans bucked his body, trying to dislodge his abuser.

'No! No! Giorgio! Please! NO!'

'Relax, Hans. Take it easy…Very easy, buddy.'

As Giorgio slowly entered him, Hans cried out in outrage and ecstasy. His brain exploded.

Hans opened his eyes. He was lying on his back between silk sheets in large bed in a room off the pool terrace. As he shifted, he gasped involuntarily at the pain.

'Ahh! Christ! Jesus!'

He lay still, hoping the pain would stop. He couldn't believe what had just happened. His first sexual experience had been with a man, and despite the discomfort, the pain, and the embarrassment, he knew that he had also enjoyed it.

Giorgio entered the room carrying a large pitcher of iced juice and two glasses. 'My boy has surfaced!' Setting the glasses down on the ivory-topped bedside table, he filled them to the brim, then held one out.

'No. I can't…I can't move.'

Giorgio grimaced, sympathetically. 'Oh, my poor boy! It hurts a little bit, the first time.' He raised his glass. 'Salud!… Just remember you're my boy now.' Giorgio said seriously. 'No Dieter or Franz.'

Hans frowned. 'Dieter, Franz?…Are they..?'

'Poofs. Don't know what you call it in German. But you don't see them anymore.'

'But I spy for them!'

Giorgio laughed. 'What do you think you can tell them that they can't find out for themselves?'

'They pay me money!' Hans retorted.

'Yeah, because they are grooming you, buddy-boy. Like a pet. Then one day, one fine day, they'll both rape you, together…'

Hans's head was spinning. So much was happening, all at once. He felt like he was drowning. Out of his depth.

'Oh, and another thing, my beautiful boy,' Giorgio added. 'Freddie is a drunken bum, not a spy.'

CHAPTER TWENTY-EIGHT

Anna had not seen Jose since his abortive attempt to kiss her. He had stopped helping Carlotta around the Mueller's house, and when Anna visited the plantation he could never be found.

'He's out,' his uncle informed her, brusquely.

'Where?'

'Hunting, fishing.' He didn't hold with the pushy, rich white girl taking up with his nephew. Nothing good could come of it.

But, despite combing the forest and the river bank, Anna had not even caught a glimpse of him. Convinced he was deliberately avoiding her, she decided on another ploy to track him down. Instead of tramping through the trees calling his name, she lay in wait, hiding.

She felt guilty at her reaction to the clumsy kiss. Though it had been a bit of a shock, she shouldn't have said those things. She knew she had hurt him, and among all her friends she valued Jose most. His life was so different to any she had known. He knew things instinctively that she had only read of in books. About the animals in the forest, the fish in the river, the insects living beneath the rotting logs. But most of all, he knew what it was like to be poor. From birth Jose had learnt to have no expectations other than his everyday existence. Merely survival. For Anna that was an alien concept and it bothered her that people could feel like that.

She has lay there, hot and sweaty, under the ferns for a long time and was just about to give up, when she heard him coming down the track.

'There you are!' she cried, springing up from the ferns.

Jose stopped, startled.

'I'm sorry I said those things, Jose!' she blurted out before he could turn and run. 'I'm really sorry! Please, be my friend again!'

He looked around, then at the ground, grinding the handle of his fishing rod in the dirt.

'I'd love you to teach me to really fish! Properly, like you do with a proper rod. Please!'

Jose looked at her moodily, then turned and walked away.

'Jose!'

He looked back, but didn't stop walking. 'Do you want to learn or not?'

With a grin Anna followed after him.

They were sitting on the bank of a small river that bordered the estate. A couple of medium-sized catfish stared up at them, glassy-eyed, from the grass. Anna had gone from triumph at landing her fish to her pet topic of the moment, Freddie Sanchez.

'I thought you liked him?' Jose said.

'No. I hate him,' Anna replied.

'Why?'

'He laughed at me for getting your family to share the profits.'

'I'm not surprised.'

'And I don't trust him. The way he looks at Mama.'

'Do you think he's after her?' Jose asked, wide-eyed.

'I shouldn't be surprised. She and Papa never speak. They hardly see each other. It would be just like Freddie to take advantage of her. She's so gullible.'

Jose frowned. 'What's gull-bull?'

'Gullible. She's easily...fooled. He could say things to her and she'd believe him.'

'Are you jealous?'

'No!' Anna rounded on him. 'Don't be ridiculous...! Ridiculous!'

Jose poked the ground with his finger, contrite. 'Sorry'.

'He's so smug,' she continued, vehemently. 'He doesn't believe anything can change!'

'What things?'

'Here in Cuba. For poor people like you. I said all people should be treated fairly. That they should be equal, and he just laughed!'

Jose shrugged. 'Maybe they can't.'

'They can, Jose! My Papa's going to lead the way!' She went on, enthusiasm burning fiercely. 'Tomorrow when the harvest starts your family are going to share in the profits!'

'My uncle doesn't believe that. He says nothing ever changes.'

'Well, he's stupid..! Hasn't he ever told you about Jose Marti?'

'Who?'

'He's your great hero. He led the revolution against the Spanish! He changed things.'

Jose frowned. 'When? What?'

'Back in the last century. He inspired people. He gave them hope. Showed them things can change, if you fight for them.'

'What happened to him?'

Anna shrugged. 'He died in a battle.'

Jose pondered this piece of information, unconvinced.

'Haven't you ever read about him?' Anna said. 'About your history?'

The boy shifted his seat in the grass and picked up a catfish. He turned it in his hands, mumbling something.

'Pardon? What did you say?'

'Can't read.'

Anna was taken aback for a moment. Then brightly said, 'I'll teach you!'

Jose sniffed.

'What are you sniffing at? Don't you want to learn to read?'

'I can smell something', Jose said looking around. He sniffed again and then stood up. 'There!'

Anna stood and looked in the direction of Jose's pointing finger. Beyond the palms thick black smoke was billowing high into the cloudless sky.

'The cane's on fire!' Jose yelled.

A long chain of workers passed buckets and anything that could hold water, from the river to the burning cane. The fire had taken hold in various places and was spreading rapidly, fanned by wind created by the searing heat. Their faces blackened, Anna and Jose dashed around the fringes of the flames trying to beat them out with wet palm leaves.

Anna thrashed desperately at the blazing sugar cane, choking back tears that weren't just caused by the swirling smoke.

But it was hopeless. Within half an hour the ripe crop was reduced to acrid, smouldering ashes. The workers stood, exhausted and tearful, watching the thick pyre of smoke hanging above the ruins of the harvest that was to have changed their lives.

Jose's uncle arrived and dismounted from the horse on which he had inspected the far reaches of the plantation. He looked at them, standing ashen-faced among the charred cane. 'All gone. All gone.'

Jose sniffed the air. Among the fumes rising from the scorched crop he detected another smell. He sniffed again.

Freddie looked at his friend, concerned. Suddenly Carl had aged. He looked old and defeated. 'Arson?'

'There was petrol everywhere,' Carl replied grimly. 'In several places. Isabel's husband and his cronies, of course.'

Freddie shrugged, sympathetically. 'But you'll never prove that. They own the island.'

Carl nodded, conceding the truth of the statement.

On hearing the terrible news Esther had taken to her bed, distraught. And when Freddie had arrived at the Mueller house unannounced, Anna had immediately rounded on him.

'What are you here for! Have you come to gloat!'

'Anna, please!' her father reproved. 'Have some manners!'

It pained Freddie that the young girl whose fiery nature he'd come to admire still bore her grudge, but he didn't show it. 'Actually, I came to offer my condolences. I know that's really no help...'

'But it's very much appreciated,' Carl said.

They were silent as Carlotta entered and mutely served them coffee. Her customary happy banter absent.

'We're ruined, of course,' Carl said, when she had gone. His voice was broken. 'There's the mortgage on the house, the estate...' He sighed angrily. 'My foolish ideas! My idiotic pride!'

'Don't blame yourself for other people's failings, Carl. Perhaps, what you tried to do was right.'

Anna looked at Freddie.

Reading her puzzled expression, he continued, 'I never said I didn't agree with you, or your father's principles, Anna. I just said that some others wouldn't. '

'And you were right,' Carl said gloomily. 'How could I have been so naïve! After what I witnessed in Germany?' He looked at Freddie, appealing. 'What am I do to?'

'Forgive me for prying, but have you no capital?'

'No...None.'

Freddie hesitated, then went on. 'What about...about the necklace?'

Carl looked at him, enquiringly. 'What? Esther's necklace?'

'I thought I saw her wearing it. Does she still have it?'

'Yes, yes, but she will never part with it.'

Freddie ignored the remark. Now was not the time for sentimentality. 'Forgive me, Carl. But I had it appraised when you sent it to me. I could get you a very, very good price. One that, I'm assured, would solve a lot of your problems.'

'Then she will have to let it go!' said Anna forcefully. Her tone allowed no argument.

A trace of a smile crossed Freddie's face. She got that from her mother.

CHAPTER TWENTY-NINE

Being ostracised by Isabel's circle had left her friendless and alone. But the ruin of the estate's harvest made Esther fear for her very existence. They would lose their home. Where would they go? She had seen beggars sleeping in shop doorways, and under the colonnades of the Old City. She would die before she allowed herself to be reduced to that.

Her earlier brusque rejection of the island's Jewish community made it unlikely she would find support from them. She had burnt her boats. But it was all Carl's fault.

She had grown hoarse berating her beleaguered husband. Finally, she had run out of words, and retreated to her room, leaving Klaus in the care of Nanny Price. In her depression, even her little pet could not console her.

She fingered the necklace at her throat.

'It's the only way, my dearest,' Carl had said to her. 'It's the only thing that can save us.'

It was also the last link to her radiant past. The beautiful Esther Goldberg, the jewel of Vienna's society. Now, all that had vanished. Along with her dreams. And it was the thing she had worn that night. With him.

Taking a deep breath, she rose and walked slowly to the door.

Freddie waited, expectantly, with Carl and Anna in the salon. He had been roused from his bed by a breathless messenger, very early in the morning.

'Mrs Mueller wants you to go to her house at ten o'clock sharp, this morning,' the boy had said. No details. Just the summons. From Esther, not Carl.

Sensing an occasion, he had quickly shaved and put on his best cotton suit. He was just leaving when Conchita arrived, having come to tidy his room.

'Where you going?' she asked

'To the Mueller's. Mrs Mueller wants to see me.'

'That bad woman? You no go.'

'I think I have to, Conchita. It could be important. They are having…a few problems.'

'Good', she said.

With his old car being in for a much-needed repair, and his credit with the city's cabs having run dry, he walked briskly to the Mueller's home, speculating about the summons.

'Esther point blank refuses to give it up,' Carl had told him, a couple of days earlier. 'She refuses to discuss it anymore,' he added, helplessly.

She must have changed her mind, Freddie thought, as he walked. That was the only explanation. And, of course, typical of Esther, the drama would have to be played out on her terms.

He had arrived there and waited with Carl and Anna awaiting Esther's entrance. He and Carl both rose as the door of the salon opened. Esther entered regally, wearing a simple gown of pure white flowing silk. The necklace sparkled at her throat.

A frown of irritation crossed her face on seeing Anna seated there. But her serene composure returned instantly. This was her moment.

'My dearest,' Carl began.

Ignoring him, Esther turned to Freddie. 'Mr Sanchez,' her tone was cool and dignified. 'I believe that you have suggested a solution to resolve our present…perilous situation?'

Freddie nodded. 'I told your husband that I could get a good price for a certain item. A sum that would enable him to buy your present home, and provide an income for quite a while.'

'And your commission?' she asked.

'Absolutely not!' Freddie said, genuinely offended. 'I wouldn't dream of taking anything! I made the offer as a friend.'

Esther's eyes were fixed on his face. Her hand went to the necklace. 'And this is the certain item?'

Holding her gaze, Freddie replied. 'Yes. It is.'

She stroked the necklace. 'It has enormous significance for me, Mr Sanchez.'

Freddie was aware that Carl and Anna were watching the drama intently. 'I realise that, Mrs Mueller. I didn't make the suggestion lightly.'

Intent on wringing the last ounce of pathos from the scene, Esther went on, 'It may be a bauble to you, but it holds many precious memories for me…Irreplaceable moments, you must understand.'

Anna glanced at her father, puzzled. Deeply uncomfortable, Carl interjected. 'My dearest, we're all well aware of the sacrifice it must be for you.'

Esther didn't even look at her husband, her eyes were on Freddie. Her hands went behind her neck. Slowly, she unclasped the necklace, and cradled it in both hands for a moment. Then she held out her hands to Freddie. Her eyes burned into his. Remember the time you first saw it, they said.

As he took the necklace their fingers touched. A spark of memory ignited momentarily, as she planned it would.

Anna heard the catch in Freddie's voice, 'Thank you…I'll do the very best I can for all of you,' he said.

Without a word, Esther turned and walked out of the room. Mission accomplished. The tragic heroine's story complete. Locked in her room again, she wept 'til exhaustion took over, and she fell into a sleep of vivid dreams.

Anna couldn't sleep that night. A full moon was shining through the curtains, turning night into semi-day. She got up and stared at the glowing disc through the glass. Earth's tiny offspring. It looked enormous. Huge and portentous. Some ancient societies believed such events were omens. It seemed like one tonight. She drew the heavy drapes across the window and went back to bed.

But sleep wouldn't come. She lay awake turning the events of the morning over and over in her mind. She had seen the way her mother had been with Freddie. There was something intensely personal in her behaviour towards him. Something to do with the necklace. And she saw that Freddie had been affected by it. Her father had sensed it too. She'd seen his embarrassment. How he tried to intervene.

Something had happened between the three of them when she was still a baby. When she was too young to understand. But she was beginning to understand it now. Her father's coldness after Freddie had rescued them from the ship. How her mother completely ignored him. She thought about the furious rows she'd heard in the hotel, without being able to hear many words, except that the name 'Freddie' was mentioned a lot. She recalled how Esther had rushed her and Klaus away, without thanking Freddie for saving her from the rabid dog at Isabel's party. It was as if she was ashamed, embarrassed, about them being seen with him. About Freddie being seen with Klaus.

She sat up. She understood now, and wondered why she hadn't seen it sooner. And she realised, with a shock, that she was jealous.

CHAPTER THIRTY

For once, Freddie had got up early and was about to leave to pay a visit to the fence, Alfredo Santini. He knew Santini would be still in the casino, where he spent every night until the morning. Checking the necklace was in his inside pocket, he was picking up his hat and cigarettes, when there was a knock on his door. Opening it, he was surprised to see Anna standing there.

'Anna! What a pleasant surprise! Come in!'

Anna didn't return his smile. She walked to the centre of the little room, heart pounding in her chest. She had not slept at all last night and, combined with walking in the heat of morning, she was feeling light-headed. She stood, her emotions in turmoil. What was she doing here? Why had she come?

Earlier in the morning she had tried to question Nanny Price about the past, which she was too young to remember. She had come straight out with it.

'Nanny, what happened with Mama and Papa and Freddie when they were in London?'

Nanny Price's eyes had widened in surprise, but her calm expression returned immediately. 'I'm sure I don't know what you're talking about.'

'Something happened. They fell out, didn't they? What was it about...? Was it about Mama and Freddie?'

'I don't know what you've been hearing,' Nanny's voice had assumed its strict tone, reserved for chastisement, 'Or what nonsense your little head has dreamed up, but I assure you that's just what it is, nonsense!'

Mrs Price returned to her embroidery, her stern face fixed firmly on. Anna knew it was useless to try and push further, but Nanny's reaction had confirmed her suspicions. She was determined to confront her dilemma head on.

But she had rushed here, without really settling in her mind what she was going to say. And now she was there, still undecided. She tried to push aside her feelings on seeing Freddie again, but looking into his pale-blue eyes, she panicked. She looked away, breathing heavily. Torn between throwing herself into his arms, and beating him furiously around the head. How could she be jealous about something that happened so long ago? Yet she was.

Freddie looked at her curiously. 'To what do I owe this pleasure...? Would you like a coffee? I'm afraid I don't have any squash.' He looked at her serious face, turned away from him. The girl was obviously disturbed about something. He felt himself getting nervous.

'Anna?'

Her voice came back after what seemed like an eternity. 'I forbid you to ever set foot in our house again!'

Freddie's voice registered his profound shock. 'What? Pardon?'

Anna was silent, shocked at herself.

'Anna? What do you mean? What have I done?'

Suddenly it all gushed out. 'Whatever happened in the past, Papa has tried very hard to build life for us here! He has tried make a happy home for us all. And he doesn't deserve you trying to ruin it again!'

Freddie felt a flush of guilt wash over him. The old guilt, resurfaced. Anna was an intelligent, perceptive girl. And, yesterday in the salon, she must have seen the past as she watched Esther, with barely concealed emotion, hand him the necklace.

'Ruin it?' Freddie spread his arms wide, trying to reduce the emotional tension in the room. 'I'm not trying ruin anything, Anna. I was just on my way to get your father enough money to buy your house, and to put food on the table for quite a while.'

She rounded on him. 'Because you want to have an affair with Mama again, like before! She's weak-willed and gullible, and you think she's going to be so grateful that you can seduce her again!'

A sliver of anger and injustice stabbed at Freddie. He wanted to blurt out the truth. To justify his actions. But they were not justifiable to a young girl just starting out on her own emotional journey. He could barely justify them himself.

'Anna,' he began solemnly, 'I can assure you, my hand on my heart, that whatever happened in the past will never be repeated again. I promise you that.'

'I don't believe you. I saw how you looked at Mama yesterday.' She looked at him fiercely, with tears forming. 'I'm warning you, if you set foot in our house again, I will tell Papa about you!'

Freddie frowned, 'Tell him what about me, Anna?'

'I'll tell him you molested me!' she cried.

Before Freddie could respond, Anna dashed from the room.

Going to the door, he shouted, 'Anna! Anna! Come back!'

He heard her footsteps clattering down the stairs, as her mothers had when she had come asking for his help. He shook his head, with a deep sigh. Mother and daughter so alike, so different.

The sale of the diamond went smoothly. Santini knew the people on the island who liked to parade their wealth. So, with the house purchase secured and the rest of the money in the bank, Esther should have felt reassured. But she was still isolated with no one to confide in. For a moment she had felt alive again at the prospect of seeing more of Freddie, but she had not seen him since giving him the necklace. He and Carl had carried out their business away from the house, at Freddie's insistence, Carl told her. That saddened and puzzled her. She sank into depression.

Her once constant companion, little Klaus, now irritated her, and she left him in the charge of Nanny Price. She told herself that, with Hans and Anna no longer needing much of her attention, the governess could earn her keep looking after her needy, youngest son. Confused at the rejection, Klaus began having nightmares, and panic attacks, which Carl had to sedate regularly.

Esther's depression was not helped when Carl informed her that he planned to help Freddie with his 'hospital for the poor.' Though the island's health service was considered the best in the Caribbean, many of the rural poor struggled to find adequate treatment. Carl had seen the improvised graves along the roads leading to Havana, of sick people trying to get to hospital in the capital.

'You're a famous professor!' she wailed. 'You should be running a hospital!'

'Perhaps, my dear, but Isabel has managed to close all those doors for me here. As, sadly, she has for you,' he added sympathetically.

Esther rounded on him, briefly rekindling her fire. 'Because of your insane ideas! You have destroyed my life! And now this final indignity! Get out of my sight!'

Carl knew better than to prolong the conversation. In truth, to his surprise, he found that he preferred the way things were turning out. He looked forward to working Freddie. They would become pioneering partners in medicine, as they were once destined to be.

For Anna's apart, after many nights crying herself to sleep, agonising about running to Freddie's arms for forgiveness, she instead redoubled her efforts at her studies. As the weeks passed, satisfied by Freddie's absence that she had helped keep the family together, she lost herself in school work, determined to be a star pupil when she went to Havana University.

Since her father's clash with the plantation owners, Anna's interest in politics, and workers' rights in particular, had blossomed and grown. A natural champion of the underdog, she devoured the sometimes-tortuous writings of the early social reformers. Marx and Engels in particular.

Silly schoolgirl crushes were for children. She would devote herself to politics and helping people. Love was for the weak. Like her mother.

CHAPTER THIRTY-ONE

Carl heard about the attack on Pearl Harbour on the radio. In December 1941, 353 Japanese war planes attacked the American fleet in Hawaii, sinking many ships and killing over 2000 Americans. Two days later, Cuba joined America in the Second World War. The island that had been their salvation was now at war with their mother country.

As the Mueller's sat down for dinner that evening, Hans arrived late, flushed and agitated. 'Did you hear, Papa? Cuba has declared war on Germany!'

'Yes, Hans. Sit down, please. You're late.' The war was a subject he didn't want to discuss in front of Esther.

'Will we have to leave and go back home!'

'What?' said Anna. 'Are you crazy? We had to leave Germany or be put in the camps!'

'That was because Mama was Jewish! She's a Catholic now!'

'She's still Jewish!' Anna responded.

'No, she isn't!'

'She is by birth! Isn't that true, Mama? We haven't heard anything about our family in Austria, Hans! Nothing from Grandpapa and Grandmama! Maybe they have been taken –'

'Stop it!' Esther cried. 'Stop it, Anna!'

What Anna said was true. There had been no letters, or messages from her family, since they had been in Cuba. Esther had tried to block it from her mind, but without Isabel or Freddie to distract her, thoughts of what had happened to her large, distinguished family kept bursting through. She had vivid, terrifying dreams, day and night. Only the contents of Carl's medicine cabinet were able to keep them, hazily, at a distance.

'No, Hans, we are not going back to Germany,' Carl said. 'This is our home now.'

'But can we just carry on living here, Papa?' Anna asked.

Carl glanced at Esther, then smiled at his daughter to reassure her.

'Of course, Anna. Yes, of course.'

The next day Carl visited Freddie. As he explained his concern, Freddie brewed his special café Cubano with beans he said he'd handpicked from the Sierra Maestra mountains.

'It was alright when the war was just in Europe, but now it means we are aliens here.'

Freddie poured the coffee into small cups. He had already realised the implications for the Mueller's, and done some research among his government acquaintances.

'Yes...' He heaped sugar into both cups. 'I hear the Americans have started interning Japanese, and Germans. And Italians.'

'They could deport us to America. Or even back to Germany.'

'No, no, I'm sure they wouldn't do that, Carl. Apparently, they are talking of internment camps here, for some people.'

'My God, that would kill Esther.'

'But with your reputation, Carl, – '

'What? After Saint Isabel destroyed it!'

Handing him a cup, Freddie went on, 'You're highly thought of in medical circles here, Carl. I know some of the doctors are glad to have their rich patients back, after Isabel destroyed your practice, but there's still a lot of respect, believe me...You're a legend here, as you were in Berlin and London. People will speak up for you.'

Carl sighed. 'What with Hans going around like he runs the Hitler Youth here?!'

'Yeah, that could be a problem, for him...' He sipped the strong, sweet coffee. 'But maybe his friendship with Tony Trevianni's boy –'

'That gangster.'

'It could help, Carl. Tony has many American friends who have 'special' influence here.'

'You mean the ones who run the hotels, and the casinos and the brothels? The Mafia.'

Freddie lit a cigarette. 'Tony's Italian, but I can't see him, or any of his friends being interned. And Hans and Giorgio seem very close.'

Throughout the month fear and anxiety about their future filled the Mueller's house. Angry spats between Anna and Hans resounded through the corridors. Esther was only able to cope with large volume of pills from Carl's dispensary. Mrs Price, for once shaken out of her natural composure, found Klaus irritable and scolded the child for the first time in her life.

Just before Christmas the Mueller's were called into the immigration department. Esther was so agitated she was unable to speak, so Carl was given permission to be with her. She was interviewed by some bored, minor official who spent most of his time staring, unashamedly, at the trembling bosom beneath her fine, silk blouse.

Anna's hatred of Hitler and the Nazis was so very genuine, the interviewer cut her interview short. But Hans had a problem. If he wasn't to be interned, he had to denounce the Fuhrer.

'My pop will help you, Hans,' said Giorgio. 'But you've gotta play ball. Come on, my little cute Nazi,' he teased. 'Say after me, Adolf Hitler is a ruthless, murdering dictator!'

Hans shook his head. 'No.'

'Adolf isn't here. He won't hear you. Say this, "I saw his S.S. troops murder children in the street."'

'No, I didn't.'

'Pretend, dude. I won't be allowed to visit you in the camp. I will have to find another...companion. That would be a shame.'

The prospect of losing Giorgio was enough for Hans. He would retract his statement after Germany had won the war, if he was ever questioned about it.

With the family anxiously waiting to find out if they were going to be interned, Christmas was once again a bleak affair. Esther insisted on Carlotta bringing her meal in her bedroom, but she ate nothing. Hans wolfed down his meal, and was picked up by Giorgio straight afterwards. Carl and Anna gave up on a desultory game of chess, while Mrs Price tried to play snakes and ladders with an increasingly fractious Klaus.

But Freddie proved to be right. Early in January Carl was told that his family were free to live in their home. But they had to report each week to the authorities, had to carry their identity cards at all times, and they were not allowed to leave Havana.

CHAPTER THIRTY-TWO

Giorgio dangled a set of keys before Hans's eyes.

'What are those for?'

'My apartment, buddy-boy,' Giorgio grinned.

'Your apartment?' Hans repeated.

For a twenty-first birthday present Tony Trevianni had bought Giorgio a small apartment in an exclusive block along the Miramar, overlooking the ocean.

'I need to do my own thing, Pop,' Giorgio had pestered. 'The house is too crowded. I need space.'

'This is your home!' his mother, Bella, insisted. She had married the mobster when she was young, and bringing up the kids and running their opulent home was all she knew. 'We're family, Giorgio!'

She neglected to add that she also liked flirting with all the young men that Giorgio regularly brought home. The handsome German, Hans, in particular. Her husband was an old man. After bearing him three children, he was no longer interested in her body. The young men's bodies tempted her, and she often arranged to be in her swimsuit when they arrived, because she knew she still had a great body, and young men seemed to find older women sexy. But she was still Tony's wife. And Tony was the jealous type, with a violent temper.

As an orphan himself Tony had mixed feelings about 'home'. In his youth he'd been free to do exactly as he pleased, and it hadn't done him any harm. He over-ruled his wife.

'The boy needs his freedom. Sow some wild oats, y'know?'

'But Tony! An apartment?' she protested.

'It's a present, for Christ's sake! I'm his father! He's twenty-one!

'Why can't he rent? He makes lots of money!'

That was true. Giorgio was beginning to build a regular clientele for his drugs, with Hans' help as his main courier. The money was pouring in.

Tony lit a cigar. 'I didn't hear you complaining when I bought you that diamond necklace. The apartment's chicken feed.'

Giorgio's first house guest was Hans. Since his 'seduction' by Giorgio, the two had become inseparable. Hans chose to think of the act as a seduction, rather than the ugly word 'rape', which was actually what it was. He was at peace with himself now. He was a homosexual. A poof. Giorgio had told him many stories about the Hollywood elite. Male heart-throbs who had millions of adoring female fans. He showed Hans a magazine with a photo of two very famous men in swimming trunks relaxing by their pool, beside a big villa.

'What, those two? Really?' Hans said, incredulously.

'Yeah. They share that big house. Raving poofs!'

Hans felt liberated and sophisticated at being in such famous company. And Giorgio made him feel very special, lavishing gifts on his latest conquest, which caused problems at home.

'Where did you get that watch?' his father had asked, when they had finished breakfast, and Hans was preparing to go to school.

'It was a present,' Hans replied, a little defensively.

'From whom?'

Hans was silent.

'That Trevianni boy?'

'He's not a boy!' Hans responded. 'He's twenty-one!'

'And you're just sixteen,' Carl went on, raising the topic that had troubled him for some time. 'He's too old to be your friend. You should find some friends your own age.'

'The Trevianni's are very wealthy and well-connected, Father,' Esther interjected.

Carl's voice was rising. 'The father is a gangster!'

'No, he's not!' Hans responded angrily. 'He runs a casino!'

'Full of gangsters! You've got to give that back!'

'No! I won't! It was a present! I won't give it back!'

Carl rose from his seat. Hans was growing tall and his father no longer towered above him. 'Do as I say!'

'Carl, it's a Patek Phillippe!' Esther was indignant. 'It's very expensive!'

'All the more reason he should give it back!'

Hans was defiant. 'Well, I won't! And you can't make me!'

He hurried out the door, slamming it behind him.

Carl looked furiously at his wife across the table. 'As my wife I expect you to support me, not undermine my efforts to keep that boy from going off the rails!'

'Your wife?' Esther screamed. 'Who you have almost reduced to being a pauper! Who drove all my friends away from me! Who left me alone, friendless, keeping Freddie away from the house! Your wife who you have driven almost to suicide!'

Carl rubbed a hand over his face, wearily. Suddenly tired of it all. 'There are more than enough pills in the surgery to do the job.'

Esther stared at her husband, eyes wide in astonishment.

'If you want,' Carl continued, all life drained from his voice, 'I can tell you which will be a most quick and effective.'

He left the room. For a moment Esther stared after him, disbelieving. Then she collapsed on the table, head in arms, sobbing.

With the freedom of Giorgio's apartment, the sex became intense and wild. Long day and night sessions fuelled by booze and drugs.

'And remember,' Giorgio said, as he and Hans were lying naked and exhausted on the bed, 'if I see you with anyone else...Like that Dieter guy, or Franz. Anyone.'

'Dieter and Franz have disappeared. They left when Cuba entered the war.'

'Good...But, I mean like anyone.'

'I don't want anyone but you, Giorgio.'

'Good. 'Cos if I caught you, I'd beat the crap out the both of you.'

Hans stroked Giorgio's chest fondly. 'Relax. I really don't want anyone else...Do you?'

'No way, Jose!'

Reassured, Hans snuggled up to Giorgio's tanned, muscular body. 'That's good, amigo.'

Giorgio rolled away, stood up and started to pull on his pants.

'Where are you going?

'Things to do.' Giorgio said abruptly. 'Ain't you got some drops-offs to do?'

Hans felt a little put out at the sudden change of mood. 'Is anything wrong?'

'Nah. See you later.'

Wriggling into his T-shirt, Giorgio headed for the door. 'And, remember, don't fuck around, lover.' Giorgio made a pistol of his hand and pointed his forefinger at Hans. 'Capiche?'

As the door closed Hans sat up and pulled the black satin sheets around him. Though the fierce afternoon sun streamed through the window, he suddenly felt chilled.

Giorgio was unpredictable, mercurial. That was part of his charm. But, for his lover, the rapid changes of mood could be unsettling. 'Lover'. Hans pondered the word. He adored Giorgio. Idolised him. But with the adoration came a feeling of nakedness and vulnerability. He wrapped the sheets more closely around his chest. What if Giorgio grew tired of him?

Threw him over for one of his many acolytes? How could he survive? He sat, as the sun carved deep, black shadows in the sheets surrounding him, feeling very young and alone. He had so much to learn about love and grown-up emotions. Outside his family, well his mother really, the only other love he had felt was for his Fuhrer. At the image of Hitler, standing proudly in the black limousine, he felt suddenly guilty. His love for the Fuhrer had nothing to do with what he and Giorgio did.

He got up quickly and showered. Giorgio was right. He had a lot of drop-offs and payments to pick up. He'd learnt quickly that junkies don't like to be kept waiting.

CHAPTER THIRTY-THREE

Carl was frustrated that war-time restrictions meant he was not allowed to leave Havana to help Freddie at his free clinics in the countryside. Most of the city's doctors were private, and they competed fiercely for the middle-class patients who could pay. The state system for the less well-off, he knew, was unreliable and riddled with corruption.

'A free clinic!' Esther cried. 'You have just begun to get some patients back!'

Despite Isabel's sanctions to all her circle, some of the Europeans knowing Dr Carl Mueller's reputation, had secretly come back to his practice. It was not much, but enough to keep them afloat.

'I know,' Carl said. 'That's why I can afford to help some of the poorer ones.'

'So, I am going to have to endure hordes of beggars and thieves coming to the door, filling the house with their rags and stench, and stealing what valuables we have left!'

'They are not thieves, Esther. They are just people who need a doctor.'

'How do you know? As soon as they found out, they will all be round here. I can hear them all now chattering among themselves in the dark little alleyways about what they can steal.'

'They can wait outside in the vestibule.'

'While I will have to creep out the back of the house, I suppose?'

'I haven't noticed you going out all, ever.'

'All because you –'

'We don't want to go down the road again,' Carl insisted.

'No? No! About how you destroyed my social circle of the best people on the island!'

'You mean those rich, prejudiced, opinionated, racist, parasites!'

Esther snatched a marble ashtray from the table and hurled it, furiously, at Carl. It exploded on the wall behind him.

Having heard the crash, Mrs Price emerged from her room. Klaus peered out behind her, fearfully.

Carl looked at the shattered ashtray on the tiled floor, 'Well, that's one thing they won't be able to steal.'

As one of the brightest pupils in her year, Anna was determined to go to university next year, and begin her career in politics.

She had seen the poverty of Jose's family on the plantation, and knew it was widespread on the island. Plantation workers only worked four months of the year, in harvest time. For the rest of the year, they and their family had to survive on what they could grow on the meagre plot around their houses.

On her walk to school Anna saw the men, and boys, who had walked miles to the city to join the city's homeless, begging from rich American tourists. Some country girls came for the bright lights, and swelled the ever-growing population of women who made a living hiring their bodies to executives, salesmen, tourists and college boys from New York to California.

Anna knew Cuba had a strong economy, mainly from selling sugar to America, and from tourism. Many of the plantations and sugar mills were owned by wealthy US corporations, and most of the profits went to America. Visiting Hollywood film stars had made famous the Mafia-run nightclubs and casinos that fleeced the thousands of tourists in opulent surroundings. Sugar, sex and glamour had made Cuba rich. And yet so many lived in poverty.

Despite her mother's vehement opposition, Anna admired her father's 'poor' clinic. In the morning before going to school, and when she returned home, Anna talked easily to the patients waiting for her father, using the colloquial Spanish she learnt from Jose. Generally, she found, they were as hungry as they were ill.

'What do you think you're doing, Anna?' Esther asked, one evening at dinner. 'Have you asked Carlotta to bake extra bread to give to those beggars.'

'They're not beggars, Mamma.'

'Have you asked her?'

'Yes. I ran out of food from the garden.'

'You've been giving them our fruit, as well?'

'Some of them are very hungry.'

'So, we are running a free food market, as well your father giving them free treatment!'

Carl touched Anna's hand. 'Anna, that's very kind, and I'm sure they appreciate it, but I'd rather they came here because they are ill, not because they are hungry.'

'Some of them are both, Papa.'

'I understand that, Anna. But your mother is right. We just can't feed all the hungry in Havana.'

'Your Father is right, for once.'

'Well, I shall, feed them all when I get into politics.'

'We don't want you studying politics,' Esther responded. 'Women have no business in politics.'

'So, what do you want? For me to marry a rich famous man, like you did?'

'Anna, please,' Carl said quietly.

'It is none of your business, but I was in love with your Father.'

'Yes. In love with his fame.'

'How dare you speak to me like that? Go to your room immediately, and don't come out until I tell you.'

'I'm not a child anymore, Mama. I'm planning to go to university next year.'

'Are you letting your daughter speak to me like that, Father?'

Carl was also perturbed, but not about Anna's attitude to her mother. 'Anna, can we talk about this later? Politics can be rather dangerous here. There was a confrontation last week. Some people got seriously hurt.'

Anna looked at him. 'Papa, you taught me that sometimes you have to fight for what you believe in. You have, and so will I.'

CHAPTER THIRTY-FOUR

Since they first met, Freddie knew that Carl's vision was that his children would grow up to be responsible, caring adults. Like their father. But, with Esther encouraging Hans' friendship with Giorgio, their eldest son was already diving into the underworld of the city. If he was in Germany, Hans would have been a devout member of the Hitler Youth. In Havana, it was the ruthless world of the Mafioso that aroused the young man's passion for excitement and adventure.

Freddie knew that Hans had already taken his first steps down that dangerous road, and it was doubtful that Carl would be able to stop him. Hans was as stubborn as his mother. But so was Anna. And it was Anna that Carl had come to talk to him about.

'You know much more about the politics here than I do, Freddie. How difficult and divisive, and dangerous it is. I have talked to Anna about not getting involved, but she seems determined to become a... er, a champion of the poor.'

Freddie lit a cigarette. He didn't like where this conversation was heading.

'She's a headstrong girl, Carl.'

'Like her mother. But for Anna it's about other people, not herself...I really want her to go into medicine, Freddie. I think she would make a brilliant doctor. Better than me. I told her that was the best way for her to help people. Poor people.'

'Maybe she'll come around to that.'

'No, she seems determined. She said only politicians can make things better...Or worse, it seems...There are lots of political groups here, and they all seem to be at war with each other. Someone was hurt last week. It seems very dangerous.'

'Always has been. But that's politics, Carl. It's the same the world over.'

'But I thought maybe...I know you tease her about her politics, but I think, really, she has always looked up to you...'

Freddie flicked his ash on the floor.

'You haven't been to our house for quite a while...I wondered if you would like to come for dinner at the weekend?'

'I, er...No. Not this weekend.'

'Well, anytime, Freddie. Carlotta can cook up a wonderful meal at the moment's notice.'

Freddie was thinking about Anna's threat. The fiction of him molesting her. Given his past history with Carl, what would happen if Anna went along with her lie? Right in the middle of dinner? And what would Esther think? Would she believe it?

He had betrayed Carl once. Would they believe he could do it again?

'I don't think...I think Anna would...' Freddie looked out to sea, looking for inspiration. A large freighter was just disappearing over the horizon. He watched the funnel disappear and wished he was on the ship at that moment. 'She's very bright, Carl. I'm sure, she would it, er, see it was prearranged...I think she could get angry...'

'Well, just come for a meal, then. No politics.'

'Carl, I...I would feel uncomfortable. In case...Please, I'm sorry, but I really don't want to intervene. I'm sorry.'

Carl sighed. He didn't understand Freddie's reluctance. He and Anna seemed to get along well, except when he made fun of her idealism. But she must know that was just his joke, really. Maybe, it was Esther. Perhaps, it would remind her of times they had spent having dinner together, before...He sighed, got up and put on his hat.

'Well, I'll keep trying.'

Freddie watched his friend walking away. He was as concerned about Anna as Carl was. Politics was a very dangerous game on the island, and Anna was such an idealist she was bound to get into trouble if she went down that road.

CHAPTER THIRTY-FIVE

Hans couldn't bring Giorgio to his home because his father thought Giorgio's father was gangster. And, of course, they couldn't get up to the things they enjoyed at Giorgio's. What really annoyed Hans was that his sister had begun to bring home groups of friends who congregated in Anna's bedroom, talking politics. Their heated debates could be heard everywhere in the house.

One afternoon he knocked on Esther's door, and went in when she called.

As usual, she was reading a book. 'Hans, how nice to see you.' She placed a silver bookmark in the exotic romance she was reading. 'Have you come to talk to your Mama?'

'Mama...

'Come and sit by me.'

He went and sat beside her. She put down the book and took his hand.

'I don't see much of you these days. We used to be so close.'

Hans smiled.

'It's that friend of yours, isn't it? The one you spend so much time with.'

He smiled again. 'Yes...I have decided that I'm going to live at Giorgio's apartment.'

'Oh? Really, Hans? Why is that?'

The thought of her son leaving home had never occurred to her. If she ever thought of it at all, she assumed that he would live at home until he met a girl, got married, found a home, and then had children. That she would dote over.

'I need some...freedom, mama. I'm not a child anymore.'

Esther looked at her son. He was growing into a tall, handsome young man. Just like his father had been. He would be a catch for any of the island's privileged young women.

'I can't bring any of my friends here.'

'You mean girls? Bringing girls home?'

'Yes...Anyone. They would fight with Anna's hangers-on.'

'Hangers-on?'

' Her 'friends'. She treats them all like her disciples. You can hear her upstairs. She has the loudest voice.'

'Yes. I know your father doesn't approve.'

'Well, why doesn't stop her?'

'He has tried, Hans. But you know what a stubborn girl she is.'

'Well, if she can do what she likes, so can I...I'm leaving school.'

'Leaving school? When?

'Straight away.'

'Hans, I think you had better talk to your father about this. You know he wants you to go to university.'

'I don't want to go, Mamma. University is for wasters like Anna's friends, talking about Communism and revolution and all that. Giorgio is a businessman. He wants me to be his partner...I thought perhaps you could talk to father about it. If I mentioned it, we'd only get into another blazing row.'

She squeezed his hand with both hers. 'Please, don't get me involved, Hans. Your father and I never agree about anything...I think you had better talk to him yourself, really.'

'Well, will you at least give me your support, mama. If I mention it at dinner tonight, you will back me?'

'Well, yes, of course.' She pushed his fringe from his forehead, and stroked his cheek. 'If that's what you really want.'

'Thank you.' He got up to leave.

'I will miss you, Hans.' She kept hold of his hand. 'I don't have anyone to talk to.'

Hans leant down and kissed her hand. 'I'll come back and see you, mama. Every day. Well, often.'

At dinner he was surprised when Esther told Carl that Hans had something to say to him. Brusquely, Hans outlined his plans to his father. Carl knew, from Freddie, that his son was already involved in Giorgio's 'business'. It was to do with drugs, and the two young men had support from Tony Trevianni. His bribes kept the police at a distance, and Hans out of the internment camp.

Quite to Hans' surprise, and to Esther's, Carl hardly put up any resistance. He knew his son was bright, but wasn't interested in studying. University would be a waste for him. In a way Carl was grateful that, with Hans living away, Giorgio's 'business' wouldn't involve anyone in the Mueller's home. As a father, his main concern was his daughter, Anna.

When he was not in the countryside at one of his clinics, Freddie liked spend the afternoon at his favourite bar overlooking the harbour. There he could enjoy the coffee that he told everyone he had hand-picked from the Sierra Madre mountains. On that day, the distinction between sea and sky was indivisible. He gazed out. Looking into infinity.

Conchita had cooked a chicken stew, which he would warm up if she had customers that evening. She insisted he ate every day to combat the alcohol. He went along with it, though he no longer tasted anything these days. Would nicotine get him before the alcohol? He took a sip of the coffee, and then a long drag on his cigarette. He'd read, years ago, that cigarette companies knew smoking was bad for you. As a doctor, he believed that anyway. But as the Babe Ruth advert said to the customers, 'There's not a cough in a carload.' He put the cigarette to his lips, and took another deep lungful of the poison.

'Oh, look Anna. It's Freddie!'

Freddie turned. Carl was approaching with Anna by his side.

'Hello, Freddie,' Carl said. 'We were just out for a walk, to look at the sea. Can we join you?'

Freddie thought about saying 'No', but instead waved a hand at the seats. They both sat. Freddie glanced at Anna. She was staring ahead, out to the ocean.

'Hello, Anna.'

'Hello,' she said, brusquely, without looking his way.

'So very different to the first time we met here, isn't it, Anna?' Carl said.

Anna gave a perfunctory nod to her father. Freddie sat silently, sure this meeting was not accidental.

'How things have changed...' Carl went on. 'We were just talking about Anna going to university next year.'

Freddie stubbed his cigarette butt on the cobbles. He glanced at Anna. She was still studying the distance.

'Anna tells me she's thinking about studying politics. Not medicine...Personally, I think that's a shame.' Carl breathed in deeply at the silence around him. 'I'll go and order some drinks.'

'There's a waiter, Carl.'

'I think I'll go and see what they have to eat. What do you want, Anna?'

'Nothing, Papa.'

'Oh. Another coffee, Freddie?'

'No, thank you, Carl.'

As Carl stood up, Freddie avoided his gaze.

'Well...' Carl walked briskly towards the open door of the bar, and disappeared through the bead of curtains.

Freddie and Anna sat in silence. A warm breeze was rippling the sea. They both stared out at the waves.

After a moment Freddie turned to Anna. 'I don't know if you know, Anna, but I'm sure this meeting wasn't a coincidence.

Your father wants me to warn you away from studying politics. I've already told him it's not my business. I really don't want to get involved...So, if you'll excuse me. Say 'goodbye' to your father.'

Freddie stood up, about to walk away.

'Freddie?'

He stopped and turned to look at her.

She was looking at him for the first time. 'I...want to say...I am so very, very sorry. For what I said to you the last time we met.'

He shrugged. 'Forget it.'

'No. What I said was disgraceful. Appalling. I was angry. Frightened. I was just being a little child...I would never have done that, really...Please, forgive me. Freddie?'

He looked at her. It should have been Esther, asking his forgiveness for vilifying his name, his honour, for destroying his career. But it wasn't. That would never happen.

'Goodbye, Anna.'

Anna rose. 'Freddie! Please!'

He turned back. 'You're forgiven, Anna...Now go and change the world.'

As he walked away, Anna watched him, feeling guilty, and sad.

CHAPTER THIRTY-SIX

It was the first time that Hans had left Havana. Though he had never driven before, they took turns to drive Giorgio's Buick convertible to the far east of the island. Driving the winding country roads with the sun on his back and his lover beside him was exhilarating. Having done his drug round for the week, Hans was relaxed. His customers could wait a few days for their next trip to paradise.

'It's the only place to surf in summer,' said Giorgio. 'Havana's no good. Here, onde grandi, mio amore.'

Hans frowned at him.

Giorgio put his hand on Hans' thigh. 'Big waves, my love!'

The country roads were deserted, apart from the occasional peasant cart. As Giorgio's hand rose to his crotch, Hans gunned the straight 8 into a sharp bend. Lumbering towards them, blocking the road, was an American army truck.

Hans froze at the wheel.

'Fuck!!' screamed Giorgio. He wrenched the wheel, spinning the car sideways. The world spun round and round, and then down, as the car careered backwards into a small gully. Three American trucks thundered past. They looked at each, shocked, and then started to laugh.

'Jesus!'

'Fuck!'

'Where the fuck did they come from?'

'From Guantanamo Bay, I guess.' said Giorgio. 'The Americans have a navy base there.'

'Well, thanks guys! They didn't even stop to help.'

Giorgio laughed, 'They've got a war on, Hans. Fighting our guys.' Giorgio pulled a bottle from glove compartment. 'Need a shot after that.'

Later, as they lay on the empty beach, watching the first stars appear above, Giorgio put his arm round Hans, 'Tomorrow, mio amore, I'll teach you to surf.'

Hans snuggled to him. 'Those guys who nearly killed us today, y'know they could die any day.'

Giorgio grinned. 'Shall we go down to the bay and sink their ships? Like Pearl Harbour.'

'Cuba's on their side, Giorgio.'

'We could be spies. Do you want to be out there, frightening with your Nazis?'

'You wanna fight with the Italians?'

'No way. We're losing anyway. I'd rather be here.'

A year or so ago, Hans would have rushed to help the Fuhrer conquer Europe. He loved his homeland, but his life was elsewhere now. 'So am I. I'd rather be here.'

Giorgio stroked Hans bare chest. 'Did you bring any coke?'

'Haven't you got any?'

'Sold it to the Americans at the casino. My Dad says it makes them rash gamblers.'

'I have some.'

'So, let's live a little. Life is for living.'

When Giorgio became twenty-one, Tony Trevianni let his son sell coke at his casino. When the punters were high, he said, they felt invincible. They lost laughing. Anyone else trying to deal drugs was shown the door by the muscle.

Buying the coke from Giorgio, Hans dealt on the streets, taking over Giorgio's customers. He charged what he could get and was gradually building up a lucrative business, getting new customers among the lower middle-class.

Some of the young, black Cubans, who weren't allowed into casinos, had pockets full of dollars from the tips they got from tourists. The attractive ones, like Juan, made much more escorting lady visitors, and sometimes men, around the sleazy back streets of the city, where the hotel receptionists didn't ask for I.D.

Juan was one of Hans best customers. He bought to treat his clients, and Hans charged him accordingly, which Juan was not happy about.

'Here comes that robbing Nazi again,' he said to his friends, as Hans approached.

Hans knew Giorgio only got the best produce. All the punters knew that. 'You don't want, Juan, go elsewhere.'

'I see your Italian buddies have chucked in the towel, huh!'

It had been announced on the radio that the Italians had surrendered. Hans was annoyed the tide of the war seemed to be turning against Germany. Now the Allies had landed in Italy, Hitler was fighting on his own in Europe.

'We don't need them!' he said arrogantly. 'They're cowards!'

'Yeh? Well, the Yanks are kicking your butt. You guys are gonna lose, period!'

'No way, we'll win! Germans don't lose!'

Juan pointed at Hans bag. 'Bet your stash, you do. You thieving fucking Nazi!'

'Shut the crap, you fucking stinking nigger!' Surrounded by Juan's friends, Hans knew that was the wrong word. Before he could move, Juan grabbed Hans' hair and headbutted his nose. Hans felt blood gushed down his throat and out of his mouth. Juan's fist crashed into his temple.

'You'll lose this time, you fucking Kraut!'

As Hans fell, he felt the kicks coming in. Then nothing.

When he came round, it was daylight. He was alone in the shaded alley, having laid unconscious all night. His head felt dizzy. His face swollen. He could taste the dried blood in his nose and mouth. Struggling up, he looked around for his bag. It was nowhere. The bag of coke was gone.

'Fuck!' he yelled. 'Fuck!'

His wallet was open, empty, on the ground. Having no cash, he had to walk the long way back to Giorgio's apartment. As he walked, trying to avoid the blazing sun, he told himself what Giorgio would do to Juan. That guy was crazy to rob him when Giorgio's dad had men who killed for a living.

Juan was slumped in the stern of Giorgio's motor launch, a thick iron chain around his chest. After just finished a very lucrative session with two older American women, Juan had been grabbed as he left the hotel. Giorgio had brought, Vince, the casinos best 'muscle' along to help. As Hans drove them to the harbour, Juan had tried to reason with them.

'He called me a stinking black nigger,' he kept repeating. 'A stinking nigger. That's bad, man. I'm a Cuban. I'm a proud man. Not a stinking nigger.'

'If that's what he says you are, that's what you are!' said Giorgio. 'Now, I want you to apologise to my friend Hans. For kicking the shit out of him with your friends.'

'It was just me. No one else did.'

'Well, you did a good job. If they let stinking niggers into my dad's casino, he'd make good security, eh, Vince?'

Giorgio cut the engine of his motor launch a couple of miles from the harbour. It was a calm, starry night. The ocean was quiet. The only sound was Juan whimpering.

Giorgio held the end of the thick iron chain that was tied round Juan's chest. 'Chuck him over.'

Juan screamed as Vince picked him up and tipped him over the side.

As Juan surfaced, Giorgio said, 'Now I want you to apologise to my friend.'

Juan was frantically treading water. 'I'm sorry!' screamed Juan. 'I'm sorry!'

'Again! Louder!

'I'm sorry, Hans!' Juan yelled. 'Please, believe me, I'm sorry!'

'Well, Hans? What shall we do to him?'

'I'm your best mark, Hans!' screamed Juan. 'Always pay top dollar!'

Hans leaned over the side. 'So, who is going to win the war, Juan?'

Juan head went under. He surfaced and spat out the water. 'You guys. You Nazis!'

'Say again!'

'You guys. You Germans! You win!' He went under again. Giorgio dragged him up. 'So, Hans, what shall we do?'

'He's understands now. He's a good punter, Giorgio.'

'Okay, buddy.' Giorgio started to pull on the chain to bring Juan on board.

'Thanks! Thanks, Hans,' gasped Juan, clinging onto the side.

'Oh, no, fuck it,' Giorgio said. 'My dad would kill me.'

He chucked the chain over the side, kicked Juan away and started the engine.

Juan screamed. 'No, no!'

As the boat moved away, Hans leapt over the side, swam and clung onto Juan as he was going under again.

'Hans!' cried Giorgio! 'What'd you doing!'

'No, Giorgio! No!' Hans shouted.

'Oh, fuck!' said Giorgio. He threw the lifebuoy to Hans. 'You fucking chicken!'

CHAPTER THIRTY-SEVEN

Esther was very bored. Since Isabel and her circle abandoned her, no one ever visited. She rarely saw Carl except at dinner. But that didn't matter. They had nothing to talk about. She was tired of pampering Klaus, who was becoming more and more irritating. Her library of romantic novels, which she often re-read, reminded her of her youthful desires and dreams, all of which had come to nothing. For some reason she didn't understand, Freddie no longer visited them. Perhaps, he still carried a torch for her, and seeing her would be distressing. She hoped that was the case. He was still an attractive man. Even more now he had matured. Maybe, she could call on him? She had done, once before, when she wanted his help with Carl's crazy idea about the plantation workers. And look what that mad scheme had done to them!

But what say to Freddie about why she was visiting him? Could she really think of starting it all over? Her heart beat faster thinking about that. She could talk to him about Klaus, their son. But did he even know? Carl said he had never discussed Klaus with him. But Freddie must know, after the way she attacked him at Isabel's party. He must.

She could take a taxi, but it was always horribly humid outside. So, she would arrive hot and sweating, not cool and elegant as she was at home. She could throw herself at him, but what if he rejected her? A hot, sweaty woman, past her best. No longer the belle of Belgravia. To be spurned by Freddie. Again. No, it was out of the question.

Hearing Anna coming down the stairs, she opened her door, and beamed her daughter.

'Anna! Good morning. Do you know, we haven't spoken together for ages? Maybe...maybe you'd like a game of canasta, and we can catch up with each other?'

'Thank you, Mama, I am going out.'

'I just thought it would be lovely spending some time with my daughter.'

'Is there anything you particularly wanted to talk about, Mama?' It was such an unusual request from her mother.

'No, just...Well...You seem to have a lot of friends. Have you met, any, young men that you particularly like?'

'Mama, I am working hard to get into university. I don't have time for...that kind of thing.'

'It isn't school today. Where are you going? We could talk.'

'I'm going to meet some friends.'

'Your Communists!'

'My friends.'

'Your father has told you not to get mixed up with those people. They are dangerous.'

'I have to go, or I'll be late. Good morning, Mama.'

As Anna left the house, Esther returned to her room. Pouring herself a whisky, she picked up book that she had read several times before. She would ask Hans, next time he came, to go and buy her some more books.

Earlier that year Anna had joined the JC, the Young Communists, and, though still at school, she went to all their rallies. As there was a presidential election at the end of the month, the JC were meeting on the wide steps of the University where most groups held their rallies. Anna was pleased that the steps were crowded with young people all the way down to the bottom. She could feel the excitement in the air.

Anna hadn't seen Jose for over a year. Carlotta told her that Jose had found work in one of the sugar mills which paid better and was more regular than cutting cane at harvest. But she hadn't expected to see him at the rally.

'Anna!'

Jose was making his way through the crowd towards her, waving. He had grown much taller and broader. What her mother would call a handsome young man.

He held out his arms, smiling. Anna put out her hand. Jose shook it with both hands. To Anna the easy familiarity they used to share, when they were younger, seemed too intimate now.

'Jose! How lovely to see you! What are you doing here?'

'I've joined the worker's union, Anna. We here in support.'

'That's wonderful.'

'I'm actually on the committee.' He laughed, and leant in closer. 'Because you taught me to read, Anna...'

Anna smiled. 'I'm glad I helped.'

'You're in the JC?'

'Yes.'

'Have you read all your Marx and Engels?'

'I have. It was hard.'

'Of course.' He shook his head, 'I tried, but it's too tough for a peasant like me.'

They walked together nearer the top of the steps, where one of the main speakers was just starting to speak. Before he had finished his first sentence several youths, nearby, started to yell abuse.

'Quiet!' Anna shouted.

Others joined in, on both sides. The speaker was now drowned out as the two sides began to hurl insults at each other. A fist was thrown and a fight erupted in the crowd. As the melee engulfed them, Jose put a protective arm around Anna. Surrounded by a sea of angry and frightened arms and legs, Anna heard the youth beside her cry out in agony. He stumbled over, screaming, blood pouring from a wound in his side.

Anna bent down to help him, putting her hand on the wound. 'Jose! Help!'

Jose ripped off his tee-shirt and handed it to Anna. She tried to staunch the flow of blood with the shirt, but the brawling mass of people engulfed her. As she fell to the ground about to be trampled, Jose grabbed her arms and yanked her up. He wrestled his way out of the heaving crowd. Away from the mayhem, they stopped for breath, with the brawl still happening on the steps.

'You okay?'

Out of breath and shocked, Anna nodded.

'Fascists thugs...!' She gasped.

Anna's clothes were covered in blood.

'I'll get you home,' said Jose.

'No.'

'It's too dangerous, Anna. There's no point staying. The rally's over!'

Through his surgery window, Carl saw Anna being helped to the door by a bare-chested black man. He rushed to open the front door, concerned.

'Professor Mueller. I brought Anna home from the rally.'

Carl looked at him, puzzled.

'It's me, sir. Jose. There was a fight at the rally.'

'Oh, Jose! Come in. Come in.'

Carl looked at Anna's bloodstained clothes.

'Someone was stabbed. Anna tried to help. She's not hurt. Just shaken, I think.'

As Carl helped the shaken Anna into the surgery, Esther appeared in the hallway. She looked questioningly at the semi-naked black man.

'Mrs Mueller. It's Jose. Jose.'

'Oh, I didn't recognise you. You've grown. What's happened?' She brushed past Jose into the surgery.

Carl was laying Anna on the chaise lounge.

'Put your feet up,' he said.

Esther looked at Anna's clothes covered in dried blood.

'Anna! What happened? Are you hurt?'

'She's not hurt, my dear. She's just in shock,' Carl said. 'She needs to rest. Can you pass that blanket, Jose?

'What happened, Anna? Is that blood?'

Carl covered Anna with the blanket. 'Just lie still, Anna. Breathe gently.'

'Jose saved me,' Anna managed to say. 'I was being trampled.'

'What happened? Anna?' said Esther.

'We were at a rally,' Jose explained.

'A rally?' She rounded on Anna. 'What did I tell you this morning! What did I say!'

'Not now, my dear, please,' Carl said. 'She needs to rest. We can talk about it later.'

'Father, she cannot mix with those people anymore! Tell her!'

Carl insisted. 'My dear, she needs to rest. She doesn't need to be stressed.'

Anna rose up. 'I will mix with who I like, Mama. You can't stop me!'

Esther glared angrily at her husband, 'Tell her!', then swept out.

'Lie down and rest, Anna. Please.'

Anna lay back down and Carl took her hand to feel her pulse.

'I don't care what she says, you can't stop me, Papa.'

CHAPTER THIRTY-EIGHT

Giorgio found Hans sitting on the apartment terrace, smoking, looking out over the ocean.

'Hey, bud. I just heard your big white chief killed himself. Killed his broad, then shot himself,' said Giorgio.

'There's no way Hitler would have done that. He would have fought to the end. He was a fighter.'

'He was a fruitcake, if you ask me.'

Hans took a drag of his cigarette and ignored the remark.

Giorgio sat beside him. 'Will you guys be going back to Germany now?'

'No. I shouldn't think so. I wouldn't go anyway. The place is wrecked, they say.'

'Yeah, well, if you get into a fight make sure you're going to win it.'

Hans got up. 'You wanna coffee?'

'A beer. You must be sorry your guy lost.'

'Do you know, Giorgio, I don't really care. I'm happy here. I did when we first came here. I wanted to be back there fighting. But I was a kid then. I'm grown-up now. And I like it here.' He put a hand on Giorgio's shoulder. 'Want that beer in bed?'

Giorgio grinned. 'You're still like a kid after that. Can't get enough.'

'Like you said, Life is for living!'

Giorgio got up and hugged him. 'I bet Anna is pleased. You said she hated the guy. Der Fuhrer.'

'She's got enough to hate here now. She's crazy about politics.'

'Another fruitcake.'

The phone rang in the bedroom as they went inside.

Hans picked it up. 'Hello. Oh, hi, Bella.' He listened for a moment, then turned to Giorgio, concerned. 'It's your mom.'

Giorgio was already stripping off. 'Tell her I'll call back.'

'No. It can't wait, Giorgio. It's about your father.'

When Tony Trevianni died of a heart attack at a party celebrating the end of the war, Esther told Hans she couldn't go to the funeral.

'There is no way I can go...I didn't know him. I only met him once at Isabel's party...And Isabel and all her women will be there. I couldn't bear it. They'll be looking at me and talking amongst themselves...I just couldn't bear it, Hans.'

The day after the funeral Hans came back to tell his mother about it. Esther was full of questions about Isabel.

'Yeah, they were all there, Isabel and her cronies.'

'Did she ask about me?' Esther asked.

'Yes, she did. At the wake. She came over and asked if you were still living with that communist.'

'What?'

'She meant Papa.'

'What did you say?'

Hans grinned. 'I said you were both very happy together, like a young married couple.'

'Hans! You didn't say that?'

'No. I just said you were fine...Actually, it was very strange, Mama. When I arrived at the funeral I saw this woman standing there. She was all in black, wearing a big hat and a veil over her face. For a minute I thought you had changed your mind and decided to come.'

'What? Why?'

'She was even wearing a necklace like yours. The diamond one. It was only when she lifted the veil, I knew it wasn't you'

'Well, who was it?'

'Bella. Giorgio's mother.'

Esther frowned. 'Does she look like me?'

Hans shrugged. 'Yeah, sort of. Same height, same sort of build, but she has bright red hair. Like Rita Hayworth. Very attractive.'

'Unlike me, I suppose.'

'I didn't say that, Mama. You are very attractive, you know that. Giorgio thinks so.'

'Hah. You never bring him round. I never get to see him.'

Hans laughed. 'Mama, you are not going to get off with my best friend!'

'No, I'm far too old. Like an old maid.'

'Rubbish. I've got to go.'

She got up and took his hand. 'Won't you stay a little longer?'

'I've got things to do. And I'm not going to stay here all day telling you how beautiful you are, so there, Mama.'

Giving her a kiss on the cheek, he left his mother feeling all alone again.

CHAPTER THIRTY-NINE

'I really need to know what has happened to them, Carl! I haven't heard from them since we landed here. Maybe they don't even know I am on this god-forsaken island!'

'Esther, the war has only just finished. I have tried to call people, but it's chaotic in Austria. Vienna is divided up between the Allies, and they don't seem to be working with each other. It's impossible to find out anything.'

'Well, you will have to go yourself then.'

'Me? My dear, it wouldn't be easy to do that.'

'You mean you won't even try? Even for my family! To find out what happened to them!'

'There is no way we can afford that, I'm afraid. The boat fare, the travel.'

'It's my parents! My grandparents! I need to know! They have money. They have friends in government. I'm sure they found some way to escape. They could be anywhere. And they have no way of knowing where I am! I sent them letters, but... I'm sure the Germans, those Nazis, stopped all the post. That's why they didn't reply.'

Both Carl parents had died before the war, and he had little contact with his other relatives. Having listened avidly to news of the war, Carl was fairly certain that the worst had happened to his wife's family. A wealthy Jewish family would have been a prime target for Hitler's Gestapo. They had fine houses filled with priceless possessions, a treasure trove for ruthless occupiers. But he couldn't tell his wife that. Besides, he had no real proof. Maybe they had escaped? Some people had. They could be in England, or America. He had no way of knowing.

'Yes, I'm sure they did stop the post. So, they could be anywhere.'

'Exactly! I need to know!' Esther said. 'If you go there, you could find out...! When you find them, we could go back home and live in Vienna again.'

'I'm sure it wouldn't be the same, Esther. Living there. Not after the war.'

'We could ask Han for the money. He could pay for you to go.'

'Hans? Don't talk to me about him.'

'Why not?'

'I am not going to ask him!'

'He makes a lot more money than you, and you are supposed to be a top professor of medicine!'

'Your son makes money by selling drugs, Esther! Illegal drugs!'

'Well, I will ask him myself then! I will phone him now!'

Carl sighed. He knew, once she had the idea, he would never hear the last of this.'Esther, if I did go, I would have to be away for weeks. Months even.'

'I'm sure I could manage on my own. We do nothing but argue together anyway.' She looked determined. While Carl was away, she realised, she and Freddie would be on their own. 'A change could do us both good.'

Hans was more than happy to help when his mother asked him. Since he had rescued Juan from drowning, his drug business had boomed. And he really enjoyed the fact that his father would have to take his 'dirty' money to go there.

Freddie and Carl had met the day before Carl left, in Freddie's favourite café by the harbour.

'I hope you have a good trip, Papa, he said!' Carl exclaimed to Freddie. 'He's obviously enjoying every minute...Taking money from a drug seller! But Esther insisted. I knew she would become hysterical if I didn't take it...Freddie, I am very ashamed.'

Freddie thought of the abortion that helped the Mueller's leave the ship, which Carl didn't know about. Would he have approved of that, if he'd known? Knowing Carl, most probably not. Two wrongs seldom make a right.

'You could be looking for a needle in a haystack, Carl, from what I have heard about Europe.'

'But I feel I have to go. Esther could be right. Her family had contacts. Money. They could be sitting somewhere in England, or America, not able to contact their only daughter.'

Freddie guessed the real reason Carl didn't want to go. Though he had not seen Anna since her apology to him, he knew she had just joined the University, and was very much involved in the skirmishes between the rival political groups. That was what Carl was really worried about. And, of course, leaving his wife on her own.

Carl finished the rest of his coffee. He looked at Freddie, uncomfortably.

'Another one?' said Freddie, finishing his own cup.

'Freddie, if I go...I know Nanny Price and Carlotta can run the house between them. They are both very capable. And I'm sure Hans will give his mother more than enough to survive on. He would revel in that...Anna is so consumed with her meetings and rallies, and she doesn't get on with her mother anyway...It's Esther I am worried about. She has no one to lean on. She has no friends. No one she can confide in. I give her pills to help calm her when she goes into her moods...But if I'm not there...I, er...'

Freddie looked into the distance, over the waves lapping the harbour wall. He knew what was coming. After what they had been through, knowing their past, he couldn't believe they could be here now knowing what Carl was about to ask him.

Freddie looked at his friend. Aware of the look, Carl turned to him.

'Of course, I will look after her, Carl.'

CHAPTER FORTY

Hans often didn't know whether Giorgio was serious, or joking.

Would he have left Juan to drown? Was his lover a killer, or a joker? Perhaps he'd never know. But with his drugs business now booming, he was surprised when on his birthday, Giorgio said, 'Hans, I've asked Juan to take over your customers.'

'Juan? Why? It's doing great, Giorgio. What's the problem?'

'I just wanna show you something, birthday boy.'

He drove them to the casino that Giorgio's father had set up before the war. Hans was excited as Giorgio led him up the steps, through the extravagant foyer, into a huge, crowded space.

'This is the main gaming room.' Giorgio swept an arm around the windowless space, lit by huge, sparkling chandeliers. On each wall, gold curtains draped large, baroque mirrors making the place seem even bigger. Well-dressed men and woman in furs, crowded every part of the room around the rows of roulette tables, and the lines of slot machines against each wall.

Giorgio grinned. 'Happy Birthday! This is your new hunting ground, bud!'

'What?' Hans' eyes wandered round the room. He knew about the casinos in the city, but until now, because he had been under-age, he had never been in one. This was Giorgio's birthday present to him.

'Giorgio! Really? What, you mean I can sell drugs here?'

Giorgio nodded. 'All yours.'

'Thank you! It's amazing. Wonderful. It's much better than I even thought. All these people. So glamorous...And I can sell stuff here?'

'Not here. Not at the tables. In the men's restroom. They blow their minds in there. Then come back and blow their wallets on the tables.'

After Tony Trevianni died his American associates decided to make his son, Giorgio, assistant manager of the casino. Now he was handing his old business to Hans.

Germany had lost the war. Hitler, The Fuhrer, had committed suicide. The shattered country was now divided between the Allied Forces. A few years ago, this would have devastated Hans. He had hoped to go back to a victorious Germany, and take his part in the New World run by the Nazis. Now, that childish dream was gone. But Hans didn't mind at all. He was part of the adult world now. The world ruled by the big boys. And he wanted to be a 'big' boy as well.

In his newly acquired Cadillac Convertible, Hans drove his father and mother to the harbour. Freddie was already there, standing beside the stairs leading to the deck of the trans-Atlantic liner bound for Hamburg. This was a moment Hans wouldn't have missed for the world. His father was going to Austria to find Esther's family, all paid for by himself. Giorgio said the trip was a waste of time, and he agreed. Being half-Jewish, he had finally accepted the appalling things the Nazis had done to millions of Jews. But he didn't really know his relatives. They were just part of the millions. He had really only funded the trip in order to please his mother, but also to humiliate his father. His criminal activity was now supporting the family and he knew his father truly hated that.

'I am surprised Anna isn't here,' said Freddie to Carl.

'Apparently, she helping some friends stop a rally by the Fascists at the University,' Carl said, unhappily. 'It will probably end in violence...Oh, Freddie, how I wish...' He shook his head. There was no need to go on.

Since President Grau was elected two years ago, the bribery and corruption in government had grown out of control. People complained, but Grau had co-opted two rival political groups who used violence against the opposition, but also against each other. The people called them 'Gangsterismos'. They had shot some of their opponents in the last few months and opponents like Anna were in their sights.

Freddie took both of Carl's hands. 'Good luck, my friend. Write, if you can...' He glanced at Esther. 'I'll look after things here for you.'

'Thank you, Freddie.'

Carl gave Esther a brief embrace. 'Goodbye, my dear. Take care.'

Esther said nothing. Her face was expressionless.

Hans held out his hand. 'Have a good trip, Papa.'

Carl hesitated, and for a moment Freddie though Carl would refuse. Then he took his sons' hand.

'And good luck.' Hans' smile had a hint of triumph.

As they watched Carl walk up the stairway, Hans looked at his mother and Freddie standing together. He vaguely remembered, as a very small child, being pampered and played with by a lively, beautiful young woman. His mother. But she had suddenly disappeared. He knew, now, what had changed the atmosphere in the house. What caused the rows, the endless recriminations and the bitterness, which was his background as he grew up. With Freddie around and his father gone, maybe he and his mother would rekindle their affair? It would nice to see his mother happy, for once.

Carl turned and walked slowly up the stairs to board the ship. He looked tired and emotionally drained. It would be a tiring trek through war-ravaged German to Austria. A journey that might end with tragic news, but whether he wanted to go, or not, he knew Esther had to be pacified. As he had said to Freddie, as a plea not a statement, 'It's Esther I am worried about...'

Freddie could see why. It was the first time he had seen Esther since Anna had threatened him not to come to the house. As usual, Esther was elegantly dressed, as if saying 'goodbye' to royalty on their private yacht, but her face looked pallid and drawn. For Freddie she now looked who she was. A mother of three, though still beautiful, approaching forty, with no friends, in a loveless marriage, and deeply depressed.

Feeling his gaze, she looked up at him. Those vivid eyes had grown dim, almost grey. She smiled at him, hesitantly. 'I would really like some company for dinner tonight.'

CHAPTER FORTY-ONE

Leaning against his police car, the newly-appointed Captain Ramos watched the confrontation at the rally escalate. It seemed to be mainly middle-class students fighting the workers. He had been brought up in the poor district of Havana, but being a policeman made him different. He was a worker, but he wasn't supposed to take sides. It had taken him many years to become a captain, which was as far as he would probably go. The people who got to the top were more ambitious, even more ruthless, more vicious than him. And the President encouraged them. Better to have the gangsterismos inside the building rather than outside fighting to get in. Ramos was apolitical. A survivor. And he'd survived so far.

As the gunshot boomed through the crowd, people began to scatter in all directions. Ramos unloosed the strap on his holster. With the chaos all around him it was impossible to see what had happened. A young woman ran towards him. She grabbed hold of his sleeve.

'There's someone shooting! Help us!'

'Is anybody hurt?' Ramos asked.

'I don't know. Let's go and see!'

'Where's the gunman?'

'I don't know! Let's go and look!'

Ramos didn't move.

'Come on!' She tugged hard on his sleeve.

Her nails were biting into his skin. He took her hand off, roughly. 'You'd better go home, before you get hurt.'

'You're a policeman. You're supposed to protect us!'

'Go home!'

The woman made a grab for his gun. 'If you won't – '

Ramos grabbed his gun, and pushed her away. 'Go home! Before I arrest you!'

'Me? I didn't shoot anyone!'

'Go home, I said! Now!'

The woman stared at him. 'You're as bad as the rest! All cowards! All corrupt!'

'I will tell you one more time. Go home, or I will arrest you!'

'You're a corrupt coward!' She turned and disappeared into the dispersing crowd.

Ramos watched her go. She didn't recognise him, but he remembered her fighting him, as he helped her from the ship. She had knocked his cap into the harbour, and she had laughed about it. Anna Mueller was someone to watch out for.

In company he liked Hans was naturally gregarious, and he mingled easily with the punters of the gaming room. They were mostly American. Though now the war was over, with Havana called 'The Pearl of the Caribbean', other nationalities, mainly British and some European, began to arrive.

But Gunter was the first German that Hans met in the casino. He was playing roulette, gambling large stakes, and generally losing. Recognising the accent, Hans stood watching at the table. After the war, Germans generally kept themselves to themselves. Gunter didn't seem to care. A German with a lot of money was as welcome as anyone.

Hans followed him into the men's facilities, which had a sumptuous lounge, with small alcoves. The lavatories were in the adjoining room. He held out his hand, and greeted him in German.

'May I introduce myself. I am Hans. I recognised the accent.'

Gunter shook his hand. 'Gunter.'

'Where are you from, Gunter?'

'Munich. Originally.'

'I was from Berlin. Before the war.'

'You wouldn't recognise it now.'

'No, I'm sure. Very...sad.'

'Yes...You watched the table, Hans, but you didn't play. Do you work here?'

Hans nodded. 'I do business here.'

'Business?'

'I supply something that makes people happy.'

'Ah.'

'You like to be happy?'

'I am always interested in being happy.'

They sat in a booth, while Hans prepared two lines of coke. Men passed by, but took no notice. It was Havana. Anything went in this city. Hans handed Gunter a rolled-up dollar bill.

'Did you fight in the war, Gunter?'

'Yes...Well, yes and no.' Gunter inhaled a line. He rubbed his nose. 'Good stuff...'

'Yes and no?'

'I was a quartermaster, for the army.'

'You seem to have done very well from it.'

'There were many items left afterwards...'

'Are you here on holiday?'

Gunter inhaled the second line. He rubbed his gums with the rest. 'Business is my holiday, Hans.'

'Ah, I see...You probably know, Gunter, Cuba has a lot of unrest, politically.'

'That's why I'm here. You have several rival groups. They oppose the president, but also each other. So, they want weapons.'

'Yeah, there was a fight today at a rally. Someone was shot... My crazy sister was there. She calls herself a revolutionary. I told her to stay away, but...'

'It sounds dangerous. Does she have a gun?'

'No. I don't think so.'

193

'Would she like one?'

CHAPTER FORTY-TWO

After the ship had sailed and they could see Carl no longer, Hans drove Esther back home. She seemed a little more animated than when he had picked her up to take his father to board the ship. He took her to front door, expecting to go in with her, but she put her hand on his arm.

'I would ask you in, Hans, but I'm feeling so exhausted. I think I will go straight to bed. It was so difficult, so very difficult, getting your father to go at all. Right until the last minute I thought that he would change his mind.'

'I hope not after I paid for the ticket.'

'Thank you so much for that, Hans.' She gave him a hug. 'You don't know what it means to me.'

'Yes, I do, Mama. And you are so very welcome. I hope he comes back with good news.'

'I hope so. It will be so good to see my parents and grandparents again.'

'Of course, it will. Now straight to bed and rest. And have sweet dreams. I will call in tomorrow.' He took her hands from around his waist, and gave one a swift kiss. 'Auf Weidersehen, Mama.'

She watched Hans drive off, with his customary squeal of tyres, then hurried inside to see Carlotta about the dinner she wanted her to cook.

After giving Carlotta special instructions, she went to her room to prepare for the evening. Esther knew that when Anna was out with her communist friends she was generally out all evening. So, after so many years she and Freddie would be dining alone. That had first happened when Carl had been called away on a medical emergency, and Freddie was already on route to the

Mueller's house in Belgravia. When he arrived, Freddie politely said that they should make it another night, when Carl was at home. But she had insisted he stay as he had made the long trip across London. Given that they had spent several evenings privately devouring each other in Carl's company, he didn't take a lot of convincing.

She had worn the necklace that night. That now had gone. Freddie had sold it to keep their house. And so had the dress, which, sadly, no longer quite fitted her. She had to find something special. Something a little décolleté, though definitely not too obvious. She didn't want to scare him away, like she had done the first time. In Vienna, as a child, her parents had spoilt her and she been brought up to always have what she wanted. Her grandmother's advice to her grand-daughter was, 'Men rule the world, so it's a woman's privilege to make them pay.'

Within six months of her marriage she realised she had made a mistake choosing the studious Carl, but by then she was pregnant with Hans. She was a mother in a marriage with little love, or even affection in it. So, she returned to her novels which showed that true romance did really exist. When she had her daughter, Anna, she spoilt her and vowed to guide her into finding the true love that she been denied. She would live her life through her daughter. But Anna had been born a tomboy, and nothing Esther could do would change that.

And then she met Freddie. He was so young, so passionate. So carefree. He loved music and dance. So unlike Carl. She had found the heroic lover of her romantic novels, and she wanted to see him always, forever. After their first wonderful night, she expected him to call. When he didn't, she began calling him at all hours, telling him that she was desperate, suicidal, calling him out of lectures, and causing him to neglect his studies. She even wrote letters, saying that she couldn't live without him, that they should run away together. She said it wouldn't matter if they were poor, they would be together. She knew now she had demanded too much of Freddie at the time. She would not let it happen again.

Anna was still furious. She found that the student who had been shot had been taken to hospital, but the police seemed to do nothing to find out who shot him. After she had confronted the policeman, she lost her friends in the confusion, so she returned home. Hearing laughter from the dining room she entered and found her mother and Freddie laughing together over their meal.

'Anna?' said Esther, clearly not pleased. 'I didn't think you were coming back so soon.'

'Obviously not!'

Esther frowned. 'Anna?'

'How did your meeting go, Anna?' said Freddie calmly.

'What are you doing here?!'

Freddie seemed a little put out by her aggressive manner. 'Your mother kindly invited me for dinner.'

'And my father has only just left the island, Mama!'

'I noticed you didn't come to see him off,' said Freddie.

'But you did!'

'Yes. He's my friend, Anna.'

'Oh, yes, I'm sure!'

Esther rose. 'Anna, how dare you speak like that to Mr Sanchez! How dare you! Go to your room! Or better still, leave the house!'

'And leave you two having your private tête-á-tête!'

Anna ducked and the wine glass shattered behind her. As Esther snatched up a plate, Freddie got up, putting out his hand to stop her.

'Esther, please! Please, let me handle this.'

Esther stood, with the plate trembling in her hand.

'Anna.' said Freddie quietly. 'Please – '

'I have been to try to stop fascists taking over this island. A man was shot there. He's in hospital. And all you can do is... is...' She stopped, staring at him.

'What?' asked Freddie. 'Please, just sit down, Anna, and we can all talk together calmly. I'm sorry if things got out of hand at the meeting. But I've told you that politics is a very dirty game here. Your father and I warned you not to get involved – '

'Because you don't care! You just think people should know their place. They should just keep quiet while thieves and fascist thugs in government just rob this country!'

'Anna, I don't think this is the right time to – '

'You just don't care, do you! Either of you! You just don't care! It's all about you two! I'll leave you two to your...assignation!'

Anna ducked again as Esther hurled the plate at her. She stormed out through the hall, leaving the front door wide open as she left. Nanny Price came out of her room, concerned. Freddie went past her to close the door. She glared at him as he went back to the dining room, where she could hear Esther sobbing hysterically.

CHAPTER FORTY-THREE

Jose was standing at the bar ordering drinks for his friends, when Anna walked in like she was being pursued by a demon.

'Anna!'

'There you are. I thought this was your bar.'

Jose smiled. 'I wish I owned it. What are you doing here? Do you want a drink?'

'Please. A large one.'

'You look upset.'

'Can I talk to you, Jose?'

'Yeah. Okay. Look, go and sit in the corner. I'll bring the drinks.'

Jose took his friend's drinks back to their table. 'My friend is a bit upset. I'm going to talk to her.'

'Your girlfriend?'

'No way. We kind of - played together, when we were kids.'

'Yeah?'

'My aunt's the cook at her parent's house.'

'She's no kid anymore. I'd play with her anytime.'

Jose laughed. 'Back off.'

He walked over and sat next to Anna. 'Nice to see you. Never seen you in a bar before.'

'I don't drink.' Anna took a long gulp of the iced drink.

'Careful, there's rum in there.'

'Really? What is it?'

'Cuba libre.'

'It's nice.'

'That was the slogan of the war!' said Jose.

'The last war?'

'No. When we kicked the Spanish out. Ages ago. See, I've been learning about our history. Like you told me to.'

'Good,' she said, clearly distracted.

'So, what's the problem?'

Anna finished off her drink. She toyed with the empty glass. 'Did you hear about the rally today against the Fascists?'

'Yeah. I heard some guy got shot.'

'They were waiting for us. They'd bought weapons. Baseball bats, knives, guns. And the police just stood there and did nothing.'

'That's what they do. No point in getting involved in politics.'

'This island is run by gangsters, Jose. The President and his family are just filling their pockets. And letting us fight among ourselves...There is no other way, Jose. We have to have an armed revolt.'

Freddie had called Mrs Price and Carlotta to help him with Esther. She was lying on the chaise-lounge in the living room, between sobbing and moaning. Freddie had seen that before, many years ago, when he told her that they must stop their relationship. He knew he couldn't handle this on his own.

'Could you both please help her to bed? That's the best thing. I'll go into the surgery and find something to help her sleep. I don't know if Anna is coming back tonight, but I don't want Mrs Mueller awake if she does...I'm sure it will all blow over tomorrow.'

Mrs Price sniffed dismissively, but Freddie didn't have time to deal with her prejudices now. She obviously knew the truth about Klaus, and clearly blamed Freddie for the whole wretched situation.

'Of course, Mr Sanchez,' said Carlotta, kindly. 'Then I'll clean up the mess in the dining room,' She was sorry that the dinner she had prepared with such care was sitting, half eaten, on the table. Mrs Mueller had looked so excited and energised as she told her what to cook for the evening. No one had told Carlotta the whole history, but she knew something had happened way back that still affected the family. And Mr Sanchez was part of it.

'Where is Klaus, Mrs Price?' said Freddie.

'He's in bed.'

'Good.'

He left the women to deal with Esther and went to the surgery. The door was unlocked, but the medicine cupboards weren't. He looked through the desk drawers, and searched the room, but couldn't find any keys. Promising to apologise to Carl when he returned from Europe, he borrowed a large knife from Carlotta and forced opened the cupboards, until he found what he was looking for.

Esther was in bed in her nightdress, half-sitting up, when he came in.

'Oh, Freddie! Freddie, I am so sorry! So sorry! Our wonderful dinner tonight and – That crazy, stupid girl ruined it!'

'Not to worry, Esther. Please, just relax. I have some pills to help you sleep tonight.' He handed her a glass of water and two pills. 'Take these. I got them from the surgery.'

'Carl gives me some of these, when I get...overwrought.' She swallowed the pills dutifully.

'Good...Now, I'll leave you to sleep.'

'No. Please, Freddie. Please stay. It was our evening...Please stay.'

'Alright. Until you go to sleep.'

She put her arm out of the covers towards him. He went to the bed and held her hand. She put her other hand on his.

'You could lay beside me. Until I fall asleep.'

'I don't want to disturb you. I'll sit in the chair.' He leant down and kissed her on the forehead.

'You will come back? Another evening?'

'Of course, I will.'

He sat in the chair opposite. She lay back, her eyes fixed on him. Maybe Anna had come at the right time, he thought.

Anna finished another Cuba libre. She had finally stopped talking politics and was staring into space.

Jose looked at her profile. His friend was right. Anna wasn't kid anymore. She was a beautiful young woman.

'So, Anna...You didn't come to talk to me about politics. You've got lot of friends to talk about that.'

Anna looked at him, and lifted her empty glass.

'You sure?' he said.

'Cuba Libre. Free Cuba!"

He went to the bar. As the drinks were being poured, he watched Anna who was still staring vacantly, clearly worried about something. He brought the drinks back and sat beside her.

'So?'

Anna took a sip. 'My father sailed to Europe today. To find my mother's family.'

'I know. My aunt told me.'

'My mother insisted he go. He didn't want to...'

'Well, it's a long journey...And he might find bad news.'

'But my mother insisted. Became hysterical, as usual.' She looked at him. 'You know what happened? Years ago? With my mother and Freddie Sanchez?'

He nodded. 'Oh, yeh. You told me once. We were down by the river, fishing.'

'Tonight, when I got home, my mother was entertaining Freddie Sanchez.'

'Er...Entertaining?'

'They were having dinner together.'

'Oh, okay.'

She took another drink. 'My father will be away for months...'

'So, you worried it might start up again?'

'My mother insisted that my father went, and the same evening, the very same evening, she and Freddie are having dinner together.'

Jose shrugged.

'There is something going on between them. I saw it when she gave Freddie the necklace.'

'The necklace?'

'After fire, the fire at the plantation, Freddie sold my mother's diamond necklace, so we didn't lose the house. When she gave it to Freddie, I saw something between them. I even challenged Freddie about it. I accused him of trying to break up our family.'

'What did he say?'

Anna thought for a while. Thinking back to when she confronted Freddie at his home.

'Did he deny it? Well, he would, wouldn't he, I guess,' Jose said.

'He said...Nothing.'

'So...what can you do?...Are you gonna talk to your mother?'

'Hah!'

'To him...? To Freddie...?'

'I don't know what to do, Jose...'

A popular Cuban band was on the jukebox, playing a very catchy tune, 'Mambo Infierno".

Anna finished her drink and suddenly got up. She wandered, a little unsteadily, to the centre of the bar and slowly began to dance. She signalled to Jose to join her, like they used to dance at the plantation when the workers had finished the day's work. Jose got up. He was very good at the mambo.

CHAPTER FORTY-FOUR

Hans found his mother lying on the chez lounge in the shaded conservatory, a book in her lap. A large ceiling fan was circling above her. She opened her eyes when he came in, and yawned.

'Hello, Mama. When I was driving here, I thought I saw that doctor guy, Freddie, walking towards the harbour with Klaus,' Hans asked her. 'I must have been mistaken?'

'No. Freddie, Dr Sanchez, has taken him out,' Esther said briskly. 'He said he thinks Klaus should get out more. He is a doctor. He should know.'

Freddie had come to see how Esther was coping after the confrontation with Anna last evening.

'Did you sleep?' he asked her.

'Yes. I don't what you put in those pills, but...

'Good. Very good. I was wondering...Does Mrs Price, does the nanny, ever take Klaus out for a walk?'

'No, no. She hates it out there as much as I do.'

'Well, you know, it's not good for a... He should...I was thinking that...'

'You want to take...our son, for a walk?'

'Yes, Esther. I would like to...You could come as well.'

'It's far too hot and noisy for me, Freddie. But...if you want to...' Esther sat up, and stretched. The book fell off her lap. 'So, off they went.'

Hans picked up the book. 'That's a bit strange,' said Hans. 'I don't remember him ever talking to Klaus. But it's about time Klaus went outside,' said Hans. 'Poor kid.'

'He is not a poor child, Hans. Klaus is your brother. He was brain damaged at birth. That's why we have to look after him. He wouldn't, doesn't understand...the world.'

'And how are you, mama? Are you coping without my father being here?'

'Perfectly well, Hans, thank you.'

'Does Freddie, Dr Sanchez…?'

'Your father asked him to make sure that I am taking my medicine. For my nerves. That's why he came around.'

'Right. Good. Is Anna here?'

'I believe so, yes. She didn't come until it was nearly morning. She didn't say where she had been…I think she's in her room, probably sleeping. We didn't speak, but she looked exhausted.'

'I'll be back in a minute,' Hans said, then went upstairs and knocked on Anna's bedroom door.

'Who is it?'

'It's Hans.'

'I'm trying to sleep, Hans.'

'I wanted to talk to you. About the shooting yesterday.'

'Come in. It's not locked.'

Anna sat up as he came in. Hans sat on the bed beside her.

'Are you okay? You look a bit…Mama said 'exhausted'.'

'I'm fine,' she said quickly. 'What about the shooting? Do you know who did it?'

'No. But it seems to be getting much more dangerous, going to those whatever, meetings.'

'If you're going to try and persuade me not to go - '

'No, no. No, what I was wondering is…if you would be interested in this?'

From his bag he took out a small black pistol. 'It's a Walther PPX. The best little hand gun around. It's semi-automatic. The German police used it. Rumour is that Hitler used this kind of gun to commit suicide.' He smiled, 'And he only had the best.'

Anna frowned. 'That's unusual for you to say that, Hans.'

'Ah, well. He did go too far. He should never have attacked the Soviet Union for a start. Not while fighting the British and the Americans. I guess, the power got to him, and he went a bit crazy.'

'He was always crazy.'

'We're not going to argue about that, Anna. What do you think of the gun?'

'Where did you get it?'

'That's a secret. But I can get you any amount. All kinds of guns. If your group feels like they need them. Which after the shooting, maybe they do.'

'Hans, you're not saying you've become a communist, or a socialist, all of a sudden?'

'No, no. I just thought…I care about you, Anna.'

'But you would sell these to the fascists, as well?'

'If they ask for them. There are some sharks around here selling stuff, but I could give them the best price.'

'So, my brother has become an arms dealer?'

'I'm a businessman, Anna. I don't take sides.'

'You just make money. No matter who gets hurt in the process?'

'That's business, Anna…Business isn't about morals. I'm not interested in politics.'

'Some people say your kind of business is all politics, Hans.'

'So, you don't want it?'

Anna took the gun from him and felt the smooth metal casing of the gun. It seemed beautifully made, if weapons could be beautiful. 'I don't have any money.'

'For you, Anna, it's free.'

CHAPTER FORTY-FIVE

Klaus had taken a little persuading to go out with Freddie. He had seen Freddie come to the house from time to time, so he knew he was a friend. And he remembered that Freddie had stopped a dog biting Anna at a party. A policeman had shot it, and everyone was very pleased. But he was not used to talking to strange people. Nanny Price was the person he spent most time with. She used to get him up in the morning, but he could do that himself now. In a morning, after breakfast, Nanny read to him, or did jigsaws with him, or watched him doing his drawings. She said she liked those. But she never took him outside. If he wandered into the courtyard garden to look at the plants, he had to wear a hat, and wasn't allowed to spend much time in the sun. But he watched Hans and Anna leave the house all the time, and he wondered what it was like. If they went out all the time, it must be more exciting than being in the house.

Nanny had not seemed pleased when his Mama said he could go outside with Freddie. But Mama said Freddie would take good care of him. So, he was dressed in his best shirt and shorts, and told to always to wear his hat. His Mama waved at the door as they left.

Anna hid the gun beneath clothes in her bottom drawer and then went back to bed. She was tired, but she couldn't sleep. She recalled that she had danced a lot with Jose in the bar. The mambo, and then the rumba. With more Cuba Libres, she had banished any thoughts about Freddie and her mother together. There was nothing she could do. They could destroy her father. And there was nothing she could do to stop it.

She had never been to Jose's room. It was in a house in the central Havana, where most manual workers lived. Despite the hour, someone was playing a guitar softly upstairs, a slow ballad about a broken heart. There was little space to move in the room, so they sat on the bed. She remembered she was feeling woozy. Jose put his hand around her shoulders and looked into her eyes. The guitar gently played above. The last time Jose kissed her was fierce, like an animal. This time it was gentle, is if hardly daring to touch her lips. She was the one who responded fiercely. Devouring his lips, his mouth, breathing heavily, her arms tight around him. He began to respond and laying her on the bed, his hand began to explore her body.

She began to groan as he kissed her neck and responded when his hand began to explore her breasts. But as his hand slipped down over her stomach, she took hold of his hand, and whispered, 'No, Jose.'

He didn't hear, or wasn't listening.

'No, Jose. No.'

'Anna, yes! Oh, Anna!'

'No!...No! No, Jose!'

Afterwards, as they lay side by side, Jose began to cry, his arm over his eyes.

'I'm sorry. I shouldn't...I'm sorry...I love you, Anna...For a long time...I'm so... so sorry.'

She got up and rearranged her clothes.

'Where are you going?'

'Home.'

'You could stay...till the morning.'

'No. Goodnight, Jose.'

Outside the night was still. The guitar had stopped playing. She walked to the harbour and looked out over the dark ocean. She couldn't sleep now. She had changed. Too much alcohol, too much anger. It wasn't supposed to be like this. The first time...

Santa Isabel del Mar beach was a short taxi ride from Havana harbour. It was too hot for them to walk, so Freddie took a cab from a driver who owed him a favour.

Klaus watched the streets and buildings as they drove along. It was all new to him. An adventure. As they approached Santa Isabel del Mar, Klaus saw the sea and pointed to Freddie. 'Look. The sea!'

'That's where we are going.'

They got out of the cab near the beach. Klaus looked at the shining white sand and the glistening blue sea, and gasped.

Freddie took off his sandals. 'Come on, Klaus. I will race you to the sea!'

Klaus watched Freddie race across the sand towards the sea. He took off his sandals and followed. The sand was warm and soft under his feet. Freddie was already in the water, waving for Klaus to join him. Nervously, he entered the water. It was warm and gentle. Freddie splashed about in the water, so he did the same. He actually enjoyed being with Freddie.

As they walked along on the shoreline, half in the water, Freddie bent down and picked up something from the surf. He showed it to Klaus.

'It's a seashell. Have you seen one before?'

Klaus shook his head. 'No. I think in a book.'

'You see, this is like a home. For things that live in the sea.'

'What things?'

'Like...have you seen snails in the garden?'

Klaus thought and then nodded.

'Well, they're like snails, only they live in the sea.'

He handed the shell to Klaus. It was white outside, but the inside glowed with blue, green and pink iridescent colours.

'Look at the colours,' Klaus said. 'It's beautiful...Is there one in there?'

Freddie peered inside, then put his finger in. 'No. He's not at home.'

Klaus looked at him, and giggled. 'Like me. Hans always said I'm not at home.'

Freddie smiled sadly. No, you're not, he thought. He picked up another shell. 'Look. This one is different,' he said to his son.

CHAPTER FORTY-SIX

Conchita had made a very special effort. She had cleaned and tidied Freddie's room, bought a new flowered tablecloth and put a vase of flowers in the middle. She knew that Dr Mueller had gone to Europe, and was upset that Freddie was spending more and more time at the Mueller's house. With that woman. But today was special. She wanted them to be together, this night.

Hearing his footsteps on the stairs, she adjusted the cleavage of her best dress, the one Freddie had chosen. She stood up to greet him, holding his present. Freddie walked in, holding a package wrapped in brown paper.

'Conchita?'

She held out the package to him.

'What's this?

'A present.'

'Why? It's not my birthday. Is it?' He had actually forgotten when his birthday was. Was it today?

'No. No birthday...The special day.'

Freddie remembered. 'Ah...'

She went to him, kissed him on the lips, and handed him the parcel. 'Open it.'

Freddie took the package, guiltily. This was a ritual Conchita had started at the end of the very first year they had been together. Tonight was the anniversary of the night that he had found her, unconscious, battered and bleeding from a savage knife wound across her face. The night she could have died, if he hadn't known how to save her. It was almost a decade ago, but she had never forgotten the date. That night.

'I cooked a special meal for you. Your favourite. And wine.'

Freddie moved away and put both packages on the table.

'I, er...' he began. 'I'd...I'd actually forgotten.'

Conchita smiled. 'Always...But you have present? You remembered today.'

'No, er, you see...Look, er, I have to go out this evening, Conchita.'

She stared at him. 'Where? Where! Tonight? To that woman!'

'No. Yes. It's her son's birthday today. I bought a present for him.'

'For that whore's son! Tonight!?'

'I had forgotten, Conchita. Like you say, I always forget... Look, tomorrow, I'll take you out for a very special meal.'

'Tomorrow! Not tonight! Our night!'

Freddie put up his hands in apology. 'I'd just forgotten, Conchita. I'm sorry!'

'You forget our night! For that whore!'

'She isn't a whore, Conchita.'

'She is whore! She married and she's whore!'

Freddie tried to go to her, but she moved away, angrily.

'Our night!'

'Look, Conchita, I'm sorry. So sorry.'

'You forget. You forget Conchita!'

'No, no. Of course not.'

'Forget Conchita!'

Before he could stop her, she turned, raced out of the door and down the stairs.

'Conchita!' he shouted.

Not able to catch her, he went to the window and saw Conchita racing across plaza, screaming, past the crowds of tourists and the traders. They stopped as she raced by, then just carried on their lives. Things happened like that near the harbour.

'You must come, Hans. It's Klaus's sixteenth birthday. It's very special. I insist.'

Hans didn't usually go to dinner at his old home anymore. There were many restaurants in the city where he was seen as a minor celebrity. He enjoyed getting the best table and impeccable service. But his mother was adamant. Esther wanted all the family to be there.

'Is Freddie coming?'

'Of course.'

Hans was very curious to see Freddie and his mother together. He knew Freddie had been going to the house often, but he didn't know if things had progressed any further, now his father was away.

If Freddie was coming to dinner, Anna was always there. She felt that her presence would act as a barrier to anything intimate happening. After her mother had been banished from Isabel's circle, she had become even more petulant than normal. She said Klaus, her constant companion, now irritated her, and now he normally ate all his meals with the nanny, Mrs Price. So, it was a surprise to Anna when her mother started asking Klaus to join them for the evening meal. It happened a few days after her youngest brother started going out with Freddie on a regular morning walk, and they had started to bring back seashells from the beach.

'You can buy them in tourist stores, but it's much better to find them yourself,' Freddie said.

Anna was intrigued that Freddie had suddenly become interested in Klaus. He had hardly ever mentioned him before, and actually had seemed indifferent. Though they had never talked about it at all, she knew that Freddie must know he was Klaus's father.

'Well, isn't this wonderful!' said Esther, as she looked around them seated the table. Freddie had been given the seat at the head of the table with Klaus by his side, and Esther opposite.

'What a shame father can't be here,' said Anna, looking at Freddie. 'Especially on such a special day.'

'Yes,' Esther muttered.

'Have you had word from him, mama?' Anna went on.

Esther shook her head, irritably. 'No.'

'He will only just have landed, Anna.' said Freddie.

'We should really have a drink to him, and wish him 'Good Luck',' said Hans. He got up and poured everyone a glass of white wine.

'No,' said Esther, when Hans reached Klaus.

'He is sixteen now, mama,' He filled Klaus's glass.

Anna raised her glass, 'To dear papa!'

'To my good friend, Carl!' said Freddie.

'Good luck,' said Hans.

'Good luck,' they all said, and drank to the absent Carl.

Esther handed Freddie a small bell from the table. 'Freddie, will you ring the bell for Carlotta to bring the first course.'

Though all the silver tableware had been sold, long ago, to help with their finances, Carlotta had produced a marvellous display of flowers as a centrepiece. And much to Klaus's annoyance, Esther had chosen his clothes for the evening, complete with a bowtie.

'I want to open my presents before we eat, mama.' Klaus said, tugging at his bowtie.

'Klaus, I think we should wait until – ' Esther began.

'Oh, please, let him open them, Esther,' said Freddie, sensing Klaus's irritation. 'It is his birthday.'

Esther nodded. Freddie brought the presents, one by one, from the sideboard. He brought his present the last. Klaus opened the packet. Inside was a book of illustrations of seashells.

'Shells!' said Klaus.

'Look at the drawings, Klaus.' said Freddie, flicking through the pages. 'They're wonderful, aren't they? I bet you could draw the shells you have.'

'I could,' Klaus said, excitedly. 'Yes, I could!'

After dinner, despite the late hour, Klaus insisted on getting out his drawing book and began drawing one of the shells in his collection. So, it was quite late when Freddie returned home. He had hoped to come back earlier to have a drink with Conchita, and try to make it up to her. There were no lights on in her room, but he knocked anyway. There was no reply. He tried the door, which she generally locked at night. It was open and he went in.

Conchita often took her clients back home with her, and she kept her room immaculately. Like his own room, it was small, with the bed dominating the space. She was not in bed. Disappointed, Freddie went upstairs to his room. Conchita's present was still on the table, unopened. Finding a bottle, he poured himself a large whisky, and sat at the table. He toyed with the package. He would leave it, until he could open it with her. He took a long drink, then lit a cigarette, and sucked in the smoke deeply.

Hearing footsteps on the stairs, he got up. He was sure she wouldn't come upstairs to see him, so he opened the door to go to see her. But it was Ramos coming up to his room. Sometimes, if he was on a nightshift, he came to have a drink with Freddie. He had come a few days ago and told him that Anna had tried to steal his gun at the rally. He hadn't arrested her, but he warned Freddie to keep an eye on her.

'Ramos?'

'Senor Sanchez.'

Freddie opened the door and Ramos walked in.

'I'll get a glass.'

'No, I don't want a drink...Senor, some fishermen pulled Conchita from the sea a little while ago.'

'God! Is she alright? Is she in the hospital? I'll go and see her now.'

'No…' He shrugged. 'She's in the mortuary, senor.'

It was late at night when Freddie approached the hospital. He knew the mortuary was in the basement. He had been there before to put a name to some of the homeless peasants who only he knew the identity of. It was a grim room. Reflecting its use.

He didn't want to do this. Visiting the victim of the crime that he had committed. He wanted to turn away and go to the ocean and drown, like Conchita had done. He could do that later. After he had seen her, and arranged for her funeral.

He stopped at the door. Beyond it was the body of a young woman who he had once saved, and then casually destroyed.

The room was empty, except for a trolley on which lay a figure covered in a white sheet. Going to the trolley, he pulled back the sheet covering the head. She was a peasant, a whore, so, they hadn't bothered to close her eyes. He couldn't close them now because rigor mortis had set in some time ago. Conchita stared at him, unseeing.

The seawater had caused her scar to pucker even more. She wouldn't have liked that. He put his arms around her slight frame and lifted her so he could hug her. Holding her tightly, his body started to tremble as he began to cry. He gently kissed the scar from the forehead to the mouth. Covering her face with his tears.

CHAPTER FORTY-SEVEN

He had waited outside the main steps of the university for an hour. At times he wanted to leave, but told himself he had to stay. They had been friends for a long time and he didn't want that friendship to end. It was nearly a month since he had danced with her at the bar, and then taken her to his room. After she had left him, he felt so ashamed. So furious, so angry with himself. At first, he decided he wouldn't try to see her again. Of course, she would never want to see him either. Yes, they had both had far too much to drink, but he had lost control. He had been in love with Anna for a long time, but what he did was not love.

At first, when they were children, he had been in awe of her. She had taught him the history of his island, and how to read. Then gradually, he began to teach her things about the world he lived in; the laws of the countryside, the different animals and insects. He showed her how to fish. How to trap and shoot animals for food for his family. When his relatives came home from their work on the plantation his brothers, sisters, and he and Anna used to play outside, while the older women cooked the evening meal. They all loved to dance to his uncle's guitar. Jose had showed Anna how to mambo. And he had fallen in love.

It was difficult, but he had promised himself to do it, so he would. Then she could decide. He had hoped she would be on her own, but he saw her coming down the steps with a group of other students. She had seen him at the bottom of the steps, so he couldn't just slip away. His legs were trembling. He could do nothing, of course, and just let her pass by. But at the last minute, he stepped forward.

'Hello, Anna.'

She could, probably would, reject him entirely. She might just ignore him. Or, she could call him names. She could tell her friends that he was a rapist, right to his face. She stopped.

'Hello, Jose.' She turned to her friends. 'I'll see you later.'

Jose was surprised that she stayed. They watched her friends walk on. He still couldn't look at her. 'Anna, I just have to say that I - '

'You don't have to apologise, Jose...You apologised...at the time.'

'But I want to – '

'No, Jose, please. Please...It happened. It's very sad, but it's over...There's no point in...'

'I know you can't forgive me. I know that. But, I would...I would still like to be your friend...Like we used to be.'

She reached out and touched his arm. 'Of course, Jose. We'll always be friends.'

He felt a tear on his cheek, and rubbed it away roughly.

'How's work?' she said, lightening the mood.

'Not so good,' Jose said, pleased to change the subject, to avoid breaking into tears. 'Some of our union leaders, they're as bad as the President...You were right what you said about the island. All the corruption. The gangsterismos. The crooked politicians. They're all the same. We need an armed revolt. And I want to be part of that.'

Carlotta let the man into the house, and took him into the conservatory, where Esther was pretending to read. For days, Klaus had been pestering her about why Freddie had not come to see them recently. Klaus wanted to go to the beach again to find some more shells to draw. As Freddie didn't have a telephone, Esther had decided to go round to see him herself. But she was waiting until Anna left for university that day. Her mother never left the house, so Anna would certainly want to know where she was going.

She couldn't tell Anna she was going to see Freddie. Anna seemed to be there whenever Freddie was around. It felt like she was spying on them. Watching. She was always at dinner when Freddie was invited to join them. And, when Klaus had gone to bed, Anna would engage Freddie in heated arguments about the politics of the island until he left, which was always quite quickly. Esther felt cheated of his company.

She had decided to take a taxi to Freddie's home, and tell him she had come because Klaus missed him. It would be the second time they had been alone since Carl left. She was happy that Freddie had taken Klaus under his wing. He actually seemed to like him. When they were at dinner together it seemed like a happy family, except for Anna's brooding presence. This time she wouldn't be there.

Esther looked up when Carlotta entered. There was a policeman behind her.

'It's a Captain Ramos to see you, senora.'

Ramos took off his cap. 'Senora Mueller. I believe your family know of Dr Freddie Sanchez.'

Esther sat up. 'Yes.'

'I think you would like to know that Dr Sanchez is in hospital, in a coma.'

CHAPTER FORTY-EIGHT

Giorgio stroked Hans' chest. 'So, this Gunter guy is queer?'

Hans shifted in bed to face him. 'You mean, am I screwing him?'

'Are you?'

'No. He's a good old-fashioned German. A businessman. He just sells guns...Would you mind, if he was?'

Giorgio grinned. 'Could be fun.'

'I thought you said I'd never find another man in your bed.'

'That was 'first love', babe.'

'So, you don't love me now?'

Giorgio gave him a long kiss on the lips, and slipped his hand down to Han's groin. 'Does he have a gun as big as this?'

Hans sighed and relaxed into the moment.

'You should be careful though. If you're selling guns to both sides, well...it might go off in your face. Like this will!' Giorgio said, as he slipped down the bed.

'You could have a...uh!' Hans gasped, 'A piece...of the action. Ah!'

Giorgio looked up. 'Is that nice...? No, my associates wouldn't like that. They prefer to keep business in the family.'

The phone rang beside the bed. Giorgio leaned over and picked up the receiver. 'Yeh? Oh, hi...' He put his other hand over the phone. 'Talk of the devil.' Giorgio sat up. 'Yeh. Yeah..? Really...? Wow! Really?

Hans got up. Sometimes these calls went on for a while. He walked into the bathroom and cleaned his teeth. He looked at his body in the mirror. He was tall, fit, toned and bronzed. His hair had been lightened by the sun. He smiled, wryly, to himself. The perfect image of the Hitler Youth.

'Hey, lover boy! Great news!' shouted Giorgio.

Hans went back into the bedroom, feeling very aroused.

'Gee,' said Giorgio, looking at his body. 'You could fly a flag on that!'

'What's the news?'

'The Mob are coming to the Hotel Nacional for a meeting. A big conference! Just before Christmas.'

'Really? Wow! Are you invited?' asked Hans.

'No,' said Giorgio. 'It's only for the top brass. The big boys.'

'Oh.'

'But they want me, us, to provide the girls.'

'What, tarts? Whores?'

'But, only the best. And a couple of queers too.'

'Me and you?'

Giorgio shook his head. 'Nah. Best to stay away from that. Far too risky. Some of those Mafia guys can get a bit rough and nasty.'

'Oh, well. We can certainly find the girls...So, an arms dealer and a pimp.' Hans laughed, sarcastically. 'My father would be so proud!'

Carl was exhausted. Travelling across war-torn Germany and Austria would have been extremely tiring and complex, even for a man half his age. He was held up constantly by soldiers of all four Allies, examining his papers, wondering why he had come all the way from an idlyllic Cuba to a ravaged Europe. As he didn't speak much French, or any Russian, he was sometimes held for questioning until a translator could be found. Food and transport were always difficult to find as well. He hadn't thought he would find so many people homeless and starving in his homeland.

Thankfully, Hans had given him a substantial amount of dollars, which he managed to keep hidden. That helped a great deal. Finally, arriving in Vienna, he found that Esther's parents' house had been mostly destroyed by an air-raid. All the belongings, the expensive paintings and the fine silver, had all been looted before then by the Nazis. There was nothing left of the home Esther loved.

Finding anyone to ask about the family seemed to be impossible. He tried to find answers at the Allied Council, which ran the city, but they were totally unhelpful. He was just one man looking for a family, among thousands of others. Hearing a rumour from a neighbour, he travelled the length of the country, in a rapidly worsening winter, chasing it down. And found nothing.

If the family had escaped the concentration camps, which he doubted, they had disappeared. They could be anywhere. In Europe, England, or America. He had tried to phone home, but communications outside Europe were impossible. He wrote a letter to Freddie, explaining the situation, and asked him not to say anything to Esther until he arrived back home.

He had not had much time to think about what he had left behind. He had left his wife in the care of her ex-lover. Freddie was a very capable doctor, and would be able to deal with Esther's constant mood swings with the drugs in his surgery. But what was happening to them both emotionally?

Knowing that his task in Austria was impossible, he decided that he should begin the long journey home. He felt ill, emotionally and physically. He just wanted to get home. To whatever he would find.

CHAPTER FORTY-NINE

It was strange dream. He seemed to be in a strange bed with Esther hovering over him, stroking his face, straightening his hair, rearranging his pillow, kissing his cheek.

He heard voices outside.

'Can I go and see him? I've done a drawing for him.'

'Not now. He's asleep, Klaus.'

'He's been sleeping for ages.'

'He has to get better,' Nanny Price said. 'Sleep is good for him.'

Freddie opened his eyes. At first, he didn't recognise the room. Then he remembered. He was in Carl's bedroom. After he had taken the overdose, he had woken up in hospital, semi-delirious with a fever. Esther had persuaded Hans to take him to the Mueller's to recover. He tried to persuade them to let him go home. But Esther was insistent, and Hans was much stronger than he was.

Hearing the door open, he closed his eyes again. He didn't want to be there. He didn't want to be anywhere. Someone came near to his bed. He could smell Esther's perfume. She stroked his face. He faked a little snore. She kissed his cheek, then walked away and closed the door.

He kept his eyes closed, but then Conchita was there, lying naked in the mortuary. Her beautiful body looked untouched, almost childlike, but the sea water had furrowed and crumpled her face, so the long scar was much more prominent.

What he needed was a drink, but they wouldn't give him one. It had nearly killed him, almost. Another few hours would have been enough. If only someone hadn't come into his room, he would be with Conchita now. Not that he believed in God, like she did. But they would have been out of it, together. At peace at last.

She had been wearing his favourite dress, and had cooked his favourite meal. Bought him a present that he hadn't even opened. What had driven him to reject her, on that special night for her? That very special night they had always celebrated. Because it was Klaus's birthday. His son. His mistake. And Conchita had paid for that. He covered his eyes with his arm, and wept.

Anna's female friends noticed it first. Jose saw them chatting among themselves when Anna's political group met at her home, to make plans to oppose President Grau's re-election.

The whole of the president's family, his friends and hangers-on, were bleeding the island dry, while the president let the two opposing political groups fight it out on the streets. There were rumours of money being sent abroad to foreign banks, of the president's wife spending sprees, and her plans to build a huge mansion for herself and her husband.

Jose was concerned of course, but what really concerned him was the women exchanging glances when Anna went off to one of her many toilet breaks. Or when she occasionally felt nauseous in the meetings. Worried that Anna was ill, he decided to talk to the women, when Anna was out of the room.

'Do you think that Anna is ill?' he asked.

The women looked at each other. Like most men, Jose clearly had no idea about women.

'No. We think she's pregnant, Jose,' said one.

'Why?'

'She goes to the toilet a lot, and she keeps getting sick in the meetings.'

'Is that a sign?'

'Absolutely.'

Jose went through the rest of the meeting not really listening to the discussion. He hadn't noticed Anna showing interest in any other men. She seemed totally committed to her cause, and had even persuaded some of the others to buy guns from her brother, Hans. He knew she carried hers, concealed, whenever she went out. If she didn't have another man...He had to talk to her.

CHAPTER FIFTY

After Hans had saved him from drowning, there was nothing Juan wouldn't do for him. So, providing the best girls in the city was child's play. But Giorgio thought that he and Hans should see them themselves. The mob had said they would have their own girls flown over from Las Vegas, but Giorgio's associates had promised to supply the best. Cuban women, they said, were the most glamorous and sexy around.

The young men vetted the girls in Giorgio's apartment. Each girl stripped, and was asked what type of action she was up for. Juan had supplied a vast variety; white, mulatto, black, small, tall, thin, voluptuous. Since being with Giorgio, Hans had never really noticed women sexually. But watching these amazing young women parade before him, he began to see the attraction, and Giorgio noticed.

After they had chosen, and the girls had gone, Giorgio poured two long Cuba Libres, and took them to Hans on the terrace over-looking the ocean.

'So, the Nazi stud is bi, is he?'

'What?'

'I noticed a bit of movement down there, when some of the girls...'

'Bi?'

'Bi-sexual. Fancy both.'

'No, no. I was probably thinking of you.'

'I notice girls, Hans. Just haven't done anything about it. I think my mom put me off, walking about naked half the time.'

'Really? Stark naked?'

'Yeah, in the pool, in the house. I think maybe, as she got older, she wanted to keep my pop's attention. She was only about fifteen when she had me. He liked them young...So

226

when I think about screwing a girl, I keep getting images of my mother naked. That kind of puts me off, you know?'

Hans remembered Giorgio's mother, giving him the eye at the Tony Trevianni's funeral. 'She's pretty attractive. She looked stunning at your pop's funeral. All dressed in black.'

'So, you'd screw her, would you?'

'Me? No. No way!'

'Good.' Giorgio took a drink, and licked his lips with his tongue. 'But I'd fuck your sister.'

'Anna?'

'She's cute. Sexy cute.'

'You go near my sister, I'll shoot you.'

Giorgio laughed. 'Hey, Mr Arms Dealer!'

'I mean it,' Hans pointed two fingers at Giorgio's head, like a gun.

'Gee, okay. You lay off my mom, I'll lay off your sister...But how about some of those girls?'

'What? You mean, try them out, for the big boys?'

Giorgio grinned. 'It's the least we could do, for our American buddies.'

Jose decided to wait behind after the meeting to be alone with Anna. It wasn't easy to bring the whole thing up, but he had to know. They were still in Anna's bedroom where they held their meetings. Anna had arranged chairs around a table near the window, as the bedroom was now her campaign office. Jose had not got up from the table as they others left. He and Anna had not been alone together in a room since the time in his own bedroom.

'I thought it was a good meeting,' he said.

'You think so? It's not going to be easy defeating Grau. He's got the newspapers on his side. He talks on the radio.

The police do what he says. They let the Fascists break up our rallies.'

This wasn't how this should go, thought Jose. How did he get to talking about them? 'But it's...it's not all about politics, is it?'

Anna looked at him, quizzically. 'How d'you mean?'

'Well...I...er...Well, you...'

'Are you...what about me, Jose?'

'I thought maybe you were ill, you know, so I asked the girls.'

Anna stopped tidying up her papers. 'Oh?'

'They think you're pregnant.'

Putting the papers down on the table, Anna sighed, and sat on the bed.

'Are they...right?'

'This isn't anyone's business, but my own.'

'But, if they are...'

'Jose, I don't want to get into this. Could you please go?'

He had gone this far. He had to know. 'I just want to know if you are...If it's mine, Anna!'

Anna put her head into her hands.

'I just want to know,' he said, more gently.

Her hands were still in covering her face. 'Yes.'

Jose sat back in his chair, overwhelmed with guilt.

Anna put her hands down and looked at him, a glint of tears in her eyes. 'Could you please go, Jose..? Please.'

Suddenly, Jose leaned forward eagerly. 'I love you, Anna...I love you. I want to marry you.'

'No.'

'I could support us. You could still go to the university until...'

'No, Jose. No. I'm only just nineteen. I have my whole life ahead of me. I have a lot to do. I don't want a baby.'

'But...Well, your mother could look after it, maybe?'

She glared at Jose. 'My mother! Look after a baby!'

'Well, Mrs Price, then. The nanny...Or one of my sisters could look after it, at the plantation.'

'Jose! I don't want a baby. Yours, or anyone else's.'

'So... But how...? '

Anna got up, and opened the door. 'Please.'

Jose knew he had no right to question her decision. It wasn't her decision to become pregnant. It was his vanity, his stupidity, his brutality. He got up. Anna moved away from the door, so not to be near him.

'I am so, Anna. I am so sorry...'

Anna turned away, and looked out of the window. Jose left, and closed the door behind him. Anna stared through the window, but saw nothing.

CHAPTER FIFTY-ONE

When Freddie awoke again, it was morning. He sat up, feeling a lot better. The fever had finally disappeared. While he was recovering, he had sensed that Esther's flirtation increased steadily as his health improved. The re-arrangement of his pillow and bedclothes had slowly moved to touching his arm, straightening the collar of his pyjamas, stroking his face, to see if his fever had gone. The kiss on the forehead had now moved to his cheek. Freddie was determined to go before she expected him to reciprocate.

He heard someone being sick in the bathroom next to his room. Getting out of bed, he looked around for his clothes. He found them in the wardrobe with Carl's. Needing a cigarette and a large whisky, he got dressed quickly, but when he tried to open the door it was locked. Had Esther locked him in!

He tried the door again, then began to bang on it and shouted.

'Hello! Hello! Esther!'

There was noise on the stairs. Then a key in the lock. Esther opened the door.

'Freddie, you're up.'

'Yes. Why did you lock me in?'

'Ah, well, Freddie. That policeman, the one who came and told us you were in hospital, well, he said...he said that you had tried to kill yourself.'

'So, you thought that I'd sneak away and try again?'

'Freddie, we all love you. I know it was awful about that poor girl, but...

'Thank you for looking after me, Esther, but I've got to go now.'

At that moment Anna came out of the bathroom, looking pale. Glancing at them, she hurried down the stairs.

'Well, stay and have breakfast,' Esther said.

'No.'

'A coffee then?'

Freddie knew Carlotta made coffee almost as good as his own. He nodded, 'Okay.'

As Freddie was drinking his coffee in the dining room, Klaus came in with some shell drawings.

'I copied them from this, Freddie,' he said, showing the shell book Freddie had bought him. Freddie looked at them both and was very impressed. Klaus had reproduced an exact replica of the drawings in the book.

'They are very good, Klaus.'

Anna came in. 'I'm going out, Mama. Tell Carlotta I won't be here for dinner.'

'Don't you want any coffee?' asked Esther.

'No, Mama, I've gone off coffee.'

'I think Freddie should come for Christmas dinner next week, Anna,' Esther said. 'It would be nice to have a man in the house at Christmas.'

'It would be nice if Papa were here, Mama. We used to have a lovely time with him.'

'Well, he can't, Anna! I have not heard anything from him.'

'I want you to come for Christmas,' said Klaus to Freddie.

'Klaus, I promise I will be here for the Christmas meal,' replied Freddie. 'But I have things to do at home now.' He looked at the women. 'There will be a lot of patients who haven't had any treatment while I've been ill.'

'They should go to the hospital, like you did,' said Esther.

'I don't think they would get the same treatment as I did.'

'Because he's a doctor,' said Klaus. 'Like Papa.'

Anna looked at Freddie. 'Are you going back today?'

Freddie held up his cup. 'When I've finished this.'

Anna nodded and left.

Watching Anna go, he wondered why Esther seemed not to have noticed the clear signs that her daughter was pregnant. Maybe she had, but hadn't mentioned it to him.

He wondered who the father was. Though there were other young men in Anna's group, Jose seemed to be a regular companion. Jose was a tall, very handsome young man. He didn't have the same education, and wasn't as intelligent as Anna, but that counted for nothing, as he knew. Physical attraction could be paramount, at any age. When he was only just a bit older than Jose, he had fallen for Esther, and he could well see Jose feeling the same for Anna. Did he know? Were they happy about the situation? Somehow, he couldn't see Anna as a mother.

Hans lay back in bed. The woman he and Giorgio had just shared had gone to take a shower.

'Joe 'Bananas' Bonanno. Charles 'Trigger Happy' Fischetti. Albert 'The Mad Hatter' Anastasia. They're all in town, Giorgio!'

Hans enjoyed the names these gangsters gave each other, and he was thrilled they were in Havana. For him, even though he wasn't allowed to join them, it was like having royalty in the city.

'And many more. From all over the States, apparently.' said Giorgio.

They had heard about the gangster world through Giorgio's father, Tony. He used to regale them with tales of the deals and the feuds, which always involved a lot of violence, and often in death. Like Tony, most of the gangsters came from Italian families, like the top man, 'Lucky' Luciano. He had been deported from America to Italy, after the war, but he was still the guest of honour at the conference.

These men were businessmen, of all the illegal business in America. They ran the drugs, prostitution and the gambling, in the casinos, and the streets. As a drug-pusher, and an arms dealer, Hans felt a small part of their world.

'Ain't it nice being part of the underworld, Giorgio. Not like normal people.'

'Who'd want to be that? Normal?'

'What's that word, for people like us?'

'Happy?'

'No. Yeah, but something, like abnormal, or something, er, deca...?'

'Deca...What? I don't know.'

'Decadent, that's it, Giorgio. We're decadent.'

Giorgio climbed onto him. 'And ain't it fun, dude?'

CHAPTER FIFTY-TWO

Freddie walked up the stairs, and stopped for a moment by the door. He knocked. A young woman in a skimpy nightdress opened it, and looked him up and down.

'You looking for fun?'

'No,' he said. 'A girl...A woman I used to know lived here.'

'Oh, yeah. I heard she drowned...Sorry.'

'Could I...Could I just look at the room? She was a very close friend.'

The woman shrugged and stepped aside. 'Sure.'

Freddie walked in. The room was untidy. There were clothes on the bed and floor, unwashed pots crowded the sink and table. He sighed. Conchita would be horrified.

'I haven't had time to tidy up yet.'

'Yes. Well, thank you,' he said. He left and walked up to his room. There was letter outside on the floor. He picked it up and went in. It was from Germany. The letter was brief. Carl said he had found nothing. It didn't look good, but maybe there was still hope. But he was leaving to come home straight away, as he couldn't do anymore.

Throwing the letter on the table, Freddie locked the door, which he never did usually. He lit a cigarette, and looked around the bare room. It was still the same, just as it was when Ramos found him, unconscious on the floor. The pill bottle was still beside the bed. He picked up the bottle. It was empty. From his pocket he took out the bottle he had taken from Carl's surgery. He put it on the chest by the bed. The whisky bottle on the floor which he had been drinking before he passed out, was empty.

He looked in the places where he used to hide the bottles from Conchita. They were all empty. Then he remembered Ramos drank rum. On night duty around the harbour, Ramos sometimes looked in to have a drink with Freddie. Looking in the cupboard under the sink, he found a nearly full bottle. He didn't like rum. Having been brought up in England in the clubs he went to everyone drank scotch. But rum was better than water for taking the pills. And the alcohol would help.

The image of Conchita's drowned face re-emerged. He sat down on the bed, and pulled the cork out of the rum.

It would be Christmas next week. He had told Klaus he would be there for Christmas dinner. He and his son had become friends. They walked on the beach and found shells that Klaus drew very well. But Klaus was a child. He hadn't known Freddie for long, so he would soon forget. Maybe with Carl's guidance, his son would become an illustrator. You didn't have to behave like an adult to be able to draw.

Carl had put the date at the top of the letter. Freddie reckoned he would probably be home in a few days, a week at most. So, Carl could take care of it all; Klaus, Anna, and Esther. As he put the rum bottle to his mouth, there was a knock at the door. Lowering the bottle, he waited. No one knew he was there. Maybe it was a patient. Someone in need. Well, he thought, there were many people in need, the whole world over. He couldn't help them all. He kept silent, waiting for them to go away, with the bottle in his hand. The knock was repeated, more firmly. A pause, then repeated again.

He waited for the sound of them going away.

Then a voice he recognised came from outside the door.

'Freddie? Freddie?'

Freddie frowned, and put the bottle down. Pushing the pills into the drawer beside his bed, he went to unlock and open the door.

'Anna! How nice to see you.'

'Can I come in? Please.'

'Sure, yes.'

Anna walked in and Freddie closed the door, uneasily. The first thought that crossed his mind was that he was about to get another roasting from Anna, about trying to break up the Mueller's marriage while her father was away. He thought he had better get in first, get rid of her, and then...and then nothing.

'I am very sorry, Anna, I put you and your mother to all that trouble. You really didn't need to. It was so, very, very kind.'

'I didn't come for that.'

'Look, Anna, I know, while I was ill. I know...Well, I think your mother...I tried not to encourage her. But –'

'Could I sit down?'

'Of course.'

Anna sat at the table, and looked at the letter, open in front of her.

'But I promise, I didn't honestly -' Freddie continued.

'Is this from my father?'

'Yes. He didn't find anything about your grandparents, I'm afraid. He'll be here very soon. In a week. Maybe even in time for Christmas. That will be so nice for you all. For all of you to be together again. All the family.'

'I didn't come here to accuse you of trying to seduce my mother again, Freddie.'

'Oh...? Oh.'

'I have a problem. Which perhaps you may be able to help me with.'

'Well, I will, if I can.'

'I am pregnant.'

Freddie nodded. 'Yes...What does your mother - ?'

'She doesn't know. As you know, my mother doesn't care about other people and their problems. I'm sure she doesn't know.'

'Ah. Yes.'

'I don't want to have the baby, Freddie...If my father is arriving soon it's even more important that I...I would have no choice if he was here. I would have to have the baby.'

Freddie sat at the table. He lit a cigarette. She looked at him.

'Freddie, I am asking you - '

'If I will abort the baby.'

'Yes.'

He watched the smoke from his cigarette drift upwards to the grubby ceiling. 'You know it's illegal?'

'Yes. Another student had it done, a few weeks ago. She died, sadly. The person who did it was arrested.'

'Does the father - ? '

'He has no say. It's my decision.'

'Is it Jose?'

'That's none of your business,' she said sharply.

'Oh. Right.' The thought of Jose making love to Anna had crossed his mind several times, making him deeply envious.

'I came to you because I think I can trust you. I don't want to die like that poor girl did. My father has said, many times, what a brilliant doctor you are...I know I am asking you to break the law, Freddie. It may even be against your principles, of course...In which case, I'm sorry to have asked you...But I need help, Freddie. Really...I don't think anyone will know. Except us.'

Freddie shrugged. He stubbed out the cigarette. He thought he would like to have a drink of the rum, but that wasn't appropriate. The rum would help Anna.

CHAPTER FIFTY-THREE

When Freddie was fighting against Franco in the Spanish Civil War in Catalonia, that province made abortion legal. Maybe it was the danger of the war, or the prospect of not being alive tomorrow, but unwanted pregnancies were common. Being a doctor, he had been asked to perform several abortions. When he came back to Cuba he soon became known as the man to go to. And they did. Women from the backstreets, and ladies from the mansions of Miramar.

Freddie knew that if he made a mistake, even if the patient was Senora Isabel Luisa Gonzales Rio de Cruz, he would be arrested and imprisoned, though her name would never be mentioned, of course. But, to him, this patient was far more important than the head of the island's social elite.

'You want me to drink all that?' Anna asked.

'That's all I've got, I'm afraid. The rum. And one of these pills,' said Freddie, taking the pill bottle from the drawer by the bed. One of the pills that would help take his life, but not at a moment. 'You won't feel anything.'

Anna gave a little guilty laugh. 'Sorry. Rum was how I got pregnant in the first place.'

Freddie smiled. 'It's a common side effect.'

He prepared the bed, lying a large towel over the sheet. One of the towels that Conchita had always washed spotlessly. He watched Anna empty the glass. 'Okay. Well, when you're feeling drowsy, just take off…your pants, and lie on the bed.'

Having boiled a pan of water, Freddie got the equipment out of his cupboard, and sterilised it all. By the time he was finished, Anna was lying on her back on the bed, her eyes closed.

'How are you feeling?' he asked gently.

Anna didn't open her eyes. She sighed, 'Sleepy'.

'Well, have sweet dreams.'

As Carl said, despite never having finished his qualifications as a doctor, Freddie was a natural. The procedure was over, successfully, in a few minutes. As Anna lay dozing, he cleared away everything, then sat at the table, lit a cigarette, and finished off the rum from the bottle. She would wake in a while. He was sure she would be fine.

He gazed at her for a long, long while. She was lying on her side, like a baby. Foetal. At peace. Eventually, he went over, and moved a long strand of shining, black hair from her face and placed his palm on her forehead. She was cool. Taking her slender, tanned wrist, he pressed his fingertips against the soft skin of her pulse. It was strong. Like she was.

His own heart was beating heavily, almost stifling his breath. A teardrop of sweat trickled through the fine hair on his chest to his belly.

He remembered lying naked beside her mother, in a passionate embrace. So different to this. Anna was as physically beautiful as Esther, but she didn't seem to know it. If she did, it didn't matter to her. Lifting her hand to his lips, he kissed the moist palm, reverently. Like a penance.

Anna was suddenly awake. 'What are you doing!' It was an accusation, not a question.

Freddie felt his cheeks blushing. 'I was just checking your pulse.'

'No! You weren't! You were kissing me! You were kissing my hand!'

'I, er...I just...It was just a friendly gesture...' He felt foolish. There was nothing sensible he could say to her.

Anna sat up and put her feet on the floor. She winced, and grabbed her stomach.

He was relieved to go back to his professional mode. 'Have you got cramp? It often happens.' He opened the pill bottle and offered one. 'Take one of these. It will go. You will have to take it easy for a day or two. Nothing too strenuous.'

Anna swallowed the pill, and stared at him.

Freddie moved away and sat back at the table, feeling under intense scrutiny. 'You may have a little cramp for a while. But everything is fine. Really.'

'Thank you. But I don't want to talk about it. Ever again.'

'No, of course not.'

He thought of just blurting it out. That despite all their rows about politics and their different view of the world, that he was simply just in love with her. A crazy thought.

Anna got up, and put on her pants. 'Could you go and get me a taxi, please?'

The thought suddenly vanished. 'Yes. If you're okay. Yes, of course.'

As he was going out, Anna said, 'It would be better if you didn't come for Christmas. You could send note. Say you're feeling a bit ill...

'Yes, if you think....'

'I will smooth it over with mama...I'm sure my papa will get in touch with you when he gets back.'

Freddie nodded and went out, unhappily, to call a cab. The kiss was a big mistake.

CHAPTER FIFTY-FOUR

As dawn broke on New Year's Eve, Carl's ship docked in Havana. With Freddie's room close by he decided to call on his friend to tell him his news, and to find out what had gone on with his family while he was away.

Freddie was asleep when he arrived, but he got up, very happy to see Carl.

Even though it was early in the morning, Carl asked for a glass of whisky with his coffee. 'I didn't want to say it in my letter, in case anyone else saw it.'

'Mauthausen?' said Freddie, pouring a generous whisky for his friend. 'Never heard of it.'

'It was a concentration camp near Vienna.'

'All of the family?'

Carl nodded. 'A neighbour told me just as I was leaving. I was able to check the records. All of them, I'm afraid.'

'Will you tell Esther?'

'No. I say what I said in the letter. That they escaped and could be anywhere.'

'I think that's wise, Carl. She can still have some hope then.'

'I'll pretend to send letters looking for them. She'll soon forget. She never saw them after we were married, you know.' He took a sip of the whisky. 'What about Anna? Have you seen much of her?'

Freddie poured himself a whisky as well. 'Yes…Yes, a few days ago.'

'Oh, at Christmas. Did you go there for a meal?'

'No. I wasn't feeling very well.'

'Too much celebrating? With Conchita?'

Freddie took a long drink. 'No…' He swallowed, trying to get rid of the image of Conchita's dead eyes looking up at him. 'She died a few months ago…She drowned.'

'Oh, Freddie. I am so sorry...'

And I would be dead too, if it wasn't for your daughter, Freddie thought. He had considered it when Anna had gone. The pills alone would have done it. But the realisation of what he felt for her stopped him. It was a feeling that had been growing for months. Years really. He had loved the little girl with her vitality and love of life, when she first came to the island. Even when she had hit him on the nose, and knocked Ramos's hat into the sea. He had watched her grow, listened to her plans to change the world, to help the poor, free the oppressed. He had argued with her, from his own experience of how the world worked, but he couldn't help admiring her fierce determination. He had to admit that he was in love. But there was nothing he could do. Her reaction to him kissing her hand was not just distaste. No, it felt like revulsion. Utter revulsion.

Carl finished his drink and got up. 'You must come this evening, for New Year's Eve!'

'Oh, no, Carl. You should be on your own with your family.'

'No, no. Hans won't be there. And Anna probably won't be. I will need your company, Freddie!'

Hans wasn't there. He and Giorgio were going to a lavish party at the Hotel Nacional, where the Mafia conference had been a big success. Anna had spent the day in her room, studying. She had arranged to go to the Old Town with some friends for the evening, but when her father arrived, unannounced, she decided to spend it with him.

In the afternoon, Carl briefly told her and Esther about the devastation in Europe, but concentrated on the lie about Esther's relations. 'It might take some time, but I'm sure we will find them, eventually. So, I think tonight is a time to celebrate. We can look forward to next year with hope.'

'Oh, that's great news!' said Esther.

'I looked in on Freddie this morning. His room is near the harbour. I invited him to join us for dinner.'

'He wasn't here for Christmas!' said Klaus, who had been listening, while drawing a shell at the table. 'I like Freddie.'

'I was so worried that he might be ill again,' said Esther.

'You maybe know he lost his friend, his girlfriend, a while ago. He looked so sad and lonely.'

Anna got up. 'It's so wonderful that you're back, Papa. And with such good news. But I'm afraid I have arranged to go out this evening.'

'Oh, Anna, you must stay! Your father has just arrived back!'

'I'm sorry. I didn't know, Papa.'

'Not to worry, Anna. We'll have a lot of time to catch up.'

'Of course. I am so glad you're back, Papa.' She gave him a little kiss on the cheek, and went back to her room.

She didn't want to be around when Freddie arrived. Before she had gone to him, she had tried the old remedies; hot gin baths, herbal medicines, punishing abdominal exercises. Even falling down the stairs, which she believed her mother had done trying to get rid of the unborn Klaus.

It had been very hard to go to see him. He was a fine doctor, but he knew her well. Though she knew she could trust him, it was shameful. It was embarrassing that he should see her like that. He had been kind, professional. The 'thing' had gone well. She didn't even like to give it its own name, an abortion. After a couple of days rest, she felt fine. She was very grateful to him for that.

But then the kiss on her hand. It was so unexpected. Caring, but so passionate. It startled her. And his reaction when she challenged him, ashamed, embarrassed. She had never seen him like that before. He was usually so cool, politely cynical, so worldly-wise. A few years ago she had gone to his room wanting to throw herself into his arms. For him to declare his love for her. Now, she believed, he had. And she didn't want to see him again.

How would her mother and her father understand such a relationship? Freddie had been a part of a dark past that her parents never spoke of. But it was there in front of them. Klaus. He was a constant reminder of the betrayal of his wife and his friend. It had caused the loss of a deep friendship between the two men, which had taken many years to heal. She remembered the hysteria her mother used to have when Freddie's name was even mentioned. Now, it seemed, her mother was wanting to recapture that same passion again. That was obvious by how she cossetted him during his illness. She knew her mother would destroy her father once again, given the chance. Anna knew that wasn't likely any more, but there was no way she would take her mother's place.

Even if she really knew herself, which she didn't, there was no way she could show Freddie what she was feeling. They had so many differences. He called her naïve, she called him cynical. She believed she could help change the world for the better. His retort was 'Plus ca change plus c'est la même chose.' Two sides of a coin, spinning.

There were more important things to do. Cuba was changing. People were becoming restless. They wanted change. She was determined to be part of that.

CHAPTER FIFTY-FIVE

Hans was sitting on the terrace, watching the wind blow the waves into white peaks. Giorgio was in the bedroom, injecting heroin into his forearm. He had been doing this for a while, and had asked Hans to join him at first.

'Come on, man. It's great. Much better than coke.'

Hans could see the euphoria it created, but saw the depression afterwards, so he refused. There was something about the injection. The needle seemed so invasive and left marks on the skin. He was very sensitive about the way he looked, loving the smooth, velvety surface of his arms, his whole body, tanned from the sun. He didn't want to spoil that beauty. Why Giorgio wanted the heroin, he didn't know. He had everything, but wanted that as well. Maybe it was because he had everything, he just wanted more. To see how far he could go.

Giorgio came out, and handed a drink to Hans.

He took the glass. 'A storm's coming.'

Giorgio sat beside him, and took a joint from his top pocket of his shirt. 'In more ways than one. Someone got killed yesterday.'

'Oh? Who?' asked Hans.

'Don't know. One of those groups. Some political stuff.' He lit the joint, and took in a lungful. He breathed out. 'Probably someone you sell weapons to.'

'That's what they're there for.'

'You shouldn't get involved with politics, man. Too violent.'

'What about the Mafia?'

'That's just business, dude.'

'So is politics. There's an election coming, Giorgio. It's a battle.'

'Are you allowed to vote?'

'Don't want to. Don't take sides. Bad for business.'

Giorgio handed Hans the joint. 'Some people were talking in the casino about that new guy, Castro . He's around a lot.'

'In the casino?'

'Nah. No way. He's always in the papers. On the radio.'

Hans breathed out the smoke. 'Anna's not keen on him.'

'You see her much?'

'Sometimes. When I go to see my mother.'

'She's very beautiful.'

'My mother?'

'Your sister, dude. Though your mum's cute as well. Did she ever walk around naked like my mom?'

'What? No way! Jesus!' Hans shook his head to get rid of the thought. 'No, Anna said Castro's all talk and no action. He keeps saying, "It's better to die on your feet, than live on your knees."'

'That's so true, man. The mob would agree to that.'

'She said he nicked it from some Mexican guy, Zapata. He was like a revolutionary. Like she is.'

'It's dangerous out there. You should tell her to back off.'

'Tell my sister to back off! No way, Buster!' He took another drag, held it inside and let it slowly drift out.

'I gave her a gun.'

'Don't stop her getting killed.' Giorgio yawned, placed a languid arm over Hans shoulders and kissed his cheek. 'You wanna look out too. People don't like you selling guns to their enemies.'

'But if I'm selling guns to them as well, what's the difference? Relax, Giorgio. It's just politics.'

He turned to Giorgio. His eyes were closed. Giorgio was very relaxed.

Carl was surprised to see his wife appear at the breakfast table. He and Anna often had breakfast together, but Esther normally slept late, and had Carlotta bring a tray to her room. But she was there today, immaculate in an ivory, silk housecoat, like she was receiving royalty. She waited until Carlotta had left the room, then looked across the table at her husband.

'Are you going out with Freddie again today?'

'Yes, my dear, I am.'

'Are you going out to minister to those 'poor' peasants?'

'Freddie goes to see people who can't get to the city. The poor get ill as well, my dear. I like to help him.'

'You go out with him, but you don't invite him here. He hasn't been here since New Year's Eve!'

'I have asked him, believe me.'

Carl had asked Freddie several times, but he had always declined, on some pretext or other. But Freddie had asked Carl to bring Klaus to the beach, so they could collect shells, which had become Klaus's passion. He had also asked Carl to bring Klaus's drawing book too and, sometimes, Carl watched contentedly as the father and son drew shells on the beach together. It was something he hadn't expected, when he returned from Europe, and he was thrilled that Freddie had started to take an interest in his son. But he had never questioned him about why he wouldn't come to the house. He assumed it had something to do with Esther.

Esther looked at him, angrily. 'Well, I don't believe you!' said Esther. 'You take Klaus to see him, but you don't want him here. Isn't that right, Anna?'

Anna looked uncomfortable. 'I've no idea, Mama.'

'It's true. You know, I nursed him, while you were away. We got on very well, as he was getting better. Very well.'

'I'm pleased to hear it, my dear,' Carl said, calmly.

'I think you haven't asked him because...we...we got very close...I think you're jealous.'

'My dear, I am not jealous that you and Freddie got on well. I am very happy. Freddie and I are good friends. I have asked him to dinner many times, my dear. But I can't force him.'

'Huh! Huh...! Well ask him tonight. Ask him especially for me! Say I insist!'

Anna looked at her watch. 'I'm going to be late.' She got up, leaving her breakfast unfinished.

Carl rose too. 'I must go as well. I'll walk you to the University, Anna.' He would ask Anna, on the way, if she knew of anything that had happened while he was in Europe that kept Freddie away from the house. He turned to Esther. 'I will ask him again, my dear. But I can't promise that he will come.'

'I have to dash, Papa. I will see you later. I won't be home for dinner tonight, Mama,' Anna said, and added, 'If he comes, please give him my regards.' She hurried out of the room.

Giving Esther a brief smile Carl also left. She sat alone for a while at the table. What did it matter that Carl would be hurt? He showed no interest in her at all, except to prescribe her medicine to calm her mood swings. No wonder she had them, living with a man with no feelings, no passion. She'd wondered if the drugs were actually meant to dilute her passion, her real feelings. So, she had stopped taking them, flushing them down the lavatory in her bedroom suite.

She pushed away her plate. Getting up, she walked down the hall to her suite. Inside, she picked up the glass she had left when she went to breakfast. She took a drink.

If Freddie didn't come tonight, she would go and see him herself, the next day. It was time the whole situation was sorted out.

The doctor took ages to arrive. Hans thought at first of not calling anyone, because of the heroin. But he'd tidied everything in the bedroom away, and then called his home. Carlotta told him that his father had gone with Freddie to the countryside. He called Giorgio's home. Giorgio's mother wasn't in, but the butler gave him the name of the family's regular doctor, so Hans called him, then went back to Giorgio and waited.

Giorgio lay on his back on the terrace, foaming at the mouth. Hans wiped it away. He wouldn't tell the doctor about the heroin. But if he didn't, how would he know how to treat him? It must have been really bad stuff. If you didn't really trust your supplier, just like coke, they could mix it with all kinds of stuff to increase their profits. He didn't know where Giorgio got his.

He cradled Giorgio head on his lap. 'Giorgio! Giorgio! It's alright. You'll be okay.'

He felt himself crying. His shoulders shook. Giorgio quivered and his eyes opened as if looking at Hans. Hans leant down and kissed his lips. They felt cold.

CHAPTER FIFTY-SIX

Assuming that Carl had really asked him, which he promised Esther he had, Freddie didn't respond to her demand that he came to dinner that evening. So, the next morning she took a taxi to his room by the harbour. Her marriage, the whole of her life, was a sham. It was time she took control. She sensed, she knew, that the feeling between them was the same as it was all those years ago. Freddie had said nothing while he lay convalescing at her home, but she could see it in his eyes, his expression. And she knew, being the man that he now was, there was nothing he would do to hurt his friend, Carl, again. It was up to her to persuade him.

Freddie hadn't been in contact with her, but he had persuaded Carl to take Klaus to see him at the beach, quite often. He had become very much involved with his own son. Their son. It seemed like his message. That they were a family. It was what he wanted, but would never be the first to say it.

The divorce would be difficult. Anna would be angry. She cared deeply about her father, and would be upset that he had been betrayed once again. But Anna was heavily into her politics, and would get over it soon enough. The house was a problem, but she knew Hans was wealthy enough to find Freddie, Klaus and her an apartment to rent. Hans always supported her against his father, and would be happy to do it. Freddie might object at first, but there was no way they could all live at his pokey little room by the harbour. If they couldn't manage, she knew Hans would always be there to help out.

She got out of the taxi, and walked through the tourists bartering with the locals for girls, drugs, or whatever. The sooner she could get Freddie away from this squalor the better. At the top of the stairs, she paused, getting her breath back. Calming herself, she knocked.

The elite of the city, and Carl, Esther, and Anna Mueller, went to the funeral. Carl and Anna were there, reluctantly, because Giorgio was Hans best friend. Esther was only persuaded to go by Hans, who promised that Giorgio's mother had warned Isabel Rio de Cruz and her group to behave themselves.

Freddie didn't want to go, because he loathed mixing with the city's elite. But he had known Bella for many years. He had performed an abortion on one of her daughters, and two on herself, which she made Freddie swear that her husband should never find out about. Her only son, Giorgio, had been her favourite, and Freddie wanted to support the grieving mother.

Standing at the back of the church, he intended to slip away after the service, but when he gave Bella his condolences at the door, she insisted that he should come back to the villa for the wake, just for a little while.

Bella buried her son with his father in the family vault, in the prosperous part of the cemetery. The tomb was topped by a marble angel, said to have been modelled on her. Standing beside her, Hans could see the resemblance, of how she must have looked when she was first married. He thought of her walking naked at her home. Today, she was dressed in black, a colour that suited her olive skin. Her lustrous red hair was hidden by her hat and veil. When the coffin began to disappear into the ground, she wiped a tear from under her veil. Hans took her hand and gave it a little squeeze. As the priest muttered a final blessing in Latin, Hans found himself, instead of thinking about Giorgio, wondering if Bella's underwear was black too.

Since Giorgio got hooked on heroin their relationship had suffered. He still loved him, as a friend, a confidante, but sex, which had been such a crucial part of their love, had all but disappeared. He had one-night stands with some of the boys, and girls, he'd met when he and Giorgio vetted them for the

Mafia conference, but that was just sex. Pure and simple. He needed more. He looked at his mother standing opposite. She was swathed in black too. Bella and his mother were very similar, and about the same age. Would going to bed with Bella be like sleeping with his mother?

The wake was held at the Trevianni's palatial villa in Miramar. Anxious to leave, Freddie drank the toast to the departed Giorgio, then said a warm goodbye to Bella. Having done his duty, he stole away from the throng and had reached the front door, when he heard Esther call him.

'Freddie! Freddie!'

There was no way to escape. She came to him, took his arm, and led them both outside into the lush, tropical front garden.

'It's so lovely to see you,' she said. 'It has been such a long, long time.'

'Yes.'

The other day as Freddie was walking back from the market, after buying his special brand of coffee beans, he'd seen Esther arrive at the harbour in the taxi. He'd stopped and watched her go the block where his room was, and go inside. When he and Carl were out running their clinics in the countryside, Carl had told him that Esther had insisted he go for dinner at the Mueller's. Carl repeated that she was very insistent. There was something about his tone that made Freddie uneasy. He questioned Carl, who eventually said that Esther thought he, Carl, was jealous and didn't want Freddie to go to their home to see her. Which was far from the truth, Carl said.

'You're free to come anytime you want, Freddie. Even if I'm not there. Esther never leaves the house. She loves your company,' Carl said. 'It might help her depression, and the violent outbursts she has. It affects everyone in the house, especially Klaus,' he added.

Freddie had looked at him. Was Carl suggesting he wouldn't mind if he and Esther started their liaison again?

Esther had taken him out of sight of everyone, behind a large pink jasmine bush. The flowers fragrance and her perfume were a heady mix.

'So, you sold my necklace to Mrs Sanchez?'

'Ah, you saw.'

'You could hardly miss it! Paraded around on that heaving bosom of hers!'

'Her husband made the highest bid.'

'It was 'our' necklace, Freddie. Don't you remember? You must.'

'That was a long time ago, Esther.'

'What did you think to my note?'

Freddie feigned a frown. 'Your note?'

'I came to your room the other day. You weren't there, so I left a note. I slipped it under the door.'

'Well, I didn't see it, Esther,' he lied. 'It must have blown away, or got under the rug or something.'

Taking both his hands in hers, she moved closer and looked into his eyes. 'Well, it said that you have been avoiding me, Freddie Sanchez.'

Freddie said nothing. He could hardly deny it. He looked about, anxiously.

'And I know why.'

'Esther - '

Esther put her fingers to his lips, silencing him. 'It's all right. I understand. I sure Carl does, as well.' Reaching up, she put her hand behind his head, and leant him towards her to kiss him.

Freddie jerked away.

'Freddie, no, it's all right.'

'No, Esther. No!'

As he started to move away, she grabbed his sleeve, and held him back. 'I want you, Freddie! I love you! I will leave Carl. We can live together. With Klaus if you like! We can get married. We can be a family. A real family!'

Abruptly, all the anger, all the hurt, and the bitterness, suddenly, overwhelmed him, and he burst out, 'I don't love you, Esther! I never have! I love your daughter!'

CHAPTER FIFTY-SEVEN

Carl was surprised when Esther met him in the hall one morning. Ever since the funeral, and her bizarre behaviour at the wake, she had hardly spoken to anyone in the house. She spent all her time in her suite, hardly touching the small meals that Carlotta brought her. This morning she stopped him on his way out.

'Are you going to see that…appalling man, again?'

'You mean Freddie? Yes.'

'Don't give him my regards.'

Esther turned and walked with extreme carefulness down the hall, as if she might fall off a tightrope at any moment. Carl shook his head. For some weeks he searched the house for bottles, glasses, but had found nothing. She'd had the lock changed to her suite, which is where she kept it. He believed she got the drink from Hans, who called round one or twice a week to see his mother. As the first-born, she had always doted on Hans, even when Anna came along. Mother and son were like minds. Having money and being admired was what Hans learnt from his mother's lap, unlike Anna who hated getting dressed up, and having to behave like a little princess for visitors.

When Hans wanted to join the Hitler Youth, Esther had supported him, despite Carl's objections. Now Hans was aiding her new dramatic role, which Carl assumed was the abandoned lover.

Carl picked up his battered Panama hat and left. Something had happened that turned his wife against his best friend. One moment she was insistent that Freddie came to see her, but, after the wake, she couldn't bear to hear his name even mentioned. Once, Carl had tried to ask her about what had happened, but she flew into such a violent rage at the mention of it, he never referred to it again. And Freddie wouldn't talk about it either.

After the wake, he had gone to see Freddie straight away, after the sedative he gave Esther had put her to sleep. Freddie seemed surprised to see him. He said he had no idea why Esther had gone berserk. He had hardly spoken to her. She had said something about him selling the necklace to Bella, which annoyed her, but he couldn't explain why Esther hated him now. As he half-joked, it would take Sigmund Freud to find out what went on inside Esther's head.

Esther had not spoken to Anna for several days, feeling unable to face her. She had no idea whether Anna and Freddie were having a relationship. Anna was out a lot of the time, she assumed at the university, or at one of her political demonstrations, but they could be meeting instead. Finally, she plucked up the courage to confront her, after breakfast.

'That man,' she began. 'That man said...at the wake, that he is in love with you.'

'What? Sorry, Mama. Who?' Anna knew who she meant, immediately, but she couldn't believe that Freddie had said that to her mother.

'At Giorgio's funeral, at the wake, that doctor friend of Carl's told me he is in love with you.'

Anna tried to appear shocked. 'Really? Do you mean Freddie? That's silly. He must have been joking, Mama.'

'Why would he joke about that?'

'I've no idea.' Anna shrugged, trying to make light of it.

'Do you see him often?'

'No, Mama. I don't see him at all. Not since before the funeral.'

'Has he not said anything to you?'

'Nothing. Never. It was a just joke, Mama.'

'Why would he say that to me? Such a hateful thing.'

'I don't know...' Anna decided to probe. 'What were you saying to him?'

'What do you mean?' Esther said, defensively.

'Maybe it was something you said, that made him make a joke.'

'I don't know what you mean...I didn't say anything. He just came out with it. "I am in love with your daughter".'

'Just like that?'

'Yes.'

'Out of the blue?'

'Yes. Exactly.',

It was very strange that Freddie would say that, Anna thought. It was a cruel thing to say. Esther must have been pursuing, propositioning him. Anna knew that her mother had been pestering her father for weeks to get Freddie to come to the house again. And then, after the funeral, she wouldn't even mention his name. She must had propositioned him at the wake, and he had turned her down, in the most hateful way possible. That would explain her awful behaviour at the wake, and her drinking.

'I'm sorry. I can't help you, Mama. He has never said anything like that to me. There's no reason why he would. And I never ever see him.'

'So, you're not having an - '

'Mama, please! No. Please believe me...Look, I have to go to a lecture...Mama, I sure it's nothing. I promise you, it's just a very nasty joke by a stupid and cruel man.'

Anna smiled and left the room. She picked up her briefcase from the bureau in the hall. So, the kiss was what she thought it was.

CHAPTER FIFTY-EIGHT

Entering her room, Esther picked up her glass. Sitting at her dressing table, she looked into the large gilt, tri-mirror, turning her head, this way and that. She was over forty now. It was annoying that men wore better than women. Men could get more attractive as they aged. Women? Her cheeks were fuller than she wished. She lifted her chin. The skin below was not as firm as it was. She smoothed her cheeks. Tiny lines were beginning to appear each side of her mouth. Her voluptuous figure, so much admired when she was younger, was becoming matronly. She took her drink and went to sit by the window. Outside the jacaranda's abundant blossom was as blue as the sky beyond. Fresh and vibrant, as she was when she first met Freddie.

It didn't matter whether, or not, it was a cruel joke that Freddie had played on her. She couldn't bear the thought of them sleeping together. The Freddie she used to know was kind, gentle and caring. The word 'gentleman' was made for men like him. So, to see him so vicious, so absolutely determined to crush her, was truly devastating.

'I don't love you! I love your daughter,' he had said, defiantly. She was beginning to believe it. Anna was beautiful, as she used to be. And she was much more intelligent, a lively a companion for someone as worldly as Freddie. It was the worst thing he could say to her. He had destroyed her, just as she had crushed him all those years ago.

And now she realised, that at the wake, Freddie had finally got his revenge.

Freddie decided to lay low for several days after the funeral. He had no idea if there had been any repercussions about his declaration to Esther. What he said wasn't premeditated. The words flew out before he knew what he was saying. All he knew was that he had to stop Esther's fixation with him, which he'd watched growing while he was convalescing at the Mueller's. Telling the truth seemed like the best way. He was in love with Anna. He hadn't said it to her, but Anna's reaction told him she knew. It seemed she loathed him for it. So, it didn't matter if she knew what he'd said to her mother.

Carl had been to see him a few hours after the wake. He said Esther had gone berserk, and he wanted to know what had happened between him and Esther. She had been very distressed and he wanted to know if Freddie knew any reason why. Freddie deflected the question, making some flip remark about Freud. So, Esther had not said anything to him, which was a relief. He didn't want yet another emotional problem between him and Carl.

If he had told the truth to Esther all those years ago, when he decided to tell her they mustn't betray Carl again, it wouldn't have worked out any less of a disaster for him that it did. Instead, trying not to hurt her, he had told her he loved and adored her, though frankly, he was actually bored with her frivolous inanity, and realised he had made a stupid, reckless mistake. Her dazzling beauty, her vivaciousness, her sparkling sensuality was so intoxicating at first, he ignored the fact that the vibrancy hid an interior as empty as a Faberge egg.

He realised, now, what he'd said at the wake was a cruel and heartless thing to do. But he couldn't take back what he said. He remembered the venom of the words. They were meant to hurt. There was no way it could be seen as a joke. After all those years, he had finally avenged his betrayal. Even drinking a full bottle of whisky couldn't hide the fact that he utterly despised himself.

CHAPTER FIFTY-NINE

By the time Carl and Hans had taken Esther home from the wake, Hans felt he had to go and apologise to Bella for the way his mother had ruined the occasion. Esther had suddenly appeared, howling like a banshee, into the crowded lounge. She ran round the room scattering people, glasses, and a valuable vase, then rushed to Bella and tried wrench off her necklace. Bella fought her off, and Esther ran out to the garden and hurled herself into the pool, screaming that she wanted to die!

Hans and a couple of other men, dragged her out, and she collapsed on the floor. Every time he, or his father, tried to comfort her, she began again, screeching, howling, arms and legs flailing. They had to carry her out through the crowded guests to the Hans open-topped limousine, and Carl had to hold onto her while Hans drove them home. Carlotta undressed her and put her to bed. Then Hans fed her a glass of brandy, while Carl went to prepare a syringe with a strong sedative.

When Hans got back to the Trevianni's house, Isadora, Bella's youngest daughter, was saying goodbye to the last of the mourners. Everyone eyed him curiously as he reached the door.

'Is Bella – ?'

The daughter coolly indicated inside. People were talking among themselves, looking at him, exchanging gossip. It seemed like Esther's rampage had clearly upstaged the main event.

Feeling very guilty, he entered the lounge. Bella was seated on a sofa in the large lounge which led out to the pool and garden. She had clearly been crying a great deal. Her eyes were red, her immaculate makeup smeared. She got up when she saw him, and put her arms out. He went to her and, tentatively, put his arms around her. She clung to him, tightly. He hugged her closer, enjoying the deep musk of her perfume.

'I am so sorry,' he said. 'I am so sorry.'

She leant against him for a while, then softly said in his ear, 'Could you pour me a drink, Hans?'

They sat on the sofa with their drinks. He couldn't explain what had happened. His mother had not made any sense. But she had said something about the necklace.

'What? So, it was hers?' said Bella.

'I guess that's why she tried to take it off you. I know she gave hers to Freddie and he sold it.'

'I didn't know. I wouldn't have worn if I had known.'

'I'm sure that wasn't the reason why she went crazy. I'm so, so sorry about that...'

Bella smiled. 'Giorgio would have laughed about it. He liked crazy things.'

'Yeah, he did.'

'Did he make you a little crazy too?'

'A little.' He took cigarette case from his pocket.

'You smoke?' Bella said.

Opening it, he showed her the white powder packed inside. 'Ah.'

'Perhaps this make us feel a little better?' he suggested.

Bella smiled. 'Oh, a whole lot better.'

Hans slowly opened his eyes. The crimson sheets surrounding him, blazed in late afternoon sun. He closed his eyes against their fire and remembered, what he could, of the last twenty-four hours. Was it twenty-four? It could have been forty-eight, for all he knew.

She had been wearing black underwear. Then nothing, but the necklace. Would Giorgio have been delighted? He thought so. It was quite a way for Hans to celebrate the passing of his first lover.

Cocaine increases the sex drive. This woman, old enough to be his mother, would have gone all evening through the night and all the next day, if he, a young fit man, hadn't fallen asleep, totally and utterly exhausted. He tried to think of a word for Bella. Insatiable, voracious, rapacious. Just like her son.

He yawned, stretched, and looked at his tanned arms above him. Handsome, young, rich, happy, and like Giorgio did, he was living life to the full.

The villa was quiet, apart from the hum of the pool generator cleansing the pool. He got up, pulled on his white underpants, and went downstairs.

'Hello?' he called. There was no response. He looked into the large kitchen, where Isadora was making a large orange juice.

'Hi, Isa.'

She pointedly ignored him.

He wandered outside. Bella was lying on a sunbed by the pool, in a bikini. The gardener and pool cleaner, Nico, tall and tanned, was clearing the water with a net on a long pole. Hans sat beside Bella.

'Good afternoon,' said Bella wryly.

Hans smiled. 'I was a little tired.'

'Really? We'll have to train you up, Hans.' She called out, 'We will have to get this young man fit, Nico!

Nico smiled and carried on cleaning the pool.

'Nico is fitness trainer, as well.'

Hans thought about asking the question, but didn't.

Bella read his mind. 'How do you think I keep my shape?'

'Well, he does a wonderful job.'

She took a sip of her daiquiri. 'I've decided I am going to sell the apartment.'

'Giorgio's?'

'I don't need it...Do you want to buy it?'

'Er, well, I...'

'Or would you like to stay here with me?'

Hans looked at her. She didn't seem to be joking.

'Really..? I don't think Isadora would like that.'

'She's getting married next month, at last. So, she won't be here, Hans...And I don't want to stay here on my own in this big place...What d'you say? No strings attached.'

CHAPTER SIXTY

Even though Freddie no longer came to Mueller's home, Carl kept up his friendship with Freddie. He was concerned that his friend had turned back to drink after a period of, for Freddie, almost total abstinence. On their trips to Freddie's countryside clinics, Carl always drove and, while he did, Freddie insisted he brought him up to date with his family.

To his surprise, Carl said that Hans had begun an affair with Giorgio's mother, who was about the same age as Esther. Freddie knew she had always had a penchant for younger men; the two abortions he'd performed on her were from boys not yet out of school. But he was surprised about Hans.

'I always assumed Hans and Giorgio were in a 'special' relationship.'

'That he's a homosexual?' said Carl. 'I think he is, but knowing Giorgio, they probably did both.'

Hans was apparently still selling drugs, but Carl suspected that his main business was selling arms to the warring political factions in the city. People were still getting shot on a regular basis. The government didn't seem to care, and Hans was reaping the benefit.

Though he didn't say it to Carl, Freddie was most interested in Anna; about her, and her politics. After graduating from the university, she was now working for a law firm that specialised in helping the poor in court.

'Her latest case is about the nine hundred workers dismissed from the canning factory. Illegally, she claims.'

'She's probably right...She could make a fortune working for the right people,' Freddie said.

'Try telling her that...She has joined a new political party. The Orthodoxo Party,' said Carl.

'I heard about them on the radio. Their main spokesman's Fidel Castro. He's very eloquent, but terribly verbose. Some of his speeches go on for hours. If you can't say what you believe in ten minutes, you really just like the sound of your own voice...Is Anna going to stand at the next election?'

'I hope not,' said Carl.

So did Freddie. Even though she was not interested in him, almost every day he woke up thinking of her. He cared for her. Wanted to protect her from her own headstrong beliefs. But he knew that it was her courage, her commitment, that had first drawn him to her. And now all he could do was stand at a distance and hope.

Jose had not seen Anna for a long time. He knew that she had aborted their child. His child. But that was her choice. He both accepted it, and resented it. He guessed the operation was probably performed by Freddie, because Anna refused to talk about him, or even mention his name. It was a curious relationship between the two of them. First, she adored him, now she seemed to hate him, but she wouldn't say why. It could be just about the abortion. Or, maybe it was still about what she thought happened between Freddie and her mother, when she was a child in London.

He met her again at the protest about the dismissal of hundreds of other workers at the canning factory. As a trade union representative, he was one of the first to be sacked. Anna was training to be a lawyer, having abandoned her idea of an armed revolt. She knew that the people of the island were growing sick of the corruption at the centre of government, and believed that the Orthodoxo Party could win the next election.

He and Anna joined the new party at the same time. Now they were producing political leaflets for the party in the attic of the Mueller's home. Her father first objected to his home being used for political purposes, but when Anna said she would leave home and go and live with a friend, he relented. With his wife closeted away with her booze, he didn't want the one person he could really talk to in the house to leave.

Working close to Anna, quite often alone, Jose never once thought of touching her, never mind anything else. If their hands accidently touched, while they were collating the leaflets, he always moved away to do something else. He still loved her, but he had made the wrong decision once. Never again.

'Shall we go for a drink?' said Anna one evening, when they had finished packing leaflets into a box to give to the others to distribute the next day.

Their favourite bar was crowded, and, of course, the music was playing. He ordered drinks, and when he handed her a Cuba Libre, she put her hand over the glass, and smiled at him.

'Let's mambo, Jose,' she said.

CHAPTER SIXTY-ONE

Hans climbed out of the pool, and took the towel that Bella held out to him. He towelled down in front of her, as she lay on the sun-lounger.

'You have a beautiful body, Hans.'

'So, have you.'

'When I was your age.'

He leant down and kissed her lips. 'No, now.'

She smiled. 'You swim very well.'

'Giorgio taught me.'

'Tony thought he could have been an Olympic swimmer, but he loved fooling around too much. He loved holding his sisters under the water. I often had to tell him to let them go.'

Hans towelled himself down. 'Yeah. He used to do that with me too,' said Hans.

'That was just his way,' said Bella. 'His fun.'

Giorgio was a bully and a bit of a sadist thought Hans, but he still missed him. He had lost his lover and his best friend, but Bella had lost her first-born, her only son. Her Giorgio. Every day she told him of a memory of him that came back to her. When he did that or this. It was actually becoming a bit of a bore, but she was a sexy woman, who let him share her mansion. So why worry? He sat on the lounger next to her and picked up his Cuba Libre.

Bella reached out and stroked his chest with her fingers, letting her red, manicured nails slightly dig into the flesh. She felt sorry for Hans. Like Giorgio did, he clearly adored his mother, and was very worried about her. Apparently, she spent every day on her own, reading trashy novels, and drinking.

She knew that Hans felt guilty that it was he who kept supplying his mother with drink. He had started it to help her get over something that Freddie Sanchez had said at Giorgio's wake.

'She wouldn't tell me what he said. It was personal, she said. Just between them. I said I'd confront Freddie about it, but she said, 'No. Please leave it.'

'If you didn't take your mother booze, Hans, what do you think she would do?'

'I don't know. Go crazy, I guess. I don't think she takes the medication my father gives her. I think the booze just keeps her...'

'Fuzzy.'

'I know she's got this thing about Freddie...I think perhaps, years ago when they were in London...Well...'

Bella had seen Hans' backward brother, Klaus, and guessed exactly what had happened. She was surprised that Hans didn't seem to see it.

'I think she believes Anna is sleeping with Freddie.'

'Your sister! That would be really upsetting for her...Is she?'

'No. But Mama thinks she is. I asked Anna. It's not happening...In fact, I think she's sleeping with that black guy, Jose.'

'Do you have a problem with that?'

Hans got hold of her hand. She felt him squeeze it.

'It's not...it doesn't seem natural.'

'You are so naïve, Hans. Haven't you slept with a black girl?'

'Well...yeah. With Giorgio.'

Bella released her hand and stroked Hans' stomach.

'Sounds like your mama needs some company. To take her mind off things.'

Hans sighed as her hand slipped lower. 'She won't see anyone, Bella.'

'I think she needs someone to take her mind off Freddie. How about Nico?'

'Nico! No. I can't see my mother...'

'Nico is a trained masseur, Hans. And he loves older women. That's how we met. He's very romantic. Recites beautiful poetry. But he's too old for me now.'

'But he's still, well...He's not even European.'

'He's not black, Hans. He's mulatto. He could be Italian. An Italian Clark Gable.'

'Yeah...He does look a bit like him.'

'Suggest it to her. It could make Freddie jealous...Your mother loves you. Talk to her. Introduce them, at least.' She slipped her hand down the front of his trunks. 'I'm sure she'll listen to her favourite son.'

As she got hold of his cock, Hans stopped her hand. 'Don't do that, Bella, when you're talking about my mother!'

Squeezing his balls, she said, 'Like that Greek guy who screwed his mother.'

'No, stop it, Bella!'

Bella sat up. 'Nico will know.' She called out. 'Nico who was that Greek guy who fucked his mother?'

Without stopping cleaning the pool, Nico called out, 'Oedipus.'

CHAPTER SIXTY-TWO

In 1940 the writer, Ernest Hemingway, had come to live near Havana. His novel, 'To Have and Have Not' had made the island sound like an exciting place, full of intrigue, romance, and just a little dangerous. So, after the war, the Americans came in their droves. The hotels and casinos flourished. El Paseo del Prado, the harbour and the Old Town were packed with stalls, bootblacks, pimps, prostitutes, fruit vendors, music and dance. Even the ragged beggars, haunting the doorways of the cathedral and churches, got a little piece of the action. It was an island of dreams.

Freddie knew that most people of the island hated the everyday political corruption. Whichever government was in power, they all played one side against the other, and when they couldn't beat them, they paid them to join them. But that didn't seem to matter. Cuba's was one of the most advanced countries in Latin American. Capitalism flourished, but trade unions were powerful, wages were good for many, and the brilliant sun was always shining. Life was good. So why bother? Hurricanes came, occasionally, but like political corruption, they were expected. You picked up the pieces, rebuilt, and life went on.

'How did Anna take the election result?' said Freddie, as he and Carl were driving to one of the countryside clinics.

Carl kept his eyes on the road. After a torrential rainstorm, the country roads could hold unpredictable hazards.

'Very badly. She couldn't believe it.'

Freddie had seen Anna at Giorgio's funeral, but not to speak to for a long time. Not since that stupid kiss. But he knew that she had been working hard for the Orthodoxo Party; printing leaflets, campaigning, going to demonstrations, writing articles for the Orthodoxo radio station, but it didn't surprise him that they lost the election. In fact, the Orthodoxo' were next to last, only just beating the Communists.

'Maybe she'll move on, and concentrate on her law career instead,' Freddie said, more in hope than expectation.

'I doubt that,' Carl said. 'She and her political friends got very drunk afterwards, but when Anna sobered up, she seems even more determined.'

Freddie shook his head. He loved Anna's fierce idealism to create a better world. He remembered he'd had that when he was growing up. But time, and events, can be a brutal enemy of ideals.

Since he returned to the island in the late Thirties, Freddie had seen how turbulent and violent Cuban politics was. Having just come from war-torn Europe, he knew it was pretty much the same the world over, but here it was not uncommon for some political leader, a union representative, or even a police chief, to be found shot dead in the street.

'I worry about her.'

'So do I, Freddie.'

'Because, I don't think her kind of...ideal world, her socialism, will ever happen here.'

'I'm afraid, Freddie, she and boyfriend, Jose, seem determined to prove you wrong about that.'

Freddie scowled at the countryside speeding by. The mention of Anna and Jose together made him jealous. He was surprised that Carl seemed so unconcerned that Anna and Jose were now an item.

'I just hope they're taking precautions,' Freddie said.

'You think...?'

'This is Havana, Carl. Not genteel middle-class England.'

'Well, then I hope so. I'm not really a believer, Freddie, but I really think abortions are dreadful. An abomination.'

'Yes,' Freddie muttered.

Anna rose from the table after having her birthday dinner with her family.

'Thank you all so much for the presents. But I won't be home tonight, so please don't worry about me.'

'It's your birthday, Anna,' said Esther. 'I'd thought perhaps you would stay. You hardly ever have dinner with us.'

Anna smiled at the hypocrisy. She knew that Esther hadn't had dinner with Carl and Klaus for a long time.

'Mama, I said I'd celebrate it with my friends as well tonight.'

'You hardly sleep here at all, Anna. Where are you staying tonight?'

'With a friend, Mama.'

'Which one?'

Anna shrugged. 'I have lots of friends. Could be any one of them.'

Esther looked across at Carl. 'Any one of them?'

Carl rose and followed Anna out. He stopped her at the front door. Taking her by shoulders, he gave her a peck on the cheek.

'Happy birthday, Liebchen.'

'Thank you, Papa.'

'You and your friend...You are taking precautions?'

Anna smiled sweetly at him. 'Papa, you know 'nice' girls don't have intercourse before they are married.'

Carl smiled. 'This isn't Berlin or London, Anna. People call Havana the sex capital of the Caribbean. So...'

'Of course, Papa. I know that.'

'Good.'

He watched her go and went back into the dining room. Klaus had already gone to join Nanny Price, who read him stories before he went to bed.

Esther had her irritated face on. 'She's told me she hasn't seen him, but I think it's Freddie!'

Carl frowned. 'Freddie what?'

'I think that's who she is sleeping with. In that horrible little room!'

'Esther, it is not Freddie.'

'How do you know?'

'I see him a lot, Esther. I would know if he was lying.'

'Like you knew how he deceived you in London!'

'We don't want to go into that again!'

'He is just doing it to spite me!'

Carl sighed, 'I have work to do in my surgery. I shall see you in the morning. Or the afternoon, or whenever.'

After he left, Esther drained the rest of the bottle of wine into her glass, and drank it all in one go.

CHAPTER SIXTY-THREE

Bella put the magazine down and stretched. Looking around the palatial room, which led out to the pool and the exotic garden beyond, she felt very happy. She had money, lived luxuriously on a beautiful island, and had a handsome, sexy young German as a lover. This afternoon, at her suggestion, he had gone to introduce a potential new lover to his mother. She was eager to know what had happened.

Hearing his sports car screeching up the drive, she got up and went to the drinks bar. When Hans walked in, she handed him a martini.

'So, how did it go?'

'Perfect! Nico gave her a little bow, and kissed her hand as if he was back in the olden days. Just like Clark Gable would have done.'

'Beautiful! What did I say?' said Bella. She sat down on a sofa. 'How did Esther behave?'

'She was a little drunk, as usual. But she loved it. She was actually like a little kid,' Hans went on excitedly. 'We went into the garden – You know, it's the first time she has been out of the house, well – for ever! Nico began telling her about the plants. He knows a lot, doesn't he?'

'He's a natural, Hans. He can talk about anything.'

'Certainly a charmer.'

'You fancy him yourself?'

'Not anymore, Bella.' He sat down beside her, and put his arm around her shoulders. 'Not since meeting you.'

Bella gave him a little kiss. 'You've gone off men?'

'It was only Giorgio, really. To be honest.'

'I know. He was like that. Magnetic...Did you leave them alone? Nico and your mother?'

'Yeah. I was trying to think of an excuse to go, then Anna came and wanted to talk to me. So, I left them to it. Afterwards, they were chatting away in the conservatory, and it seemed a pity to interrupt, so I just left.'

'You hardly ever see Anna. What did she want?'

'She was moaning that the police broke up another demonstration about the president. She says people think he's more corrupt than the last one. '

Bella took a drink. 'They're all corrupt, Hans.'

'Anna thinks there's gonna be another election.'

'Another one?'

'She reckons maybe that's why Batista came back from America.'

'Oh yeah, he invited us to his estate. For his homecoming party.'

Hans stopped. He had taken out his tobacco case and was rolling out two lines on the coffee table.

'Yeah? Really? I didn't know you were part of that scene, Bella.'

'Tony was part of it. The whole Mob bit. We just played the game, Hans. At the time Batista was in power. Maybe he will be again. Who knows? But as Tony used to say, "Just show me the dollars!"'

Bella rolled up a dollar and sniffed a line.

'I gave Anna a gun, you know.' Hans confessed.

'You worried about her getting hurt?"

'Yeah.'

'But it's what she wants to do, Hans. You can't stop her. She cares about people. The poor people. It's her life, I guess.'

Bella rubbed the rest of the line against her gums.

'I didn't come from money, Hans. My parents were poor workers. Tony dragged this little girl out of the gutter...So why don't you take this dirt-poor Cuban peasant upstairs, and put her in her place?'

Jose's rented room was small and much less comfortable than Anna's bedroom, but there was no way they could be seen to sleep together at her home. When they got together again, Jose always let Anna lead the way in bed. Their love-making was at first slow, both well aware of the disastrous first time. But now they felt like proper, passionate lovers.

As they both lay, satisfied and a little breathless, Anna shifted in bed and nestled against Jose's bare chest.

'Hans told me my mother thinks I'm sleeping with Freddie.'

Jose grinned. 'Are you?'

Anna hit him hard on his chest. 'Bastardo!'

'Hey. That hurt.'

Anna kissed the spot better.

'Does she really? Has she asked you?'

'No. She hardly ever speaks to me, but she keeps making cutting remarks about him whenever I'm around.'

'She'd probably rather you slept with Freddie than her white, middle-class daughter sleeping with a black dude.'

'I don't know about that. She has just employed a masseur. And he's mulatto.'

'Really?'

'It's the guy who does Bella's garden. Hans is very worried about her drinking, so he suggested Nico. Apparently, he is supposed to be a trained masseur. He gives her a massage twice a week, and does the garden as well.'

'A massage?' Jose questioned.

'Whatever...If it helps.'

'And are you supposed to tell Freddie, to make him jealous?'

'Who knows? Maybe. God knows what goes on in my mother's head.'

Jose stretched, and gave her a kiss. 'Gotta move. Gotta work.'

She watched him get out of bed. A working-class black Adonis who worked twelve hours, and spent the rest of the day trying to help her to change society. For his people, his mother, his younger brother and five sisters, who all worked at the plantation, who he hardly ever saw nowadays.

She propped herself up in bed. 'Hans saw Batista last weekend.'

'Yeah?'

'At his estate. Very impressive, apparently.'

'Did Batista want drugs, or guns?'

'Who knows? Maybe both. It was a party. Bella has known him for ages, when her husband was in the Mafia. He said Batista has gold telephones! People are dying in the gutter, and he talks on gold telephones!'

Jose fastened his trousers, and slipped on a tee-shirt. 'You think he's going to run for president again?'

'Why else would he come back?'

'Did Hans say anything?'

'Nothing. But Batista showed him a telescope that Napoleon owned, apparently. Gold telephones and Napoleon's telescope!' Anna said, sarcastically.

'We could put that in our newspaper, and on the radio station. People wouldn't like that.'

'Yeah, and a lot of people will love it, Jose! That's what they expect of people in power. Mansions, gold telephones, while they live in a one-room tin shack with a thatched roof with holes in it!'

Jose smiled. 'Or a tiny little rented room.'

She threw a pillow at him. 'Get to work, peasant! We have work to do tonight. We're going to win the next election!'

While Carl tuned in the radio station, Freddie made his special coffee for them. On Sunday evenings, despite his disillusion with the island's politics, Freddie always listened to the regular radio broadcast of Eduardo Chilbás.

'Eddy' Chiblás was an elected senator, and was very popular among ordinary people. He talked about creating a proper democracy, about freedom from the rampant corruption, and the violence that seemed to be getting worse every day. He was also the leader of Anna's party, the Orthodoxos.

'Anna believes he will be president after the next election,' said Carl. 'He seems to be about the only honest man in the Congress.'

'Maybe he is. But they have to win the election first.'

'Freddie Sanchez, always the pessimist.'

'In Cuba, like everywhere else, Carl, there are rich and poor. And, somehow, the poor never seem to win.'

Born in Havana from a middle-class Cuban father and an educated English mother, Freddie hadn't always been a cynic. He'd had a great childhood. His parents were very open-minded and allowed him to play on the beach, and in the nearby forests with friends from all over the city. Freddie was a natural leader. If something exciting was happening, like playing pirates, or hunting dinosaurs, it was generally Freddie's idea. And he was always the pirate captain, Blackbeard.

At first, he was sad when he was sent to a boarding school in gloomy, rainy England, but he soon became a star pupil, both academically and in sport. Having been brought up to believe in helping people, he began to study medicine, and, as a pupil at St. Barts, Freddie became acutely aware of the difference between the health, and the treatment, of the rich and the poor. His idea was to go back to Cuba and set up a proper hospital for the poor, for the families of the sort of children that he had played with as a child. Strangely, the man he was pouring coffee for had helped to destroy all that, but now, that same man was helping in him in his makeshift, countryside clinics.

As they listened Chiblás began his broadcast attacking the government and the gangster groups they aided and supported. He was expected to produce evidence of embezzlement against a particular minister.

But instead towards the end he paused, then said, very passionately, 'I urge the people of Cuba to awaken, in the name of economic independence, political liberty, and social justice! People of Cuba. Rise up and walk! People of Cuba, wake up! This is my last loud knock."

Then a loud bang! And another, and another. Then silence.

'Were those gunshots?' said Carl.

CHAPTER SIXTY-FOUR

They waited in the long queue, in the baking sun, to file past 'Eddy' Chiblás's bier at the university's Hall of Honour.

Anna had her head buried into Jose's arm. 'Crazy, crazy!' she mumbled.

Jose hugged her. 'It wasn't to him, Anna. "I am dying for the revolution. I am dying for Cuba." That's what he said when they took him to the hospital.'

Eleven days after his last broadcast, 'Eddy' Chiblás had died in hospital from the three gunshot wounds he had fired into his own stomach. Inside the Hall of Honour, several of Orthodoxo's senior members, including the Party's young firebrand, Fidel Castro, were standing guarding by the coffin as it lay in state.

After they had paid their respects and emerged onto the steps outside, Anna sat down, tears staining her face.

Jose lit a cigarette, 'You okay?'

'I just need a minute, Jose.'

He nodded, stroked her hair, kissed her forehead, and went to talk to a friend.

Anna took out a handkerchief and blew her nose, then noticed someone standing beside her. She looked up.

'Hello. A very sad situation...' said Freddie. He had just emerged from the hall.

'Why are you here?'

'Out of respect. I always listened to his broadcasts.'

'You surprise me.'

'Yeah, well, there are many things you don't know about me, Anna.'

'I'm sure...,' she said, indifferently.

Feeling dismissed, he said, 'Goodbye,' and began to walk away.

'He could have been president next year,' she called after him.

Freddie stopped and turned to her. 'Yes, maybe...' He took a step back towards her. 'Who will take over now? In your Party? Castro?'

'Eddy' could have been president...We could have won. We could have transformed this island!'

'The Anna I used to know would still think she can.'

Anna got up and faced him. 'Oh, really?' She got closer and almost whispered, 'What you said to my mother at Giorgio's wake was appalling. Disgraceful. Disgusting. You know she has become an alcoholic.'

Freddie nodded unhappily.

'Why did you say it? Just to hurt her? To stop her pestering you?'

'Yes, I did...When I was recovering from the fever at your home, she seemed determined to start it all over again. And at the wake she...She just...I just had to stop her, Anna...So I just said that...But it's...' He took a deep breath, sighed, looked away.

Anna looked at him. She was also breathing deeply. 'But it's just...what?'

He shook his head. 'Nothing. Nothing at all.'

Jose had noted the conversation and came over. He glanced at Freddie. 'You okay?' he asked Anna.

'Yes...' She took Jose's arm. 'We were just talking about maybe Castro taking over.'

'No. He's far too young,' said Jose. 'And too fond of his own voice.'

'He's very passionate,' said Freddie. 'Passion can move people. 'Eddy' Chiblás knew that. So does Castro...

'Yeah,' said Jose.

'Good luck with your campaign,' Freddie said, and walked away down the crowded steps.

Jose put his arm around Anna's shoulders. 'Shall we go and have a Cuba Libre to celebrate Eddy's life?'

Anna smiled. 'And for the revolution.'

They followed Freddie down the steps. He turned, briefly, at the bottom, looking back towards them. And then moved on.

At home, Carl felt very much alone. Esther was now besotted with Nico, who was a masseur, a gardener and who knows what else? Anna worked all day at the law firm, or was out campaigning for the new election, and Klaus spent the days playing games with Mrs Price, or drawing in his sea-shell book.

It was only when he went helping with Freddie's clinics, or taking Klaus to the beach to look for shells with Freddie, that he came alive.

'I've lived in Vienna, London, Berlin. I never dreamt of living by the sea,' he said. He was seated beside Freddie on the warm sand. 'But you never know what's waiting for you beyond the horizon.'

'No matter how much we plan. We're in the lap of the gods, Carl...and the politicians.'

Carl half-laughed. 'Will the election change anything?'

'Maybe...Have you listened to any of Castro's speeches on 'Voice of the Air',

'Not really. Politics scares me here, Freddie.'

'He's very passionate, magnetic. He has thousands of listeners, apparently!'

Klaus rushed up and gave Freddie a shell. 'Look at this Freddie! Such a lovely pattern!'

Freddie stroked the shell. 'It's beautiful, Klaus.'

'What's it called?' asked Carl.

Klaus had already looked up the shell in his book. 'An angel wing!' he said proudly.

'Well done, Klaus,' said Freddie. 'Can you go and find the other one? Then you'll have a full angel!'

Klaus laughed, and then ran off towards the sea, eagerly.

'Anna is very excited, of course.' Carl said. 'The Orthodoxos are doing pretty well, it seems. She and Jose have been out among the workers in the slum areas, and all the people are very much for them. She really believes this time they are going to win.'

Freddie grinned. 'Onward the revolution, Carl!'

Minutes later Klaus appeared, breathless, holding out a shell to Freddie.

'Look!'

Freddie took it. 'Bravo, Klaus! A full angel!'

The next day, about to lose the imminent election, General Batista staged a bloodless military coup and became the de facto dictator of Cuba.

CHAPTER SIXTY-FIVE

Freddie saw Ramos approach as he was drinking coffee and whiskey at the harbour café. Ramos sat down beside him without invitation. He knew that Freddie was the 'go-to' man for abortions, and if he heard the rumour that Freddie had serviced one of the wealthier patrons of the island, he expected a little reward for his silence. Freddie had not been busy for a month or two, so he wondered why Ramos had stopped.

'Senor Freddie, how are you?'

'Very well, thank you, Ramos.'

Ramos waved at the waiter standing by the door of the café, and ordered a drink with a gesture. He waved his hand towards the harbour, 'I was thinking about the time I helped you get that family off the ship.'

'Really? The Mueller's. That was a long time ago.'

'I remember because I didn't get anything for it.'

'Because I didn't get any money that time.'

'No.'

Freddie didn't know where this was going, but he played along. 'I was very grateful for your help that day, Ramos.'

'That family. You knew them before, in Europe?'

'Yes. In London.'

'I've never been to London.'

'You wouldn't like it. It's cold and wet.'

'You have stayed in contact with them.' It wasn't a question.

'Yes. Professor Mueller helps me at my clinics out of town. He is brilliant. We are very lucky to have him.'

'Good. Very good.' The waiter arrived. Ramos took the drink from him and swallowed the rum at one go. 'Do you see the daughter at all?'

'Anna. No. Not for a long time.'

'You have fallen out?'

Freddie shook his head. 'No. We just...don't mix in the same circles.'

'No. You're not a terrorist.'

'Sorry? Anna is not a terrorist!'

'She tried to take my gun from me one day.'

'To shoot you?'

'No. Someone got shot at a demonstration. She wanted me to help.'

'That sounds like a reasonable request...Look, Ramos, I'm sure Anna doesn't like what Batista is doing. Many people don't. He's banned some newspapers. He's against free speech. He's a dictator, Ramos. Cubans don't like that.'

'Some Cubans...I have just been re-assigned to the Military Intelligent Service.'

Freddie stubbed his cigarette butt in the ashtray. The M.I.S. were basically the island's secret police. 'Should I congratulate you on that?'

'My job now is to root out terrorists, and, er, silence them. I think you maybe should tell the Professor that. So, he can tell his daughter to be...silent.'

Anna lay on her stomach in the wet undergrowth. Jose was lying close by. There were about ten of them in a line. They had been there, hidden doing nothing, for a long time. Not a movement, no contact. Ahead of them, twenty yards away, the American Korean veteran stood, rifle in hand, looking their way.

Before the election Anna had been convinced that her party would win. She and Jose had toured the city, the suburbs and the countryside, distributing leaflets, and talking and listening to people. Everyone knew that the President, Carlos Prio, was weak and corrupt. For her, the peaceful revolution was on its way. She had first thought of standing for the Congress herself, but she was rising fast as a lawyer and believed she could do more good fighting for the poor in the courts.

After the suicide of Eddy Chiblás, Fidel Castro had become the party's main spokesman. People flocked to hear his speeches at rallies, and listened to his regular tirades against the president on the 'Voice of the Air' radio station. At twenty-five he was seen as too young to be the next president, but Anna knew he was the voice of the people.

One evening, after a day's campaigning, she raised her Cuba Libre in a toast. 'It's going to happen, Jose. Because the people want to end it, once and for all!'

Batista's bloodless coup had been a complete surprise to her, and her group. Batista was an ex-colonel, well-known and respected by the military. The army supported him straight away, prompting the now ex-President Prio and his family to flee the island on a private plane.

The new regime began to bring in censorship of the press and the radio, though Batista still allowed the political Party's to exist, giving the appearance that the island was still a democracy, rather than a dictatorship.

Which was why Anna was waiting in the long grass, feeling very wet, and a little bored. She moved her head to wink at Jose.

'Bang! You're dead!' The veteran had his rifle trained straight at her. 'The sniper would've got you right between the eyes.' He approached the line. 'D'you know how long the Gooks would lay there in ambush? An hour? No way. A day?' He shook his head. 'As long as it took.'

It was the first time they had been out to the countryside. All their training, so far, had been done in the University grounds, mostly at night, away from prying eyes. They had been taught unarmed combat, the use of a compass, map reading, the use of guns and knives, and had spent hours crawling on their bellies through the dust of the courtyard.

One evening within weeks of Batista's coup, Anna told Jose, 'They want us to be part of a cell. There will be about ten of us.'

Jose smiled, 'That's not enough for a revolution.'

'There'll be other cells, idiot! But we won't know who they are. In case the M.I.S interrogate us.'

Their cell had produced anti-Batista leaflets, and helped to transport the printer from hideout to hideout. They had had a few near misses, narrowly escaping secret police raids, which happened all the time.

On their way back from the long day's training, Jose said, 'All this training, Anna. When is something going to happen?'

The next morning, they were told.

CHAPTER SIXTY-SIX

Esther was surprised and, at first, nervous that Bella had asked Hans if she could visit his mother. She had only seen Bella once, at the funeral and the wake for Giorgio. Though she couldn't really remember it all, she had made a terrible scene after Freddie had told her he loved Anna. She had, apparently, tried to tear the necklace off Bella's neck.

'She wants to see you. To get to know you, Mama. That's all,' Hans had said, reassuringly. 'She was the one who suggested that Nico could help with the garden. And that's worked out very well, hasn't it?'

And there Bella was, seated in the living room, being served a cool drink by Carlotta. Both women had spent a lot of time preparing for the meeting. Esther had gone for her favoured chiffon. Bella had chosen silk.

When Carlotta had gone, Bella looked out at the garden. 'Hans said Nico has done wonders with your garden,'

'He is a marvel,' smiled Esther. 'Thank you for suggesting him.'

'Yes.' Bella looked straight at Esther, meeting her eyes. 'He's a marvel at other things too.'

Esther looked away, and gave a little cough.

Bella sipped her drink. 'When I'd had my third child, my late husband, Tony, he stopped having sex with me. Just like that. I was nearly twenty-five. Much too old for some men.'

'Oh, no, surely not. You're very beautiful…'

'Well, thankfully, your son seems to think so…How old were you when you met your husband?'

'Er, well, nearly twenty.'

'When did you stop…making love?'

'Well, really…I…I don't think…'

'I'm sorry. I'm being too forward. It's the Italian in me.'

Esther toyed with her glass. She was pleased she had topped up her fruit drink with a little vodka before Bella arrived. 'Carl is much older than me. And...erm, certain things happened.'

'He had an affair?'

'No, no. Nothing like that. Carl is...Carl.'

'You had an affair...?' Bella put up her hands in apology. 'Sorry again. Italians talk about love a lot. It's natural to us. Please, it's not my business. Shall we change the subject?'

'I, er...' Esther wanted to mention Freddie, to find out if Bella knew anything.

Bella went on, 'Thankfully some young men prefer older women. And I prefer younger men. They are generally very eager to please...Like Nico was. But he's too old for me now.'

'But surely he's...only in his thirties?'

'Yes. And he's very handsome. He's a good lover. It was good while it lasted, but that was some time ago...I always fancied your Hans.'

'Oh, yes?'

'He always seemed so proud and arrogant when he came to the villa with Giorgio. Very Germanic. But when he came back to see me after the wake, to apologise, he seemed so shy, so bashful. He is very adorable.'

Esther rushed in. 'I'm afraid I believe I made a terrible fool of myself there! At the wake. I really do apologise. Really. I should have phoned to say sorry.'

'No need. No. You'd had a bad experience.'

'Well, er...'

'Freddie can be very spiteful.'

'Oh...? You and he...?'

'No, no. He's far too old for me...He and Anna aren't together, you know.'

'Really?'

'Hans has talked to Anna. Nothing has happened, believe me. It was just a cruel insult.'

'Oh.'

Bella picked up her bag and took something out a small package. 'I bought you a present. To show there are no hard feelings between us.'

She handed the package towards Esther, who got up and took it.

'Thank you. Shall I..?'

'Of course.'

Esther opened the package. Inside the tissue paper was her necklace. 'Oh! Oh! No, I can't take this! No.'

'I believe it's very dear to you. To me it's just diamonds, and I have too many of those anyway.'

'Please, no, I couldn't!'

Smiling warmly at her, Bella rose. 'Of course you can, Esther.' Bella took the necklace from her and put it around Esther's neck. 'There, where it should.' Throwing out her arms she hugged Esther. 'Remember life is for living!'

Mrs Price had done a wonderful alteration on the dress. It fitted perfectly, just where it should, and where it shouldn't. With Carl away for the day, out with that man in the countryside clinics, she was now ready. She stood up as the doorbell chimed. The diamond necklace glistened above the red décolletage as Nico entered the room.

CHAPTER SIXTY-SEVEN

Anna lay huddled next to the sleeping Jose, in the dark farmhouse. In the blackness, she could hear people whispering. Like her, some of the others lying there were too full of adrenalin, mixed with a sense of fear, to be able to rest. On what could be their last night on earth how could anyone sleep?

Two days ago, the leader of their cell had contacted them. 'He wants us to take a train to Santiago de Cuba,' Jose told her.

'Did he say why?' asked Anna.

'No. Someone will contact us at the station there,' said Jose. 'That's all he said.'

'This must be it, Jose!'

They had boarded the train for the very long journey to the south-east of the island, carrying just enough for a couple of days. At the bottom of their rucksacks they had concealed their handguns, supplied by Hans some weeks ago.

The man, wearing the red shirt and yellow kerchief, met them at the station. Along with three others she didn't know, he drove them to an isolated farmhouse, someway outside of the city. Inside there were already about a hundred people, mostly of their age. Some were examining the weapons they had chosen from a pile in the corner. The guns were a mixture from farming shotguns to army rifles and one submachine gun. Anna guessed that a lot of them had probably been bought from Hans. It was ironic that he was supplying arms for a revolution he had no interest in.

As they were some of the last to arrive, there was little left to choose, but, luckily, there was an old Springfield rifle which Anna had trained with. Jose picked up a Winchester rifle.

'The gun that won the West!' he said.

They were then given regulations army uniforms, which they were told to put on.

'Army uniforms?' said Anna to Jose.

'There is a big army barracks in the town,' said Jose, quietly.

'But there'll be hundreds of soldiers there.'

'There's a festival in the city this weekend,' said a young man nearby, pulling on his army trousers. 'Most will probably be there. Or drunk.'

In the blackness, most of the people in the different cells stuck together, talking quietly among themselves. Where they really going to attack an army barracks?

'It makes sense,' said Jose. 'If we do it at night. Take them by surprise.'

Anna looked around, hardly able to make out her companions now. Just like herself, all of these people were committed revolutionaries, determined to end Batista's corrupt regime. They had been trained for weeks, taught how to fire their weapons, how to kill with a knife, how to break a neck with their arms, but they were not trained, disciplined soldiers. How many of them had actually killed a man? Or could? For the first time, she was scared.

It was a bright sunny morning and, on Sundays, Freddie had a ritual of going to his favourite café for a coffee, to have a smoke and to watch the world go by. As usual the owner, Miquel, brought out the cup without Freddie ordering it. He sat down opposite, and accepted a cigarette Freddie offered. Miquel lit the cigarette, took a deep drag, then breathed out slowly.

'There was an attack on the barracks in Santiago this morning, Freddie.'

'Really?'

'My friend in Santiago called. Said he was woken up at dawn by lots of gunfire.'

'In the barracks?'

'Yes. In the barracks. A lot of rebels attacked it.'

'So, what happened?'

'Nothing. It only lasted about half an hour. The rebels were shot, I think.'

'All of them?' Freddie felt his heart beginning to race.

'I don't know. He said there were a lot of bodies in the parade ground. All rebels.'

Abruptly, the world had stopped going by and had stopped at Freddie's table. He just knew that Anna was in the attack. Carl had told him how enraged Anna had been at Batista's coup, and how she intended to oppose him, using the only way that now seemed possible. A revolution. A crazy, stupid, armed resistance against a ruthless dictator, who held all the cards.

'Can I use your phone, Miquel?'

'Sure. You know where it is.'

Freddie stubbed out his cigarette and got up.

'Is something the matter, Freddie?'

'I just need to phone.' He hurried into the café, and went round to the back of the counter. Picking up the receiver, he dialled. The phone rang and rang. Finally, it was Carl who answered.

'Hello, Carl? It's Freddie.'

'Freddie? This is a surprise. It's Sunday morning. Is anything wrong?'

'Is Anna there?'

'Anna? No. She doesn't sleep here much now.'

'Have you heard from her today?'

'Today? No. Why?'

'Do you know where she is?'

'No. She's gone off somewhere for a day or two, I think. With Jose. She came home, packed a rucksack and left. What's going on, Freddie?'

'Did she say anything before she left?

'No. She seemed a bit agitated. She was just going to catch a train.'

'Where to?'

'I have no idea. Somewhere east, I think.'

'Santiago?'

'I really don't know, Freddie. Why?'

Freddie could hardly breathe. 'If you hear from her, please let me know!'

'Freddie, please, what's going on?'

'You'll hear about it on the news, Carl…I just hope I'm wrong.'

CHAPTER SIXTY-EIGHT

It was four o'clock in the morning when things started to happen. After a troubled, sleepless night, Anna was finally dozing off when she heard several people enter the farmhouse. She sat up drowsily and could see in the semi-blackness that the men seemed to be in army uniforms. Her first thought was that the rebels had been discovered and this was an army patrol sent to arrest them. As she reached for her pistol, she recognised the tall, broad figure standing beside the man holding the paraffin lamp.

She relaxed, nudged the sleeping Jose, and whispered, 'Jose! It's Fidel!'

It turned out that what people in the farmhouse had begun to believe was true.

Castro thanked everyone for being there, and for enduring the hard weeks of training, and then told them that the plan was to attack the Moncada barracks in the heart of the city.

'I knew it was the barracks,' whispered Jose to Anna.

Illuminated by the small, flickering lamp, Castro explained the simple plan to them all. In the darkness, their convoy of cars would drive to the gate nearest to the headquarters building. The commandos in the first car would disarm the guards and open the gates, allowing the convoy to drive through. They would then spread out to subdue the sleeping soldiers in their quarters.

When someone asked what they should do to the prisoners, he said, 'Treat them humanely. The life of an unarmed man must be sacred to you.'

In the middle of the group a small group of students, some of which Anna taught law to at the university, had begun to talk animatedly amongst themselves,

Castro concluded, 'With the element of surprise in our favour, the attack will be short and swift. But it is a dangerous plan. Anyone who leaves with me tonight will have to do so willingly.'

One of students stood up and spoke, 'Fidel, look at our shit weapons! We don't have the enough to take the barracks. They will have machine guns and many more men than us! We've decided we don't want to go.'

Some people began to shout at them, 'Cowards! Traitors!'

Castro shut them up with a wave of his hand. 'What did you come here for? A picnic? Lock them in the bathroom! We don't want any weaklings amongst us!'

The students were shepherded into the bathroom, with a guard at the door.

Putting up his hands for silence again, Castro said, 'In a few hours you will be victorious, or defeated, but regardless of the outcome...this Movement will triumph! Cuba Libre!'

He turned and walked out with his small group of commanders.

Anna turned to Jose. 'What do you think?'

He took her hand. 'I think we go, and attack the barracks.'

She gripped his hand and nodded.

The rebel group gathered outside, waiting for the cars to be brought from the various farm outbuildings where they had been hidden. In the blackness Anna could hear the sound of weapons being checked again, more from nerves, as everyone had checked them several times overnight.

Anna stood very close to Jose. Despite the heat of the night, she was shivering.

Jose put his arm around her. 'It will be fine,' he said.

'I love you, Jose,' she whispered.

He leant down and gave her a little kiss.

When the cars arrived, the team commanders began to allocate the detachments into them. Though they were in the same team, there was not enough room for Anna to squeeze in with Jose. Reluctantly, she had to wait for the next car.

As the farmyard was too small to organise the convoy, the cars set off separately to rendezvous on the highway to form the convoy there. Getting into the back seat of her car, Anna saw Jose's car drive off into the darkness.

Immediately it set off her car stalled. The driver swore and pressed the starter button. The engine sputtered and stopped. He swore, and tried again. The engine stalled. After the fourth time, the driver switched off the lights. Four men got out of the car to push it from behind. Another car set off in front of them before the engine stuttered then roared into life. They set off, following the red rear lights down the bumpy road from the farm.

The passengers were quiet for a while, as they tailed the car in front. Even with all the windows open it was sweltering with so many people crammed inside. Anna wished she had not put on her small rucksack, but she had figured that, whatever happened, they would not be going back to the farm.

When they reached the highway, there was no sign of the convoy. As no-one in the car knew the area, they followed the car in front, expecting to meet the convoy further on.

After a few miles people began to mutter to each other. Where were the other cars? Where was the convoy?

A few more minutes passed. Anna looked behind. 'I thought the barracks were in the city,' she said.

'They are,' said someone.

'Then we're going the wrong way,' Anna said. 'The city's behind us. Can we catch the car in front?'

The driver floored the accelerator and quickly caught the car. He flashed his lights. From the back of the car two heads appeared out of the windows.

'It looks like the students!' the driver said. 'The ones who didn't want to come!'

'They're going back to Havana!' Anna cried. 'Turn around! We're going to miss the attack!'

On the deserted road, the driver spun round, and headed back to the lights of the city. In the still dawn air, they heard the sound of echoing gunfire.

CHAPTER SIXTY-NINE

'I guess they were using some of your weapons,' Bella said. 'But it doesn't sound like they did them much good.'

They had listened to the radio broadcast about the attack on Moncada barracks, while having a late breakfast on the terrace by the pool. The report said that the attack had failed and most of the rebels had been killed.

Hans seemed preoccupied, picking at his food.

'Let's hope the President doesn't find out about your involvement with the revolution.'

'He'll only know if you tell him at one of his parties, I expect,' Hans said.

She smiled, leant over and popped a green fig into his mouth. 'I thought I was living with a young, successful entrepreneur, but who would have thought I was actually sleeping with a dangerous revolutionary?'

He chewed the fig, and swallowed it. 'I have to go and see my mother, Bella.'

'What? What, now?'

'I think Anna could have been in the attack. If she was, she may have been hurt....Maybe killed.'

'Anna? Do you think so? That she was there?'

'I'm pretty sure. She never said anything, but I guessed something was going to happen soon. I sold them a lot of guns recently.'

Bella took his hand. 'Oh, Hans. I never really met her...I don't agree with those rebels, but I do hope you're wrong. That would be awful. But does your mother know about Anna, and all that politics stuff?'

'No, no. She's like you. She doesn't care about politics. I'm sure she doesn't know what Anna has been doing. But I want to be with her...just in case...'

'Well, if you don't know anything, Hans, what's the point in going? You might just upset her.'

'I wouldn't mention it, of course. I just want to be there.'

'I think Nico's 'being there' for her, Hans.'

'Anna's my sister, Bella. I don't agree with her either, I think she's stupid. But she could be dead, or injured.'

Bella took a red chilli from her plate and bit into it. 'Well, if you play with fire...'

Hans got up, about to leave. 'I won't be too long'.

She took his arm. 'I know you sell guns to people, Hans. I don't really like it, but it's your business...Me? I'm happy with Batista. He throws nice parties...I know he's a dictator really, but that doesn't bother me. I have money, a nice house. I just care about myself, I'm afraid...And you...I thought we could have a nice day, lazing together. You've been out so much doing 'business', I've hardly seen you.'

'Bella, I really need to know about Anna.'

'Well, make some phone calls here. Find out something before you go disturbing your mother. I've got friends high up in the police. And in the army...Better to know for definite, okay?'

'Okay. I'll go and do that.'

'Perfect...And while you're up, a martini?'

Two days after the failed attack on the Moncada barracks, Freddie had no way of knowing what had happened to Anna. There were terrible rumours about what had happened to the rebels. They had either been killed in the battle, or taken prisoners and been tortured to death. A female photographer had taken horrific photos of the victims, and travelled back to Havana with the film concealed in her bra. Despite the state of emergency that President Batista had announced, one newspaper had printed them. Freddie had scoured the pictures. Anna wasn't amongst the mutilated corpses.

But what had happened to her? He couldn't just go to Ramos and ask. Feeling helpless, and distressed, he had got blind drunk and stayed that way.

In his dream bells were ringing, happily. He stopped an old woman passing by. 'Why are the bells ringing?' he said.

'It's for the dead,' she said, and shuffled on.

Above him in the bright, celestial sky an angel appeared. She had flowing white wings, but the white of her gown was covered in blood. She waved her bloodstained arms towards him.

'Come and join us. Come and join me!' she said, brightly.

Suddenly the angel became Anna. As he reached out to her, the phone finally woke him. Still in a daze, he reached out and picked up the receiver.

'Y-Yes?'

'Oh, you're there. Good news, Freddie,' said Carl. 'Anna arrived home this afternoon.'

Freddie heard himself sigh over the phone.

'Er - really?' He struggled to sit up. 'I've just been dreaming about her. Is it true? This isn't still the dream, is it?'

'No. It's real. It's me, Carl.'

'Anna is there?'

'Yes.'

'Is she alright?'

'Physically yes. She's a bit exhausted. She's just hitched back from Santiago.'

'Did she say what happened?'

'Not really. She wasn't involved in the attack. There was some confusion about cars. She didn't explain it very well, she is too distressed about Jose. She doesn't know what's happened to him. She thinks he may be dead.'

301

Freddie was sitting up now, reaching for his cigarettes. After the booze and the dream, he was slowly coming back to the surface. At least she was alive.

'I'm surprised she told you all this. Was anyone else there? Esther, or Mrs Price?'

'No. Mrs Price is in her room, and Esther is with Nico, in her room.'

'They mustn't know.'

'Of course not. I think she only told me because she's upset and worried about Jose...I've given her something to help her sleep. She's gone to bed.'

Freddie lit a cigarette, and breathed out a sigh of relief.

'Carl, when she wakes up, tell her...Tell her I'm so pleased she's safe.'

CHAPTER SEVENTY

Racing back towards the city, they could hear noise of gunfire resounding from the walls of the buildings.

'That's a machine-gun!' the driver said. 'I heard 'em in the war. Don't want to mess with those.'

'We don't have any,' said Anna.

'Maybe they stole one.'

'It doesn't look like we took them by surprise.'

As they drove through the empty streets, which were bathed in golden light by the rising sun, they realised that the sound of the gunfire had suddenly stopped. They rounded a corner and saw the barracks in the distance. The air was silent now. The driver slowed down and then stopped.

'Listen...There's no shooting.'

The sun was lighting the barracks like a film set.

'But there's soldiers everywhere,' said the driver.

'Are they ours?'

'Doesn't look like it.'

They could see that there were many soldiers in the parade ground and around the barracks. They weren't running or shooting. Several seemed to be looking at somethings on the ground, and dragging them away.

'Are they bodies?'

The rebels in the car looked at each other.

'What do we do now?' asked Anna.

'We can't just drive up there,' said the driver. 'We'd be sitting ducks.' He started to turn the car. 'I don't want to be in range of that machine gun,' he said, driving back towards the highway.

Suddenly, everyone began to talk.

'We've lost.'

'What can we do now?'

'Go back to the farm?'

'They may be setting up roadblocks.'

'We should get away.'

No one really seemed to know. There wasn't any plan for this. Anna was thinking of Jose. If she'd been in with him, they could both be dead now. Her heart was beating fast, and she was trying not to cry.

As they returned the highway, Anna made up her mind. 'Stop,' she said. 'I want to get out.'

The driver stopped, a bit surprised.

'We don't know what's happened,' she said. 'We know the attack's failed. They could be all dead, or taken prisoner. I'm gonna get rid of this uniform and hitch back to Havana.'

She left her rifle, and stumbled out of the car with her rucksack, onto the empty highway.

'This isn't over,' she said...'Whatever happened, I want to live to fight another day.'

Emotional and physical fatigue, and her father's pills, kept Anna asleep for over twenty-four hours, while President Batista broadcast on the radio, declaring a State of Emergency, and martial law. Gossip and rumour were rife all over Havana, as Ramos's dreaded MIS secret police scoured the city arresting potential rebels.

When she awoke, despite the danger to herself, Anna immediately hurried round to Jose's room hoping that, somehow, he had escaped and made his way back to Havana. But the room was locked and none of the neighbours had seen him. As she sat on the old-tiled staircase, feeling distraught and helpless, she heard someone limping up the stairs. She looked up.

'Anna?'

It was Luis, the leader of her cell who lived in the same apartment block as Jose. He had survived the attack.

'Luis!' She got up and hugged him.

He winced. 'What happened to you?'

'It was crazy. We got lost. Do you know what happened to Jose?'

'Yes.' He sat down, wearily, on the stairs. 'We went back to the farm after the attack. Jose was there with Fidel and some others.'

Anna breathed a huge sigh. 'He's alive! Was he hurt?'

'No, I don't think so. Fidel wanted to go to the Gran Piedra Mountains to start a guerrilla operation. I couldn't go. I can't walk. I got hurt in the attack.'

'Did Jose go?'

'Yes. There were about twenty of them.'

'So, Jose's alive,' she repeated.

'I don't know for how long. The army are already up there looking for them. After what they did to the ones caught at the barracks...They're not taking any prisoners, Anna! You shouldn't be here! The secret police are bound to come here. I'm going to get some things and go into hiding.' He hugged her again. 'Go! Please!'

Anna hurried down the gloomy staircase and, at the bottom, ran straight into Ramos with a group of his armed men entering the building.

'Ah, Senorita,' said Ramos, sardonically. 'Just the person I want to see.'

CHAPTER SEVENTY-ONE

Hans came in from the pool and saw the maid finishing laying the formal dinner table. He frowned at Bella who, he noticed, was wearing the dress she had just had flown over from Paris.

'Dress for dinner?'

'Yes. Your white dinner jacket and bowtie, please, Hans,' said Bella.

'Why? Who's coming? Batista?'

'No. No-one. It's just us. Please, just for this evening,' Bella pursed her lips in a kiss. 'For me.'

'What's going on, Bella?'

'Wait and see.'

A thought struck him. 'You're not...' He looked anxious. 'You're not...?'

'Wait.'

'Bella?'

'Don't be impatient, Hans. Just go.'

'But-'

'Go!'

Hans sighed, but went upstairs to do as he was told. As he showered and dressed in his tuxedo he worried about what was the special occasion. Generally, they didn't dress for the evening meal, if it was just the two of them. Quite often they had dinner out by the pool, wearing robes over their wet swimming gear. Sometimes, just robes. Or, if the servants had an evening off, nothing.

But tonight was special for Bella. Was she pregnant? Bella had told him that she had already had an abortion, so if she was pregnant she may be thinking of keeping it. Hans didn't like the sound of that. He didn't like children. They were a bore.

He went downstairs feeling anxious. Just as they settled down at the table, the phone rang.

'Leave it, Hans,' Bella said.

But Hans was already up and heading for the phone.

'Hans Mueller.' He put his hand over the receiver, and turned to her, surprised. 'It's my father.'

Bella was annoyed that the call had happened just as she was about to make her announcement. This was something she had been planning for a while.

But as Hans' father had never phoned before, it must be something important. As Hans talked on the phone, Bella poured two glasses of champagne.

'So, is she okay?' asked Hans.

'Yes,' said Carl. 'She came home late yesterday.'

'Was she alright? Not injured, or anything?'

'No...not physically. No.'

'Did she say what...happened...about the...?'

'No, not really. But she's very worried about José. She's gone round to see if he's in his apartment.'

Hans couldn't care less about José. He didn't like his sister sleeping with a black man, but he was relieved that Anna had come home safely. He guessed, from what Carl wasn't saying, that Anna had been involved in the failed attack on the barracks. Hans had told Anna, many times, that he didn't believe in politics because he thought they were all the same, right, left, whatever. But as the oldest son, he felt it was his duty to look after his younger sister.

'Tell her I'll come round to see her tomorrow. Okay? Goodbye, Papa.'

As he put the phone down, Bella stood up, holding out a glass to him as he came back to the table.

'It was about Anna –'

'Is she okay?'

'Yes. She was - '

'So, congratulations!' said Bella cutting him off.

He looked puzzled. 'What for?'

She handed him a document.

He glanced at it. 'What's all this, Bella?'

'Read it...' She was very pleased what she had done. But her late husband, Tony, had been a respected, well-trusted colleague, and that carried a lot of weight. 'You are now the manager of our own nightclub.'

CHAPTER SEVENTY-TWO

They had kept Anna waiting, alone in her cell, for hours. From the next room, she had heard Luis's tortured screams, going on for what seemed like eternity. She tried to block her ears, but the cries still got through. Finally, there was a long agonising squeal. Then silence.

She knew that they would come to her, soon. She only knew her own cell members, and apart from Luis and Jose, she had no idea what had happened to the rest. But she did know all their names. If they had escaped and gone into hiding, the police would want to get the names from their prisoners. She didn't know how she would be able to put up with torture. Trying hard not to imagine what her captors would do to her, she concentrated on Jose. At least he was safe. They might get his name from her, but he was still out there, fighting.

She didn't know what had happened at the barracks, except that the attack had failed. When she had left the car on the highway, she had said she wanted to live to fight for another day. And now she knew that Fidel, Jose and some others had gone to the mountains, the revolution would continue. With or without her. Perhaps she wouldn't be there to fight for it. In fact, she might not be here at all. From what she thought had happened to Luis, she might not be anywhere.

The key turned in the lock. A policeman entered and jerked his thumb for her to follow. She got up and swayed, almost falling as her legs gave way. Recovering her balance, she stumbled after him, her heart beating frantically, the drumming in her ears deafening.

Freddie had heard of Anna's arrest from Ramos himself. The policeman had been bragging about the number of rebels they had arrested to the customers at Freddie's usual café.

'Even your young friend, Anna Mueller, Freddie. I did tell you to warn her.'

Freddie said nothing to Ramos. He left, and phoned Carl straight away. He picked Carl up from his home, and they drove quickly to the forbidding, concrete building of headquarters of the Military Intelligence Service. On the way there, they rehearsed what they would say.

When Ramos arrived back he kept them waiting almost an hour, before he agreed to see them.

'What you're saying is quite untrue!' Carl insisted to Ramos. 'My daughter has been unwell for over three days. She has been in bed all of that time.'

'That's correct,' lied Freddie. 'Anna couldn't have been at the Moncada barracks. Professor Mueller asked me to his house for my opinion, as a doctor, actually on the day of the attack. I saw Anna. She was in bed, unwell, but it turned out it was only a minor infection.'

Freddie could see that Ramos didn't believe them, but knew he couldn't prove that.

Ramos shrugged, dismissively. He could arrest Freddie and Carl and have them tortured about where Anna really was, but they had some of the leaders, people very close to Castro, behind bars. Even now they were being tortured by his best men. And he guessed that Freddie and her father would probably die than betray Anna.

Trembling all over inside, Anna followed the guard along the bleak corridor. She looked around her. Was there any way out? Could she attack the guard and escape? He was a big man, with a gun and a baton. And she was wearing handcuffs. It was hopeless. She fought to stop crying about what was going to happen to her. Wiping the tears running from her nose, she would try to show them she was not afraid.

Turning the corner, she saw her father and Freddie waiting in the entrance. Brusquely, the guard took off her handcuffs, and disappeared down the corridor. Overwhelmed, she stumbled forward and fell into her father's arms.

Carl gave her a huge hug. She glanced at Freddie, her eyes full of tears.

'Let's go, quickly,' Freddie said. 'Before they change their minds.'

Outside, the explosion of relief hit her like an earthquake. As she began to fall, they both held onto her, feeling the shudders run through her body. When she could stand again, still holding her, they took her to Freddie's car.

Finally, when they were in the car, she was at last able to speak. 'Jose is alive,' repeating what Luis had said. 'He's with Fidel in the mountains.'

Carl and Freddie glanced at each other. On their way to the police headquarters, they had both seen the newspaper placard attached to a lamppost. It read 'Fidel Castro Dead.'

Neither one wanted to tell Anna that.

CHAPTER SEVENTY-THREE

The afterglow of the setting sun turned the ocean to purple, as Hans drove Bella along the Malecon to view their new nightclub. He looked at her. The luminous sky above them bathed her elegant profile. She looked at him, smiled and squeezed his thigh.

'Happy, my darling?'

'Ecstatic,' he said.

He was amazed and surprised at what Bella had managed to organise on his behalf. He was not in the Mafia, and they normally kept a tight rein about who ran hotels, casinos and nightclubs in Havana. But trading on her late husband's impeccable reputation with the Mob, she had arranged for them both to manage a small nightclub in the centre of the Old City.

'I don't like you selling arms, Hans,' she had said when she told him her news. 'It's too dangerous. Okay, Castro may be dead, but there are still people out there who want to get rid of Batista. He's not going to love someone who sells them weapons.'

After watching Giorgio run the casino, Hans had a good idea about running a nightclub. It was a very exciting prospect. Okay, so he wasn't going to get Frank Sinatra to perform there, but there many talented Cubans who could bring in an audience. Singers, dancers, musicians. The city was full of them. It was the atmosphere that really mattered.

'I think we want glamorous sleaze,' he told Bella, as they walked around the empty club. 'Dark, mysterious, sexy. Like the nightclubs in Germany in the Thirties.'

Giorgio had been an avid reader, often reading late into the night, while Hans slept. Shortly before he died, he had started a new book, 'Goodbye to Berlin'.

'Hey, you should read this,' he said to Hans when they were lying in bed. 'It's about Germany when you were a kid.'

Hans had never really tried to read English well, so Giorgio read it to him. They both particularly liked the story of the racy night-club singer, and her sleazy surroundings.

'But your idol, The Fuhrer, closed them all down,' said Bella.

'That's just what Giorgio used to say. I was just young and stupid then, Bella.'

'But sexy. You had a sort of shy arrogance.'

'I wish Giorgio was here now. We'd take this club right to the top.'

'We're not trying to compete with the Tropicana, Hans. The Mob wouldn't like that...And if Giorgio was here, well, we wouldn't be together, would we?'

'Yeah. Strange how something wonderful can come out of a tragedy,' he said.

As tears welled in her eyes, at the thought of her son, he took her in his arms,

'Let's make it wonderful for him, Bella. We'll call it Giorgio's.'

Anna kept to her old room at the Mueller's all the next day.

She tried to sleep, trying to forget the last few days. But sleep wouldn't come. The news of Castro's death made her believe that Jose must have suffered the same fate. Her lover was surely dead as well.

It now seemed all over. Maybe it had all been just a dream. A fantasy. Hitler and his Nazis had been defeated by a huge Allied army. Yet Castro had expected to beat Batista with a tiny group of rebels. When she thought about it now, how did they think they could take on Batista's well-trained army and his ruthless police force?

Her father had told her it was Freddie who heard she was captured, and had helped to arrange her release. She was surprised in some ways he had bothered. The attack was just pure madness, he would have said. And he was right.

Did Freddie still love her, as he seemed to have shown when they met paying their respects at Eddie Chiblás bier at the University? That was ages ago. But there was something in his expression, his eyes, when she hugged her father at the prison... She just wished she had hugged him too.

There was a knock at the door.

She sat up in the bed. 'Come in.'

Her father entered holding a newspaper. 'You ought to read this, Anna.'

She took the newspaper. On the front page, there was a picture of Castro, very much alive, with some of the rebels, surrounded by soldiers.

'That was yesterday. Castro isn't dead,' said Carl. 'They were captured in the mountains.'

Anna scoured the slightly blurred picture for the other faces, but Jose wasn't there.

'Jose isn't there.'

'No. It says there was a fight, before they were captured, apparently.'

'I need to know about Jose!' she said. 'I need to know, Papa!'

CHAPTER SEVENTY-FOUR

'A nightclub?' said Esther. She looked at the drawing that Hans had given her. It was a flamboyant sketch of just one word, 'Giorgio's'

As soon as Bella and he had finished viewing the club, Hans had insisted he drove to the Mueller's to tell his mother about the new venture.

'I don't know if Mama knows how I make a living.'

'Selling drugs and weapons?'

'Yeh. She's never mentioned anything, but maybe Anna and Papa might have mentioned it. She could know.'

'And you don't think she approve?'

'No, I don't think so.'

'Well, she's the same as me then.'

'Giorgio sold drugs.'

'But he didn't sell arms. That's much more dangerous.'

Hans honked his horn and served to avoid a group of children playing football in the road. The nightclub was in a poor area of the city, that was gradually turning into the 'go-to' place for exotic nightlife. He wanted their club to be the jewel.

'But drugs killed him,' said Hans. 'And we take them, Bella'

'As a recreation. Just for fun,' Bella insisted. 'It's not a habit. An addiction...' She blew her nose. 'I should have talked to him more.'

'It's not your fault, Bella. Giorgio was Giorgio!'

When they arrived, Carlotta took them into lounge and went to make them coffee. They had finished their drinks before Esther appeared. She sat in her usual chair, where she often watched Nino when he was working in the garden. Not that she would tell anyone, but her eyesight was not as good as it was, so she was holding Hans drawing out at arms' length.

'Giorgio's? That was your friend?' she said.

'Yes.'

'And my son,' Bella added.

'Of course, yes.'

'It will be in neon, of course,' said Hans.

'Multi-coloured, like Giorgio,' said Bella.

Esther gave the drawing back to Hans. 'It sounds very exciting, Hans. When is it going to open?'

'In a couple of weeks or so. We have to decorate. And get some entertainers. Singers, dancers.'

'Wonderful,' Esther exclaimed. 'It sounds wonderful, Hans!'

'We're going to have a grand opening night,' Hans said.

'Oh, wonderful! Can I come? I'd love to come.'

'You will be the belle of the ball, Esther,' Bella said.

'What? Really? How?'

'Yes,' said Hans. 'We are going to ask you to open the nightclub, Mama!'

Esther cried out in pleasure. 'Oh, Hans! Hans!' She threw out her arms to him. He leant down and hugged her.

Ramos shifted in his seat. He took the gun from his holster and laid it on the desk. 'I know you lied to protect her.'

Freddie looked across the desk to Ramos. The gun barrel pointing straight at him didn't make him feel any easier. Ramos had kept him waiting again in the cramped reception of the headquarters, which was busy with police bringing in prisoners. The failed attack at the barracks had galvanised Ramos's men, and they were plucking up as many people as they liked from all over the city. As he sat in the crowded reception, Freddie was thinking maybe this wasn't the time to go asking about the fate of one of the attackers?

But Carl had called him to see if he could find out about Jose.

'It's for Anna, of course,' Carl explained. 'Jose wasn't in the photo in the newspaper, but she knows he was with Castro in the mountains. There was a fight and she thinks maybe... maybe...'

'He was killed?'

'Yes. She's very worried. Well, distraught, really.'

'I'm sorry about that, but I don't know how I can help, Carl.'

'I'm asking for Anna. She asked me to ask you.'

'Anna did?'

'Yes.'

'She mentioned me?'

'She said you knew people. People in the police. She thought, maybe, you could ask around.'

Freddie drew on his cigarette. 'Anna asked you to ask me to go to police and ask about one of the rebels?'

'Mmm...Yes, put like that, Freddie, it does seem like a bit of a tall order,' Carl conceded.

'The rumour has it that they are still assassinating people, Carl.'

Carl sighed. 'I'm sorry I mentioned it, Freddie. It was foolish, of course. I should have thought. But she is so worried. She didn't want to go herself, after what happened when she was arrested. She's sure one of her 'friends' was tortured to death. She says she heard it.'

So, Anna thinks that he, Freddie, could just go to the police and ask about Jose? A rebel who took part in the attack. She wanted him, who had threatened him, and had rejected and ignored him since he kissed her hand, to go and find out about her lover? What a damned utter cheek!

'Okay. I'll do it,' he said to Carl.

'Really? Are you sure, Freddie?'

'I said I'll do it, Carl!'

And there he was, with the gun pointing straight at his heart.

'Anna wasn't in the attack, Ramos.'

'But she was there? In Santiago?'

Freddie looked away. He wasn't going to answer that. 'She has a...a lover. Jose Santana. She knows he was with Castro in the mountains, after the attack. She just wants to know if he is still alive.'

'Her lover?'

'Yes.'

'She asked you to come here to find out about a rebel, who just tried to overthrow our president?'

There was no way of knowing how this was going to go, thought Freddie. 'Yes, well. I told her that you and I are...very good friends.'

Ramos stroked the handle of the gun. He smiled at Freddie. 'I did warn you about getting mixed up with her, didn't I?'

CHAPTER SEVENTY-FIVE

Hans and Bella had invited Havana's top people for the opening of 'Giorgio's', as well as the regulars of the city's night-life scene. President Batista had declined, but had wished the couple well in their new venture.

'I knew he wouldn't come,' Bella told Hans. 'It's all too lowbrow for him, but he'll be pleased to have been invited.'

The couple had transformed the club with a Thirties theme. It was dark, with tables softly-lit to focus on the stage, where a troupe of semi-naked dancers, a rhumba quartet, and female singer began the evening.

Hans was sorry his father didn't come. Esther assured him she had asked him.

'He said, "I have never been in a nightclub",' she said to Hans. '"And I shan't be going to this one." I said, "But it's your son's nightclub! He asked me to open it. You must go!"...But he refused, Hans. I'm so sorry.'

It actually suited Esther perfectly. Her husband looked like an old man nowadays. She needed to be with someone dashing, smooth, like a film-star. Nico was exactly that. Apart from Giorgio's wake, she had not been seen in public since she was shunned many years ago by Isabel Gonzales and her set. She wished Isabel had come tonight. Now she was going to be the belle of the ball when she went on stage to announce the opening of her son's nightclub.

After much begging, Hans had finally persuaded Anna to come. He had wanted his family to see him in a new light, as a proper businessman. Not someone always living outside the law.

Nightclubs weren't Anna's scene, but she wanted to keep contact with Hans. No-one knew what would happen now Castro was in prison. Would he organise a rebellion from inside? It seemed unlikely. But whatever happened, she wanted to replace the gun she had thrown away on the night of the attack. Despite the crackdown that Batista had imposed, the city was still dangerously volatile. It was wise to be prepared.

She was sitting, uncomfortably, with her mother, Hans, Bella and Nico, at a front table. Hans looked around the crowded room, then glanced at the band and nodded. They began to play a rousing introduction.

'Are you ready?' Hans asked his mother.

Esther picked up her full champagne glass. 'You must come on stage with me, Nico,' said Esther.

'No, no,' he said. 'It is your night, Esther. It's your night.'

As Hans, Bella and Esther left to prepare for the opening announcement, Freddie suddenly appeared beside Anna. He nodded to Nico, then turned to Anna.

'Hello, Anna.'

She gave Freddie a weak smile.

Freddie sat down beside her, and said softly, 'I'm sorry I couldn't find out about Jose. I did try.'

'It's alright. I found out. He's alive, in prison with Castro and the rest.'

'Oh. That's good, isn't it...? Is he alright?,' he added.

'I think so.'

'You must be very relieved.'

'Yes...'

'At least they'll get a trial. Not like some of the others. Just butchered and assassinated.'

She turned to him. 'Thank you for trying, Freddie...I shouldn't have asked you, really. It was wrong for...for several reasons.'

'That's alright.' He gave a half laugh, and said more loudly. 'But I think the Secret Police see me as one of the rebels now.'

Above the sound of the band, Nico had been listening to them. He looked away, as the stage filled with a light. With

Hans and Bella on either side, Esther stepped into the spotlight. The belle of the ball again.

CHAPTER SEVENTY-SIX

Carl was sitting on the trunk of a fallen tree with Freddie, watching Klaus collecting shells far away on the shoreline. The young man was carrying a metal bucket to put the shells in. He had been an avid collector since Freddie had introduced him to the hobby. Klaus drew shells beautifully, but he would never make a living as an illustrator, Carl thought. Really still only a child, he would only draw when he wanted and only drew what he wanted to draw. A great talent wasted.

Despite the cool refreshing breeze from the ocean, Carl felt weary and old. Something deep inside him felt wrong. He sighed.

'That came from a long way down, Carl,' said Freddie.

'Yes...It's my birthday tomorrow.'

Freddie got up from the tree and stretched. 'Are you having a party?'

Carl attempted a smile. 'At my age?'

'Why not? Do the family know? Esther, Anna?'

'I doubt it. They're too much involved in their own lives.'

'Well, you should tell them. I'll bring you a present tomorrow.'

'No, please...Don't...Before the war in Europe, I was quite well-known. A distinguished professor. I liked being that. Just vanity, I suppose.'

'Why not? You deserved it.'

'And now...All I do is help you at your clinics.'

'For which I am very grateful, Carl.'

'My marriage is over. My wife has a young lover, who she sleeps with in my house. My own son got rich being a drug dealer and selling arms –'

'Ah, but he runs a nightclub now.'

'And my daughter...seems intent in getting herself killed for some political ideal...That's the story of my life, Freddie...Not what I intended it to be.'

Freddie lit a cigarette, and blew the smoke into the breeze. He hadn't seen Anna since the opening night of Giorgio's. 'How is she? Jose got ten years, didn't he?'

'Yes. She was very depressed at first. She was just very tired, lethargic. For the first week or two, she didn't get up until noon most days.'

'I'm not surprised.'

'But you know Anna. Now, she's helping organising an amnesty campaign.'

'She thinks Batista will give amnesty to people who tried to overthrow him?'

'That's what she's doing, Freddie. And she's going round criticising Batista and preaching the revolution to anyone who will hear. It's madness, Freddie.'

'She still believes? After what happened?'

'I think Castro's been sending secret messages about keeping up the propaganda against Batista. But, somehow, I don't think he will be able to organise a revolution, while he's spending the next fifteen years in prison.'

'But Anna believes he will?'

'And that's what scares me, Freddie.'

With American tourists flooding the island, Giorgio's nightclub was doing well. Hans was very pleased, happy not to be breaking the law every day of his life. Being top dog in drugs and weapons on the island was thrilling for a while, but you never knew when the police would turn on you. Under Batista's regime the police had become a law onto themselves, arresting, and apparently torturing, people at will.

Though Castro's 'revolution' had been quashed, there was still real hostility in the air. Some people on the island were doing very well, but the poor workers weren't. Knowing that some of the guns he had sold had been used in the attack on the barracks, he no longer wanted to be weapons supplier to a rebel army. The police wouldn't like that. As he promised Bella, he had quit.

He was sitting at the back of the club, watching Bella rehearse the dancers in a new routine.

'I didn't know you were a choreographer,' he had said to her.

'I was dancing in a club when I met Tony.'

'You must have been very young.'

'Started when I was twelve. I've always wanted to run a dance troupe.'

And she seemed to be good at it. Particularly with some of the young men. They were all in their teens, the way that Bella liked men, but knowing that most male dancers were queer, Hans wasn't really worried.

He turned as someone entered the room behind him. It was Anna. She came and sat beside him.

'I saw your car outside,' she said quietly.

'What are you doing here?' He grinned. 'I've heard you singing, so it can't be for an audition.'

She leaned closer. 'I had to throw my gun away, after the attack. On Moncada...'

He looked at her.

'You knew I was there?' she said.

'It figured.'

'There were roadblocks on the way back to Havana. So, I had to ditch it.'

'Good thing. Guns can be very dangerous.'

'I need another one. A handgun. Like the one you gave me.'

'Why?' He joked, 'Are you going to kill Batista?'

'For protection.'

'Look, Anna. Just get out of politics. Please. Your guys lost. They will be in prison for years. Don't throw your life away as well.'

'Just a handgun, that's all. Just one.'

'I told Bella I quit.'

'I'm not stopping, Hans. Armed or unarmed, I'm going on...So, Hans, please?'

CHAPTER SEVENTY-SEVEN

The demonstration right in front of the Presidential Palace was huge, noisy, and peaceful. But President Batista wasn't there to see or hear it. Warned about the protest, he had gone to his luxurious estate outside of the city. The amnesty campaign, which Anna had helped to start some months ago, seemed unstoppable. Could the president just ignore it?

Freddie stood at the fringe of the crowd. He couldn't believe that the campaign would win, though it had been going on for weeks now, and was growing all the time. Even the press was campaigning for an amnesty for the political prisoners who attacked Moncada. But surely the president wouldn't free Castro, who was becoming an idol in some peoples' eyes, after just a few months in prison? That would be incredible. Could people power influence a dictator? It didn't seem likely.

Anna would be at the front of the demonstration, Freddie guessed, leading the chants.

'Free our sons! Free our husbands! Free Cuba!' the crowd were shouting, over and over.

'Free my lover!', thought Freddie. He laughed, cynically. It was hard being an older man in love with a beautiful young woman, who was in love with somebody else. He'd resigned himself to the realisation that his feelings were hopeless. But that didn't stop him waking up in the dead of night thinking about her, holding her, making love.

He felt the need to see her, if only from a distance. He knew he couldn't protect her. Not at all. She was involved in a deadly political game, with dangerous enemies. All he could do was watch, and hope for the best.

One of the enemies was Ramos. He was standing with his troops, nearby, waiting for trouble to start, so they could wade in and break heads.

Thankfully the demonstration broke up, peacefully for once, with people going their different ways. Freddie saw Anna coming towards him, with a small group of protestors.

Seeing him, she looked surprised. 'Freddie! What are you doing here?'

Freddie laughed. 'Well, Ramos, thinks I'm a rebel now, so I don't want to disappoint him.'

'Do you think we will win? The amnesty?' said Anna.

'If I was Batista, I wouldn't let Castro leave his cell for the next fifteen years.'

'I'm very worried about Jose, Freddie.'

Like the rest of the Moncada attackers, Jose had been put in prison on the Island of Pines, fifty miles south of the mainland.

'Oh?'

'He was injured and was in the prison hospital. We exchanged letters at the start, but a few weeks ago, he stopped replying. I called the prison and they said he wasn't there. But he was! I don't know what's happened to him.'

'Just an administrative cock-up, I imagine.'

'I'm worried. I've heard some awful stories.'

'I'm sure it will be okay, Anna. I hope so.'

'Is there anyway...You could...?'

Freddie shook his head. 'I'm sorry, Anna. I don't have any contacts there.' He smiled.Seeing Ramos was watching, Freddie gave him a wave. Ramos turned away. 'I think Ramos thinks I'm leading the revolution anyway, by the back door. So...'

Anna saw the rest of the group waiting for her.

'I'd better go,' she said.

'Good luck, Anna. With everything.'

She joined her friends, and they walked away chattering animatedly.

Freddie watched her go, admiring the swaying movement of her hips, the long shapely legs, the slender ankles. Damn her! He could go and find a local whore, or take his fantasy home with him. Perhaps he would do both.

Hans sniffed the two lines of coke from the patio table beside the pool, then rubbed the rest of the powder into his gums. He was irritated. No, more than that. He was getting angry. The coke wouldn't help, but he needed the boost if he was going to confront Bella. Her Corvette had just roared into the drive.

Hearing the sound of her high heels echoing on the marble floor of the villa, he stood up. Sitting down felt too casual for what he wanted to say.

'Darling!' she called.

'Here!' he said.

Bella came out into the mid-afternoon sun, looking fresh and radiant. Wearing flowing slacks and a bright halter-top, she looked as good as when Hans first met her. Now in her mid-forties, swimming regular lengths in the pool and vigorous workouts with Nico in the gym, had kept her voluptuous figure beautifully toned. Hans desired and was annoyed with her, at the same time.

She came and kissed him on the cheek. Her rich perfume enveloped him.

'You look a little tense,' she said.

Hans moved away. 'Bella, this is third time I have eaten lunch on my own this week. And last week, as well.'

Since they opened Giorgio's, they were there every night, often until dawn. Usually, Bella and he slept late, and then had breakfast as their lunch. But since she had decided to become the club's choreographer, she had been getting up mid-morning, leaving asleep Hans in bed.

'I am rehearsing the dancers, Hans.'

'Every day? Until this time?'

'It's a new routine.'

'You rehearse dressed like that?'

'I have a shower and change. I want to look good for you, when I get back.' She went to the table and took a drink from his glass. 'You don't want me coming back sweaty and scruffy, do you? Or is that your thing?'

'I would just like you to be here, some time.'

Bella went into the kitchen, opened the fridge and took out a jug of orange juice. Taking a glass she filled it, and went out to Hans on the terrace.

'The troupe need a lot of work, Hans. They're young. Some of them have never been trained.'

'At what?'

Bella stared at him. 'What?'

The sunlight glinting off the pool blinded him for a moment. He had not intended to say it like that.

'What?' Bella repeated. 'Are you saying I'm fucking one of them. Or all of them?'

'Are you?'

'Hans, do we need to go into this? Please?' She went up to him and put her arm around his waist. 'We could have a drink, and go to bed.'

'I don't do seconds.'

Bella moved away. She turned to him and said calmly, 'Yes, I am fucking one of them. He's young. You know I like that. You were almost a teenager when I screwed you.'

'So, that's me out of here then, is it?'

'Why…? Do you want to leave?'

'No, of course not! I love you, Bella!'

'I love you to. But sex isn't love, Hans. You know that. Giorgio taught you that, didn't he?'

'But…I feel…' He didn't want to say the word jealous. That would make him seem weak.

'Look, if it bothers you, Hans, I won't do it...' She looked at him, then smiled, wickedly. 'Or we could have a threesome. Like you used to do with Giorgio.'

CHAPTER SEVENTY-EIGHT

The amnesty campaign for the Moncada rebels, spearheaded by the mothers of the prisoners, proved overwhelming. Surprisingly, Batista had signed the amnesty bill "in honour of Mother's Day". A week later several hundred people, relatives and friends, were at the harbour, watching the ferry from the Island of Pines arrive with the freed rebels.

Anna was there, though she didn't know whether Jose would be amongst the ex-prisoners because, during the last few months, she had not been able to contact him in prison.

Fidel Castro appeared first. He was handed a large Cuban flag and hoisted on the shoulders of his admirers, as the crowd broke into the national anthem.

With the crowd flocking around the arrivals it was difficult for Anna to see if Jose was there. She couldn't see him among the jostling heads. Her heart sank. What had happened to him?

Then, as the triumphant procession moved on, she saw a lone figure, limping with a stick, at the back of the crowd. She struggled through the throng and threw her arms around him.

'Jose! Jose!!' she cried. 'Oh god, you're here!'

They hugged each other, kissed, then followed after the others.

'What happened to your leg?' she said.

'I got beaten. Put in solitary.'

'That's why I couldn't contact you.'

'Yeah,' he said. 'I guess. I didn't get any letters.'

'I am so relieved, Jose. I didn't know what to think. I was so worried.'

He smiled. 'Well, I'm here now, Anna...'

'And the battle goes on?'

'Yes. Fidel talked to us all on the boat. He's forming the group. It's going to be called The 26th of July Movement. To celebrate the attack. Yes, Anna, the battle goes on.'

Esther sat expectantly. She was having afternoon coffee, alone. Normally, she had it in her room, but on the days that Nico was tending the garden she liked to watch from the lounge. Generally, he wore shorts and nothing else. It excited her, knowing his body would be hers, later.

Carlotta had just brought the coffee and Esther's favourite pastelitos, when the phone rang beside her.

It was Nico.

'Nico, you're late.'

His voice sounded rough. 'I have fever. A cold.'

'Aren't you coming?' she asked.

'No. Not today. Tomorrow, if I'm okay.'

Esther tried to stop her irritation showing. 'I was looking forward to...seeing you.'

'Tomorrow. I make it better for you.'

'You'd better, Nico.'

She put down the phone, annoyed. Taking the biggest pastelito, she took a large bite.

Hearing the front door opened, she took another bite.

Carl entered the lounge. 'Good afternoon, my dear. Do you know if Anna is back yet?' he said.

'No. She'll be out all evening, I expect, celebrating with her fellow rebels.' She stuffed the rest of the pastry into her mouth.

Carl turned to leave, not wanting to hear any more of his wife's views on their daughter.

'Eighteen months!' she said, loudly, with her mouth full. 'That's all they served. How ridiculous! They tried to bring down the president and he lets them go!'

'I didn't think you were interested in politics,' said Carl.

'Nico served under Batista in the army, when he was younger. He said he was a great commander.'

'Oh, really?'

They heard the front door open again.

'Hello!' shouted Anna. 'Papa!'

'In here, Anna!' Carl called.

Anna entered the lounge, beaming. She stepped aside as Jose entered behind her. He gave them a nervous smile.

'Jose?' said Carl. 'Wonderful!'

'It is!' said Anna. 'He was there with the rest of them. He's been hurt. I said he can stay here until he finds a place to live. He can have Hans room, can't he?'

'Of course,' Carl said.

'Thank you, Professor Mueller,' Jose said.

'Come on,' Anna said. 'I'll show you your room.'

Esther rounded on Carl, when Anna and Jose left.

'You didn't ask me about it! I do not want a criminal in this house!' she snapped.

'Jose did just the same as Anna did. But he got caught. Shall I throw her out as well?'

She scowled and got up to leave. 'You can as far as I'm concerned!'

On his own, Carl looked out at that garden that Nico kept so immaculate. He should tell Anna about Nico's allegiance to Batista. With Jose staying there, it was something they both needed to know.

CHAPTER SEVENTY-NINE

Hans rolled over and got out of the bed. Bella, lying stretched out beside him, didn't notice. Putting on his silk robe, he walked out of the bedroom. Downstairs, he poured a drink and went out to the darkened patio. It was a clear, moonless night. It would be dawn soon, but the still clear water of the pool reflected the countless stars above. Looking up into space, he wondered how many lives were going on there, millions of miles away? Were they looking at him? And what did they see?

Laying on a lounger, he tried not to listen to the sounds from the bedroom. He had reluctantly gone along with Bella's idea of threesome and, when it happened, he immediately felt he was in a competition. The guy she chose a young black dancer. He was fitter, stronger, and had much more stamina than he had. Bella really enjoyed stamina. Hans had wondered what watching her with another man would make him feel. It didn't turn him on at all. He just felt envious and jealous.

He took a long drink, and tried to think about the nightclub. That was doing very well. They were talking of renting the place next door to double the space.

'I'm an entrepreneur,' he said to the dark universe. 'I used to sell drugs and weapons. Now I own a successful nightclub in the Las Vegas of the Caribbean.'

Not like the boy in the bedroom. His dance career would be short, and then what? A gigolo? There were plenty of those on the island for the rich American widows.

Some people may think that he was, a gigolo, living in Bella's luxury villa. But he and Bella loved each other. And he wanted to keep it that way. No more threesomes from now on.

They were sitting on their favourite dead tree-trunk on the beach, watching Klaus skimming stones over the calm blue waves.

'He's getting very good at that,' said Freddie.

Carl sighed. 'He can be brilliant at a few things. But...'

'He seems happy, Carl.'

'A child's happiness.'

'Some say that's the best.'

'Was yours? The happiest?'

Freddie buried his cigarette butt in the sand. 'Until I was sent to a gloomy English public school, hardly speaking any English.'

'Still, you did well there, didn't you?'

'Yes.' He put on an upper-class English accent. 'Top of the class, old boy!'

They smiled. It was better to stop there, they both thought.

Freddie looked at Carl. He knew Carl was about twenty years older than him, but he seemed older than that recently. His fine cheeks were lined and sunken, like a frail old man. To Freddie, the doctor, he looked like someone not well.

'Are you okay, Carl?'

Carl glanced at him, then looked away. 'Fine. Yes, fine.'

'You're not ill, or anything?'

'No.'

'You would tell me, if there was anything?'

'Of course.' How was it that he, Carl, who didn't smoke, was coughing up blood, while chain-smoking Freddie looked fit and healthy? As if to prove the point, Freddie lit another cigarette.

'I'm just worried about Anna, Freddie. She and Jose are still involved with Castro's mob. The whole situation is just getting worse.'

Freddie blew out smoke and nodded. Violence had spread the last few weeks. There were frequent clashes with the police and students. Arsons attacks and shootings were common. Walking the city for some had become a dangerous pastime. Havana was an exciting city, but some of the American tourists were getting jumpy.

'If Batista thought that the amnesty would bring peace to the island, he was very wrong,' said Freddie.

'What's going to happen, Freddie? Not to me, I'm near the end of my life but...to my children?'

Anna and Hans were grown up, living their own lives. It was Klaus that Carl was thinking of, thought Freddie.

'If I'm still around, Carl – '

The air around them suddenly spilt with a deafening crack. It came from the city. Klaus stopped, a stone in his hand. He looked at them. Carl waved to him to come.

'What was that?' the boy asked, as he came to them.

'Just another bomb,' said Freddie, casually. 'But we're safe here, Klaus.' He looked at Carl and then back at his son. 'You'll always be safe.'

CHAPTER EIGHTY

In the middle of August even the air under the sparse trees of the huge Colon Cemetery was a furnace. Despite the heat, every year at the anniversary of Eddie Chiblás death many people filed past his grave to honour his life.

Among the crowd were Anna and Jose, secretly distributing leaflets of Castro's 'Manifesto to the People of Cuba.' Castro, having been censored on the radio and the press, and fearing assassination, had left Cuba for Mexico. His manifesto had been smuggled onto the island to the newly-formed members of the underground Movement of July 26th, in time for the annual homage to Chiblás.

Anna had agreed to help printing and handing out some of the fifty thousand leaflets Castro had requested.

'Jose, the revolution will only happen with the support of the people,' Anna said, when Jose had at first seemed reluctant to be involved. She knew he feared being taken back to prison, after what happened to him the first time. His injured leg had never really healed. Walking a long distance was still painful.

'I mean your people,' Anna continued. 'Not the middle-class. They're happy with things as they are.'

Jose knew that was true. As the middle-class got richer, the poor of the island were getting poorer. Under Batista corruption was again rampant. Unemployment was growing, wages of the workers were being cut. Jose's family, who were cane-cutters on the plantation, were struggling. He was doing his best to help them. Any way he could.

When Anna first joined the Orthodoxo Party, years ago, she bought a small mimeograph machine to print propaganda leaflets. It was in the attic where Anna and her brothers used to play when they were children.

'We can't print the leaflets here,' said Jose. 'They will hear us. You know what your father said about Nico. If he finds out, he could report it.'

'We'll do it when he's not around.'

Jose finally agreed. But, before they left for the cemetery, he insisted that they put the machine away behind the secret panel that Anna and Hans had found in the attic, when they first moved into the house.

'The police are raiding lots of houses,' he said. 'If they know I'm living here, we don't want to leave any trace.'

Mary Price, the Mueller's English nanny in London, was persuaded to go to Germany with the family as all the children adored her. But when the Professor decided they could no longer stay in Nazi Germany, Mary thought of returning to England, but the Professor begged her to stay with family. He said that Klaus needed her, and would be totally distressed if she left. He promised they would all get visas for America where life was so much better than in Europe, which was headed for war. Having no parents, or close relatives in England, and the fact that she loved poor little Klaus more than anyone else in the world, Mary boarded the 's.s. St Louis' with the Mueller's.

Though Klaus still thought like a child, he could now look after himself, and her job was really redundant. But she knew she couldn't survive in Cuba by herself, so she was very grateful that the Mueller's kept her on. She ate on her own, though sometimes Klaus joined her and played games with her afterwards. But generally, she lived alone. Though she had lived in the same house for many years with the cook, Carlotta, she didn't have anything in common with her. As a child she had been brought up to believe that black people had smaller brains than white people. So, she never spoke to Carlotta, except to thank her for the meals.

Even though the fans were on in her room, the heat in the house was oppressive and Mrs Price had fallen asleep over her embroidery. She was woken by an angry knocking on the door. The doorbell rang repeated.

She got up and opened her door as Carlotta opened the front door. Several policemen pushed past Carlotta, and went straight up the two flights of stairs that led to the attic.

Esther came out of her room, drowsily.

'What on earth is going on?'

'It's the police,' said Carlotta.

'The police! Is my husband here?'

'No,' said Mrs Price. 'The professor left about an hour ago, Mrs Mueller.'

The three women waited, feeling helpless and uneasy.

'I wish Nico was here,' Esther said. 'He would deal with them. How dare they come into my house!'

After a few minutes the police came down the stairs, empty-handed. Without a word, they left, leaving the front door open.

'How dare they!' repeated Esther. 'This is Anna's fault! She has to go! Both of them! They have to go.'

Ramos remembered Freddie's fiery, young friend. The girl who knocked his hat off as he helped carry her from the ship, who tried to take his gun at the demonstration. He guessed that Freddie fancied her. She was arrogantly attractive, with her thick black hair and dark piercing, intelligent eyes, which were staring at him.

Taking his gun from his holster, he put it on his desk between them. He liked that the weapon showed who was the boss in such situations.

Anna sat opposite him. His office was spartan. Two chairs, an empty desk. No filing cabinet. Obviously, not a man for paperwork. He leant back, his head framed by a large picture of President Batista hanging on the wall behind him. Since she had been led in by a policeman, Ramos had said nothing to her.

'Senor,' she said after a minute, 'why am I here? Your men raided our house. They found nothing. So, why are you questioning me and Jose, now?'

He opened a drawer in the desk, and threw a copy of Castro's manifesto in front of her. 'You've seen this?'

She recognised it immediately. 'Of course. Practically everyone in the city has seen it.'

Reaching forward, he picked up the pamphlet. 'This is illegal. It's about overthrowing the president.'

'Have you read it? It has some very good ideas in it. About restoring democracy and social justice.'

'So, senorita, you're saying you agree with this? You are part of Castro's gangsters?'

'No. But if I was, you wouldn't expect me to tell you that.'

Ramos toyed with the gun, running his finger down the ribbed metal grip. 'I could have you, er...interrogated more thoroughly.'

When they arrested her, she had expected to be interviewed in a cell like before. She tried to block out the memory of Luis's agonising screams, before he died. No way was she going to show Ramos how terrified she was. She continued to stare at him.

'You could. Apparently, the police can do whatever they want. So much for 'social justice'.'

He waved the pamphlet at her. 'We heard you were printing this. In the attic in your house.'

'Really? Who told you that nonsense?'

Ramos inclined his head and said nothing.

Anna was happy that Jose had decided to hide the mimeograph machine, before they took the leaflets to the cemetery.

'Whoever told you that was wrong,' she said. 'Or they lied... As you probably know, I am a lawyer. I work in our courts. You found nothing at my house. You have no evidence against me. You have no reason at all to question me at all.'

He looked at her. Lawyer or not, he could have her questioned till she begged for mercy. That would be enjoyable to watch.

Shrugging, Ramos stood up. Picking up the gun, he slipped it into his holster. 'Next time when we catch you, senorita, I promise you, the questioning will be much more...shall we say, robust.'

CHAPTER EIGHTY-ONE

Carl had called round to see Freddie, as he had asked him to on the phone.

'He's dead. Shot twice in the chest and once in the head,' said Freddie.

'What? Really?' Carl exclaimed. 'Was it a robbery?'

'His wallet was missing, but from the rumours, it looks more like an assassination.'

"An assassination?'

'He was taken into a back alley at gunpoint, apparently.'

'Who by?'

'It was dark. They didn't see. It was just one man, they think.'

Carl shook his head. 'Who would want to kill Nico?'

Freddie shrugged, and poured out coffee for them both.

'I don't think he was interested in politics,' said Carl. 'I think he supported Batista, but...'

'He was in Batista's army in the 30's. Maybe someone thought he was a police spy? There's a lot of them about.'

Carl sipped the coffee, and savoured it in his mouth. Freddie was right, he probably did make the best coffee in the city.

Freddie lit a cigarette. Carl blew away the smoke and coughed. He wiped his mouth with his handkerchief, and then put it away quickly in his pocket, but not before Freddie saw the trace of blood on the cotton.

'Yes, I know. The police raided our house, last week,' Carl continued.

'You said.'

'They didn't find anything, thank God. But Anna and Jose were very upset. I'm pretty sure they had been printing leaflets. Upstairs in the attic.'

'Probably Castro's manifesto. I've seen some around. Have you read it?'

'No.'

'He promises all kinds of things after the revolution. A real socialist programme. The sort of thing Anna would be involved in...Do you think Nico knew they were printing it?'

'I wouldn't have thought they did it while he was there.'

'What about Esther? Would she know?' Freddie asked.

'I don't know. She was furious about the police raid.' Carl gasped. 'Oh, my god, Esther!'

'That's why I wanted to tell you before you found out from anyone else...I don't what their relationship was like. How serious it was. But I thought it might be better if you told her.'

Carl took another sip of coffee. 'I don't know, Freddie...You know what she is like. She lives in a fantasy a lot of the time... She might not even believe me.'

Freddie stubbed out his cigarette, and wafted the remains of the smoke away. He reminded himself not to have another while Carl was around. 'How would she find out? Would the police come to tell her?'

'No. I don't think so, Freddie. Her and Nico are supposed to be a secret. I don't think the police would know.'

'Maybe it's better if Hans told her. It was Hans who introduced them, wasn't it?'

Hans put the phone down. He and Bella had already been told about Nico's killing by a friend at the nightclub, but the last thing he needed right now was to be told to go and tell his mother that her lover had been shot, dead.

He and Bella had both been shocked when they heard the news. But, at the moment, those things happened in the city. People got killed in Havana. Many of the killings were political, but robberies and drugs rivalries were also rife, especially in the Old City. And Nico spent a lot of time there.

'Poor Nico,' said Bella. 'Maybe it was drugs? He loved his Amps and his Angel Powder.'

Hans shook his head. He had promised Bella to give up dealing in drugs, as well as weapons, but Nico got his drugs from Hans, who he trusted.

Right now, it was Hans who needed reassurance. Last night he had decided to confront Bella about the threesomes. They had made love, passionately, with Hans doing everything he knew to please her.

Afterwards, Bella lay on her back and smiled.

'Thank you, Hans. That was...wonderful.'

'Thanks. You're so beautiful, Bella.'

He had sat up and lit a spliff for them to share. This was a good time, he thought. The best time. But how to begin? Without feeling...weak...jealous. Like a little boy asking his mother?

'Er...'

Bella sat up and took the spliff. Taking a deep drag, she held it in, let it out slowly and handed it back to Hans. 'Oh, Jerry wants to come over tonight.'

'Oh.'

'Okay?'

'Er, look...Bella...I'm not happy...I'm not happy about threesomes.'

Bella looked at him. 'Really?'

'I just think, we have such a great thing going on between us, Bella...'

'Exactly.'

'That...we...Well...'

Bella got out of bed and slipped on her silk robe. 'Okay, Hans. If you don't like it, fine. I'll stick to twosomes.'

He opened his mouth, but the words wouldn't come.

'You don't mind my little boys, do you?' She blew him a kiss and went into the bathroom.

Hans leant back dejectedly in bed. He was just fourteen when he left Germany, so he had never learnt the German for the expression. In Spanish he was el cornudo. The English had an ugly, stupid word for it, 'cuckold'.

CHAPTER EIGHTY-TWO

Esther had waited in the conservatory all week, growing more anxious and petulant with everyone else in the household.

Mrs Price, Carlotta and Klaus were keeping as far away from her as they could.

She had called the number Nico had given her every day, repeatedly, but the phone just kept ringing endlessly. Sitting waiting for her absent lover, she began to fantasise about what had happened. If he was ill he would have phoned, or sent a message. So why was he not coming to her?

Finally, unable to keep her frustration to herself, she hurried down the hall and burst into Carl's surgery at the front of the house.

'What have you done with Nico!' she demanded.

Carl was in the middle of examining the chest of one of his few wealthy patients, with his stethoscope.

'Esther, I am in the middle of a – '

'Have you threatened him? Have you warned him off?'

The patient began to hurriedly fasten up his shirt.

'Esther!' Carl turned to the patient. 'Excuse me, senor'. Bustling Esther out of the room into the hall, he shut the door behind them.

'Esther - '

'Have you threatened him? Is that it?'

'No.'

'I bet that's it! That's it! You're jealous!'

'Please, keep your voice down!'

Carl didn't know what to do. If he told her the truth, that Nico was dead, he wasn't prepared to see what her reaction would be to that.

'You don't want me to be happy, living in this awful place! Now you try to take away my only...my only joy!'

'I don't what's happened, Esther, I promise.'

'I don't believe you! He wouldn't just not come to see me!'

'Why don't you call Hans? He might know.'

The surgery door opened. The patient came out, headed straight for the front door and left.

'Now look what you've done!' Carl shouted. 'I've lost one of the few patients who pay me!'

Esther glared at him and then hurried back to the living room.

Carl went back into his surgery and slumped into his chair. He coughed. Taking out his handkerchief, he spat into it. The blood was thicker now.

Looking out of the window, he stared at but didn't see the vibrant, purple bougainvillea around the window frame. He had once been a distinguished medical professor in Europe. Now he was marooned on this island, treating the poor for nothing. His beloved daughter, Anna, was a revolutionary, being harassed by the police. His son, Hans, once sold drugs and weapons. Maybe still did. His youngest 'son', Klaus, would never be able to live on his own. He looked at the red-stained handkerchief. And he was dying.

The door burst open. Esther stood in the doorway and glared at him.

'You had him killed!' she screamed. 'You had Nico killed!'

CHAPTER EIGHTY-THREE

At Carl's insistence Anna and Jose left the Mueller's house after the police raid. They rented a small apartment in the Old Town, still determined to carry on with their campaign.

After Castro left Cuba for Mexico the political violence got worse in Havana. There were gun battles, bombs under cars, arson; mainly between the Far-Right groups and the Communists. Castro's demand was that instead of violence, the July 26th Movement should distribute his manifesto, far and wide, to win over people's minds.

On the night they left the Mueller's, they smuggled the mimeograph machine into Anna's little car and drove to their new apartment. Now, Jose was looking around for somewhere to store the bulky machine.

'Thank god you decided to hide it, Jose, before the police arrived.'

'You can't be too careful. The police spies are everywhere.'

'Mrs Price said they went straight up to the attic,' said Anna 'They didn't look anywhere else, apparently...Strange.'

'They obviously knew where to look...So, it can only have been Nico who told them.'

'He was never there when we were printing.'

'Your mother could easily have told him. She probably heard us.'

'And then he ends up dead...Coincidence...? Did you tell any of the others?' Anna added.

'In our group? No, I don't think so. Maybe he was reporting on others groups as well. And they found out.'

Anna nodded. That was possible. The rebel cells still liked to keep themselves to themselves, just in case they were brought in by the police for questioning. She knew there must be several more cells in the city, carrying out Castro's instructions.

She wandered with Jose around the little apartment, as Jose looked into the cupboards.

'We could perhaps build a little place in one of these,' he said.

'They say his money was stolen, but someone said it looked more like an assassination.'

'Really?' said Jose, uninterested.

'Just one man. From behind.'

'Could have been drugs, or whatever.' Jose knocked on the walls of the large cupboard.

'Mm. Where did you get your gun from, Jose?'

He stopped and looked at her.

'I saw it when you were packing.'

He shrugged. 'Where you got yours from. Your brother.' He went on knocking the walls.

'He told me he'd stopped selling.'

'I think he had. But he's just started supplying again. There's a big market out there.'

'Well, if Nico was working for the police, that's very good news for us, isn't it? I mean, no matter who shot him.'

Jose stopped knocking and looked at her. 'Very...Very good...Not for your mother though.' He went back to tapping the wall. 'I think there's space behind here.'

Hans stood at the bar watching the crowded, steamy dance floor of Giorgio's. The tourists loved the clubs' regular dance quartet, which was one of the most exciting and vibrant in the city. That was good. But he wasn't happy. Bella was dancing an improvised version of the tango with a tall, athletic American college boy. Hans felt humiliated. But this was Havana. You didn't have to care.

He saw Bella weaving her way over to him, with the college boy in tow. She leant towards him, so he could hear above the band. Her red, lush lips brushed his ear.

'Mike wants to swim in our pool. Can you lock up, Mein Fuhrer?'

'Please don't call me that!' Hans snapped.

'You might want to sleep in the spare room tonight.'

Blowing him a kiss, Bella disappeared into the swaying throng. Hans threaded his way through to the office at the back of the club. What he needed was a line of coke. He had cut back his drinking because it just made him more depressed and aggressive. After snorting two lines, he sat back in his expensive, leather office chair, and lit a cigarette.

He was jealous and resentful about Bella's regular young men, and he had decided to go back to dealing in weapons. He knew Bella would hate it if she knew, but dealing with guns made him feel big. Guns were real. Tangible. Lethal. Whenever he read about someone being killed in a political clash, he quoted to himself the words of the man who invented the atom bomb. 'I am become Death.' He didn't care about politics but, if they wanted to fight about it, he was proud to arm the conflicts in the divided city.

Life for ordinary people in Batista's dictatorship was becoming harder each day. Batista's government, propped up by the American companies who employed many of the island's workers, grew richer as unemployment grew. Police action, especially against workers who tried to organise strikes, was brutal. As uncontrolled soaring rents put people on the streets, political rivalries grew between the right and the left, which led to almost daily violent clashes.

But at dawn, as the first rays of the sun touched the cross at the top of the city's cathedral, below in the warren of Old Havana Hans counted the takings of the evening. Giorgio's nightclub was a great success. He and Bella had decided to rent the empty building next door, and doubled the size and glamour of the club. Bigger entertainers were being attracted. Profits kept rising.

Today, he was becoming 'Senor Death' again. Delivering a couple of automatics pistols to a young couple. Were they Left, or Right? He didn't know. Or care. Despite Bella's regular liaisons in bed, life could be worse.

CHAPTER EIGHTY-FOUR

Freddie wasn't surprised that it was a very small gathering for the funeral. Years ago, Nico had come from Tobago, a small island off Trinidad, well over a thousand miles from Cuba. Far too far for any of his relatives to travel. Even if anyone in Cuba knew how to contact them, which no-one did.

He watched Esther arrive in Hans' limousine. She emerged, veiled, swathed in black, with Bella by her side. Both dressed in black, they looked remarkably alike. Carl wasn't with her. It would be surprising if he were. Who goes to the funeral of your wife's lover? So, apart from Hans and a couple of Nico's friends from the Old Town, that was it. Sad to see so few for a life. How many would be there at his funeral? Probably even less.

Anna wasn't there. Thinking about it, why would she be? He was disappointed. Not having seen her for quite a while, he wanted to talk to her. Ramos had visited his local café, and told him that he had interviewed Anna about the illegal distribution of Castro's manifesto. She had denied it, of course. He was surprised that Ramos didn't seem to have to pressed her harder, because Freddie was sure that she had been very much involved. What the manifesto preached was admirable. What any humane and decent society wanted. But it was also 'an open call for revolution'. And that was illegal.

Freddie wanted to warn Anna that she was right in Ramos's sights. Not that she really needed to be told. No, in fact, that wasn't the real reason he wanted to see her. Seeing her lifted his spirits. He'd watched her grow from the feisty, fiery little girl to a beautiful, intelligent young woman, passionately committed to social reform and justice. Spending time with Anna, or even just seeing her, made him feel it was worth getting up in a morning.

But there were times when he wondered whether carrying on living was worth it. One of the reasons was Esther, who was heading towards him as they left the graveside. They hadn't spoken since his outburst at Giorgio' wake. He knew he had hurt her then, very badly. He felt a little guilty still, and he couldn't imagine why she was going to speak to him now.

'Freddie.'

It seemed she had dried the tears she had shed, copiously, at the grave.

'Hello, Esther...I'm sorry about your loss.'

Taking his arm, she led them away from the others.

'I want to talk to you...' She took a deep breath and said, 'I think Carl killed Nico.'

'What?'

'I don't mean he shot him, but he paid someone to do it.'

Freddie stopped and peered at her, but through the veil it was impossible to see her eyes.

'Carl?' he said, incredulously.

'Yes. You know people in the police. I want you to report it.'

He looked around at Hans and Bella talking to the priest at the grave, and to Nico's two friends walking away through the extravagant graves. Everything seemed normal, except for this mad woman beside him. He freed himself from her arm.

'Esther, you and I both know Carl would never do such a thing.'

'He did, I'm telling you. He was jealous...You remember how furious he was when he found about us! Do you remember? I can never forget it...But he couldn't have you killed in England. The police would have found out.'

'This is crazy, Esther. This is Carl you are talking about.'

'That's what Hans said. He said 'Where's the evidence?''

'Where is it?'

'If they arrested him, they could question him. They could find out.'

'Esther, you should let Hans drive you home, then take one of your pills, and try to rest.'

'I'm not taking them anymore. He may be poisoning me.'

Freddie could see there was no point in arguing. She was in her own world. Hans and Bella were now waiting by their car. He took hold of her arms, gently.

'Tell Hans to come to me when he's taken you home. I'll give him some pills. Is that alright? Will you take those?'

Esther nodded. 'I can trust you, Freddie, you know that.'

As he ushered her towards Hans' limousine, she held his hand.

'Come and see me sometime. Please, Freddie...I'm so alone.'

He faked a smile, 'I will.'

He watched the car pull away, puzzled. Had she forgotten what he had said at Giorgio's wake? It seemed like she had.

CHAPTER EIGHTY-FIVE

Though she loved to dance, nightclubs were not Anna's scene.

She had only been to Giorgio's nightclub once, for the grand opening. Then she had only gone because Hans begged her to. For some years he had done well in the grubby world of drugs and weapons, but when he branched out into a genuine, legal, legitimate venture, he suddenly seemed to want his family's acknowledgement. He loved having his glamorous mother opening the event. And Anna knew how unhappy he was that his father hadn't agreed to be there. But from what Jose had said, she was now aware that Hans had also gone back to his earlier, more squalid trade. Which was why she was there.

An elegant, bow-tied young man let her into the dimly-lit club. The space had expanded since she had last seen it. It was twice as big, and felt much more glamorous. The only lighting was from stylish, art-deco lamps on the tables, which surrounded a large, shiny dance floor.

Over the phone, Hans had asked her to come to the nightclub that evening, if she wanted to see him. It was early, so there were not many people inside. Just a few solitary drinkers at the bar, and one or two couples dancing to the regular band. She couldn't see Hans, so she went up to the bar.

'Yes, senorita?' the barman said.

'I've come to see my brother, Hans.'

'Ah. He's in the office, senorita. Through there. The first door.' He pointed at some lush heavy-velvet curtains at the side of the bar. She went through into a short corridor and knocked.

'Come,' Hans called. As she went in, Hans got up to meet her and gave her a kiss on the both cheeks.

'Lovely to see you, Anna.' He walked over to a small cocktail cabinet filled with bottles. 'A drink?'

355

'No. Not 'til we've finished.'

He smiled. 'You were always the most self-disciplined.'

She grinned in return. 'And you, a member of the Hitler Youth.'

'Please, that was a long time ago.' Taking his glass from his desk, he topped it up with premium Scottish whisky. 'So, what couldn't you say on the phone?'

Anna sat on the edge of the desk. She knew Hans and she didn't agree about many things, but she also sincerely believed that blood was thicker than water, and that she could trust her brother.

'I know Jose bought a gun from you recently, and you've been supplying others as well.'

Hans shrugged and sat down again at his desk.

'So, now you're back in the business, I wonder if you could get your hands on a radio transmitter?'

'A what?'

'The sort the army uses.'

He took a sip of his drink. 'Why?'

'A lot of people can't read on the island, Hans. So, they can't read Castro's manifesto.'

'Which is illegal anyway, I believe.'

'If we had a transmitter we could read the manifesto out to them.'

'That sounds like a dangerous occupation. It's very long, I hear.'

'We could read small parts of it at a time, and move the station around Havana. I think the stuff the army uses we could move around easily...What do you think?'

He took a longer drink, and savoured the taste in his mouth, before swallowing. 'I sell weapons to all parties, Anna. Right, Left, in between, whatever. I don't take sides. It's purely business...What you're asking me to do is to take one side. The side that wants to overthrow the president.'

'I'm not asking you to agree with my politics, Hans. Like you say, it's just business.'

Hans reached out and took her hand, firmly, in his. 'I may not show it, but I do care about my little sister, you know.'

She stroked his hand with her fingers. 'So, indulge her?'

The tourists took taxis to the soft, white-sand beaches a short ride to the east of the city. Freddie and Carl never went there. Their beach of rocks and meagre sand, a short walk from the Old Town, was generally deserted.

As they made their way through the rocks, Carl stopped, and coughed throatily. Wiping his mouth with the handkerchief, he put it away in his pocket. With an effort, he leaned down and picked up a pebble. He rubbed it between his fingers for a moment, feeling the silkiness honed from thousands of years. Then threw it into the sea. It didn't go far.

'I can throw further than that,' said Klaus. He picked up a stone and hurled it over the waves. A long way. The splash swallowed by a white-topped breaker.

'Very good, Klaus,' said Freddie. 'Can you find me five different shells?'

'Of course, Freddie.'

Klaus began to pick his way over the rocks, silhouetted by the sun about to set beyond the headland.

Freddie looked at his friend, concerned.

Carl was gazing at the horizon, though not seeing it. 'It's madness, Freddie. I never see her. She has all her meals in her suite. She never even speaks if we pass in the hall...Because she still thinks I had Nico killed...Madness.'

'I thought the tablets would help.'

'They don't seem to.'

Aware that Esther now believed her husband was trying to poison her, they had arranged for Carl to provide Freddie with the pills from his surgery, which Freddie would then pretend to prescribe for Esther.

'If I doubled the doze, she'd spend all day sleeping,' Freddie said.

Unable to avoid the sarcasm, Carl grimaced, 'You could treble it.'

Freddie pretended to smile at the joke. To him, Esther seemed beyond all hope. It was his friend he was more concerned about. 'I assume she doesn't know you're ill?'

Carl looked at him and frowned.

'I've seen the blood on your handkerchief.'

'Just got a little sore throat,' Carl said quickly.

'Which you've had for a long time.' Freddie added. 'I'm a doctor, Carl. Very well trained, by you. Have you been to the hospital?'

'It's too late, Freddie. They can do nothing about cancer. It kills you.'

CHAPTER EIGHTY-SIX

The courtroom stood as the judge made his way out. That was the last case of what seemed to Anna to be a very long morning. She had been the counsel defending a family being illegally evicted from their home, but half her mind was on something else. Despite her best efforts the case had been lost. Justice wasn't done this time. But Anna was sure it was coming down the line.

Last night she and Jose had collected the transmitter from Hans at Giorgio's. As they drove to deliver it to the apartment of a couple within their group, Anna turned to look at Jose. He seemed tense, looking around, and back behind.

'It will be okay, Jose. I don't think we were followed.'

Anna was hiding her own irritation. Their group had discussed who should make the first broadcast, and had made their decision. Though Anna really wanted to play her part broadcasting the manifesto to the island the couple chosen were the obvious first choice. The man learnt electronics in the army during the Second World War. His partner used to be an announcer at CMQ radio station, where Eddie Chiblás made his final, tragic broadcast. But Anna knew no one could deliver it with the passion she had.

When she first read Castro's lengthy manifesto, she said to Jose, 'This will totally change society, Jose! Giving the land to the peasants, workers having a share of the profits of industry, building decent houses for poor people - '

Jose seemed irritated. 'You did teach me to read, Anna.'

'Sorry. I'm just excited.'

But she knew she wouldn't have to wait long for her turn to be a voice of the revolution. After the first initial broadcast, the transmitter was being moved to their apartment. With the secret police combing the city, it was not safe to broadcast twice from the same place.

Overnight, the groups of the 26th of July Movement had spread the word throughout the city that today was the first broadcast of the manifesto.

Anna was very excited. She and Jose had distributed many of the illegal pamphlets, but for many of the islanders who couldn't read, radio was their main way of finding out what was happening on the island.

On her way home from the courthouse, she collected bread, cheese, ham and pickles. And a bottle of wine, to celebrate. She almost sprinted up the stairs to their apartment on the eight-floor of the building. Being at the top of the building, their radio signal was excellent.

Carl, after taking Freddie's advice, had reluctantly visited the hospital. They met for coffee in Freddie's favourite café, while Carl told Freddie about the state of his illness.

'They don't know how long it will be. Both lungs are affected...It's just a matter of time.'

Freddie touched his top pocket, where he kept his cigarette packet. But put his hand down again.

'Don't let me stop you, Freddie. It's alright. I'm sure your smoking didn't give me cancer...In fact, maybe I should try it myself. I never have. Ever. I wonder what it's like.'

'It's probably not a good time, Carl.'

'No. Indulge me, Freddie. Let me know what I've been missing all this time...' He put his handkerchief to his mouth and coughed. After a moment, he put it away. 'There's a lot of things I should have tried, maybe. But I didn't...' He put out his hand. 'So please, indulge an old friend.'

Freddie took out the packet and shook a couple of cigarettes free.

Taking one, Carl looked at it. 'Tobacco came from around here. The Mayans used it in Mexico, I think, for hundreds of years before we discovered it.' He put the cigarette between his lips.

Freddie leant forward and lit it for him. Carl sucked gently, and breathed out. He pulled a face.

'I don't much like the taste. Does it really give you a buzz?'

'It's more a habit, really. It's not like cannabis.'

Carl smiled, 'Maybe I should try that.'

Freddie was very concerned about the Mueller's. He didn't know how long his friend, Carl, had to live. But it wasn't long. The field of medicine was a long way from knowing how to treat, never mind cure, this dreadful disease. Cancer could take its time, or be a swift end. He didn't know how the Mueller family would survive when Carl had gone. It didn't seem that Esther was capable of running a household, even if they had enough money to survive on, when Carl's few wealthy patients were no longer there.

Hans, of course, was doing very well. He could certainly support the family, if only because he doted on his mother. Freddie wondered if Bella was her substitute. The women were very much alike, physically. And, when Freddie first met Esther, she had the same wild, fiery spirit that Bella still had in abundance. Like mother, like lover.

Anna was too involved in her politics to be relied on. There was no way of knowing what would happen to her. With the rise of Castro's movement, she was now more determined than ever that Batista had to be overthrown by force, not by the ballot box. And she would not give that struggle to look after her family. She could end up in prison for years. Or lie dead in the street, any day, from a gunshot.

Anna and Hans had chosen their own way. But Klaus. He was not mature enough, nor ever would be, to choose his own life. If Klaus outlived them all, his bastard son would probably spend his last days in an institution for the backward and insane. Sadly, Freddie knew there was nothing he could do about that.

CHAPTER EIGHTY-SEVEN

Anna waited, impatiently, as Jose tried to find the right frequency on their small radio. There were just bursts of static interrupted by music.

'Come on, Jose!' said Anna. 'They'll be starting any minute!'

He sat back and raised his hands. 'I can't find it.'

'Have you got the right frequency?'

'I think so.'

'Let me try.'

Jose got up slowly.

'Move!' Anna said.

She took his place at the table. Jose stood back, watching. Winding the tuning knob to the start of the dial, she started scrolling slowly forward. Halfway along the dial, a voice came through loudly, then faded.

'That's Gabriela!' She wound the knob back. Gabriela's voice came through again. 'You had the wrong frequency! It's already started!'

Gabriela was reading the manifesto. Anna sat back, listening to Castro's words.

"Cuba is my fatherland, and I shall never return to it, or I shall return with the dignity I have pledged myself to. The bridges have been burned: Either we conquer the fatherland at any price so that we can live with dignity and honor, or we shall remain without one – "

Suddenly, there were other sounds behind Gabriela's voice. The thundering of many feet running upstairs, a door being battered, cries of alarm, scuffling, a voice shouting loudly.

'Stop!' 'Get her!'

Then Gabriela's loud scream! The station went dead. Leaving just static.

Shocked and startled, Anna looked at Jose. 'They've have been raided! The police have found them!'

Jose looked away, covering his face with a hand.

Anna slumped back. 'Someone has ratted on us, Jose. They're are onto us.'

On his weekly visits, when Carlotta opened the door, Freddie always said, 'Hello, Carlotta. Is Mrs Mueller in?' Even though he knew Esther had not left the house for as long as anyone could remember, except for Nico's funeral.

Carlotta fixed him with her quizzical look. 'Of course, senor.'

She let him in, and then returned to her kitchen domain. Freddie went down the hall and knocked quietly on the door.

'Who is that?'

'It's me.'

'Come in, Freddie.'

He walked into Esther's suite. Seated on her chaise-lounge, she was dressed in an exquisite, silk housecoat, with the diamond necklace sparkling over her discreet cleavage. She extended her hand to him.

Freddie took it, and kissed it. 'You are looking wonderful, Esther. How are you feeling today?'

'So much better for seeing you, Freddie.'

As the pills he brought her were powerful, he and Carl had decided not to give her too many at once. There was no way of knowing what she would do next. Thankfully, the pills depressed her libido, also. So, they played bridge, or bezique, while Esther complained about Carl, the weather, and Anna. She seemed to have forgotten he'd told her he loved her daughter. Or maybe she hadn't, and just liked maligning Anna to him. Usually, she liked to finish by indulging herself with tales of her life as the over-privileged young woman back in Vienna.

He tried to keep his visits to about an hour, though Esther attempted to detain him longer each time. Today, as usual, Freddie pretended to listen, but his thoughts were somewhere else.

Having heard about the broadcast through the city's grapevine, he had listened to the radio as the broadcast was terminated abruptly by the police. He wondered if Anna had been there and was now being questioned by Ramos's men. But it would be too dangerous to go to the headquarters and ask. Too dangerous for Anna, if she hadn't been arrested. He told himself that, knowing Ramos, the police chief would probably have been to the café to brag to Freddie about capturing his 'girlfriend'.

Managing to escape within the hour, Freddie spent a little time with Klaus, admiring his shell drawings. As he was leaving the house, he met Anna coming up the drive.

He couldn't keep the relief from his voice. 'Hello, Anna. How lovely to see you.'

'Freddie.'

'I'm so, so pleased to see you.'

'Why?'

'Well, after the broadcast, I wondered...if...'

'That's why I'm coming to see my father. In case, well...' She knew she could trust Freddie and wanted to get it off her chest. 'They have already arrested two others of the group. I wanted to see him in case Jose and I are the next.'

'Your father isn't here.'

'Oh.'

'He's in hospital. For a check-up.'

'Is he ill?'

'I don't know,' Freddie lied. 'You'll have to ask him.'

Anna turned and walked back down the drive.

'Do you think, someone betrayed you?'

She stopped. 'Yes. They knew exactly where to go. And when.'

'Someone from the group?'

She shook her head. 'We can't believe anyone of us would... Jose, thinks it's Hans. So do the others.'

'Hans?'

'He got us the transmitter. Jose thinks he had us followed. We went straight to the apartment to deliver it for the broadcast.'

'Do you believe that? That Hans would have you arrested? He's your brother.'

'Who knows? He's been selling us weapons. Maybe he thought this would put him in Batista's good books, if they found out about the arms.'

'So, what are you going to do? Talk to him? To Hans?'

'He wouldn't tell us anything, would he?'

'So...What are you - ?'

'I don't want to talk about it, Freddie!' Anna snapped. 'I've said too much already.'

She turned and walked quickly away.

Freddie was going to follow her. But what could he say? If the group had decided to deal with Hans, to kill him. What could he do?

CHAPTER EIGHTY-EIGHT

Anna knew that she and Hans, even as children, were very different. When Hans was born his father was totally immersed in his new role as visiting professor and tutor at St. Bartholomew's. So, their first-born was left to be totally indulged by his mother, and he had absorbed her rash, impulsive nature. For them, everything was black or white, right or wrong. There was no place for nuance in their nature. The Hitler Youth was perfect for her brother.

When she was born, instinctively, she rejected her mother's gushing attempt to turn her daughter into her infant clone. By the time she could walk, she had tossed away her blonde, angelic dolls in favour of Hans building bricks and toy cars. In a short while, her mother ignored her and Anna was left in the hands of Mrs Price. It was from her that she learnt discipline, self-control, and a strong sense of duty to others.

When Klaus was born, even as a young child, Anna could feel the tension between her mother and father. At first totally ignoring him, Esther suddenly became obsessed with baby Klaus. Day and night, he was never allowed to be out of her sight. She fed him, bathed him, clothed him, and he slept in her bedroom, in her bed. Whether he liked it or not, he was never free from his mother's smothering embraces.

Feeling rejected by his mother, only reinforced Hans arrogant, egotistic nature. Everything from then on was for Hans. As they grew up, she and he fought a lot, especially about Hitler and his Nazis. But he had changed after the war. Could she believe he had betrayed his sister to the police, knowing what awful things could happen to her, if she was arrested?

After they had their discussion with the rest of their group, the argument went on between her and Jose in their apartment.

'I said we were being followed.' Jose said, heatedly. 'You kept saying we're not, but I had a sense. I knew it!'

'I can't believe Hans would do that!' said Anna. 'He's not political. He's just a businessman!'

'Well, maybe he did it for money. I'm sure the police pay informers very well!'

Anna was trying not to lose her temper, entirely. 'He doesn't need money, Jose! He's got money! Lots of it!'

'A profit is a profit! You taught me that. Was it Marx, or Engels, or someone…!' He seemed to calm down, abruptly, and sighed. 'Look, we had this discussion with the rest. We all agreed.'

'I didn't!'

Jose went to the door and opened it. 'Well, we did. It's all settled, Anna.' He went out, closing the door firmly behind him.

Since he had last been there, Giorgio's had expanded. Freddie saw that they had taken over the bar next door, and posters of their cabaret acts and the regular band were prominently displayed outside.

He had been once before, for the grand opening, when Esther was the belle of the ball. This time was quite different. Having phoned to check that Hans was at the club that evening, he had decided to go there. He didn't want to speak to him on the phone. It was too important. If he could speak to Hans face to face, perhaps he could find out the truth.

Hans was surprised to see Freddie enter the club. He knew Freddie was a drinker, but he certainly wouldn't be paying these prices. Tourists' prices. As Hans went to shake his hand, Freddie immediately asked if they could talk somewhere privately.

Taking him into his office, Hans offered Freddie a drink. His finest Scotch whisky. Surprisingly, Freddie declined, and got straight to the point.

'You heard about the police breaking up the broadcast. About Castro's manifesto?'

'Yes. I didn't hear it, but I was told. Shame,' Hans added, ironically.

'I was told that you provided the transmitter. And then you told the police about it. Even where it was.'

Hans stopped pouring his own drink. 'What?' He put the decanter down. 'Who told you that?'

'Your sister. Anna.'

'That's crazy! Why would I do that? When did you see her?'

'This morning.'

'She's crazy. Did she actually say that?'

'Yes.' Freddie went on, 'Apparently, her 'group' have decided it was you.'

'This is ridiculous, Freddie! I'm a businessman. I don't do politics.'

'Well, that's what they've decided.'

'I'm her brother. I wouldn't rat on her. I've heard what the MIS do in their 'interviews'. Especially to women.'

'I just felt I had to warn you, Hans.'

'I can't believe it...But, thanks, Freddie.'

Freddie nodded at the decanter. 'I think I've earned that drink now.'

When Jose didn't come back all evening, Anna began to think that something might be happening about Hans already. It was late. She decided to go out to look in the bars that Jose would likely to be in. But he wasn't in any. So, where was he?

She had to try and persuade him that he was wrong. People had been told about the broadcast, so they could tell others.

They wanted the whole city to listen. The secret police were everywhere in the city. They must have heard, and tracked the transmitter.

Hans would probably be at the club. He would be safe there, probably. No-one in their group would just walk into the club and shoot him. That would give themselves away. They would wait outside, among the crowd. The tourists were always milling around until the early hours. That would be the best time.

Of course, she believed in what the group were doing. She cared passionately about Castro's campaign. But Hans was her brother. He didn't believe in her cause, but she didn't think he believed in Batista's brutal regime either. Could she let this happen? Let her brother be killed? If Hans died it would destroy her mother. Probably drive her crazier than she already was. Not that she really cared all that much about her mother, but her father would have to bear the brunt of whatever Esther did. She didn't want him to go through that.

Passing a public phone she decided to call Hans, and tell him she was coming to the club to speak to him. The phone was engaged, but the club wasn't far away. She began to hurry there, through the back streets of the Old City.

Entering the street, dominated by Giorgio's neon sign, she saw through a group of tourists, the door of Hans' coupe closing. She hurried to catch him before he drove away.

Ten yards away, she was blown backwards as the car erupted in flames.

CHAPTER EIGHTY-NINE

Dazed and shocked, Anna picked herself up, unhurt apart from the fall. Hans' coupe was engulfed in flames. There was no way anyone could get near it. She could see the figure of her brother, already unrecognisable by the inferno surrounding him.

There were screams and cries from some of the tourists who had been injured by flying glass. All the rest of them were panicking. There was no point in her being there. The police would be here soon, and she didn't want to be anywhere near the scene when they arrived. She stumbled away, shaking, too numb to cry.

With police sirens wailing in the distance, she wandered the back streets for a while. Thoughts tumbled through her head, as she tried to block out the image of her brother being burnt alive. She didn't want to go back to her apartment. Right at this moment, there was no way she wanted to be with Jose. He might be sympathetic, she was sure, but underneath he would be celebrating.

She had expected it to be a gunman. That's what she was hurrying to tell Hans about. Maybe the group thought he was the police spy, but she couldn't believe it. If she told him someone was about to shoot him, he could take precautions. But there were no precautions you could take about a bomb.

As a full moon climbed over rooftops, the bells of the nearby cathedral chimed midnight. She wanted to scream, to cry. She wanted, needed, to tell someone. But there was no point in waking her parents up at this time. They were all normally asleep by nine o'clock. What was the point of delivering such dreadful news in the middle of the night? She would go to their house first thing in the morning, before their breakfast.

Bella listened as her latest stud roared off on his scooter. She lay back on her silk sheets, replete. Someone had said, sometime, that sex was so much better as you got older. If you knew what to do. Teaching young men how to treat a mature woman was part of the fun, and she was an excellent teacher.

She had fancied Hans the first time Giorgio brought him home. He was tall and athletic, with a shy, aloof, arrogance you really wanted to strip away. By the time they came together, there wasn't much she had to teach him. He had learnt most of it from Giorgio, who used to swing both ways. But, after several years together, their initial pleasure and exhilaration had gradually waned. The love-making had become predictable. Perfunctory. Hans was still very beautiful to look at, but, working late at the club, he was often too tired to be attentive to her needs.

But, after she had got him away from dealing in drugs and weapons, they now worked well together as business partners. The club was booming. She was happy as they were.

As she was drifting to sleep, the phone rang beside the bed. She picked it up, sleepily.

'Hello?' Expecting it to be Hans, saying he wouldn't be in until morning. But it was Anna.

'Bella, it's Anna...?'

There was a long pause. 'Yes, Anna?'

'I have some terrible news...I don't know how to say this... Hans is dead.'

Bella shot up in bed. 'What? What! How?'

'He was blown up, in his car. It was...It was a mistake.' Anna blurted out.

'What do you mean, a mistake?'

Anna wanted to get it out. To make a penance somehow. 'Some people, some people...thought he was spying for the police.'

Bella got out of bed, stunned.

'Hans? Hans spying for the police?' she said, disbelievingly. 'Why did they think that?'

'We asked Hans if he could get us a radio transmitter. He did, but the police raided during the first broadcast. Some people thought he told the police. I told them he wouldn't do that...But...I was going to the club to tell him, but his car just... just blew up, right in front of me...I am so, so sorry...'

Holding the phone, Bella turned to stare out of the window, too shocked to respond. The full moon blazed on the pool.

On the phone Anna kept repeating, 'I'm sorry, Bella. I tried to stop them. I'm so sorry...!'

Bella turned at a noise behind her, and gasped.

Hans walked in, looking scared and troubled.

Harry Duffin

CHAPTER NINETY

For decades sugar had been the main export of Cuba. Its production, in the cane fields and the factories, was largely controlled by large American companies, and most of the profits went straight to United States. When sugar prices began to fall in the 1950's, the companies' response was to sack many workers, and increase workloads for the rest. The workers' organisation responded with strikes, which were met with brutal violence from the police. President Batista, subsidised with huge bribes from the companies, openly supported them.

When Benny was sacked by his company, he wasn't interested in joining the protests. It was his job to earn money, somehow. At sixteen, he was the head of the family. Since his father died a year ago, his wage had kept his younger brothers and sisters just about fed. Now the family was destitute. Thrown out of the company shack, they had built a one-roomed hut from cane, with palm leaves for a roof. The family ate the small amount they could grow, or find in the forest around them. But the children were always hungry.

Benny knew there was money in Havana. The city was full of tourists. Tourists had money. Plenty of it. Money that would feed his family. Saying goodbye to his mother and his siblings he hitch-hiked to the capital.

Never having been in a city before, he was amazed by the wonderful buildings, and by the fabulous cars that whizzed along the wide streets. There was money everywhere. And he was determined to have some.

But unemployment was as bad in the city as in the countryside. Dressed in peasant's clothes, there was no way he could act as a guide to the city, which he didn't know anyway. Nor could he get a waiter's job. Even getting work clearing out the slops from the kitchens was hard to find. But everywhere tourists splashed out dollars like they were going out of fashion.

The streets, day and night, were full of young Cubans trying to earn a few dollars from the passing tourists. Musicians and dancers seemed to do the best. Not being musical, Benny's one attempt at dancing, brought laughter and derision from passers-by.

Benny was deeply unhappy and frustrated. Having come to the city to earn money for his family, he found he couldn't even feed himself. He had found a space to sleep in an old building occupied by other young unemployed, but at night he preferred to wander the streets begging. When they were drunk the American tourists could be generous, or they could be aggressive and threaten to hand you over to the police. You never knew which.

He stood in a doorway opposite a nightclub waiting for tourists coming in, or out of the club. As he watched one group approaching, a stylish, young man came out the club and got into a flashy, two-tone coupe parked outside. The man looked up and saw him, then reached into the glove compartment. Quickly, he got out of the car and hurried back into the club.

Benny approached the car. It was beautiful. He ran his hand along the smooth, gleaming side, and looked inside at the plush interior, illuminated by the neon lights from the club. The keys were hanging from the ignition. If he had that car, surely, he could sell it somewhere, and make a lot of money. As the tourists approached, he got inside the car, slammed the door, and turned on the ignition.

The pool terrace looked beautiful, bathed in moonlight, but Hans didn't notice. He took a large slug of his whisky.

'Why didn't you tell Anna I was alive?'

'She said she was going to warn you, so she must have been in on it. I didn't want her to know.'

'I didn't know whether to believe Freddie, or not. But I decided maybe to change my routine anyway. So, I left the club early. When I went out to the car, there was a guy lurking in the shadows. I reached for my gun in the glove compartment, but it wasn't there, so I went back into the club to get it...If the gun had been in the car, I'd be toast by now.'

Bella was leaning back on a sun-lounger, arms folded across her chest. 'You told me you had given up selling stuff to the rebels.'

'It was only a transmitter, Bella. Didn't seem to be any harm.'

'For them to broadcast illegal stuff.'

Hans shrugged.

'You're sure it was only a transmitter?'

'Yes. Sure, of course.'

'No guns?'

'No way.' He turned to her. 'I promised you that.'

'Yeah,' she said, sceptically.

Finishing off his drink, he raised his glass to Bella. She shook her head. He refilled his glass from the pool bar. 'I still can't believe it.'

'Neither did the guy in the car.'

'I can't believe Anna would go along with that.'

'She said she was on the way to warn you.'

Hans sat on a lounger next to Bella. 'Were you upset when she told you I'd been blown up?'

Bella sat upright. 'Of course. Of course, I was.' She reached out her hand to him.

He took it. 'I just wondered...with all your –'

'Don't go there, Hans. I love you...Though I don't always trust you.'

Hans smiled and squeezed her hand.

'But we need to get you out of here,' she continued.

'What do you mean?' he said, frowning.

'They tried to kill you with a bomb, Hans! When they find out it wasn't you, do you think they'll stop at that?'

CHAPTER NINETY-ONE

They were sitting outside the café overlooking the harbour. Sipping his unsweetened, espresso coffee, Freddie listened as Carl recounted the scene at his home earlier that morning. To Freddie, knowing that Hans was still alive and kicking, the story had something of a tragicomedy about it.

'Of course, Esther was hysterical at first when Anna told her,' Carl said. 'Telling Esther her favourite child had been blown up. But after a while, she calmed down just a little. She knew, straight away, that Anna had something to do with it. Anna tried to explain that she was actually going to warn Hans when it happened, but Esther just exploded with rage! She shrieked that Anna had killed her own brother!'

'I had warned Hans earlier on,' Freddie interrupted. 'I met Anna going to your house. She was upset and she just blurted it out.'

'I thought Esther was going to attack her. She screamed at me to hit her. She wanted me to hit Anna! Then she said "Kill her", she said. She actually said, "Kill her!"'

'Oh, Carl.'

'And in the middle of that the phone rang. I wasn't going to answer it. I wasn't going to leave the room not with Esther in that state. It rang and rang, and, eventually, Carlotta came from the kitchen and answered it. She knocked on the living room door, came in and said, "Senor Hans is on the phone".'

'Wow!' said Freddie.

'Exactly. I couldn't believe it. "Senor Hans?" I said.'

Carlotta said, '"Yes, Senor Hans. He said it's important."'

With his cup posed halfway to his mouth, Freddie listened. It really was tragicomedy.

'We were all stunned,' Carl went on. 'Anna in particular. She actually went white, Freddie. I went to the phone. It was

Hans. He didn't explain it very well, but he said his car had blown up, and that he was going to leave the island for a while. Today, in fact. He was just about to leave for the airport. He said he didn't have to time to come and see us, to see his mother. He sounded pretty upset. Obviously, he was very unnerved. Which, as you know, is not like Hans.'

Freddie put down his cup. 'So, what happened?'

'Esther was beside herself. She wanted to speak to him, of course. But she could hardly speak, she was so upset, so relieved. He had to keep telling her he was okay, and it really, really was him. She wanted him to come to see her, but he wouldn't. He said it was too dangerous...I told Anna to leave while Esther was talking to Hans, so she left, while Esther was still on the phone.'

'Did Hans come?'

'No. No...I thought Esther might calm down afterwards. But she was still furious with Anna. She said Hans had to leave the island, to leave her, because of Anna's mob of murderers! She was crying and angry that she might never see him again. She said that Anna was never allowed to come to the house again. Ever! And that Anna wasn't her daughter anymore. That she didn't have a daughter.'

Carl was slumped back, wearily, in his chair. Reaching out, Freddie put his hand on Carl's arm. In the midst of his fatal illness, his close friend's family was tearing itself apart.

Anna was too involved with the growing confrontation with Batista's regime to even think of going for Christmas at the Mueller's, not that Esther would have allowed that anyway. So, Carl arranged to meet his daughter, secretly, for a Christmas lunch with just the two of them.

As it was Christmas, Carl had wanted to take his daughter to an expensive restaurant in one of the hotels facing the ocean, not that he could really afford it. But life was short. Especially his. However, Anna insisted they went to a small restaurant in the Old Town.

Having got there early, Carl chose a table outside, overlooking the square, which was festooned with large, fiery-red poinsettias blooming in huge stone pots. When he saw Anna arrive, he got up to hug her, but Anna winced as he put his arms around her.

'What?' Carl said, stepping back. 'What is it? Are you hurt?'

Anna shrugged it away. 'No, not really.'

Concerned, he showed her to the table, and continued as soon as she sat down. 'You are hurt. What happened?'

'I'm sure you don't want to know, Papa.'

'Is it Jose?'

'No. No, of course not.'

'Anna, please. I'm your father.'

Reluctantly, she went on. 'You've heard of the sugar workers' strike?

'Of course. I'm not political, Anna, but I do know what's going on.'

'Well, we were supporting the strikers and the police attacked us. I got hit.'

'Have you been to the hospital?'

'It's just bruises, Papa.'

'Where?'

She smiled dryly, 'Everywhere really. They are very thorough.'

'You really should go to –'

'How did it go?' she interrupted. 'Your Christmas meal?'

Carl shrugged. 'Not too well. Freddie came. He tried to amuse us with some jokes, but Esther was still so angry that Hans wasn't there. So, she spoilt it, really. She blamed you, of course.'

'Have you heard from him? From Hans?'

'Yes. He's in Miami. There are a lot of Cubans there, apparently. A sort of a refugee colony from Batista.'

'They should be here fighting with the rest of us,' Anna had said.

'And get beaten up, and maybe killed?'

'You have to fight for what you believe in, Papa,' she'd said.

'I just wish...' He didn't go on. It was no use. 'A father should never have to bury his daughter.'

'I'm not dead. Just bruised.'

Carl looked around the square, and suddenly started waving, 'Freddie! Freddie!'

Standing in the middle of the square, Freddie was just lighting a cigarette. He waved and came over to them, dropping the full cigarette as he did. A ragged boy sitting in the square begging, seized the cigarette, and stuck it between his lips. A rare Christmas treat.

Freddie raised his Panama. 'Hello, Anna. Merry Christmas!'

'Not for her. She's just got beaten up by the police.'

'Papa!'

'She won't go to the hospital. Can I use your place to examine her, Freddie? I can't take her home, of course.'

'Papa, there is no need. I shall leave if you don't stop now,' she said firmly.

'Still fighting for the cause, Anna?' said Freddie, wryly. 'While your leader, Castro, is sunning himself in Mexico.'

Anna turned on him defiantly, 'Castro gave a speech on Christmas Eve. He said he is coming back to overthrow Batista next year!'

'And you believe him?'

'Yes, Freddie, I do!'

Carl shook his head and groaned. 'And the streets will be as red as those flowers in the square.'

CHAPTER NINETY-TWO

Almost a year after Castro's Christmas Eve speech, Hans read about the invasion in a local newspaper in Miami. He turned to his Cuban companion as they sat drinking in a bar overlooking the bright-blue Atlantic Ocean.

'It says, here, a small group of men landed at night on a beach in Oriente.'

'In the south-east? That's a long way from Havana.'

'Yeah. Apparently, they were attacked by the Rural Guard, and most of them have been killed. Including Castro.'

'So, Castro's dead? That's a pity,' said his companion, 'You could have done a good trade selling him guns.'

Hans had returned to his weapons trade when he got established in Miami. Since he left Cuba political unrest had got worse there, particularly among students and striking workers. He knew that the police spies had been targeting groups, and he had a lot of demand for weapons from the left-wing, but also from right-wing groups who supported President Batista.

'You sell them both weapons?' said his companion, when Hans told him about his business, after they got very drunk one evening. 'The left and the right?'

Hans shrugged. 'It's just business. It's always happened. For centuries. Finance rules the world, my friend. You back both sides, so whoever wins, you get a profit.'

'That's why I'm not a businessman,' his friend replied. 'I'm too honest.' He smiled. 'So, you're picking up the tab tonight, Mr Rockefeller!'

On New Year's Eve, Hans was waiting at the bar for the start of the huge party on the beach. He missed Bella, and had called to wish her Happy New Year, but he couldn't reach her, at home or at the club.

It felt much safer in Miami. There were a lot of Cubans working in the holiday trade. Some preferred Batista, others said they supported the dead Castro, but no one shot each other, like they did in Havana.

Anna was no doubt in the thick of it. He didn't like his sister's views, but he hoped she stayed safe. There were lots of police spies on the island, and it looked like there might be a traitor in her group. The one who said that he, Hans, was the spy and had planted the bomb to get rid of him. Whatever, he was happy to be in one piece, and to be here, waiting for tonight's party.

Anna had put the newspaper down, and collapsed into her chair, as if all the air had gone out of her body. The paper only repeated what she had heard on the radio that morning. Closing her eyes, she tried to hold back the tears.

Jose poured an expresso, and put the cup on the table next to her.

'Coffee, Anna.'

She put her hands over her face. 'What do we do now, Jose?' she said, through her fingers.

Through their network, they had heard that Castro had set off with a small army, to sail back to Cuba to invade the island. Anna was delighted. The revolution had at last begun. She waited, anxiously, all week for news. And now she had it.

The radio and the newspaper both said that Batista's troops had attacked the rebels as they landed, and that Castro and most of the rest had been killed. Everyone knew that Fidel Castro was the natural leader and spokesman for the revolution. Without his leadership there was no way of knowing what would happen.

Throughout 1956, following Castro's instructions, Anna and Jose, and the rest of the 26th July Movement, had kept away from direct political confrontation. The message was to win the hearts and minds of the people, not take on Batista's forces. Leaving the students and workers to fight with the police, the group had set out on a propaganda campaign. They leafletted, started illegal broadcasts again, and went out into the countryside to talk directly to the peasants who couldn't read.

Anna had travelled the whole of the island, talking to the peasants' families. They were only employed in the harvest and planting time, so most of the families had to survive as best they could for the rest of the year.

'You will get a piece of land of your own,' Anna had told them. 'Your children will go to school, you will have doctors, nurses. A decent home.'

The peasants of the south-east, in the Oriente Province, were the poorest of the island, and they were the most receptive to Anna's message. For they had the most to gain if the revolution ever happened.

And they were the people who spread the news, towards the end of the month, that Fidel Castro was still alive, with his men, and living in the Sierra Maestra mountains.

'And that's where we're going!' Anna shouted to Jose, jubilantly. 'To join the real revolution!'

CHAPTER NINETY-THREE

'These are really very remarkable, don't you think?' Freddie asked Esther, showing her the superb, coloured drawings and paintings of shells.

Since Freddie had first shown seashells to his son on the beach, Klaus had become obsessed with them. He was fascinated to learn about the tiny creatures that lived inside them, and by their infinite variety of shape and colour. From being a child, Klaus had a natural gift as an artist, and he had drawn hundreds of shells over the years, becoming more and more skilled as he got older.

Finally, after a great deal of persuading, to take Esther away from talking about herself, and maligning Carl and Anna, Freddie had got her to look through some of Klaus's dozens of sketch pads. She had allowed them into her ground floor suite, which she hardly ever left these days.

'I'm not an authority on art, Freddie,' she said coolly, closing the pad. 'How should I know?'

Klaus looked at him, confused.

'They are very good, Klaus,' said Freddie, reassuringly. 'You are very good. You are a very good artist. You're very good at drawing.'

It was difficult, sometimes, to talk to Klaus. Some days he seemed to understand a lot. Like an adult. Other times he seemed to regress to a more childlike state, and could become unresponsive, or petulant, just like his mother.

For a long time, it had been difficult to get Esther to pay any attention at all to their son. Knowing that Carl hadn't much longer to live, Freddie felt that he should try and make Esther take an interest in her child. Klaus's day to day companion, Mrs Price, couldn't go on for ever, and mother and son could be living in the same house for many years.

'I think we could, maybe, sell some of these,' Freddie pressed on. 'Even have a book published, perhaps.'

'A book?' she said. 'From Klaus?'

'Yes. Why not?'

Esther raised her eyebrows and looked away, dismissively.

Clearly keen to regain his mother's attention, Klaus showed Esther a delicate watercolour of an intricate shell of white and pink. It was shaped like a heart.

'That's called a jewel box,' he said, earnestly. 'You have jewels.'

Automatically, Esther's fingers touched her throat. The diamond necklace wasn't there.

She glanced at Freddie. 'I'll go and get it, Klaus. It's very special to me.'

She glanced at Freddie. Freddie looked away.

With the news of Castro's invasion the violence in Havana escalated. As the police raids grew, and prominent left-wing activists were being targeted and assassinated, Anna and Jose had decided to move to a secret basement in the Old Town. Unlike their apartment, which was bright and sunny with a splendid view over the city, the basement felt dark and oppressive.

Despite Anna's determination to go, Jose, having no real knowledge of where Castro group actually were, was not keen to make the journey right across the island to find and join the rebels.

In the gloomy room, Anna was serving up a scratch meal of beans and rice. She felt nervous now, going out into the streets, so she was using up what they had brought with them. As she piled the beans and gravy onto the rice on Jose's plate, she repeated her argument.

'Let the students fight it out with the police, Jose. We have to go to fight with Castro.'

'Anna, the Sierra Maestra is huge. We need more information before we go.'

'Some of the peasants there are bound to know where they are. You saw how keen they were when we went to talk to them.'

Jose put a forkful into his mouth, and chewed. 'I don't know if my leg will stand it, Anna,' said Jose.

'We used to live on the eighth floor, Jose. The mountains can't be any worse than you walking up eight flights of stairs every day.'

'I think, we can do a lot here, in the city, Anna.'

'But the police are closing in all the time. They don't ask questions, Jose, they just shoot you. Or worse. If anyone of our group is arrested, they could name us.'

'I'm sure they wouldn't.'

'I heard Luis being tortured to death, Jose...Some people know where we live. I feel every time I go outside someone will come from a doorway and arrest me, or blow my brains out.'

She got up, and picked up her keys and her handbag.

'Where are you going?'

'I'm going to tell my father...I'm going in the morning, Jose. With or without you.'

CHAPTER NINETY-FOUR

Esther looked forward to Freddie's visit every week, when he delivered her pills. She didn't know if the pills did her any good, but it gave her a way of seeing him. So, she dutifully took them.

He had hurt her deeply when he said he loved her daughter, but the feelings she had for him all those years ago were still there inside. She had known it from the very first moment when he rescued them from the ship. He looked older, of course, world-weary, certainly, but that, if anything, made him more appealing.

Seeing Freddie and Klaus together for the first time was deeply embarrassing. Her former friend, Isabel, had seen the resemblance immediately. So, Esther had shunned Freddie, just as she did when the truth of their liaison had come out.

Carl had thrown Freddie out of the house, and had him sacked from his course. She had been stupid, but at the time she couldn't tell Carl the truth, that she loved Freddie and wanted to be with him. There was no way she and Freddie could have lived together. His pittance as a student would not have kept them, except in the gutter. From being a child, she has been brought up to expect the very best, and it was hard to turn your back on that. Now she believed she could.

She knew that Freddie and Anna weren't together as a couple. Anna had that black boy, Jose, which disgusted her. She tried not to think about that. Poor Nico had brown skin. A mulatto. His flesh was a pale, beautiful brown, not like the monkey-dark skin of Jose. Nico was almost as light as Freddie. Freddie who had baked in the sun, he'd told her, when he was a child. Playing on the beach, swimming naked in the sea. How she would love to do that. Swim naked with him. Of course, her body was fuller now, but she still found it attractive when she looked in the mirror. And Freddie wasn't as trim and lithe as he used to be either.

She could see why Freddie would be attracted to Anna. Her daughter was the mirror image of her when she was younger. A vision that Freddie had loved, made love to, so eagerly. And she could see his attraction to her.

But had Freddie lied about loving Anna? She felt, perhaps, she had pushed him too far, too soon at Giorgio's wake? And he said the worst thing ever to reject her. But Freddie was seeing her now. He was prescribing medicine for her. So, he obviously cared. She should take her time, now that Anna was gone. Anna had gone to war and might never return. She had time.

Maybe it was fate that brought her to the island. To see him again. Taking the necklace from her jewel box, she fastened it around her neck.

When she got back from visiting her father, Anna was delighted that Jose had changed his mind about going with her. Just before dawn the next day the pair set off from the city. They knew that, after Castro's invasion, Batista's army had taken control of the roads leading to the Oriente Province. Fearing they could be picked up and arrested they left the car halfway along the journey. They hitched a lift in the back of a sugar cane lorry, then walked the last few miles to the shack of a peasant they trusted, just as the moon was rising above the distant mountain range.

They were lucky. The peasant was in contact with Celia Sanchez, who had co-ordinated support for the rebels when they landed. She was now organising the supplies to the rebel camps in the mountains. The peasant went off on his horse that evening, and came back to say that Celia would meet them at the shack, the next morning.

Celia arrived at the break of day, carrying a woman's peasant dress for Anna and peasant's clothes for Jose.

'You should wear these in case you are stopped,' she said. 'I want you take the medicine, and some ammunition to Che's camp. There are pockets sewn into the insides.'

Anna had heard of Che Guevara. He was an Argentinian medical student turned revolutionary, who was now second-in-command to Castro. She was excited that, at last, she would be joining the real rebels in the mountains.

'What about weapons?' she asked.

'You'll be given those when you get there,' Celia replied.

As she was speaking a small lorry arrived at the shack, raising a cloud of dust into the still morning air.

'He will take you to the foothills of the Sierras. There'll be a guide there to take you to the camp.'

Jose was packing two belts of ammunition into the legs of his trousers. 'These are heavy. How long will it take?'

'You should get there by the afternoon.'

'Today?' he asked.

'No, tomorrow,' Celia said, 'If you walk through the night.'

Jose blew out his cheeks.

Still maintaining the fiction that he was prescribing Esther's pills Freddie was paying his weekly visit to the Mueller's. Having seen him arrive from his surgery window, Carl opened the door for him.

'Good morning, Freddie.'

Taking off his hat, Freddie entered. As Carl closed the door, Freddie looked at him. He looked thinner and frailer than last week. 'How are you?'

Carl put out his hands and shrugged. 'Still here. Unlike Anna.'

'What?' said Freddie, concerned.

'She's gone to join Castro's rebels in the Sierra Maestra.'

'When?'

'She came last evening to tell me. She was leaving first thing this morning.'

'I'm sorry, Carl, but I can't say I'm surprised. I suppose you did try to persuade her to –'

Carl interrupted. 'This is Anna, we are talking about.'

Freddie sighed. 'Did you tell her you were ill?'

'No. Why should I?'

'Well, maybe that would have changed her mind.'

'I'm not using emotional blackmail on my daughter, Freddie. And I'm not having her going off concerned about me. She'll have enough to worry about.'

Freddie shook his head. 'I suppose Jose went with her?'

'I don't know. She said he was undecided.'

'Let's hope he did. He'd do anything to protect her. And she might need it. It's a war she going into.'

'It's one she wants to fight, Freddie.'

The door to Esther's suite opened and she came out.

'Oh, I thought I'd heard you, Freddie. I've been waiting.'

She went back inside, leaving the door open.

'Does she know about Anna?'

Carl nodded.

'I'll talk to you later, Carl.'

Freddie walked down the hall and entered Esther's living room. She patted the cushion next to her on the sofa, but Freddie sat in the chair opposite, putting his briefcase on the floor beside him. He noticed she was wearing the necklace.

'How are you today, Esther?' He reached down to open the briefcase. 'I've brought you your pills.'

Esther touched the necklace at her throat. 'I hear your 'lover' has gone off to war,' she said.

'Esther – '

391

'Unrequited love can be very painful, can't it, Freddie? I should know.'

CHAPTER NINETY-FIVE

'Hi, Hans. Coming to dance with me?' said the young, beautiful teenager, stroking Hans bare, tanned arm.

Hans put his finger down the strap of her bikini bra and gently pulled to reveal more of her appealing cleavage.

'Later,' he said.

She pursed her lips, then turned and walked away. He watched her walk down the beach, her bottom swaying to sound of Presley's 'All Shook Up' from the bar's jukebox. Later, definitely.

Hans found Miami a fun place to be. Like being permanently on holiday. He swam, sunbathed, and surf-boarded in the afternoon and, in the evening, had a regular seat at the most popular bar on the coast. Elvis Presley, and rock and roll, had burst onto the scene in America. Though Hans was in his thirties, and no longer a teenager, he enjoyed joining the young girls rocking and rolling on the sand until dawn.

Sex was easy, and plentiful. Twosomes, threesomes. Whatever he wished. He was a mature man, handsome, wealthy, and foreign. There was something mysterious and enigmatic about being a German now. He had let it be known that he had been a leader in the Hitler Youth. And he loved the rumours, which he'd helped spread, that he had been a spy towards the end of the war. Perhaps, a double-agent. Maybe CIA. Well, the young girls seemed to love it, so why disabuse them?

In business, he had made a lot of contacts with Cubans who had sympathy with Castro, and he was selling weapons to the growing number of people who were joining the revolution, both in the mountains and in the cities. And, of course, selling them to the right-wing groups as well. War was very, very good.

Giorgio's nightclub in Havana was still doing well. So far the Mafia, who owned most of the entertainment in Cuba, had left the club alone. His part of the profit was building up nicely in an American bank.

But he missed Bella. Teenage girls were cute, but they couldn't compare to a mature woman like her.

Yesterday, after Carl had told him on the phone that Anna had gone to the far side of the island to fight with Castro, he made a decision.

'I've decided to go back home,' he told his new American companion, who had recently befriended him at the bar.

'To Germany?'

Hans, who was happily merry from Cuba Libres bought by his friend, had already told him about his youth, and hinted at his contact with the German agents in Cuba.

'No, to Cuba, dummkopf! My sister, Anna, she's a rebel. Been against Batista for years. She's just gone to fight with Castro in the south. So, I think, maybe, it's safe to go back now.'

His companion was looking at him. 'Your sister is called Anna, is she?

'Yeah.'

The man frowned, 'She's Anna Mueller?'

'Yes.' Hans answered, curiously. 'Why?'

Anna and Jose found the journey up to the mountain camp, long, arduous and dangerous. During the day there were spotter planes and helicopters overhead, looking for any movement beneath. It was safer to move at night but, with the moon mostly shrouded by cloud, progress was slow. After a while their eyes became accustomed, but they had to avoid groups of Batista's troops camped in the forest. Luckily the troops, unused to guerrilla tactics, generally lit fires which could easily be seen through the trees.

Late on the second afternoon, they finally reached the camp where Che Guevara, and his small group, were based. Not that you would have noticed it until you were almost on top of it. Having been trained in guerrilla warfare in Mexico, mostly by an American marine who had fought in Korea, the fighters knew how to conceal themselves in the trees and undergrowth, so they were invisible.

'This is the camp?' said Jose. 'There's no tents, no nothing. Where do we sleep?'

'On the ground,' said their guide, Alberto. He took them over to a large tree, surrounded by bushes. Inside the camouflaged structure Che Guevara was discussing tactics with a couple of men, over a detailed map of the area.

After Alberto introduced them, Guevara took his cigar from his mouth.

'Did you bring the medicine from Celia?' he said.

'Yes,' said Anna. She lifted up her skirt. 'Sewn in here.'

'Thank you.'

Later, after they had unloaded themselves of all the medicine and ammunition they had brought, Alberto showed them a place where they could sleep. Then he brought them a sparse meal of rice, vegetables and some indefinable meat.

'How is Che to work with?' asked Jose.

'He's brilliant, very brave, but he suffers from asthma,' Alberto explained. 'Sometimes he can hardly walk if it's bad.'

As Anna and Jose wolfed down the food, Alberto told them about the rebels' routine.

'We're scattered in small groups in the mountains. Small groups are easy to hide.'

'Do the army attack us often?' asked Anna, chewing on some gristle.

'No. Mostly we attack them. They don't know the forest, so it's easy to surprise them. We maybe kill some of them, and then disappear again.'

'When will we attack again?' asked Jose.

'First, we have to get you some proper clothes and some weapons. Then we'll see what Che has decided.'

Anna had been trained, along with her group, about how to fight. How to fire a weapon. How to kill. But she had never killed anyone. Tomorrow, or the next day, she might have to do that.

Hans listened to the American's story from start to finish, then went straight back to his room. He tried three times before he finally got his father on the phone. When Carl had heard what Hans had to say, he left the house immediately, and went straight to the harbour. Freddie wasn't in his room, but he found him seated outside his local café.

Freddie shook his head, and stared at the ocean, after he heard what Carl had told him, finding it hard to believe what he'd just heard.

'Does he really, really know that?' he asked Carl.

'Hans thinks the man is CIA. Apparently, they have been watching the situation in Cuba for years. They've got people in Havana. And all over the island.'

They were silent, as the waiter brought Carl's coffee. Putting a spoonful of sugar in the cup, Carl stirred the drink, distractedly.

'There's no way that Anna knows?'

'No way, Freddie! You know Anna. You know how passionate she is about the revolution. There's no way!'

Freddie nodded. He didn't even know why he had asked the question. Anna was too honest, too sincere, to be so devious.

'Do you know if they went together?'

'I don't know. She said he was undecided.'

Freddie got up. 'I'll see if I can find out, Carl.'

'Please.'

'If it's true, Carl, and he's gone with her, Anna needs to know, now.'

CHAPTER NINETY-SIX

Through the thinning cloud, Hans watched Cuba appear beneath him. The long island seemed lush and peaceful from up above. You couldn't tell that on the ground two armies were fighting hand to hand in the thick forest to the east. In those wooded mountains, Anna was risking her life for what she believed in. He was not a revolutionary. In fact, he didn't care which side won. As long as the war went on, he was very happy. It made him money. But whether he believed in her cause or not, he had done what he could to protect his young sister. Now all he wanted was to see Bella.

He had told Bella when he was arriving and he'd hoped she would pick him up at the airport, but she told him she was busy. When his taxi pulled up at the villa, he was disappointed that Bella's car wasn't in the drive, or in the open garage. Maybe she was at the club. He could have had the taxi stop there, but it was mid-morning, when it was generally closed. She could be rehearsing the dancers, of course, but she'd said she had hired a young choreographer last month, who was amazing.

Dropping his case in the hall, he went into the kitchen. The coffee percolator was still warm, so he poured a cup and then rang the club. There was no answer. Taking his coffee and his case upstairs to the master bedroom, he saw the bedclothes were their usual tangled mess. As they often worked at the club until dawn, Bella and he often didn't get up until the after midday. So, the cleaner never arrived until late afternoon.

There were wine glasses on both bedside tables. Well, that figured. Bella hadn't mentioned it on the phone, but he was sure she was still having her young men around for company at night.

Throwing his cases on the bed, he opened the French windows that led to their balcony to let in some air. Looking down at the sparkling pool, he felt very happy to be back. He unlocked his case and opened his wardrobe. It was full of clothes. Not his.

Hans stared at them, and then rummaged through the rack. There were shirts, slacks, even a couple a designer summer suits. None of the clothes were his. He frowned. Who the hell had taken over his wardrobe?

He went to look in his drawers. They were full of someone else's underwear, handkerchiefs, and socks. Feeling angry now, he went into the bathroom. The toiletries he'd left were missing. The shaver, the aftershave, the cologne, were not his. This wasn't just a casual lover. Someone had moved into his space.

It was a long drive to Oriente Province. When Freddie had found that Jose had gone with Anna, Carl had wanted to accompany him, but he was too frail for that length of car journey. And as Freddie said, he wouldn't actually be seeing Anna. All he could do was find a peasant who would take a letter to her. From his time fighting in the Spanish Civil War, Freddie knew that the rebels were often helped by the local people. He had seen the Catalonian peasants bring food, ammunition and information to the anti-Franco fighters up in the mountains in Northern Spain. Castro's men must have communication with local people as well. He was sure he could find one who would deliver the letter.

'It's much better if you write the letter, Carl,' Freddie had said. 'She may not believe it if it comes from me. Will she recognise your handwriting?'

'I think so. Yes.'

So, Carl had written the letter with as much detail as they knew, because Anna would need a lot of convincing.

According to Hans' American, Jose had been turned when he was in prison after the Moncada attack. He had been injured in the battle and spent some weeks in the prison hospital. It was there that the police worked on him.

Ramos's uncle was the overseer at the plantation where all of Jose's family worked, so Ramos knew of the family. Jose was the oldest. He hadn't worked on the plantation since he went with his auntie, Carlotta, to be the houseboy for the Mueller's. But his mother, and her five younger children were totally dependent on their work there, and also for their accommodation. If they were sacked, they would lose their shack as well. Losing their work and their home would be terrible for them, as there was no where they could go for help. That would be bad, though many other peasants on the island were in the same situation.

But four of Jose's siblings were girls. Most by now in their teens. The youngest being just eleven. When Ramos threatened to have them all taken away and handed over to the Mafia, who ran brothels all over America, Jose reluctantly agreed that he would become an informant.

It was easy to feel sorry for Jose. A man like Jose didn't have the money, or the contacts to protect his sisters. Freddie wondered if Jose had been involved in the death of Nico, or the car bomb that should have killed Hans. Once Jose had started down that track it was difficult to turn back. If he confessed, and told Anna, the four girls would just vanish anyway. It was a no-win situation for him.

Freddie wound his car down the track to the cabin of the peasant he thought would be the most likely to be in contact with the rebels. He knew that he must insist that the letter should be given to Anna herself, and only when she was alone.

When she knew the truth, it was up to her what she did then.

CHAPTER NINETY-SEVEN

Hans was sitting on the patio, with an almost empty bottle of finest Scotch whisky on the table beside him. He was furious that Bella had not mentioned anything of this to him over the phone. She could have explained and he might have been okay with it, for the time he was away. He'd thought of getting into his car to go looking for Bella, but having no idea where she was, he opted for a large whisky instead.

Going back upstairs, he took all his usurpers clothes from the wardrobe and the drawers onto the balcony. Screwing them up he hurled them into the pool below. Then, he put all his own clothes and toiletries back where they should be. Feeling vindicated, he went downstairs again to wait for Bella to come home. And emptied the bottle into his glass.

Even under the shade of the patio, the sun's heat was stifling. He glanced at the bottle, and winced. It was probably not a good idea to have had so much, if he wanted to talk to her rationally.

The sun made the pool a dazzling, bright-blue mirror. Some of the clothes had sunk to the bottom of the pool, while others floated gracefully, like a surrealist collage. Closing his eyes, he tried to think what he would say.

The dream was very vivid. It felt real. He was on the patio when he heard a car drive up. Voices came towards him.

'What the hell!' he heard Bella shout.

Hans opened his eyes, blearily, and blinked at the sunlight. For a moment he couldn't remember where he was. Bella was standing over him framed by the sunlight behind her, like an angel, though she didn't look very angelic at the moment.

'What the fucking hell, Hans!'

As Hans tried to sit up, a young man appeared next to Bella. He was a handsome, tall, slim mulatto.

'All of them,' the man said, flatly to Bella. He looked at the pool. The pool system had sucked some of the floating clothes into the filtration vents. 'They'll be ruined.'

'We'll buy some more,' Bella said.

Hans sat up. He didn't feel like trying to stand up at the moment.

'What the hell's going on, Bella? Who is this guy?'

'I'm Max,' the young man said, and added, acidly. 'Thanks for doing my laundry for me.'

'What is he doing in my bedroom? What's going on?'

'I was going to tell you, Hans, but Max only just moved in a couple of days ago.'

'Well, tell Max to move out. Now!'

'I'm sorry I didn't have time to tell you, but it's nothing personal, Hans.'

'It seems very personal to me!' Hans retorted. 'I want him out!'

Bella folded her arms, over her breasts. 'Hans, I liked you being here. Even after I heard you'd started selling guns again. I had thought maybe you could sleep in one of the spare rooms. I didn't intend throwing you out.'

'Sleep in one of the spare rooms! What the hell, Bella! I live here!'

'That doesn't seem like it's going to work now, Hans. Sorry.'

'Bella, who is this guy?'

'I'm Bella's choreographer, at the club.'

'Fuck the club!' Hans shouted. He got up now, anger taking over from his hangover. 'Get the fuck out of here! I live here!'

Bella stood between the two men as Hans made a move towards Max. 'Not any more, Hans,' Bella said quietly.

Hans looked at her. She looked serious. 'But, Bella... Listen...About the guns - '

'Things change, Hans,' Bella interrupted. 'You've been away quite a while. Don't get me wrong, I liked having you around. We had some great times together. But I felt I needed something new, something different. I didn't think there was any need for you to move out.'

'What, while some jerk nigger takes my place? In my bed? Fuck that! Get him out of our house, Bella!'

'It's my house, Hans. And I chose who stays and who goes.'

Hans shouted past Bella. 'Don't you like guns, as well, Max? Well, you're gonna be staring down the barrel of one in a minute!'

Shoving Bella aside, Hans made his way into the house, but Max stood in his way. As Hans tried to push past him, Max took hold of him and propelled him backwards into the pool.

With a startled cry, Hans fell deep under the water, taking a mouthful as he went. Shocked and furious, he thrashed to the surface. Gasping, he yelled, 'You fucking bastard! Get out of this house, or I'll fucking kill you!'

Swimming to the edge, he scrambled out of the pool. The water had partly sobered him up. He stood up, clearly determined to beat the shit out of Max, but found himself staring at a small pistol in Bella's hand.

'No, Hans. You get out of the house. Now.'

CHAPTER NINETY-EIGHT

The farmer's donkey could only go so far up the mountain track. When the trail disappeared into thick undergrowth beneath the trees, he tethered the donkey to a branch and waited. He looked around, nervously. It was a perilous journey. The army had units in the mountains searching for the rebels. If he was found, with what his donkey was carrying, he would probably be shot on the spot. Or worse, they could torture him to find out where the rebels were camped. He didn't know that, but they would enjoy the torture anyway. One of his neighbours had already been arrested, tortured and killed by one of the army units. Then, they burnt down his shack, leaving his family homeless.

There was movement in the undergrowth. He turned towards it, swinging his shotgun from his shoulder. Three rebels emerged through the thick ferns. Two men and a woman. The tall man smiled and shook his hand.

'Juan, this is Jose and Anna,' he said.

The farmer never really wanted to know any rebel's names, but this time he was grateful. As the two men started to unpack the weapons from the donkey's packs, Juan caught the woman's eye. She looked at him, curiously. He shook his head, slightly. Taking a small folded paper from his pocket, he moved over to her and slipped it into her hand, while putting his hand over his mouth. He coughed.

'Dr Freddie,' he whispered.

She looked very surprised but, thankfully, put the paper straight into her pocket. He didn't think the others had seen. Juan was very relieved that the woman had arrived, as he had been told to deliver the letter to the woman, and thought he would have help carry the weapons to the camp to find her. Dr

Freddie had insisted that he delivered the letter to the woman, in secret. And he had done that.

When the doctor had left his shack, Juan opened the folded letter. He could speak Spanish, of course, and could read a little, but it looked like it was written in English. So, he had no idea what the letter said, but he trusted Dr Freddie, implicitly.

He thought about it. Was the doctor in love with the woman? Was it a love letter? She looked much younger than him, but even without make-up, he could see that she was beautiful. Maybe the doctor was in love with a rebel, who he might never see again? And whatever happened, Dr Freddie wanted her to know that he loved her. Juan had put the letter in his pocket and smiled.

The rain began to fall as they carried the weapons through the undergrowth back to the camp. The folded paper felt like it was burning a hole in Anna's pocket. It was clearly a note. Hopefully, the torrential rain wouldn't make it unreadable. She thought the man had whispered, "Dr Freddie", but she didn't know why the man had given it to her secretly. What would Freddie have to say to her that was a secret?

That he loved her? Well, she knew that already. Despite his constant critical quips about her 'revolution', it was there in his expression when he looked at her. He had told her mother that he loved her daughter at Giorgio's wake. At first, she tried to pretend it was just a defence against her mother's unwanted attention. But, remembering the way he kissed her hand after her abortion, she knew.

Perhaps the note was about her father? She had known for a while that her father wasn't well. He had clearly lost weight, and Carlotta had told her that he hardly ate his meals. But she had never questioned him about it. Her father was a private man. If he wanted her to know, if he wanted to talk to his daughter about it, he would have. So, she respected his wishes, and never mentioned it.

It must be that he had died, surely? As she was telling him that she was going to fight with Castro in the Sierra Maestra, she knew that might happen while she was gone. He'd looked extremely sad, but he had only hugged her, kissed her, and then, surprisingly, wished her God speed. Strange, as neither of them believed in a God.

She guessed that after seeing so many sick and dying in his life as a doctor, his belief must have slipped away, like the lives of many of his patients. For her, it was the sheer injustice in the world that convinced her. How could a Deity stand back and let brutal tyrants oppress and destroy the poor? How could a God let what happened to her mother's family? To so many of the Jews in Germany?

If her father had died, she very much wanted to be with him as he was laid to rest. But there was no way she could travel all the way across the island to be at his funeral. That would have to wait until they reached Havana, when they had won.

She touched the pocket of her soaking trousers. Perhaps, the rain had washed Freddie's words away? At the moment, that was probably the best thing.

CHAPTER NINETY-NINE

By now in his early thirties, Hans didn't expect to be going home to his mother, feeling lost and unloved, like a little boy. But that's how he felt.

He had left Bella's villa at gunpoint, and had driven away still dripping from his soaking in the pool. He drove along the Malecon in his convertible, alongside a wild and stormy ocean. The turbulent waves, lashing the seawall, were as violent as he felt. As the heavy rain began to fall the howling wind chilled him, but he didn't close the hood. Feeling cold fuelled his anger. He was so incensed.

Bella was rapacious, he knew that. She liked younger men, boys almost. But he had handled that. So, how could she throw him out like a piece of garbage? She had actually said he could stay in a spare room! How humiliating, after what they had been to each other. He thought he understood women, but not Bella. She was more like a man.

There was no way he was going to a hotel. He was wet, cold, and he had no money. But he wasn't going back to the villa, begging for his wallet.

He parked the car outside the Mueller's house. Walking up the drive, he let himself in with his key. The hall was empty. The door to his father's surgery was closed. He didn't know if his father was in there, but he didn't want to see him, anyway. He could imagine Carl's scorn when he found out what had happened. His son being thrown out by a woman as old as his own mother. No matter what he did, his father never seemed to care, or praise him.

In Germany, it was obligatory for boys of his age to join the Hitler Youth. But his father had ridiculed him when he said he actually enjoyed it. In Cuba he had derided his friendship with his beloved Giorgio, and was furious when he found out his son made a living selling drugs. He didn't even turn up for the grand opening of his nightclub, something which he should have been proud of his son for achieving.

How different to his mother. Until Klaus came he had enjoyed being his mother's favourite. He could still remember, even though they had a nanny, that his mother used to bath him, and then put him to bed and read him fairy stories from The Brother's Grimm. He loved cuddling up to her warm, soft body, peaking at the gruesome pictures of witches and devils, doing their evil deeds in the forests. But he was safe, being wrapped in his mother's arms.

At the end of the hall, Hans stopped and knocked on his mother's door.

'Mama, it's me, Hans!'

There was a rustle and then Esther opened the door. She stared at her son, looking cold, wet and wretched.

'Hans! What are you doing here? Whatever happened?'

Hans slumped his shoulders, unhappily. Esther opens her arms, and hugged him to her.

The rain had stopped when they reached the camp, and the late afternoon sun made the wet leaves glisten like a fairy glade. Anna wanted to read the note, but there were duties to be done before she could have time to herself. After they unloaded and stored the ammunition, she was asked to serve out the stew and take it to the little groups dotted in the camp area.

When she had finished, she sat with Jose and began to eat her meal quickly, anxious to go somewhere she could read the note.

'What did the man give you?' asked Jose.

Anna looked up. 'What?' she said, guiltily.

'The farmer gave you something. You put it on your pocket.'

For a moment, Anna thought of lying. But that wouldn't work. 'He gave me a note, I think.

'A note?'

'I think he said it was from Freddie.'

Jose was surprised. 'From Freddie?'

Anna shrugged. 'Yeah'.

'Why would Freddie send you a secret note?'

'It's not secret, Jose. I just put it in my pocket. It was raining.'

'He didn't want us to see him give it to you.'

'Didn't he? I don't know.'

'Are you going to read it?'

'When I have time. It's probably ruined anyway, with all the rain.'

They carried on eating in silence for a minute.

Then Jose said, 'It's very strange.' He spooned up his last piece of meat and put it in his mouth. 'Freddie coming all that way to give you a note. Why?'

'I have no idea, Jose...Freddie is...a law until himself.'

Jose licked his plate clean.

'Well, you're obviously not going to read it while I'm here.'

'No. I will, Jose...' She took the soggy paper from her pocket. 'It's just...I know Freddie cares about me. It's probably just to say...Good luck.'

'It's a long way to travel, Anna, just to say 'Good Luck'.

Anna held the folded paper in her hand, but didn't open it.

Jose looked at her, then stood up. 'Have you finished?'

'Yes.'

He took her plate. 'I'll leave you to it.'

Anna watched him walk away towards the kitchen, which was concealed in the ferns. Then, she prised open the wet paper. The ink had spread a little over the note, but it was just about readable. She recognised her father's handwriting.

CHAPTER ONE HUNDRED

Hans relaxed in the deep hot bath, the bubbles coming up to his neck. Furious with Bella, he hadn't realised how chilled he had become driving in his open car through the gathering storm. When his mother hugged him, he broke down and started to cry. Esther hugged him harder.

'Oh Hans. What's the matter?'

Before he could speak, she went on, 'You're so cold and wet. You're shivering. First of all you have to get out of those clothes and have a hot bath before you say anything else, or you'll get a cold.'

So, he had undressed in her bedroom and put on one of Esther's housecoats, while she filled the bathtub. After what he had just been through, it was lovely being looked after. Bella didn't do 'motherly'. Especially not with a gun in her hand.

'Hans, you look wonderful in that!' joked Esther, as he entered the bathroom in her housecoat, which was covered with tiny flowers. 'Leave the door, I'll get Carlotta to make you a hot rum, to warm you up inside.'

When his mother left, he'd hung the housecoat on a peg on the door, and put his foot in the water. It was almost too hot, but he put both feet in and waited till he could slowly lower himself into the water. His cold body soon became accustomed. He lay back, relaxed and closed his eyes.

Without knocking, Esther walked in holding a glass.

'Sorry, I should have knocked,' she said, pretending to cover her eyes.

Despite being covered by the bubbles, Hans quickly covered himself with his hands.

She leant over to put the glass on the tiled shelf running alongside the bath. In the flowing, silk housecoat, her full breasts were close to his face. Her figure was very much like

Bella's, though lack of exercise had now made it fuller and less toned.

'I didn't know you had come back from America,' she said, still leaning over him. 'When you have finished your bath, you can tell me all about what's happened.'

'Thank you, Mama. I will,' he said, trying not look at her breasts.

She stood up. 'You're so brown. Almost like Nico.'

'Poor Nico,' he said, sympathetically. 'So sad.'

'Yes...I really shouldn't say this to my son, I suppose, but Nico taught me to share it with him...The bath...Your father and I never did anything like that.'

'Oh,' Hans said, slightly panicked. For a moment, he thought his mother was going to disrobe and get in with him. The thought scared him, but he realised it also quite excited him.

Esther leant over again, and kissed him on the forehead. 'Enjoy your bath.'

After she left and closed the door, Hans sighed, with relief. He picked up the glass. Had he actually wanted his mother to get in the bath with him? He drank the rum all in one go.

Anna wasn't there when Jose got back from the camp kitchen. He looked around. One of the rebels seated nearby nodded and pointed into the forest.

The sound of one of Batista's helicopters broke the quiet of the camp. It was lowdown, nearby. They all looked up, but the foliage of the trees was so thick it was impossible to see it.

Jose waited until the sound of the helicopter faded away, then picked up his rifle and went into the trees to look for Anna. She hadn't gone far. He found her sitting with her back against a large banyan tree, whose perpendicular roots, growing upwards, looked like the columns of a tiny cathedral.

When she saw him, she got up and stared at him.

'Are you alright?' he said.

She had the opened note in her hand. 'Is it true?'

'What?'

'Are you really a spy for the police?'

'What?' said Jose, shocked.

'It's what the note says.'

'What? That's crazy...! Crazy...! Let me see!'

Anna moved away as he came towards her. Her hand moved to the butt of the pistol in her belt.

Jose stopped. 'Anna, this is crazy! You know that Freddie fancies you. You said that yourself. He even told your mother! He's obviously just gone mad. He wants to break us up...Maybe he wants you to leave and go back to him. I just don't know why he said that.'

'Jose, the note was from my father. He got the information from Hans.'

'Hans?'

'Hans met someone in Miami. CIA, they think. He said it happened in prison. That they threatened to kidnap your sisters, and take them away to be prostitutes in America.'

Jose looked at the ground, and then this way and that.

'Is that true, Jose?'

Finally, Jose looked at Anna. 'I wanted to protect them, Anna. The police can do what they want. I couldn't stop them... Clara is just eleven years-old!'

'Jose, why didn't you tell me?'

'There was nothing you could have done! You were only safe because you were with me...I didn't want to do it, Anna!'

Anna was breathing deeply now. At first, she didn't believe the note. She had to read it several times, to see what her father said was true. But she knew her father would never lie to her. He must believe it, and Jose had just confirmed it.

'Did you kill Nico?'

'No…I just suggested it was him. To take suspicion from me. Because of the police raid at your house.'

'When you hid the printing machine. You knew it was going to happen?'

She looked at Jose, whose head and shoulders had slumped.

'Did you plant the bomb that nearly killed Hans?'

Jose looked up at Anna, with tears in his eyes. 'He was the obvious choice…because he delivered the radio. The transmitter.'

'You planted the bomb to kill my brother?' She took her pistol from her belt.

'You're going to shoot me?'

'No. I'm going to take you to the camp, and let Ché decide what to do.'

Jose slowly slipped the rifle from his shoulder. Anna raised her gun, and pointed it at Jose's chest. As Jose swung the rifle up, Anna's finger tightened on the trigger. He put the muzzle under his chin.

'I love you, Anna.'

The crack of the rifle bullet, shattered the silence of the forest.

CHAPTER ONE HUNDRED AND ONE

Wearing his mother's housecoat, Hans emerged from the bathroom. In the sitting room, Esther had organised coffee and two large slices of cake on the coffee table. She patted the cushion next to her on the sofa. Hans thought for a moment of choosing the large armchair but, instead, he sat down beside her.

'Carlotta's rum cake,' she said. 'Your favourite.'

'Thank you, Mama. But I'm not really hungry.'

Esther took his hand in both of hers, and put it in her lap. 'Then tell me all about it.'

Feeling uncomfortable being so close, Hans told her what had happened at Bella's villa. Esther listened intently, encouraging him, squeezing his hand from time to time.

'She had a gun?' she said, when he had finished. 'Would she have shot you?'

Hans tried a smile. 'I didn't wait to find out, Mama.'

'Oh, Hans. You poor, poor boy. Come here.'

Putting an arm round his shoulder, she gently pulled his head down to her chest. For a moment, Hans enjoyed the warm softness of her breasts on his face, feeling her heart beating. He sat up quickly.

'Where are my clothes?' he said, abruptly.

Esther looked a little surprised at his reaction. 'Carlotta is drying them.'

'Can you ring and see if they are ready?'

She was a little irritated now. 'Are you going somewhere?'

'I think I should call and apologise to Bella.'

Straightening her top, she said, coolly, 'Do you think that's wise? I don't see my son settling for being second best.'

He shrugged. He didn't intend phoning Bella, but he needed to get away from his mother. As soon as he was dressed, he got in his car and drove around the city aimlessly, feeling very agitated and disturbed.

Anna stared at the prone figure of Jose. He had fallen backwards, so she couldn't see the gaping hole that had scattered his brains up into the trees. Dropping to her knees, she put her hands to her face and began to cry.

'Oh, Jose,' she muttered. 'Jose, why didn't you tell me...? We could have done something!' she said through her tears.

Slowly, she looked up. They would have heard the sound of the shot in the camp and would come looking for them. They might be watching her now from the undergrowth, seeing what had happened before approaching her. She'd show them her father's letter, and they would understand. But Jose would have been shot anyway. There was no way they could guard and drag a prisoner around, as they moved from place to place, attacking the army, and then hiding from them. Maybe suicide was the best way for Jose.

She got up and put the note in the top pocket of her fatigues. There was no way she was going to leave Jose's body where it was, to be eaten by the forest animals. She needed to go to the camp and get them to help burying him.

Suddenly, the roar of the helicopter crashed through the leaves. They must have heard the rifle shot and come back to investigate. Then, she heard rat-tat-tat of its machine gun, raining death through the foliage. She dived for cover beneath the banyan tree.

There was firing from the camp, aiming for a helicopter. She felt the 'whoosh' of a mortar landing close by. The pilot must have given an army unit the co-ordinates. She knew she had to get away from the attack. Crawling on her hands and knees along the ground, she felt a massive shock-wave lift her up, and hurl her through the ferns. Then she was falling. Huge, stinging leaves and jagged branches slapped and tore her skin. It was a long fall, through damp air and silence, except for the silent scream in her brain.

And then, blackness...

CHAPTER ONE HUNDRED AND TWO

Maria had just started her shift. She would be there until midnight, or later, if she felt like it. Having had no education, it was the best work she could get in the city.

She generally liked sex, and the boss of her brothel was more generous than most, so she had built up a tidy nest-egg for the time when she finally hung up her black stockings and suspenders. And, more importantly, she was paying for Aurora to have a proper education. Her daughter would be able to choose what job she wanted when she graduated.

From being a teenager, Maria's voluptuous figure had always attracted men's attention. Now, having just turned forty-five, she appealed to a more specialist market. Many of the male tourists wanted the young slim girls. The younger the better. But many of the teenage sailors from the American fleet often went for the roundness of her hips, the comfort of her breasts, and softness of her stomach. She wondered about that, and she mothered them into the slower, more loving side of sexual pleasure. That was most the enjoyable part of her job. Teaching young men how to appreciate a woman.

She was seated with the rest of the girls in the shadily-lit reception area, where the customers could choose who they wanted. The tall, handsome man who came in didn't look like he needed to pay for a woman's attention. Most of the girls would have done him for free.

He gave an embarrassed nod to her boss at the reception desk, and looked around the room at the six girls lounging on the plush sofas. To Maria's surprise, his eyes immediately settled on her. He half-smiled, embarrassed.

She got up and approached him.

'Hi. I'm Maria.'

'Hans,' he muttered, looking nervously around.

Maria took his hand and led him down the corridor to her room. Though he looked rather sophisticated, he was obviously very nervous. She wondered what he liked.

Even as she was closing the door, Hans was hurriedly stripping off his shirt, slacks and briefs. She turned to him. He had a great body, tanned and toned. His prick was already quite stiff.

He took hold of her, forcefully, and pushed her backwards on the bed. Before she could speak, he pulled her knickers down roughly, opened her legs and forced himself straight into her.

She gasped, surprised.

Pulling her breasts from her bra, he closed his eyes and began suck and fondle them, as he thrust in and out, crying out with each lunge.

'Hans,' she said. 'Slow down.'

But he took no notice and increased his pace, almost hurting her.

'Bella, you bitch!' he gasped. With each thrust he began to shout out a difference curse. 'Bella, you dirty fucking bitch!' 'You fucking bitch! Bella, you bitch! You fucking dirty bitch, Bella!'

With his eyes still tightly closed, he began to squeeze her breasts harder, as Maria felt him about to come.

He slowed down, groaning, and muttered, 'Oh, no! Oh, God!...Oh, No!...No!'

When he had finished, he slumped down on her, breathless, and began to cry.

It was dark when Anna woke. Thankfully the moon was shining through the trees, so she could see around her. She felt very sore, scratched and bruised, and had a bad headache. But she didn't seem to be badly injured. How long had she been unconscious? Hours definitely. Days? She didn't know.

Apart from the wind in the leaves it was silent. She remembered the attack, but she had no idea what had happened. Had they all been killed, captured, or had they escaped? The only way of knowing was to climb back up the mountain and try to find them. Looking up, she seemed to have fallen down a steep gulley. There was no way up the way she had fallen.

Holding onto a branch, she struggled up. At least she could stand and move all her limbs. She checked herself. Her knife was still in its sheath, but her gun wasn't in her waistband. She searched on the ground all around her, but it wasn't there. It must have fallen out when she fell and there was no way she could find it in the darkness.

She didn't know which way to go, so she chose to head towards the moon. The gulley turned out to be a long ravine. She kept on walking, trying not to think about the last moments with Jose. After about an hour, she still couldn't find an easy way up. But the forest was thinning out. Through the trees she saw a faint light. She crept towards it, hoping it wasn't the fire of an army camp.

The light turned out to be an oil lamp, shining through the small window of a wooden shack. Should she go and see who was there? The local peasants seemed to side with the rebels. Maybe it was Juan's shack? She hoped so.

It wasn't Juan. It was a middle-aged man called Angel. He lived with his wife and three children in the shack. They were only awake because one of the children had a fever and the mother was cradling him in her arms.

Angel was very welcoming. He gave Anna some water and piece of mango. As there was no room in the shack for Anna to rest, he took her to a little shed where the goat was kept. There was enough straw in there to make a bed for Anna.

'When it's light,' he said, 'I will show you where I think the rebels are camped.'

'Did you see the fight? Up there? Did you see the helicopter?' Anna asked.

'Yes. But I think the rebels escaped.'

'Good. Really? Did you see them?'

'No. They are up there, in the mountains...I heard some soldiers talking in the town.'

Anna thanked him and then bedded down, beside the goat. She tried to sleep, but thoughts about Jose kept her awake most of the night. The image of him lying there, dead eyes wide open, kept coming whenever she closed her eyes. Finally, having fallen into a deep sleep just as dawn was breaking, she was woken by the goat bleating beside her. She sat up. There was movement outside. Looking through the door, she saw Angel cycling away on an old bicycle.

She got up, puzzled. Going round to the door of the shack, she saw the mother, looking at the child who was tossing and turning in a small bed. The mother looked up, a little nervously, as Anna entered.

'Is the child alright?' Anna asked.

The mother shook her head.

'Where has Angel gone?'

'He's gone...to see the doctor, in the town.'

'Is there anything I can do?'

The mother shook her head. 'No...When Angel gets back he will show you the way to the rebels camp.'

Anna went outside as the rising sun's rays began to filter through the trees. Feeling hungry, she wondered where Angel had got the mango? She looked about her. Around the back of the shack she found a small mango tree. As she reached to pick a ripe mango off a branch, she heard the sound of a truck coming up the track. Peering round the corner, she saw an army lorry rattling up the track, driving straight towards her.

CHAPTER ONE HUNDRED AND THREE

Esther had waited beside her door and managed to catch Hans in the hall, on his way out of the house.

'Hans, my darling. There you are.'

Taking his hand, she stroked the tanned flesh of his forearm. 'I was thinking it would be so lovely for us to have breakfast in my suite. Just the two of us.'

Hans desperately wanted not to be there, but just pulling his arm away would be rude. Knowing what he had done with that prostitute made him shrink from his mother's touch. To his shame, he'd had sex with his mother in his mind, and with his body. He was not religious, and never went to church, but he knew that incest was a sin.

'Thank you, Mama, but I don't do breakfast. I work late at the club, so I don't get up 'til noon.'

'You're not going back to the club again surely? Not after what Bella did to you!'

'I own it, Mama. I have to go.'

She stopped stroking and pressed his forearm. 'Will you see her?'

'Maybe. I don't know.'

He took her hand and slowly released it from his.

'You're not thinking of going back to her?'

Hans shrugged.

'Hans, my darling, I can't bear you being dominated by that woman.'

'She's my business partner, Mama. We have to talk.'

'You will come and tell me what happens, won't you?'

'Of course, Mama.'

As he tried to leave, she reached up trying to kiss him on the lips. He moved his head, so the kiss was on his cheek.

She took his arm again. 'You promise,' she said. It was not a question. 'You come straight back and tell me.'

The doorbell rang. Relieved, Hans went and opened it. Freddie was outside. He looked surprised.

'Hans?'

'Freddie.' He glanced back at his mother, then turned and muttered to Freddie. 'Did you...get the message...to her?

Freddie nodded.

Hans turned to his mother, 'Goodbye, Mama!'

'Goodbye, my darling!'

Freddie entered and closed the door.

'What was that about?' Esther enquired.

'What? Just saying 'Hello'.

'It's not my pills day, Freddie, but I'm very happy to see you, anyway.'

'I've actually come to see Carl,' Freddie said.

'Oh, really? Did you know that Hans has left that awful woman and has come back home?'

'How very nice for you, Esther.'

'Come and see me afterwards,' she demanded, 'and I'll tell you all about it.'.

As she went back into her room, Freddie stood to attention and clicked his heels together, a mock German salute.

He wondered did Esther ever think about anything but herself? Did she know, or care, that her husband was soon to die of a terrible illness? Did she know her daughter was risking her life trying to bring freedom to this island? Probably not. But she had her favourite child, Hans, back now. Perhaps that would take the pressure off him? Hans was very welcome to her.

As Anna ran the hail of bullets ripped through the air around her. Somehow, mercifully without being hit she reached the forest, and started weaving through the trunks and the ferns. After a moment, the firing stopped. They must be chasing her. Could she outrun them? Having no weapon, all she could do was run.

She ran on, being lashed by branches and huge leaves, through the thickening undergrowth. Gasping for air, she looked behind her, and tripped over a concealed branch. Sprawling forwards, she rolled into the ferns. As she tried to get up she felt her ankle give way. She couldn't outrun them now.

Hiding was as good as anything the US army trainer had told them. She looked around for a suitable place. Crouching down beneath the large leaves and ferns, she slipped her knife out from its sheath. Maybe she could take one of them out, if nothing else.

She waited, trying to calm down her breathing, and listened. The soldiers were shouting amongst themselves. Some ran on into the thickening forest, the others spread out to search.

Peering through the leaves, she could see one soldier heading her way. She gripped the knife, trying to remember the words of the trainer. If they were facing you, straight to the heart. Facing away, pull back their head and slit the throat from ear to ear. Could she do that? Could she kill someone? She knew that she had nearly pulled the trigger on Jose. It was what she joined up for, to fight or to die. Now, it looked like she was about to do both.

The soldier approached. He hadn't seen her yet, but she knew he must at any moment. She would have to spring out and surprise him. Straight to the heart. She tensed her body to leap.

Suddenly a shot rang out, echoing through the forest. The soldier turned away to see what was happening. Anna waited. She didn't know who was firing, or at who. As the soldier called out to the others, a bullet tore into his skull, sending bits of his brain all over the leaves, and onto Anna's face.

She heard the other soldiers shouting out to each other in panic. Then heard them running, away. She waited, wiping slivers of grey matter from her hair and cheeks.

'Anna!' she heard someone call.

Slowly, she stood up. Two of her unit emerged through the trees.

CHAPTER ONE HUNDRED AND FOUR

Knowing that Carl's illness made him unable to leave the house, Freddie had come to tell him about giving the letter to Juan, the farmer.

'Anna should have your letter by now,' Freddie said.

'If she believes it, she will have to confront him.'

'At least she has the upper hand now, Carl.'

'I'm very frightened, for both of them, Freddie.' Carl shook his head. 'Poor Jose. I feel so angry, but I feel so sorry for him. Being threatened yourself is one thing,' he said. 'But your family is quite another.'

Freddie nodded. For him it was Anna he was concerned about. 'Have you thought about your family?'

'What about them?'

'Have you told them how ill you are?'

'No.'

'They must have seen you, recently. You've lost weight. You look...frail. Have they not said anything?'

'Carlotta knows, I think. Anna maybe knows, in her sort of way. But she has never said anything. Not even hinted when she told me she was going away to fight with Castro.'

'That's her...her passion, Carl. A wonderful thing to have, if you think about nothing else.'

Carl nodded.

'But I'm sure she really loves you,' Freddie added.

'I think so...I hope so. She was always my favourite, Freddie. Anna's always been the favourite...' Carl smiled, then looked at Freddie, closely. 'With everyone.'

Freddie looked down, picked up his cup and drank the dregs of the coffee. What he did with Carl's young wife helped to ruin their marriage, and now he was helplessly in love with Carl's daughter. Why would he have driven all that way to tell

Anna that her lover was in fact a spy? A traitor. He wanted to say, 'I love Anna, Carl. I love your daughter. Sorry, I can't help that.' But that wouldn't help here, now. It never would. Instead, he said, 'What about Esther?'

'I haven't told Esther. She just cares about herself. And you, of course. And now Hans.'

'I just do my best to placate her, Carl.'

Carl took a sip of his coffee. 'I don't suppose that you would, er...go back together, after...'

'Good God, Carl! No! I was young, foolish, and naïve. You've no idea how much I...You have no idea...'

'She was an enchanting young woman, Freddie. I was so foolish. So much flattery, so much passion...So much beauty...'

'Only skin deep, sadly.'

Looking tired, Carl sighed and leaned back in his chair, 'It's Klaus I'm really worried about.'

Freddie looked at him, earnestly. 'I will take care of him, Carl. Of course. While I'm around. And if Anna...Well, if everything works out, for the best...I'm sure she will look after him too.'

Carl gave a little smile. 'I'm sure Klaus will be very happy, being looked after by you two.'

Miraculously, none of Ché's unit had been killed in the attack. They had scattered, and then regrouped further away from the camp. It was then that they noticed Anna and Jose were missing. So, Ché had sent two of their best snipers to go and look for them.

'We heard the shooting,' said Garcia, who was helping Anna back to the new camp. 'And saw you running.'

'Thank God. I thought I was finished,' Anna said.

She explained what had happened with Jose, and had to explain it again to Ché when they reached the new camp.

'We would have had to shoot him anyway, Anna,' he said. 'Prisoners we let go. Spies, no.'

'Jose knew that,' Anna replied.

Escaping the army attack, the rebels had left what food they had in the old camp, so Anna found a place to sit, and busied herself breaking down and reassembling the sub-machine gun she had taken from the dead soldier, trying to forget how hungry she was.

But thoughts of Jose kept going round and round in her head. She knew he had been preoccupied for quite a while. If ever she asked him how he was, he was evasive and became more withdrawn from her. The love-making was less intense, more occasional. But she had put that down to the pressures they were under acting as a secret cell in the city, expecting to be arrested at any moment.

She now knew why her interview with Ramos has been so cursory. It wasn't because he was concerned that she was a lawyer. He had interviewed them both to take attention away from Jose.

It was hard to forgive Jose. She suspected, now, that he had killed Nico to explain the police raid on her home. And he had admitted to her that he tried to blow up her brother.

But she could understand his reason. She knew his four beautiful teenage sisters. Young Cuban girls, maybe because of the mix of Spanish and African blood, were sought after by Americans. Some girls went willingly to America to earn a living selling their bodies, but she knew that others were taken, willing or not. Batista's police were a law unto themselves. There was nothing Jose could have done about saving them.

As night came, she lay down to sleep on the ground with her weapon beside her. But sleep wouldn't come. Only tears.

CHAPTER ONE HUNDRED AND FIVE

Hans knew it was no use trying to phone Bella again. Either she wasn't in, or she put the phone down as soon as she heard his voice. Driving to the night-club, he saw Bella's Chevrolet Bel Air parked outside and pulled in behind it.

As it was mid-afternoon, Giorgio's wasn't yet open for punters. He opened the front door and walked in. In the evening Giorgio's had one of the most stylish décors in the city, but in the daytime lit by bare light bulbs, the club seemed more like a faded courtesan.

Max was rehearsing the dancers on the stage. Seeing Hans enter, he stopped and followed him through to the back of the club to the office. Bella was sitting at her desk looking over the accounts. She looked up when Hans entered, but didn't seem surprised.

'Ah, Hans.'

'Bella. We need to talk.'

Max walked in, aggressively.

'It's alright, Max,' Bella said, putting up her hand. 'I'll deal with this. Go back to your rehearsal.'

'You sure?'

Bella waved him away. Giving Hans a menacing look, Max left.

'Help yourself to a drink,' Bella said.

'Too early.'

Bella raised her eyebrows. 'Then sit.'

But Hans remained standing. 'I kept phoning, Bella, to apologise...For everything...'

Leaning back, Bella took out a cigarette from a pack. Hans pulled out his lighter and leant forward to light it for her.

He went on, 'I mean, it was such a shock, Bella. Coming back and finding...I didn't know. You never said anything.'

Bella blew out a smoke-ring, staring at him, impassively.

'If you've had said something, Bella...Well, maybe, I'm sure, I could have got used to it. I mean, erm, I am quite happy to sleep in the spare bedroom...Really...Like you said. I'm happy to do that.'

'That was before you threatened Max with a gun.'

'I was just angry then, confused...I'd had too much to drink...You see, I thought we had something. Us two...I love you, Bella.'

'I don't think Max is going to sleep easy, knowing there's a man in the next room who wants to shoot him.'

'You know I wouldn't do that!'

'I might. He doesn't.'

Hans was beginning to look desperate. 'Please, Bella. Let me come back...I love you...I don't care how, whatever you want...Just, please...'

'I bet Esther was delighted to see her son back home.'

'Please, Bella...Please.' Hans pleaded.

Bella stubbed out her cigarette. 'I don't like men who grovel, Hans. I may be tough, but I'm not a dominatrix.'

Hans stood there, tears welling in his eyes. 'Bella...'

'Oh, and leave your key when you go, for the club.'

'What? I own this place, Bella.'

'Yeah, well, since we're doing so well the mob have taken a big interest. I said I'd give them your share.'

'You can't do that!'

'You don't argue with gangsters, Hans. I'll pay you a fair price.'

Hans left the club into blazing sunshine. Sitting in his open car he broke down and wept, as tourists wandered by staring.

That evening, as Maria came in for her shift at the brothel, she found Hans already there, waiting for her in reception.

Anna had taken part in many demonstrations where fighting sometimes broke out. She had even seen people being shot beside her. But violence was never the aim of those rallies.

In the attack on the Moncada barracks her rebel group had arrived too late to take part in the fight, so she had never fired a gun in anger. But today was different. Today an armed battle was going to happen. And she was going to be there, amongst it.

The army unit, that had attacked the rebel camp with mortars, had been tracked down. Inexperienced, or neglectful of guerrilla tactics, they were camped down the mountain in a glade in the forest. An easy target.

'Ché wants those mortars,' she was told, as the rebels were divided into small units.

Before they left, she checked her sub-machine gun for the last time. It was an M3 which she had fired in training. Used in the Second World War and Korea, it was light, but had to be regularly cleaned to stop it jamming. That was the last thing you needed faced with an angry enemy.

The sun was getting low in the West as they approached the army camp. On a silent signal, the units fanned out, keeping the sun behind them, making it harder for the soldiers to see them against the glare.

The air of the forest was humid, but Anna crouched in the wet ferns, her heart beating rapidly, couldn't feel the sweat pouring down her. She watched the soldier's line up, getting ready for a meal. Sitting ducks.

Silently moving the gun, she took aim at people she didn't know. All with mothers, fathers, friends, lovers. Should she aim above their heads? They would all panic when the firing started, and most probably run away. Leaving the mortars behind.

Her finger tightened on the trigger, waiting for the shrill bird-song that was their signal to attack.

CHAPTER ONE HUNDRED AND SIX

Freddie was delighted. Thrilled. He had expected to wait months, maybe a year, before he got a reply. But there it was. He read the letter, and re-read it, to see if it really said what he thought it did. Then, putting on his hat, he left his room breezily. He didn't bother to phone the Mueller's. With the cancer was spreading Carl never left the house. Freddie wanted to see Carl's face when he told him the news.

'A book?' interrupted Carl, as Freddie was still reading the letter.

'Yes,' Freddie said. He showed Carl the publisher's letter. 'They want to publish them. They are going to get an expert on conchology to write a little piece about each shell.'

Carl shook his head. 'A book of Klaus's drawings,' he said, disbelievingly. 'I didn't even know you had sent them off, Freddie.'

'I didn't tell you because I didn't know what would happen.'

As the conflict between Batista troops and Castro's rebels increased, Freddie had become more and more concerned about Anna. His first thoughts on waking up was wondering how she was. Every day, whatever he was doing; treating a patient in his country clinic, visiting Carl to give him some extra pain-killers, or just sitting outside his favourite café, gazing at the ocean, images of Anna came back to him. And they were especially strong, when he took Esther her weekly medicine. Mother and daughter were peas in a pod. Esther was older and much fuller now, but staring into her eyes was looking at Anna.

'I can see love there,' Esther said, one time, as they sat together on the sofa.

Freddie had smiled. Yes, there was love there.

When he heard about Castro's successful attack on the army garrison at Uvero, he avidly read all the newspapers and listened to the radio broadcasts about the battle. But there was no way of knowing whether Anna was one of the rebel casualties that were reported killed. He didn't know if she was alive or dead.

He needed something to distract him, to take his mind away from a person, and a situation he could do nothing about. So, he had gathered all of Klaus's shell drawings together and had sent them to an American publisher.

Carl was holding the letter. 'Shall we go and tell Klaus?'

'Maybe we should wait and just show him the book?' said Freddie. 'That will be more of a thrill for him.'

Putting the letter on the desk beside him, Carl said, 'I wonder if I'll get to see it.'

Maria tied the blindfold round his eyes. Very timidly, Hans had suggested it the second time he'd come to see her. After he asked the question, he had stood looking like a young boy expecting to be refused.

'You see...Your body is like...like hers...If I couldn't see...'

It was strange request, but she'd had catered for many needs in her long career, and this one amused her. Hans never told Maria who the woman was, but when he began to teach her German words, it became obvious.

'Ich liebe dich,' she said.

'Ja.' he whispered.

Unbuttoning his shirt, she stroked his tanned chest.

'Du bist wunderschön, Hans.'

Hans began to breath more heavily. 'Danke.'

Reaching down to his crotch, she pretended to act shocked, 'Du bist sehr hart, naughty junge!'

Feeling angry and hurt at his treatment by Bella, the first time Hans had used Maria in a brutal way to release his frustration. He wanted his power back, and he had been very rough until the last few moments, when he slowed down, moaned and then began to cry when he had finished. Maria had thought about asking the owner to ban him, but then he came with his strange desire and seemed very relieved when Maria agreed.

The first time with the blindfold had been very quick. He must have been thinking about it a great deal. But gradually, he relaxed into the part and the experience became pleasurable for them both. Now, Maria looked forward to their regular sessions together, and she enjoyed learning another language, even if they were mostly words you wouldn't say in public.

Hans had finally accepted that his life with Bella was over, and had thrown himself into his arms dealing. Castro's invasion had re-fuelled the rivalries on the island, and he had difficulty keeping up with demand from all sides.

Bella's quite generous offer for his half of the club meant he had cash to buy a place of his own. He knew he had to get away from home, from Esther. With his business deals he spent a lot of time out of the house, but his mother was often waiting for him when got back, whatever the hour.

'I can't sleep, Hans', she would whisper, as she met him in the hall. 'I am worried about what's happening. All this fighting in the streets. Please, come and have a drink with me until I fall asleep.'

Knowing she could easily throw a tantrum and wake all the house if he refused, he would sit on her bed, holding her hand, listening to her abusing Bella, his father, the island in general, until she slept. One night, watching her laying asleep, he made a decision.

As Maria and he were getting dressed again, he said, 'I'm buying an apartment over-looking the sea.'

Maria was a little surprised. 'You're leaving home?'

'Yes...Why don't you move in with me?'

'Me?' Maria was even more surprised. 'Why?'

'You don't have to do this. I make enough money to keep you.'

She was pulling her stockings up, and fastening them in her suspenders. 'You mean with you as my only client?'

'Well, sort of, yes.'

'Do you know how much my daughter's American college fees are?'

'I make a lot of money, Maria. I can easily afford them.'

Maria stood up, and straightened her basque over her tummy. 'Thank you, Hans. That is really very flattering. But where will I go when you get bored with me playing your Mutter?'

CHAPTER ONE HUNDRED AND SEVEN

Anna quickly found that being a part of Castro's rebel army was not for the weak, or the faint hearted. The rebels were fighting a much bigger army, who had more and better weapons, supplied by the Americans. Being trained in guerrilla tactics, the rebels were more skilled at fighting in the forest, but when you were attacked by helicopters and planes all you could do was dive for cover. There was no way you could fight back against them, even if you could see them through the dense foliage. You dived down, and if you believed in a God, you prayed. Anna didn't pray.

She was just angry that the aircraft were being fuelled and re-armed at the nearby American base in Guantanamo. Although America wasn't in the war, it supported the fascistic regime of Batista against the people of the island.

From the first day in the camp, high up in the mountains, she learnt to sleep in a corn-sack in her camouflaged hide-out. The camp often got soaked with the tropical rain, became intensely humid during the day, and was surrounded with flying insects, both day and night. Meals were irregular and, when they did arrive, they were often sparse. Being hungry, tense and sometimes very afraid, was her daily life.

But sleeping was the worst time for her. Almost every night she was troubled by intense, dreadful nightmares of being chased by someone who looked like Jose. Occasionally, she was woken by someone in the middle of the night.

'Sorry, Anna, but your screaming is keeping everyone awake.'

Try as she might, when she fell asleep again, the nightmares returned. There was always blood. Much blood. In her dream, she remembered what her father said as they sat in the café near the square.

'And the streets will be as red as those flowers in the square.'

Freddie was often there too in her dream. Sometimes Jose and Freddie merged into each other. And she killed them both, in the square. She was always thankful when it was time to get up, and begin the next task.

Despite the hardships, on those days when she thought she should leave and go back to look after her sick father in Havana, she stayed on because people were beginning to join them. Each day more eager peasants enlisted to fight against Batista. Anna felt that, with the will of the people, the war was turning in their favour.

With his rebel army growing, Castro decided to go from defence into attack. Anna had been part of the team who captured the mortars from the army camp in the forest. As she predicted, the soldiers queuing up for food were taken by surprise and fled, even though she fired above their heads.

But the attack to take the garrison at the coastal town of El Uvero was totally different. The three-hour battle was frightening, yet exhilarating. With bullets flying around you, the thought that you could be killed at any moment meant you just battled for your life. You killed, or were killed. She aimed to kill. And did.

She was elated when they won the battle. But killing the enemy soldiers didn't help her nightmares.

'Do you know how ill Carl is?' Freddie asked.

Esther plumped up the cushion on chaise lounge, and settled back on it.

'Hans has left, you know,' she responded. 'He came back home, then he just left again. I don't know where he's gone. I hope not back to that dreadful Bella,' she said, unconsciously touching the necklace Bella had given back to her.

'You realise Carl is very ill?' Freddie persisted.

He thought it was time to take on Esther's indifference to her husband's illness. She must have known that he was seriously ill, but she never mentioned it all in his weekly visits to give her the medicine. Did Freddie expect a reconciliation between them? Did Carl even want that? He hadn't said. Freddie knew it was none of his business, really, but he couldn't let it go on.

'I do miss Hans,' Esther replied. 'We used to have some lovely little talks at night, when he came in. I'm sure he liked it too. I don't know why he left.'

'Well, I hope you didn't offend him,' Freddie said. 'Hans is the only way you're paying your bills, now Anna has gone.'

'I'm sure I didn't offend him. He actually seemed quite shy.' She smiled. 'Imagine, being shy in front of his own mother.'

Realising the conversation was going nowhere, Freddie got up to go.

'You're not going so soon?'

'I have patients waiting,' he lied.

'Of course, when Carl...is gone. Well, you and I –'

'Goodbye, Esther. I'll see you next week,' he said, opening the door.

'Or before. Whenever you like,' she said, as Freddie went out, closing the door behind him.

She settled back on her cushion. Two men in love with her, she thought. Just like when she was young.

CHAPTER ONE HUNDRED AND EIGHT

He had shown her round the impressive apartment and they were standing in the lounge, by the picture window overlooking the ocean.

'So, do you like it?' said Hans.

'Very much,' Maria said. 'Who wouldn't?'

'So, would you like to live here?'

Maria smiled, 'Hans, we have been through this. You know why. Thank you very much. I'm very flattered, but no.'

He tried to persuade her again, but Maria was adamant. The argument settled they went to sit on the shaded patio. The sea was calm today, like a blue mirror. Maria picked up her Dr Pepper.

'So, your sister is fighting with Castro. She's very brave,' Maria said.

'Very stupid,' said Hans.

She shrugged. 'What does your brother do?'

'Klaus? Nothing.'

'How old is he?'

'Oh, a few years younger than me.'

'Does he go to college?'

'No...He does nothing.'

'Why is that?'

Hans picked up his drink, and said off-handedly, 'He's just...strange.'

It was Sunday, Maria's day off. She worked in the brothel six days, but not on the Sabbath. Having brought up with religion, she always went to Mass on Sunday morning. Believing in God, she felt that he had helped her when her mother died. She was a beautiful teenager, and because of her stunning looks, it was very easy to drift into prostitution.

That could be a hard life, but the first pimp she had, her first lover, was a kind, generous, lazy young man. He had no education, no proper job, and was happy that Maria was content to earn enough for both of them. When he died of a brain tumour, shortly after Maria had their baby daughter, she went to work in a brothel. The one she worked in now.

The owner, twenty years older than her, was her second real lover. After their affair faded out after a few years, he was happy that she carried on working in his establishment. He knew she had a special something, and let her keep most of her earnings. Which was how she had given her daughter a decent education, and was now paying for her to go through college in America. Maria felt that God had looked after her. She knew her life could have been so much worse, and she went to Mass to thank him.

Generally, she spent the rest of Sunday pampering herself, and meeting her girlfriends for a late lunch. Today, she'd let Hans persuade her to go and look at his new apartment.

They had not had sex. Maybe later, she thought, after he had taken her for an expensive meal. She had brought the blindfold and the outfit he liked best. The one he liked to imagine his mother wearing.

She was curious at Hans casual remark about his brother. 'Strange? How is he strange?' she asked.

Hans looked embarrassed. 'He's...well, he's backward. He behaves like a child. Like a ten-year old.'

'Oh, what a shame.'

'He fell on his head, or something, when he was a baby. So, he just stays at home with Mrs Price.'

'Mrs Price?'

'The nanny. She brought us all up...Mama used to bring him up like a pet, but then she got bored. So, he spends all day with Mrs Price. I said he should get out. See as bit of life...

Maybe if he did...' He looked at her, suddenly. 'Maybe if he had sex. It might wake him up.'

Maria frowned. 'I doubt it. It'd probably scare him to death.'

But Hans had got the bit between his teeth now. 'No. No. He should try it. The pampered little shit.'

'You sound a bit jealous, Hans. Did he take your mother's attention away from you?'

'No, really...' He looked at her. 'If it was someone like his mother. She used to cuddle him and stroke him all the time, when he was younger. Someone like that.'

Maria put down her drink, and stared at him. 'Are you looking at me?'

At daybreak in their forest camp, Ché gathered his small group of rebels together. Anna stood looking around at them. They were a tightly-knit unit having fought in several skirmishes, and the successful battle at the Uvero garrison. She was very proud to be a member of such a team.

'We are marching to the Escambray Mountains, today,' Ché told them.

People looked at each other. Escambray was halfway across the island, towards Havana. Over three hundred miles.

'A second front has been established there, from various factions,' Ché said. 'Fidel says it is very important that we, the Fidelistas, are in control of that.'

Castro's invasion of Cuba had gradually caused an uprising of people against Batista throughout the island. In towns and in the countryside fierce protests were beginning to erupt. Rival political groups, often violently at odds with each other, had united together in the forests of Escambray.

Ché went on, 'After all the hardship we have endured this far, we don't want to let those groups stage another coup. As Fidel says, Revolution, yes. Military coup, no!'

This was greeted by loud cheers from the group.

'So, where are the lorries?' shouted Alberto, the joker of the group.

The rebels laughed, and then went about packing their gear for the long trek.

The march took six weeks. Through forests, swamps, often with little food or water, and, with clashes with the retreating army units. Anna was thrilled when many of Batista's soldiers just put up their hands and joined the growing rebel army.

After they finally set up camp in the Escambray mountains, they were able to relax for a moment.

Anna had just established her own space in the camp, and was stretching out to go to sleep in the shade, when Alberto came over. He was holding 'El Cubano Libre', the newspaper that Guevara had set up to counteract the propaganda that Batista's controlled-press was disseminating. It had reports from all the towns and cities on the island.

'Anna, your last name is Mueller, isn't it?' he asked.

'Yes.'

'Is your father a professor of medicine?'

Anna sat up, a little concerned. 'Yes.'

Alberto handed her the paper. 'I think you should read this.'

CHAPTER ONE HUNDRED AND NINE

Freddie knew that it wasn't going to be easy, but he had not expected that evening to end as it did. He almost immediately realised how foolish he had been falling for Esther's bewitching beauty, and her almost childish vivaciousness. That evening he knew Carl was at a faculty dinner. So, exasperated with Esther's incessant demands, he had gone round to tell her that what had happened was not going to happen again. As he expected, she had not taken his rejection well.

'I don't believe you, Freddie! I don't! I want to marry you! I'll leave Carl! We can live together. I don't care if we can't live on your money. We can get by somehow!'

'I am so sorry, Esther, it is very wrong of us. Very wrong of me! I should never have...Please, Esther, we have to think about Carl. How it will hurt him! We have to stop, now.'

It was useless arguing. She was oblivious. Frustrated and unable to make her understand, he was just about to leave when Carl arrived, having left the dinner because he was feeling a little unwell. Suspicious that Freddie was there alone with Esther, he asked her what was going on. That's when she told the lie.

'Get out of my house!' shouted Carl at him. 'If it wasn't for my wife reputation, I would have you put in jail for what you have done! But I will have you barred from the course. And I will make sure that you never, ever, have a career in medicine!'

After almost twenty years, Freddie could still remember Carl's words. What had happened with Esther had destroyed his hopes of becoming a respected physician, had helped ruin a marriage, and produced a backward child that Carl had treated as his own son. Now Carl Mueller was his closest friend, and Freddie was his principal carer in his last few weeks of life. Strange how life turned out, Freddie thought.

Over the month he saw Carl becoming gradually weaker. They had set a bed up in his surgery, so he didn't have to struggle upstairs. Carlotta looked after him when Freddie wasn't there, and Mrs Price and Klaus came to see him each day. Esther never came to see her husband. When Freddie asked why, she blamed Carl for Nico's death, for ruining Freddie's career, and for not telling her that her family had almost certainly been killed in the Nazi concentration camps.

Carl was in constant pain because he didn't want to be constantly drowsy with pain-killers, to become dependent on them. He still wanted to be able to think, to feel, but Freddie could see that the end was near.

From Carl's face that morning, Freddie could see that the pain had finally become unbearable. Carl's voice was weak, so Freddie had to lean close to him to hear.

'I remember...' Carl whispered, 'I remember in the war, Freddie...men with ...their innards...hanging out...'

Freddie put his hand on Carl's withered arm and stroked it. Knowing that Carl had served as a doctor in the First World War, he knew his friend had seen many terrible things.

Carl struggled on, 'They were crying...crying out…but….I had no, no...no morphine left...The pain...' He began to cry softly.

Leaning forward, Freddie put his arms around his friend, and held him.

'Freddie...'

The two men looked at each other. They had discussed this eventuality some time ago.

Knowing that Freddie had enough morphine in his bag to quietly end his life, Carl whispered, 'Please...Freddie, please... now.'

With sobs wracking his body, Freddie hugged Carl close.

CHAPTER ONE HUNDRED AND TEN

The full moon silvered the mountain range against the black of the night sky. It illuminated Anna, as she sat outside her tent with her comrade, Alberto.

'It's very dangerous to go, Anna. There'll be troops and police everywhere in the city. It's too risky.'

She knew Alberto was right, of course. Fidel's revolution was going well. Victory was in sight. They may reach Havana in a few weeks, but there were still casualties among the rebels. Having seen some of her comrades die, Anna knew that she might not live to enter Havana. But her father was being buried there tomorrow. And she felt so guilty.

Anna knew that her father was very ill went she left to join Castro's army. Whenever she went back to her family home, she had seen him getting thinner and weaker. But he had never mentioned it. He was a stoic, never complaining about troubles that affected him. Living with her mother was one of the crosses he had to bear for many years. She wondered how much Esther had cared for Carl in his last few days. Maybe not at all.

'I owe my father a lot, Alberto...It's why I'm here, and not looking after him, while he was dying. He didn't ask me to. He didn't ask me to stay, because he knew this was my...my...'

'Mission?'

Anna nodded. 'Like his was medicine...He didn't try to stop me. He knew what war was like, Alberto. He was in the First World War. He knew how horrendous it was...is. But he didn't try to stop his daughter going to war because, because...That's why I have to go...'

Dark clouds covered the moon, shrouding the camp into invisibility again.

Alberto got up. 'I'll drive you as far as I can.'

Havana's Necrópolis de Cristóbal Colón is known as one of the world's most captivating cemeteries. It is enormous, grandiose and eccentric.

'The Cristóbal Colón?' said Freddie. 'But Carl wasn't Catholic.'

Esther had gathered Freddie and Hans together to discuss the funeral arrangements.

'Everyone gets buried there,' she said. 'Everyone important.'

'If they are Catholic,' said Freddie.

'I am.'

'But you're not being buried, Mama,' said Hans.

She looked at him. Hans shrugged and avoided her eyes. The look was enough.

'I am the next of kin, Freddie. I think Carl would have wanted that.'

Knowing that Esther had never visited Carl when he was dying, Freddie said spitefully,

'Why, did you ask him?'

Despite Freddie's objections, it was Esther's event. She had it her way. Mrs Price altered Esther's most elegant black dress, which she wore with the diamond necklace. On his mother's instructions, Hans paid for the most magnificent wreaths for the coffin, and Carlotta was made to scrub Klaus to within an inch of his life. Esther wanted to put on a show.

But there were few people at the ceremony. The family, Carlotta, a few of Professor Carls' poorer patients and an elegant woman Freddie didn't recognise. It wasn't Isabel Luisa Gonzales Rio de Cruz. 'La Isabel' exerted a powerful influence among the elite and none of her circle came.

Freddie stood a step back from the small group surrounding the flower-festooned grave of the man he had helped to die. His heart thumped heavily inside the damp cotton shirt and linen jacket. Reaching inside the jacket, he felt the butt of the gun he had brought from Hans. He hadn't fired a gun since he'd fought against Franco in the Spanish Civil War. It felt foolish to have one now, but he was prepared to give up his life to defend her.

He looked around him, anxiously. She would come, he felt it. Despite the danger, she would come.

CHAPTER ONE HUNDRED AND ELEVEN

At his mother's command, Hans had organised a lavish wake at the Hotel Riveria owned by the top Mafia mobster, Meyer Lanski. How absurd, Freddie thought. The sort of place Carl had always totally avoided.

Despite Esther's insistence, Freddie declined her invitation, lying that he felt very unwell. Esther allowed him not to attend, after he promised her to visit her as soon as he felt better.

'We have so much to talk about,' she said, unconsciously stroking her necklace, as she got into the rear of the hired black limousine.

Freddie took off his hat and mopped his brow, as the limousine drove away. He couldn't care less what Esther wanted to talk about, except it was bound to be something he didn't want to hear. He turned to look at the cemetery. Anna hadn't been at the funeral. That was wise. But he had an instinct. Getting into his car, he drove quickly to the Mueller's house, and let himself in.

'Anna!' he called, as he entered in the hall. He started to look in every room, shouting her name. All the downstairs room were empty.

Going to the foot of the stairs, he called, 'Anna!' He listened. Nothing. Maybe he had got it wrong.

Years ago, he remembered being told about the attic. It was the safe place that the children used to play in, away from the prying eyes of the adults. He bounded up the stairs and arrived at the attic door, out of breath.

'Anna,' he called. When he got his breath back, he tried the door. It wasn't locked.

The large room was empty, apart from the piles of accumulated junk. Toys the children had played with, then abandoned; dolls, games, drawings scattered on the floor, a toy rifle, a rocking-horse with a swastika draped over one eye. They were together with old pictures, ornaments and bits of furniture the family had discarded in the twenty years they had lived there.

He looked around. There was a hidey-hole there somewhere, someone had once said. It was where the original gangster owner had hidden when he fell out with the mob. Not that it did him any good. But it was well hidden.

'Anna,' he said quietly. 'It's me. Freddie. I'm on my own.'

He waited. Nothing. Going to the door he was about to leave, when he heard the hidden door open in the wall. Turning, he saw Anna emerge.

She smiled. 'Freddie, what a shrewd man you are.'

Freddie shrugged. 'I knew you would come.'

When Maria refused to introduce his brother, Klaus, to sex Hans stopped seeing her out of spite. So, as the hearse and the funeral party arrived at his father's graveside, he was shocked to see Maria standing among the mourners. Dressed tastefully in black, she stood out among the other mourners; the poor that Carl had looked after for free.

Taking his mother's hand, he led Esther to the grave. Maria gave him a look as he approached. It was embarrassing, but arousing, seeing Isabel and his mother together in the same place.

'Who is that?' Esther asked him, quietly.

'Must be one of Papa's patients.'

'I don't remember seeing her at the house.'

'He saw people at their homes as well, Mama.'

Esther looked around at the other mourners. 'She looks very elegant.'

'Mm,' said Hans, evasively.

After the service, Hans saw Maria making her way over to them, and was about to hurry his mother away.

'Senora Mueller!' Maria called.

Esther stopped.

'I am so sorry for your loss.'

'Thank you...' Esther said.

Maria extended her hand. 'Maria Roderiques.'

Esther took her hand. 'Esther Mueller...This is my son, Hans.'

Hans put out his hand. 'Senora. Hans Mueller.'

Maria took his hand and squeezed it with both hands. 'I am so pleased to meet you, Hans. I am so sorry about your father.'

'You were one of my husband's patients?' Esther enquired.

Still holding Hans' hand, she said, 'Yes.'

'He never mentioned you.'

'Professional discretion, I expect,' she said, releasing Hans hand at last.

Hans stood there as he heard his mother say, 'Thank you for coming. You must come to the wake, Maria. It's at the Hotel Riveria.'

'Thank you. That's most kind,' Maria said, smiling at Hans.

CHAPTER ONE HUNDRED AND TWELVE

Standing by the attic skylight, Freddie watched thunder-clouds gathering in the early evening sky.

'There's a storm coming,' Freddie said.

'That's good,' Anna replied. 'The police won't be out in that.'

Going back to his seat in the dilapidated armchair, Freddie looked at Anna, sitting astride the rocking horse. Apart from the time the teenage Anna angrily told Freddie never to come to their home again, and the dreadful time of her abortion, they had never spent any length of time together, despite having known each other for nearly twenty years. Now he had spent the whole afternoon with her, after promising to take Anna to the cemetery when it was dark. It was blissful time for him.

It seemed Anna wanted to get to know him more. She was particularly keen about his time in the Spanish Civil War, which was similar to the fight she was engaged in.

'We were mostly fighting in Catalonia. In Northern Spain,' Freddie said. 'That was where most of the left-wing groups were. Socialists, Communists, Marxists, Anarchists. And the Basques, and the Catalans. They all wanted to break away from Spain, but sadly, they spent a lot of time arguing amongst themselves. That's why I left. Even if they won, I could see them going on to fight each other.'

'That's what Fidel doesn't want to happen. That's why he sent Ché to Escambray. To take control of the different factions there.'

'Has he?'

'Oh yes. He has. Fidel and Ché are a powerful duo.'

She went on about Castro plans for the revolution, that she was sure they would win.

'We will nationalize factories, banks, and businesses.'

'The Americans will love that,' Freddie joked.

Anna pressed on. 'We will have affordable housing, fair rents, healthcare, education for all children.'

Freddie mocked, 'Sounds like paradise.'

'You fought for it in Spain, Freddie!' she said, a little irritated.

'Did I?'

'Yes. You did!'

He stared at her beautiful eyes, then looked away, his gaze wandering among the discarded objects. The debris of the Mueller's life. He thought of his friend, Carl, lying in the earth. His throat thickened.

'Maybe…maybe, I was just…just fighting to get away… from myself… Hoping for a stray bullet.'

Anna stared at him. 'What…? Why?'

There was suddenly a commotion downstairs. Raised voices, commands. Orders!

'It's the police!' Freddie said.

'Quickly!' Anna said. She opened the door to the hiding place. Taking out her pistol, she ushered Freddie inside. Following him in, she was closing the door when Freddie pushed past her.

'Freddie!' she hissed.

Freddie grabbed the cup he was using for an ashtray, and hurried back into the hiding place. Anna closed the door. The place was small. Good for children. Cramped for two adults. They stood face to face, listening to the noises from below in the house. Both tried to calm their breaths.

'I hope Jose didn't tell them about this place,' Anna whispered, in the darkness.

Remembering he had a weapon too, he reached for it, brushing Anna's breast as he did.

'Sorry,' he whispered.

Freddie knew this could be last moment he would ever be with Anna again. He could feel her face close to his. As he heard heavy footsteps coming up the stairs, he just wanted to hold her and find her lips. To show her what he felt.

The attic door opened.

CHAPTER ONE HUNDRED AND THIRTEEN

At the Hotel Riveria, Esther insisted that Hans sat between her and Maria, at the lavishly decked table. During the meal the two women leant across Hans, talking constantly. Maria seemed very interested in Esther's background in Austria, and loved the idea of Vienna.

'I would love to speak another language,' Maria said. 'How do you say, er, "I love that very much," she said to Esther, touching Hans' arm.

'Ich liebe das sehr,' said Esther.

'Ich..liebe das..sehr,' repeated Maria.

'Wonderful,' Esther said.

Leaning across Hans, Maria secretly squeezed his thigh. 'What about, "I'd like some more, please."

'Ich hätte gern noch mehr, bitte,' Esther said.

Squeezing his thigh harder and higher up, Isabel began, 'Ich hätte...'

'Gern noch' Esther prompted.

'I think it's about time for the...for the...,' said Hans, abruptly.

'The eulogy, yes, of course, Hans,' said Esther. 'Yes.'

Maria and Esther turned to him, attentively. Hans cleared his throat, and began to address the audience; Klaus, Mrs Price and Carlotta. 'Well, we've all come here today to –'

'Hans, please,' said Esther. 'You must stand. For the eulogy.'

Hans hesitated. Tucking his napkin into his trousers, he stood up, leaning forward with his hands on the table, hoping his erection didn't show.

They waited, feeling each other's stifled breath in the darkness. Freddie couldn't see her, but their bodies were almost touching.

He wondered if she could feel his heart thumping. A mixture of fear, and desire.

The police had briefly searched the room but, as there was nothing to see, they left. The sounds in the house gradually faded away. Finally, they heard the front door slam. Anna gave a huge sigh. As she opened the hidden door the sunlight, shining through a gap in the thunderclouds, blinded them.

They looked at each other and gave a little laugh of relief.

'Sorry,' he began.

'What?'

'About my fag-breath,' Freddie said.

'God, Freddie, I must smell like a pigsty,' Anna replied.

Freddie sat down again. He wanted to say it was the most beautiful smell he'd ever smelt, but got out his cigarettes instead.

'That's a bad habit.'

He shrugged. 'When they get back from the wake, we'll have to wait until they all go to bed. 'Til it's really dark.'

Anna nodded. 'I thought we'd had it, Freddie.'

'We'd have gone out guns blazing though, Anna. Just like in the cowboys.' He lit the cigarette. 'Jose obviously didn't tell them.'

Anna looked away.

'Do you want to talk about it?'

She shook her head. 'No...No.'

Freddie blew out the smoke. 'I think we'll make it, Anna.'

'It's so good of you to help.'

'Why wouldn't I? Carl's my friend. I loved him. And you love him too.'

'I do...I wish I'd...' Suddenly yawning, she said, 'I was travelling all night. Didn't get much sleep.'

'You should try.' He looked around. There wasn't a comfortable space. 'Have my chair.' He started to get up.

'No, sit.'

Anna picked up two cushions, and put one at his feet. She stood holding the other cushion, and nodded at his lap.

'Do you mind?

Did he mind? God, did he not mind! He tried to sound as casual as possible. 'Sure.'

She put the cushion on his lap, sat down and rested her head on it.

'Night.'

'Goodnight,' he said. He put his hand on her head, and stroked her hair, gently, until she fell asleep.

CHAPTER ONE HUNDRED AND FOURTEEN

The storm was raging by the time Freddie's car arrived at the cemetery. Clinging onto the umbrella, Freddie took Anna to Carl's grave, past the towering shrines for the dead that appeared like eerie ghosts as the lightning flashed above.

Anna couched down on the sodden earth. Freddie stood behind covering her with the umbrella, keeping the rain off her as best he could. When the lightning flooded the scene he looked all around, but he was sure no police would be out in this.

He could hear her crying, but the rolling thunder drowned out her words. When she had finished, she stood up, and she took his arm.

'Thank you,' she shouted above the storm.

They splashed their way back to the car. Anna tucked herself into the passenger well and Freddie covered her with rug. She felt his arm.

'Freddie, you're soaked!'

'It's warm rain. Not like in England.'

He started the car and headed out of the city.

Anna moved the blanket so she could see him. 'You've got a gun, Freddie.'

'Yeah. I got it from Hans. If we meet an army patrol, we go down fighting, no?'

'Yes. I guess we do.'

The thunder and lightning had moved on and the rain finally stopped. He drove through the bumpy, flooded road, glad that his Dodge Custom was built like a tank, and could handle poor roads. Though he was concentrating on the road, he could feel Anna looking at him.

After a while, Anna said, 'Freddie, that stray bullet you mentioned...that you went looking for in Spain...Did it have anything to do with something that happened in England?'

Freddie kept his eyes on the road and drove on in silence.

She went on, 'It's a long time ago, but I can still remember. You used to play with us, me and Hans, when you came to our house.'

'You remember that? Really? You were very young.'

'You were quite a celebrity. Papa talked about you a lot. Mama quite obviously adored you...Then you just suddenly disappeared. And we weren't even allowed to mention your name...'

The car was struggling up an incline. Freddie changed to a lower gear.

'You play with Klaus a lot. Taught him to draw those shells. He's very good. He loves you, Freddie...It's obvious that Klaus is your son...'

He looked at her, and then back at the road, swerving to avoid a pothole.

'You and Mama had an affair. And Papa found out?'

'God, these roads are terrible!' Freddie blurted out.

'Papa once said you were a special student. That you would go far...Did you ever graduate?'

Freddie began to shake his head, reliving something that he didn't want to remember. 'No...No.'

'Why didn't you become that special doctor, Freddie?'

'Please, Anna...Don't. Please.'

'Why did that special student want a bullet to end it all?'

Suddenly, Freddie stopped the car. He put his hand to his face and began to cry.

Anna got up from the well, and put her arm around his shoulders.

'Freddie?'

Freddie put both hands on the wheel and stared ahead. 'It…
it wasn't an affair…I knew it…I knew it was stupid. I knew I was
being crazy…! But she was so…dazzling, Anna. So dazzling…!
It was my birthday. She invited me to dinner. I thought Carl
would be there. I thought it was a birthday celebration…
But he wasn't there. He had a conference away from London
that night, so, there was just her…I was surprised because she
opened the door for me. She took me into the lounge and said
"I gave the servants the night off, because I wanted to give you
your present." She was wearing a white robe, silk, I think. She
opened the robe…All she was wearing was…the necklace.'

'Oh, god!'

'That was the first time…The only time, Anna…She called
me a lot afterwards. On the phone. Sent me letters…I couldn't
even get on with my studies…On the next time when I knew
Carl wasn't in, I went round to tell her that I was sorry…That
she was beautiful, and it was wonderful and all that, but it was
a terrible mistake. I told her we mustn't hurt Carl. But she
wouldn't listen. She wanted us…She wanted us to run away
together…'

'Oh, Freddie.'

'I tried to reason with her, but she began to become
hysterical…Like she does. She wouldn't listen to me at all. Then
Carl came in. He'd left his meeting early. He could obviously
see that Esther was very upset…She was in floods of tears…'

'Oh, god, no, Freddie,' Anna said. 'No!'

'So…she told Carl that…that I raped her.'

Anna gasped in anger.

'Carl made sure that…I could never finish my course…He
had a lot of influence, Anna, everywhere in England. None
one would take me…' He laughed through his tears. 'I couldn't
even get a job as a hospital porter.'

'Freddie!' Anna was crying too. She took him in her arms, cradling him. They stayed together until Freddie crying stopped.

He sat up, suddenly. 'We'd better get going.'

It would be dawn soon, and Freddie wanted to get Anna safe, back to her comrades.

CHAPTER ONE HUNDRED AND FIFTEEN

Hans was livid. He didn't think Mrs Price or Klaus had seen it, but Maria and his mother must have. It was the biggest erection he'd ever had. He felt like he did as a schoolboy, hiding his burgeoned manhood behind his satchel as he left the school assembly.

After the wake, he dropped his mother and the rest at home, and went round to the brothel. Maria had told him she wasn't working today, but was going there to chat to the other girls.

She was sitting in the reception talking to two women. Hans motioned to her.

'I'm not working today, Hans.'

'We need to talk,' he said brusquely.

They went out to a nearby café and sat outside. Hans waited until the waiter had taken their order, then he rounded on her.

'What the hell do you think you're doing! Coming to the funeral!'

'I just wanted to pay my respects,' Maria said calmly.

'You didn't know my father!'

'I wanted to see your mother, as well.'

'Why? Why?'

'Close your eyes, Hans.'

'What?'

'Please.'

Reluctantly, he closed his eyes.

'Ich hätte gern noch mehr, bitte.'

Maria's accent and intonation were perfect. It could have been his mother sitting there. He opened his eyes and looked at her.

Maria smiled. 'I thought it would make it better for you.'

'I'm not coming to see you again!' Hans snapped. 'That's over!'

'That's a shame.'

'I thought you were going to tell my mother everything! I was terrified.'

'Poor Hans…So, that's it then?'

'Yes.'

'Mmm. Just after I found a girl who might be just the one for Klaus.'

They drove on in silence for a while. Freddie was aware that Anna was looking at him, earnestly.

'I think you'd better get down again, Anna. There may be patrols out now the storm's gone.'

Anna got down into the well, and covered herself with her blanket, but he could see she had left a tiny space where could look at him as he drove.

Suddenly, driving round a sharp bend, Freddie braked, and came to a shuddering stop.

'Shit!' he muttered. He put his hand in his pocket for his gun. 'A patrol,' he whispered.

Anna pulled her gun from her holster. She couldn't believe that she and Freddie might just die here, now. Before…

There were three soldiers with submachine guns pointed at the car. Freddie wound the window down. 'Good morning!' he said.

The soldier in front leaned into the window, his weapon pointing at Freddie's face. 'Where are you going?' he said.

'I'm just going to see a patient. I'm a doctor.'

The soldier looked inside the car and immediately saw the blanket covering something in the well.

'Get out of the car,' he said. 'Please.'

'I'm actually in a hurry. The patient is very ill.'

'And I want to know what you have got hidden in there, doctor. Down there. It is guns. A bomb? Get out of the car!'

Anna suddenly pulled back the blanket. 'Alberto!' She said, springing up to the passenger seat.

Alberto looked at her. 'Anna! You came back?'

'I said I would.'

'Everyone was worried at the camp.'

'Where is it? The camp?'

'There's a track further down the road, to the left. Just a couple of miles.'

'I'll see you there,' Anna said. She looked at Freddie. 'Drive on, driver.'

Freddie gave a huge sigh, started the car and drove on.

'So, you have control of these roads now,' he said.

Anna grinned. 'Yes, in Escambray. I told you we were winning.'

They saw the turning on the left and Freddie drove down it. It was a track, muddy and rutted, but Freddie knew the Dodge could handle it.

After a moment, Anna said, 'Can you stop?'

'We're not there yet.'

'Just stop, Freddie. I can walk from here.'

'Oh, okay.' He stopped the car, puzzled.

'Can you turn the engine off?'

'But - '

'Please.'

He turned off the engine.

She turned to look at him. 'My mother and father helped to destroy your life – '

'Oh, no, well - ' he began.

She put her hand up to stop him. 'But you saved us from the boat,' she said. 'You had the necklace. You could have just kept it, and let us sail away... It's worth a fortune. Which you could have done with, I think.'

'I would have just drunk it away, Anna.'

'And yet you saved us... Why did you do that?'

Freddie looked down the track, at the forest at either side. 'Your mother lied to your father. He didn't know what had happened. He could have put me in prison, Anna. I could have spent many years in there. A respectable professor, and his young wife, against a poor Cuban student. Who would the court have believed?'

'He helped to destroy your career.'

'He didn't know. He was lied to...I might have done the same...

'But you saved us.'

'I had to try to save him, and his family. He didn't know, Anna.'

'Did you ever talk about it? Here?'

'No...But I think he knew. Sort of.'

Anna got out of the car.

'Oh, goodbye,' Freddie said, surprised.

'Can you get out, please, Freddie,' she said quietly.

Very curious, Freddie got out. Anna came and stood in front of him. She looked around, then taking his arm, she led him into the forest. Freddie was very puzzled now. Did she think he might go back and tell the police where the camp was? Surely, she knew he wouldn't do that? She led him to a clearing.

'I won't tell them where the camp is, Anna.'

'Is that what you think?'

Freddie shrugged. He had given Anna his gun in the car. 'You'll need it more than me,' he'd said. Not that he would use it anyway.

Anna came close to him. He was about to speak again, but she put her fingers to his lips. 'You don't know, do you?' she said.

'Know what?'

She reached up and pushed a lock of his hair back from his forehead. 'Freddie, I hated you from the moment you picked me up and dragged me off the boat.'

Freddie attempted a smile.

Then her fingers ran softly down his cheek. 'And loved you just as much.'

Before he could speak her lips met his. It was a long kiss. Twenty years in the making.

CHAPTER ONE HUNDRED AND SIXTEEN

It was a three-hour drive back to the city, but Freddie couldn't remember driving there. Because he was either crying, or laughing. Crying because the woman he had loved since she was a teenager, that woman, had just told him she had loved him too! And he never knew.

Anna told him as they lay wrapped together, naked, in a clearing in the undergrowth.

'I thought you'd had an affair with my mother, and you wanted to start it again. That's why I came round to tell you never to come round to our house again, do you remember?

'Oh, yes. I was very surprised.'

'I said I didn't want you to hurt my father again. But I was just jealous really...I thought it was just an adolescent crush, at first, but I kept wanting to be with you, to touch you. So, I didn't want to see you anymore.'

'You were always pretty aggressive when we did meet.'

'It was that, and because of your...world-weary, cynicism. Which you haven't lost!'

Freddie laughed. 'I've just taken a rabid revolutionary back to her army camp! How world-weary and cynical is that?'

'Well...' Anna grinned. 'You were just after her body!'

He ran his hands down her back. 'Which I have.'

The love-making had been more than he had wished for. Poor dead Conchita had shown him how to treat a woman, and Anna rejoiced in his expertise and his love.

As he drove back to Havana, his laughter kept breaking through as he recalled the way Anna had led the way. Who knew that the serious, committed revolutionary had a wicked, raunchy sense of humour? Which he'd never seen before.

After their first kiss, she pulled back and said, 'Freddie, is that a gun in your pocket, or are you just pleased to see me?'

His laughter echoed through the trees. 'I don't quite see you as Mae West, Anna!'

As they lay together afterwards, he said, 'I hope...I know you'll win, Anna. But, please, be careful.'

'You could come and join us, Freddie.'

'What?'

'You fought in Spain. You know about how to fight in the forest. The countryside.'

He shook his head. 'Even if I did believe in your cause, I'm told old, Anna...' He decided to say what he felt. 'I'd spend so much time looking out for you, that I might catch that spare bullet.'

She smiled. 'You could be our medic.'

'It's not my fight. It's your future.'

Then they slowly made love again.

It was a bright morning by the time Anna was ready to leave. They got dressed and stood holding each other.

'Wait for me,' she said.

'I've waited all my life, Anna. I can wait a bit longer. Just come back. Don't take any risks.'

'No stray bullets.'

He watched her walk off through the trees. As she turned to wave to him, the sunlight rose above the mountain top and burst into the forest. He raised his hand to shade his eyes, but she was invisible to him.

CHAPTER ONE HUNDRED AND SEVENTEEN

Hans drove his white, open-topped Corvette along the Malecon.

Alongside him the ocean was a flat, sparkling, mid-blue. It was beautiful day. A great day to get laid. Not that he would tell Klaus that. No. He was just going to show his young brother his apartment which overlooked the ocean. Klaus liked the sea. He collected boring sea-shells and did drawings of them. Very boring. Well, after today, he may be fascinated by something a lot more interesting.

He had left Maria and her work-friend, Claudia, at his apartment, while he went to fetch Klaus. He didn't know if he approved of Maria's choice. Claudia was one of the youngest girls in the brothel. She was small and very slim, which he didn't care for.

'She's only just sixteen,' Maria had said. 'She's very popular with the older men, but I thought Klaus would prefer someone closer to his age.'

Maybe she was right, but from what he saw of Claudia, she looked more like a boy than a girl.

Maria tried to reassure him, 'Someone like me would be too intimidating, Hans. I've told her to act younger, as if she's just a young girl. Just playing about. There's no point in just stripping off and getting on with it. He's got to think it's a game. I told her to take him on the balcony to look at the sea. Then she could suggest sunbathing and take her top off. I said to her, "Don't wear a bra."'

'You could hardly tell,' said Hans. 'She's got hardly any tits at all.'

Maria laughed. 'I'm sure he wouldn't want to be swamped by my melons…! I don't suppose he's ever seen a woman naked. He's bound to be interested. I said to Claudia, "Ask him if he

467

wants to touch them." He'll probably get an erection, and she can take it from there.'

Hans wondered what would happen next? Afterwards? If Klaus was like most boys, he would be thinking about girls all the time from then on. He didn't know if Klaus had ever played with himself. Boys that age usually did. But Klaus was different.

He would talk to Klaus about it of course, afterwards. Man to man. To let him know it was normal. He could introduce him to other girls. Proper girls with good bodies. Klaus would no longer be that little boy that his mother used to dote over, and cuddle and fondle all the time. Like she used to do to him, before Klaus arrived.

Pulling up at the Mueller's house with a squeal of brakes, he sat back and looked at himself in the rear-view mirror. He was feeling rather happy with himself. He had liked Maria's impersonation of his mother. She got her voice and the German language really well. He was handsome, had got rich selling weapons to violent rebels, and, okay, he had a prostitute to play his mother so he could screw her. There were worse things in life than that.

Freddie left it a couple of days before he obeyed Esther's instruction to go to see her. He wanted to be alone for a while soaking up, wallowing in the experience of being with Anna. The next morning, when he woke up, his first thought was that he had dreamed it all. Then he saw the white flower, the mariposa sitting in a jar on the table. Anna had put one in her hair, and given him one to remember her.

Not that he needed anything to remember that ecstatic experience. There are times in people's lives that are their happiest moment, and yet they don't know it. Freddie would remember his until his final breath.

Now, more than ever, he was concerned about Anna. He had always been anxious when she went to fight for Castro's revolution, but that was just an abstract notion that he would never be able to reveal his love for her. That was a relationship he never believed would happen anyway. Now, he could see their life together. He was sure Castro and his army would win the battle against Batista, but there would be other rebel casualties before the victory. More stray bullets. Not believing in any God, he still prayed for Anna's safe return.

But return to what? Would she get the revolution she had set her heart on? Would she get the new society she dreamed of? With free education, free health care, houses that people could afford, a society of equals? Or would Castro become just another dictator, like many other conquerors, and rob the island and its people, like the man he had overthrown?

If he did, Freddie could see Anna taking up arms against her former leader. He knew loving an idealist meant that there would be discussions, disagreements, arguments, fallings out, and reconciliations. Having lived alone, apart from the arrangement with Conchita, that was an experience he had really never known. But he was so looking forward to it.

Walking up the path to the Mueller's house to visit Esther was an experience he could have well done without. He was in love with a visionary. What would her fantasist mother have dreamed up for him?

CHAPTER ONE HUNDRED AND EIGHTEEN

'Ich liebe das sehr,' groaned Maria.

Hans grabbed her breasts and was just coming to orgasm when Klaus burst into the bedroom. Seeing his brother and the woman wrapped together naked on the bed, he cried out and ran out of the apartment.

Scrambling up, Hans grabbed his shorts and ran into the lounge. Maria followed him in. Claudia was in the room, crying.

'What happened?' said Hans said angrily, struggling into his shorts.

'I'm sorry!' said Claudia, frightened at what Hans would say.

'What happened, Claudia?' Maria said, kindly, protecting her friend.

'I took him out to the balcony like you said. We looked at the sea. He seemed very shy...So, I said it's very hot, shall we sunbathe...? He didn't say anything, so I took my top off. He just stared at me. At them. So, I put his hand on them...'

Hans went out onto the balcony.

Claudia went on, still crying. 'He looked a bit scared...I said "It's alright. It's nice." Then, I put my hand on his on his trousers - '

'On his cock?' Maria said.

'Yeah.'

Hans was looking both ways over the balcony. 'Christ!' he shouted.

'Sorry,' Claudia said.

Running out the apartment, Hans saw the lift was at the bottom. Racing down the stairs, he ran onto the sidewalk. But there was no sign of Klaus.

He looked up. Maria was looking at him from the balcony.

'My car keys!' he shouted.

Maria went back inside. As Hans waited, he realised he had come into his white shorts.

She threw down the keys, and he jumped into his car. Not knowing which way to go, he decided to head for the Old City. He drove along the long stretch of the Malecon, looking anxiously to either side. An oncoming car blared its horn, as Hans Corvette veered towards it. He swerved back onto his side of the road, and slowed down.

Where the hell was he? He could be anywhere. Maybe he had gone into the city. In which case he would never find him. Klaus had never been out alone, and didn't know the city at all. He probably didn't even know the address where he lived. So, he would be lost. Hans began to panic at what his mother would say.

'Oh, Christ, bloody Klaus!'

Esther was wearing her best silk robe, with the necklace sparkling on her bare neck. Freddie thought, God knows what she was wearing underneath. Nothing? Like his birthday present? He hoped not. That was thirty years ago. Even Esther, with her warped sense of reality, must realise that wasn't appropriate anymore.

She asked him if he would like a drink, but Freddie said 'No'. He wanted one very much, but he wanted to be stone cold sober today.

'Coffee, then?'

He said 'Yes.' Anything to delay the conversation.

When Carlotta had gone to make the coffee, Esther rose and opened a cupboard. She took out a candleholder with seven holders on it and showed it to Freddie.

'You looked surprised that I have a menorah.'

'I am.'

'I asked Hans to get one for me.'

'I thought you had given up that religion? When you married Carl?'

'I did…But when Hans told me about the news films he'd seen after the war…About the…concentration camps, you know…'

Freddie nodded.

'Hans couldn't believe it. He said it was horrible… Horrible…I thought maybe my family…They have never been in touch, Freddie. Not after all these years…So, I like to…from time to time, to remember them…All the wonderful times we had.'

When Carlotta had served the coffee and left, Esther patted the cushion next to her on the settee. Freddie ignored it, and took his coffee to stand by the window. There wasn't much to see, but he wanted to keep a safe distance.

'Poor old Carl,' Esther said. 'He wasn't a romantic…If I had known that then…But he was so handsome, and so famous. Every girl in Vienna wanted him. But I knew he wanted me. Well, all the men wanted me…And when he left for England, well, I suppose I was impetuous, but I had to go after him…I was so young…Naive…I didn't know about real romance, until I met you.'

'I don't know where this is going, Esther – '

'Please, let me finish, Freddie…I know I did something wrong. Very wrong. Something that hurt you…But you hurt me, you know. I knew we should be together. You said so. But then you said you didn't want to hurt Carl. But he would have got over it. He wasn't romantic, like us…But now…You can't hurt him now, Freddie…We can be together now, forever.'

It was hard to know what to say to her. He wanted to tell her the truth. That he had been seduced by her ravishing looks. Her beautiful body. And that he was naïve, as well. Should he also tell her that he hated her vacuous obsession with herself?

Even when they were having sex, that was what he called it not making love, he hated a part of himself for playing the role of the romantic lover. In that moment, he might have agreed with her, that they should be together. He couldn't remember. Maybe he did...

But perhaps, now, he should tell her the truth? Now it didn't matter...She would be angry, furious, but she couldn't hurt him anymore...He could tell her that he had just made love to her daughter. Real love. That they were going to be together...She would find that out soon enough, when Castro had won, and he and Anna started living together. Yes. Maybe that was best. She should know the truth now, rather than later.

'Freddie?' She put out her hand towards him.

About to speak Freddie saw, out of the window, Klaus walking up the path with a policeman holding his arm.

CHAPTER ONE HUNDRED AND NINETEEN

'She was a very rude girl,' Mrs Price told Klaus, when his mother had told the nanny what had happened. 'Forget about it, Klaus. She was just very rude.'

Nanny put him to bed, and Freddie gave him a pill. Klaus fell asleep knowing that he didn't like rude girls.

The next day, Freddie took Klaus to the beach. It was the best place to calm him. Freddie needed calming as well after what had happened with Esther, when they had sorted out the incident with Hans.

For once, Klaus was not interested in shells.

'Why did Hans leave me with that rude girl?' he asked Freddie. 'And what was he doing with the other one?'

Shaking his head, Freddie said, 'Your brother is a bit strange, Klaus...'

Picking up a shell, he showed it to him. 'Hey, look at this. You've drawn a wonderful picture of one like this. It's going to be in a book.'

'What? What book?' Klaus asked.

Freddie remembered he hadn't told him. 'They are making a book of your paintings.'

'Who? Who is?'

'A publisher. People who make books.'

'Really? I want to see that.'

'You will, very soon.'

Freddie was happy that Klaus was easily distracted. He didn't really want to explain sex to a man as innocent as a ten-year old.

He was furious with Hans. They had nearly come to blows when Hans turned up and found Klaus had told them what had happened.

'You may as well have taken him to a brothel!' said Freddie.

'She is not a prostitute!' Hans snapped. 'Claudia is a friend of Maria's. You know Maria, Mama. You invited her to the wake. Does she seem like a prostitute to you?'

'No. She seemed very respectable,' said Esther. 'But it does seem very odd, Hans, what happened.'

Freddie remembered Maria at the funeral. He vaguely recalled a woman like her who was a friend of Conchita. She was a prostitute. But he couldn't be sure if it was her. What he did know, if Klaus was to be believed, that the other girl had shown Klaus her breasts, had made him feel them, and tried to touch his penis as well. Why would Klaus lie about that? He just wouldn't.

'What the hell do you think you were playing at, Hans!' said Freddie. 'You left Klaus alone with this girl. Who then attacked him.'

'She didn't attack him. She was just trying to be friendly.'

'By touching his cock!'

'Freddie,' said Esther, a little shocked.

'That's what she did!'

On the ropes, Hans decided to defend himself. 'Klaus needs to grow up. He's got a man's body. He needs to have sex.'

'No, he doesn't! He's a child!' Freddie said, angrily.

'Have it your way!' shouted Hans, and stormed out.

They heard him slam out of the house, and listened to the sound of his car roaring away.

Freddie sighed. 'I think I'll have that drink now.'

'Help yourself,' Esther said.

Going over to the cabinet, Freddie poured himself a large whisky. He turned to Esther, 'How about you?'

She touched the necklace. 'I'm waiting for you to answer my proposal, Freddie.'

CHAPTER ONE HUNDRED AND TWENTY

As Christmas approached and Ché Guevara's army reached the centre of the island, they were met by cheering crowds of peasants, who presented them with flowers and little gifts. Some even offered them their homes to sleep in.

For the first time in months, Anna was able to sleep in a proper bed. A local landowner, who her father had treated in the early days, invited her to stay with his family, and share their Christmas meal with them.

'Please stay. Professor Mueller, your father, saved my life,' he said.

Knowing the rumours that Batista was planning a last stand, throwing everything, troops, tanks, and aircraft at the rebels, Anna accepted. She could do with a good night's sleep, and a real meal.

It was very late after she had finished the large festive feast with the family. As she was going to bed, she saw a telephone in the large hall. She asked the owner if she could make a call.

'Of course, of course. Please. As long as you like.'

She dialled the number, not knowing what Freddie was doing on Christmas Day. The phone rang, and rang. As she was about to put the receiver down, it was picked up.

'Hello?' said Freddie.

He sounded slightly drunk.

'Merry Christmas, Freddie!'

'Jesus Christ!' he exclaimed. 'Anna…! How?'

'I'm staying at someone's house. I just wanted to talk to you.'

'Oh, God, how are you? Are you still staying safe?'

'Of course. Don't worry, I'm coming back to you, Freddie.'

She decided not to tell him her news. It was not news to tell on the phone. 'How is everything? How are you?'

'Not bad for a man about to get married next week.'

'Sorry?'

'It was your mother's Christmas present to me. She's decided we are getting married next week.'

Anna shouted into the phone. 'What?'

'Sorry, I shouldn't have said it like that. She must be taking some of Carl's pills. Seems like she's hallucinating. I've taken all the other pills Carl had, but she must have some hidden away.'

'Why does she think you are going to marry her?'

She heard him pouring a drink.

'It's a long story. After your father's funeral she wanted to talk to me. I put it off, but, when I did go, she said now Carl wasn't there, we could be together, as we should have been all the time.'

'What did you say?'

'I told her the truth.'

'About us?'

'No....No, I thought that might be too much for her, Anna, at the time. But I told her I had never loved her. Ever. I'd made a terrible mistake that night. And I've lived to regret it ever since...I even told her she is stupid, vain, self-centred, and said I wouldn't marry her if she was the last woman on earth.'

'What did she say to that?'

'She laughed, and said I was joking. That it was just "my way" she said...She's started making all the arrangements. Asked Mrs Price to alter one of her dresses as a wedding gown.'

Anna gasped. 'This is crazy.'

'I'm afraid so. I asked her about the pills, but she denies taking any. Maybe...I don't know, Anna...Maybe she's gone mad, finally...'

'Oh, poor Mama!'

'If she doesn't come round, maybe she'll understand when we start living together.'

'Oh, I really want that, Freddie! I love you so much!'

She heard Freddie suddenly start crying, as he said, 'I never thought I'd hear you say that to me. It's a miracle.'

Anna was also crying. 'I will come back, Freddie. It's my Christmas promise to you.'

'You'd better, or I'll come and haunt you in Heaven.'

'I'm not sure that's where I'm going.'

Freddie laughed. 'Come and join me in Hell then.'

Anna laughed and cried at the same time. 'Merry Christmas, my love.'

Hans and Maria laid side by side, naked, on his huge bed. Replete. Maria had become more than a mother replacement now, and Hans enjoyed her company.

Hans stretched. 'I'm thinking of leaving Cuba.'

'Why?'

'It looks like that Castro guy is going to win. He's captured nearly all the island now.'

'So?'

'I've heard some of his speeches on the radio.'

Maria yawned. 'They go on for hours.'

'I don't listen to them all, but I don't think I'd fit in with his society.'

He got up, went to the window and looked down on the communal pool. A couple of tourists, sunbathing, looked up to see a naked man standing at the window. Hans waved to them, allowed them a few more moments to admire his tanned, athletic body, then turned away to pour himself a drink.

'I'm an entrepreneur. Entrepreneurs need freedom. Freedom to flourish.'

Maria sat up, yawned and spread her arms wide.

'You have great tits,' Hans said.

'Thank you,' said Maria brushing that aside. 'And you don't think Castro would approve?'

'I bet he'd love them,' he joked.

'I mean about entrepreneurs?'

'He's talking about everything being collective, all in it together. That sort of thing. Not like in America, where it's everyone for themselves. Dog eat dog.'

'So, you're going to move to America?'

'Yeah. I liked Miami. There's a lot of stuff going on there. Stuff I could get involved with.'

'What about your family? Your mother? Would you take her? And Klaus?'

'I mentioned it to her on Christmas Day, but she's so busy getting ready for the wedding.'

Maria stared at him. 'Wedding? What wedding?'

'She's marrying that doctor guy. Freddie somebody.'

'Freddie Sanchez?'

Hans nodded. 'Whatever makes her happy.'

'I'm surprised.'

'I think they knew each other way back. Back in England.' He shrugged. 'So...'

'I'm surprised you're taking that so lightly.'

'Why?'

'Well...you and...your mother.'

'That was just a phase, Maria. After Bella, you know...Now, I've got you...Actually, I think Mama's going a bit crazy. But that's Freddie's problem.'

Maria got up. 'I'm going to get a shower.'

'I'd like you to come with me.'

'What? To America?'

'You'd love it.'

'But I'm very happy here, Hans.'

'Yeah, but when Castro takes over...I'd really like you to come.'

'As a mother substitute?'

'No. No, Maria! Not at all. I like you being around.'

'Hans, I think Castro's ideas for the island are great.'

'What? Really? I'm surprised.'

'I might even be able to get a proper job.'

'Wow!' Hans finished his drink, and began pouring another one.

'And my daughter has just graduated. She can't wait to come back and join the revolution.'

Maria walked off to the bathroom, her naked hips swaying.

CHAPTER ONE HUNDRED AND TWENTY-ONE

'Ché's called us the 'suicide squad', Alberto said to Anna. 'After we take the top of the hill, Batista's troop train is going to be right below us. Bang-Bang!'

'What about the troops up there?'

'If they're anything like the others, they'll just give up and walk away.'

'That would be nice.'

As Alberto walked off to talk some of the others in the small unit, Anna checked her weapons again. She had a Thompson sub-machine gun, the Glock semi-automatic pistol she had bought from Hans, and the Colt handgun that Freddie had given her when she left him in the forest.

Anna stroked the gun. Nestled the cool metal against her cheek. She couldn't believe how she had got it all wrong about Freddie. All her suspicions about his motives towards her mother. He had made one mistake, prompted outrageously by her mother, and had regretted it ever since.

She was so glad he and her father had put it behind them, and become very close friends. It was a shame that Carl hadn't lived to see the revolution succeed, and for her and Freddie to be together. She knew he would have liked both of those things.

Since the time that she and Freddie had made love in the forest, Anna had found it difficult to concentrate on being a soldier. Luckily, many of Batista's troops were surrendering, or just disappearing from the garrisons. But she knew she was getting careless. Which was why she had volunteered for the mission. It could be dangerous, and that would focus her mind.

They set off before dawn. When the sun rose, it would be behind them, and right in the eyes of their enemy. Perhaps these troops would just surrender, or disappear? But they were

481

meant to be part of Batista's special forces, with a reputation to protect.

As her unit approached the summit a hail of machine gun bullets split the air around her. Anna crouched behind a tree.

This lot are not walking away, she thought.

The trunk of the tree clattered as the bullets ripped into it. Dropping to the ground, cradling the sub-machine gun, she slithered sideways on her belly through the ferns. Her unit were returning the fire now. Slipping the butt of the gun onto her shoulder, she took aim and let off a volley at where the shots had come. Then she moved on again, quickly, as they returned her fire.

Taking up another position, she was raising the muzzle as a bullet crashed into her chest. Rolling over from the impact, she felt the blood seeping from the wound. She thought of Freddie as her eyes closed. And the stray bullet.

'You are leaving, today?' said Esther.

Hans had gone round to see his mother, as soon as he heard the news that General Batista, and his family, had fled the country early that morning.

'It's New Year's Day, Mama,' said Hans. 'Perfect time to make a new start.'

'But you'll miss the wedding, Hans.'

'I'll come back for it. I will send you some money, when I start my business over there to pay for it.'

She put her arms around him, and hugged him closely.

'Hans, I shall miss you so much. So much!'

Hans felt her soft body pressed tightly against him. He was glad he was going, for that reason as well. Castro's Cuba wouldn't be for him, he was sure, but he knew that wanting to screw your mother, even if she was mad, wasn't right either.

'I will call you when I arrive,' he said, taking her arms from around him, and giving her a brief kiss on the cheek.

Now that the President had gone, there was no point in hanging around. Hans had his passport and his money. That's all he needed. He knew he would miss Maria, but there were lots of women in Miami, just waiting for him.

He drove through the streets, weaving through crowds of people, who were shouting, singing, dancing and shooting guns into the air to celebrate. Celebrate, he thought, because you don't know what's round the corner.

It was only a short drive to the airport. He would leave the car there, and arrange for it to be put on a boat to sail to Florida.

He was surprised that just outside of the city there was a road block, manned by four men dressed like guerrillas. He stopped his car and they approached casually.

'Diego!' Hans called, recognising the leader. He had sold arms to the man some months ago. 'How are you? A great day for you, hey?'

'Perfecto, Hans! Get out of the car, please.'

'I've got a flight to catch, Diego.'

'Out please, Hans.' Diego said calmly.

'Hey, look, I'm on your side, guys.'

Diego raised the gun. It was the one Hans had sold him.

'Hey – '

'Out.'

Hans got out of the car. 'I don't understand, Diego.'

'It's not far to the airport. You can walk.'

'What?'

'Give me the keys, please.'

'You're taking my car? You can't do that.'

'Keys.'

Realising he couldn't argue, Hans gave Diego the keys.

'Wallet.'

'What!'

'Wallet, watch, rings.'

'You're robbing me! You guys are not supposed to do that! You're supposed to be the good guys!'

'Just paying your taxes before you leave, Hans.'

One of the other men took Hans' briefcase from the passenger seat, and went through it. He opened the large manilla envelope with all Hans money inside, and pocketed it.

'Hey! That's my money! You can't take that! How will I pay for the flight?'

'Then maybe you'll have to stay,' said Diego, getting into the driving seat. 'Who knows, maybe you'll like it?'

The other three climbed into the open-topped car.

'Adios, Hans.'

Revving the engine, Diego spun the car round and headed back to the city. The men waved as they drove off, leaving Hans standing furiously alone in the road.

CHAPTER ONE HUNDRED AND TWENTY-TWO

Freddie poured a cup of his favourite coffee as he listened to the noisy celebrations going on outside on the harbour. He had heard on the radio that Batista had flown away that morning, taking his family, and much of the island's wealth with him, no doubt stored in a friendly, foreign bank account.

It was hard to believe, he thought, that only two years ago Fidel Castro had landed with just a few exhausted men, and yet had defeated a well-equipped, vastly superior army, which was supported by the Americans. It was a truly a remarkable success.

He had become disillusioned with politics years ago, but he was thrilled that Anna's revolution had won. Today was January the first. The start of a new year. And a new regime for the island. Would it be what Anna hoped, and fought for? Time would tell.

Whatever, he was certain that Anna was alive. She had phoned only a few days ago and, according to the news, there hadn't been much fighting since then, apart from the rebels' successful attack on the troop train. That victory had sealed Batista's fate. Freddie didn't really believe in destiny, but he knew that Anna was alive. And that, very soon, they would be together, starting a new life, in a new year.

Sipping the coffee, he looked at the package. He smiled, sadly, remembering that Carl liked his coffee the best. And Carl would have loved to have seen what was in the package.

It had arrived yesterday, but Freddie wanted to wait until New Year's Day to show it to Klaus. That seemed the perfect day.

The hardbacked book was even more beautiful than he had thought. Every page had a large illustration of one of Klaus's drawings of seashells, with a small text explaining each shell.

Freddie had looked at the images many times, remembering how Klaus's first attempts had steadily grown into such magnificent pictures.

He finished his coffee. It was time to show his son.

'What's all that noise, Nanny?' said Klaus.

Outside there was the sound of cheering, laughing, singing, and people playing instruments.

Mrs Price looked up from sewing Esther's wedding dress. She didn't listen to, or care about what was happening outside of the house.

'It some people having a celebration.'

'They sound very happy.'

He hadn't been out of the house since the time Hans introduced him to that rude girl. When he escaped from her, he had wandered the streets not knowing where he was. There were so many buildings towering above him, but he didn't recognise them. Having no idea where his home was, he thought he could ask someone. There were so many people around. A lot were sitting at tables eating and drinking outside. Some girls, with very little clothes on, stood in doorways, talking to men who passed by. Everywhere, people seemed excited. This was the city where he lived. It seemed new and fascinating, but rather scary at the same time.

He had jumped, alarmed, as a big car honked as he crossed the street. The man inside shouted something to him. He didn't know what it was, but the man sounded angry. Getting out of the car, the man walked towards him. He was wearing a uniform. He had put Klaus in his car, and taken him home.

Outside, he heard the celebration getting louder. Peering from the front window he saw a group of people passing by the house. They were shouting, laughing, singing and dancing. One of them raised a gun in the air and fired it. What were they doing? Where were they going? They looked so happy, he really wanted to join them.

He left the room and raced up the stairs to the attic. Excitedly, he searched among the piles of toys, and finally found it. As he got to the bottom of the stairs again, Mrs Price was standing there, looking concerned.

'Klaus, what are you doing?'

'I'm going outside to join those people, Nanny. They look so happy.'

'You can't do that. You have to stay here.'

'No, I want to go, Nanny. Please.'

'No, your Mama wouldn't like it.'

Laughing, he raised his gun. 'I'll shoot you if you try to stop me.' Pushing past Mrs Price, he rushed out of the house.

Mrs Price followed him to the door. 'Klaus! Klaus!' she shouted.

But he was gone, waving his gun in the air.

CHAPTER ONE HUNDRED AND TWENTY-THREE

Freddie had to force his way through what seemed like the whole of Havana, heading for the Plaza Cívica. People sang and danced in the street, kissed and hugged each other, and fired guns, not in anger, but joyfully, upwards into the blue sky.

He felt as excited as the rest. Overjoyed that he would get to see Anna very soon, and delighted that he was going to show Klaus his own book.

Mrs Price was standing at the open front door of the Mueller's when he arrived, with a handkerchief to her eyes.

'Oh, Mr Sanchez!' she cried. 'Thank goodness!'

'What's the matter, Mrs Price?'

'Klaus has gone!'

'What do you mean?'

'He got excited by all the people and he ran off to join them.'

'Did you see which way he went?'

She pointed. 'That way. He had a toy gun, I think.'

The city was so happy and jubilant Freddie couldn't see Klaus getting into any harm, but he didn't know the city, and would easily get lost. He held out the package to her. 'Hold this, Mrs Price. But, please, don't open it.'

'What is it?'

'It's for Klaus.'

Freddie turned and headed off to find his son.

Among the winding, narrow streets, Klaus seemed to have lost the people. He could still hear their noise, but he found himself alone in a small square. It looked very pretty with all the red flowers in every corner. He thought maybe they were put there for Christmas. But Christmas was over, and he wanted to find the people, and join in the fun with them.

Then he saw a man appear at the other side of the square. He was wearing a uniform. Klaus didn't like men in uniforms. Maybe the man would take him back home, and he would miss out on all the fun. Raising his gun, he pointed it at the man.

Ramos was in his office when he heard the news about Batista fleeing the island. Hurriedly, he began collecting papers that would be used against him if it came to a trial. Looking out of the window, he saw a crowd heading towards the building. With Batista gone, he knew it wouldn't be long before people came looking for him. There were many people in the city who had suffered under him, and would be looking to take their revenge. And they were here right now.

His car was parked outside the front, so, he couldn't use that. With the papers under his arm, he fled down the corridor, and left by the rear entrance. But he was in uniform. Very proud of his position, Ramos never appeared without his uniform. Now, he needed to find some new clothes, so he could blend in with the rest.

It seemed people had left their cafes and shops to join the celebration. So, he headed for the nearest square where he knew there was a tourist shop that sold expensive men's clothes.

As he entered the square, he saw a young man at the opposite side. The man was raising a gun at him. Ramos dropped the papers and snatched his pistol from its holster. He took aim and fired.

CHAPTER ONE HUNDRED AND TWENTY-FOUR

Havana airport is not far from the city, but after walking three miles in the blazing sun to reach it, Hans was dripping with sweat. He stood in the shade, getting his breath back and trying to cool down, though that was not really possible in the humidity.

On the long trudge there, he went through the various scenarios ahead of him. Thanks to Castro's rebels, he had no car and no money. Over the last few years he made money selling arms, mostly to the rebels, some of whom had just robbed him. He couldn't see him selling arms in the new regime Castro had promised. Drugs? He had contacts, but didn't fancy spending years in the prison on the Isla de Pinos.

He had drawn all his money from the bank earlier in the month, suspecting that Castro would win and take over the island. He had hoped to leave taking Maria with him. Sadly, that didn't happen.

He couldn't even pay rent for an apartment now. And the thought of going back to live in the same house as his mother worried him. Though now she was marrying Freddie, it wouldn't really be convenient for him to stay there anyway. He still wondered about that situation. Freddie had said that it wasn't happening, but his mother said that was just one of Freddie's jokes.

All he knew was that he had to leave the island. Having no money made it difficult if you couldn't buy a ticket, but he was halfway to the airport when his car was stolen, so he carried on, hoping his charm would pay off.

If that didn't happen, he thought maybe he could steal a boat and sail to Florida. He didn't know how to sail a boat, and didn't know how to navigate. It was only ninety miles, but if you went the wrong way Africa was a long way off. A plane was definitely the best option.

It was difficult for Freddie to see through the crowd of happy, jubilant people in the Plaza Cívica. Pushing through the mass of bodies, he headed for one of the old Victorian lampposts. He scrambled up as far as he could and looked around. At least Klaus was tall and blonde, so he should stand out, but Freddie still couldn't see him. There was no sign. Maybe Klaus had got lost? He didn't know the city. And he didn't know where the main square was.

Freddie climbed down and pushed through the crowd again. Avoiding several women, and men who wanted to dance with him, he wandered into the back streets, where there were less people gathered.

At the end of a narrow street, he recognised the little square where he had met with Carl, and had a row with Anna. The bright-red, Christmas poinsettias were still in every corner. Reaching the square, he saw just ahead of him, Ramos pulling out his gun. At the other side of the square was Klaus, pointing his toy gun at Ramos.

There were a lot of people leaving Havana that day. Mainly tourists, some having come to the end of their vacation, and others leaving because of the political situation. It was not clear what would happen on the island, and people didn't want to get caught in the turmoil that could happen.

Knowing he had to put on a show, he went to the gentlemen's restroom, and stripped off his shirt and slacks, then washed himself thoroughly. He had to look as good as he could.

Finished, he took his comb from his top pocket, and smoothed his hair. Looking in the mirror, even feeling tired and angry, he still looked tanned and handsome. He would have to be if he wasn't going to have to stay in the island, with no prospects.

When, at last, he found a seat in the busy waiting room, he surveyed the crowd. They were mainly couples, or groups. He needed to find a woman on her own. A wealthy one.

He tried some young ones, about his age, but they weren't interested in talking to this handsome young man who approached them. Maybe he had been too forward, too needy?

After an hour, he saw her. She was in her mid-fifties. Tall and elegant. She was far too thin for his liking, but she was going over the edge of the hill, and might be grateful for the attention.

'Ramos!' screamed Freddie, as Ramos aimed at Klaus. Freddie hurled himself at him. Locked together, the two men tumbled to the ground together. Ramos's shot whistled close to Klaus's head, and slammed into the stonework behind him.

Reacting quickly, Ramos spun round on the floor and fired a shot at his assailant. He was about to fire again, when he saw who it was. He scrambled up, surprised.

'Freddie?'

Seeing what had happened, Klaus was running across the square. Ramos turned his gun towards him.

Still lying injured, on the ground, Freddie cried out. 'He's my son, Ramos! It's a toy gun!'

Freddie screamed again as a shot rang out.

Ramos spun round, holding his arm. Four men were rushing into the square, heading straight for him.

'There he is!', they cried. 'Murderer! Murderer!'

Ramos fired a shot at them, then raced away out of the square. The men followed, yelling abuse and firing at him.

Hans lit the woman's cigarette. Then lit his own. He had had enough change in his pocket to buy the woman a coffee, and they had found seats in the small airport café.

Her name was Nora. She was an English traveller and writer, who spent most of her time travelling the world, writing about her adventures. She was well travelled, but it was the first time she had been to the Cuba.

'I'm an entrepreneur,' Hans said. 'But the rebels, those thugs, have just stolen my car and all my savings, on the way here.'

'You mean Castro's revolutionaries.'

Hans shrugged.

'So, you're leaving Cuba, for good?'

'I don't think...'the revolution' approves of my kind of capitalism.'

The woman took a long drag of her cigarette, looked closely at him, and blew the smoke into the air. 'You live in here, Hans, but I think I can hear a trace of a...German accent?'

He nodded. 'We arrived here on the s.s. St Louis. Twenty years ago. From Hamburg.'

'Ah, yes. Really? I remember that. It must be a fascinating story. Perhaps you could tell me more...' She reached out to stroke his hand. 'On the plane?'

Hans took her hand, and smiled his gratitude.

Klaus crouched beside Freddie, who was still lying where he fell.

'I'm sorry, Freddie! I didn't know that man. I didn't know it was for real!'

'That's alright, Klaus. As long as you are okay...'

Klaus nodded. 'I'm okay. But you're hurt, Freddie.'

Freddie coughed and felt blood in his mouth. 'I need help, Klaus. I don't think I can walk on my own.'

'I'll carry you, Freddie. I'll give you a piggy-back.'

Klaus helped Freddie up. The young man bent over. Freddie managed to climb onto his back, and put his arms around Klaus's neck. The young man had a broad, strong back and he set off, easily, across the square.

'I'll tell you which way to go,' Freddie said.

After a moment, Klaus chuckled.

'What's funny?' said Freddie.

Klaus laughed again. 'It's like you're the shell, Freddie. Protecting me.'

Despite the pain, Freddie smiled.

CHAPTER ONE HUNDRED AND TWENTY-FIVE

Twenty-four hours after the dictator, Batista, fled the island, Ché Guevara led his army in the capital, Havana, waving from the top of a captured tank. All along the parade the streets were alive people and with noise; horns, sirens, whistles, trumpets, church bells, and everywhere the cry of 'Viva la Revolution,'

In the third vehicle, Anna Mueller stood smiling, waving her left arm to the crowd. Her right arm was in a sling, protecting the wound from the bullet that smashed into the muzzle of her gun on the attack on the hill.

She was as thrilled as everyone else, but she couldn't wait to embrace Freddie. When the procession reached the Plaza Cívica, Anna climbed onto the bonnet and looked around, but there was no way she could see Freddie among all those people, even if he was in the crowd.

Freddie was actually lying in the bed that Carl had died in, in the Mueller's house. Sitting on a chair beside him, Klaus was showing him pictures from his book. Klaus couldn't read all the words, but he knew the shells and their names by heart.

'That's an Apple Murex,' said Klaus. He grinned, 'It doesn't look like an apple.' He turned over the page. 'That's a Dogshead Triton. That doesn't look like a dog's head either, does it, Freddie? Not really.'

Freddie smiled at his son, and closed his eyes.

Anna leapt from the jeep, and she made her way through the massed crowd. Many people wanted to hug her, but when they saw she was injured, they made a path for her. When she was clear of the crowd she began to run. The injury hurt, but she didn't care.

When she reached the harbour, she raced up the stairs to Freddie's room. The door wasn't locked, but he wasn't there. She then tried his favourite café.

'Freddie? He hasn't been here today yet,' said Manuel, the owner. 'He's celebrating, eh? Viva la Revolution!'

She ran to Sloppy Joes. Maybe Freddie was celebrating with one of its famous twelve-year old whiskies? The bar was crowded, but he wasn't there.

Walking quickly, holding onto her injured shoulder, she made her way to the Mueller's house. She rang the bell and waited.

After a moment, Carlotta opened the door.

Anna went to her and hugged her, 'Carlotta! How lovely to see you.'

Carlotta began to cry.

'It's okay, Carlotta. I'm home!'

Carlotta began to sob. Anna held her tightly.

'What's the matter, Carlotta?'

As she holding Carlotta, Mrs Price came out of her room.

'Miss Anna!' she said, surprised.

Anna broke away. 'Mrs Price! Nanny! How are you?'

Without speaking, Mrs Price went to the surgery door and opened it, but stayed outside, looking at her.

Puzzled, Anna went to the door. Inside, Klaus was sitting beside Freddie, who was lying, stretched-out in the bed, his eyes closed. Klaus turned over a page of the book and looked at his beautiful illustration.

'That's an Angel Wing, Freddie. That's our favourite, isn't it...?' He sniffed, and reached out to touch Freddie's hand. 'I bet you can see angels now...'

CHAPTER ONE HUNDRED AND TWENTY- SIX

A thin tropical mist shrouded the Colon Cemetery, masking the vast, elaborate monuments to the dead. The mourners had drifted away, leaving just Anna and Esther beside the grave. Slowly, Esther sank to her knees, sobbing.

'Freddie!' she cried. 'Oh, Freddie!'

Anna stared blindly out at the mist, seeing nothing. She didn't know what the future held for her. Whatever it was, it wasn't what she had planned. The revolution had happened. That was what she had wanted most for years, and fought so hard for. But for the moment that didn't matter. Nothing did.

As the tears trickled down her cheeks, she stroked her belly. The baby wouldn't know him, but she would tell it all about its father. About Freddie. Her Freddie.

How he rescued them from the ship. How he saved her life from the rabid dog. How he loved her, and never told her until...

She saw Esther take the diamond necklace from around her neck.

Esther kissed it, like a sacred religious relic. 'Freddie,' she whispered. Dropping the necklace onto the coffin in the grave, she got up, and without looking at Anna, walked away.

Anna stared down at the necklace, lying in the middle of the dark coffin. As the sun broke through the mist, the diamonds sparkled in the sunlight.

She picked up the shovel, stuck in the pile of earth beside her, and began to fill the grave, until the diamonds shone no more.

THE END.

**With special thanks to the late Rod Davis for his
wonderful cover design.**

Also by Harry Duffin

The Tribe: Birth Of The Mall Rats

by

Harry Duffin

The Birth of The Mall Rats is the first story in a compelling series of novelizations of the global cult television phenomenon, The Tribe.

The world began without the human race. Now, after a mysterious pandemic decimates the entire adult population, it looks as if it will end exactly the same way. Unless the young survivors – who band together in warring Tribes – overcome the power struggles, dangers and unexpected challenges in a lawless dystopian society to unite and build a new world from the ashes of the old.

Creating a new world in their own image – whatever that image might be…

Chicago May

by

Harry Duffin

Fleeing her abusive father in Ireland, young May Sharpe chases her dream of a new life in America. Arriving penniless and friendless in 1919's New York, May has to choose between honest poverty, or crime.

Beautiful May is sharp as a tack, and in just two years becomes the 'Queen of Crooks'. But in the midst of her successful criminal career, May is forced to re-examine her morality, and has to make a decision.

A decision which threatens, not only her new-found fame and fortune, but, her young life.

Jail Tales:

Memoirs of a 'Lady' Prison Governor

by

Chris Duffin & Harry Duffin

As the first woman governor into HMP Strangeways and the notorious Dartmoor Prison, Governor Chris Duffin was a ground-breaker. In 'Jail Tales' she recounts some of the many stories and incidents from her twenty-year career both as a lowly 'screw' and as a prison governor. Whether it's flying out of the UK with a briefcase full of class A drugs, talking to the BBC News in her nightie, displaying a naked hunk's willy on her office wall, or having Myra Hindley as her tea-lady, these tales will amuse, entertain and definitely change your view of life behind bars.

ALSO AVAILABLE

Keeping The Dream Alive

by

Raymond Thompson.

The fascinating inside story about the making of the cult television series, The Tribe.

An intriguing memoir charting the life and times of how someone growing up on the wrong side of the tracks in a very poor working class environment in post-War Britain was able to journey to the glittering arena of Hollywood, providing an inspirational insight into how the one most likely to fail at school due to a special need battled and succeeded against all the odds to travel the world, founding and overseeing a prolific international independent television production company.

With humorous insight into the fertile imagination of a writer's mind, the book explores life away from the red carpet in the global world of motion pictures and television - and reveals the unique story of how the cult series 'The Tribe' came into being. Along with a personal quest to exist and survive amidst the ups and downs and pressures of a long and successful career as a writer/producer, culminating in being appointed an Adjunct Professor and featuring in the New Years Honours List, recognized by Her Majesty Queen Elizabeth II for services to television.

The Tribe: A New World

by

A.J. Penn

The official story continues in this novel, set immediately after the conclusion of season 5 of The Tribe television series, with The Tribe: A New World effectively becoming Season 6 in the continuing saga.

Forced to flee the city in their homeland - along with abandoning their dream of building a better world from the ashes of the old - the Mall Rats embark upon a perilous journey of discovery into the unknown.

Cast adrift, few could have foreseen the dangers that lay in store. What is the secret surrounding the Jzhao Li? Will they unravel the mysteries of The Collective? Let alone overcome the many challenges and obstacles they encounter as they battle the forces of mother nature, unexpected adversaries, and at times, even themselves? Above all, can they build a new world in their own images - by keeping their dream alive?

The Tribe: A New Dawn

by

A.J. Penn

Following the many challenges in the best selling novel, 'The Tribe: A New World', the Mall Rats find themselves faced with an even greater struggle as they try to unravel the many unexplained mysteries they now encounter - in the equivalent of Season 7 in the continuing saga.

What was the real mission of the United Nations survival fleet? Who is the enigmatic leader of the Collective? What really did occur at Arthurs Air Force Base? Is there something more sinister to the secrets revealed on the paradise island where they are now stranded?

Forced to resolve the agonizing conflict in their personal lives, the Mall Rats must also decide which path to take and whether or not to confront the ghosts of their past in their battle to survive against an ominous adversary. With the very real threat of human existence becoming extinct, can they endure against all odds to secure a future and the promise of a better tomorrow? Or will they suffer the same fate as the adults who had gone before and perish?

The tribe must fight not only for their lives but face their greatest fears to prevent the new world plunging further into darkness - and ensure hope prevails in a new dawn. And that they keep their dream alive.

The Tribe: R(E)volution

by

A.J. Penn

In the sequel to the critically acclaimed best selling, 'The Tribe: A New Dawn' and 'The Tribe: A New World', 'The Tribe: (R) Evolution' is the third novel in the long awaited continuing saga based upon the cult television series 'The Tribe'.

What secrets lay hidden in the ominous Eagle Mountain? Who are The Collective? And will the identity of their enigmatic leader be revealed?

Where is safe if invaders of faraway lands, intent on expanding their empire and fracturing alliances of all those struggling to rebuild and survive, ruthlessly pursue their own vision for the future and quest to gain domination and absolute power?

How does The Broker and The Selector fit into all the mystery surrounding Project Eden? Does anyone survive The Cube and the nightmarish Void?

Can the Mall Rats overcome all the unbearable challenges and obstacles they encounter to build a new and better world from the ashes of the old? Will they conquer their adversaries and ever recover from the heartache and agonising conflicts they experience in their personal lives?

Facing the very real threat of human extinction - can they endure? Adapt? Evolve? Survive? And keep their dream alive?

About The Author

Harry Duffin is an award-winning British screenwriter, who was Head of Development at UK independent, the Cloud 9 Screen Entertainment Group, from its foundation in 1994. During that time he was the script executive responsible for seven major television series, including 'Swiss Family Robinson' starring Richard 'John Boy' Thomas, and 'Twist in the Tale', featuring William Shatner.

He is co-creator of the UK Channel Five teen-cult drama series 'The Tribe', which ran for five series, numbering 260 episodes. The 'Tribe' has been sold world-wide, and has a growing international fan base.

Before joining Cloud 9, Harry worked extensively in British theatre and UK television, for both the BBC and ITV.

He was on the first writing team for the BBC's 'EastEnders'. And while writing for Granada Television's 'Coronation Street', he won the Writers' Guild Award for Best TV serial.

harry.duffin26@gmail.com

www.harryduffin.co.uk

216 Conchita Freddie's
commits suicide, drowns "woman"

Lightning Source UK Ltd.
Milton Keynes UK
UKHW011019171222
414082UK00002B/342